Badge *of* Respect

A NOVEL

by

TAMARA TILLEY

Badge of Respect

By Tamara Tilley

Copyright © 2014 Tamara Tilley

Library of Congress Cataloging-in-Publication Data is on file at the Library of Congress, Washington, DC.

ISBN–10: 0692349944
ISBN–13: 978–0692349946

Cover design by Tamara Tilley & Scott Saunders
Cover images: iStock Photo

ARCHER
PRESS

OTHER BOOKS BY TAMARA TILLEY

FULL DISCLOSURE
ABANDONED IDENTITY
CRIMINAL OBSESSION

TO WALTER
MY BIGGEST SUPPORTER
I LOVE YOU
♥

mother did nothing to comfort her. Struggling to free herself, Joanna pulled on the seatbelt wrapped around her but it was no use. When she realized her legs were pinned behind her father's seat, she became hysterical.

"Daddy! I can't get out!" Joanna cried. "My legs are stuck! Help me Daddy!"

But he too was incredibly silent.

Joanna looked past the front seat to see the hood of their car crushed and smoking. The windshield was pushed in and pieces of twisted metal hung from the roof of the car like angry claws.

Petrified, Joanna tried again to free herself, but the safety belt pressed against her chest and the door was crushed against her shoulder, making it hard for her to move. Joanna cried again and again for her parents but they didn't answer. She could see them through the smoke that began to fill the car, but still they did nothing to help her.

It's a nightmare. That's what it is. Quickly, Joanna squeezed her eyes shut and waited. But when she opened her eyes, the nightmare had not gone away. Closing her eyes again, she tried to wish it all away. That's when she felt a hand take hold of hers.

"It's all right. I've got you now. You're going to be okay."

The voice was deep and kind. Joanna looked to see a policeman staring at her. He smiled and squeezed her hand. "I'm going to stay right here with you, Sweetie, until the firemen can get you out, okay?"

She nodded timidly.

Smoke continued to fill the car. Loud voices yelled and hollered around her—scaring her even more. A fireman in a

PROLOGUE

It was the perfect day. Joanna, along with her parents, was on her way to a fancy restaurant to celebrate her mother's thirtieth birthday. Joanna and her father sang "Happy Birthday" while her mother laughed, begging them to stop. Everyone was having such a good time until her father cried out for God and slammed on the brakes. In that instant, her mother let out the most chilling scream Joanna had ever heard.

She had no time to react. The next thing Joanna heard was the horrifying groan of bending metal and the terrifying sound of shattering glass. Dazed and confused, she tried to shake off the deafening sounds that swam around her as a pain shot through her chest.

"Mommy, it hurts," Joanna screamed. "Help me, Mommy!"

But her mother didn't answer.

Joanna gagged on the smoke that began to fill the car, and her chest hurt every time she coughed, but still her

Acknowledgements

My family and friends have been so supportive of my writing from the very start. They have been a constant source of encouragement and have never allowed me to give up.

To my family–Walter, my Moms, Christopher, John, Jennifer, Alex, Lorelei, Addison, Trey, Jackson and our soon-to-be new edition–I love you more than words can express.

To my friends–Vicki, Michele, LeAnn, and all my Hume Lake connections, thank you for your continuous encouragement.

To Bob Phillips and MaryLu Tyndall–for your encouragement, advice, and wiliness to help me with my journey. Thank you.

To Jeanne Halstead, Charlene Ponzio, and Michele Nordquist–thank you for your tireless efforts in editing. I appreciate your wiliness and dedication. Words cannot express my gratitude.

To Scott Saunders–Thank you for your invaluable help with the cover design. Your professional touches were just what it needed.

To Terry Mowers – Your words of wisdom were greatly appreciated.

To my Lord and Savior, Jesus Christ–I pray people will see you in each and every story I write.

bright yellow suit spoke to the policeman holding her hand and told him he needed to back away. Joanna clutched his fingers even harder, afraid he would leave, but he smiled and gave her hand a reassuring squeeze.

"Work around me," he said to the fireman. "I'm staying right here."

"Then get this blanket around her," the fireman instructed. "We need to get the jaws-of-life in here, and we're running out of time."

The policeman turned to her and smiled. "What's your name, Sweetheart?"

"Joanna," she said through sniffles and tears.

"Hi, Joanna, my name's Matthew. I'm going to put this blanket around us, okay? That way the firemen can help to get you out." Matthew gingerly laid the heavy blanket across her and pulled it over both of their heads.

"It's so dark," she whimpered.

"I'm sure a big girl like you isn't afraid of the dark," Matthew said to her in a kind voice. "But I'll tell you a secret that helps me when I'm scared. If you close your eyes and sing your favorite song, the darkness doesn't seem so scary. Can you do that for me, Joanna?" he asked while squeezing her hand. "Can you sing a song while the firemen work around us?"

She nodded her head slowly, and quietly began to sing "Happy Birthday". It wasn't her favorite song, but it was the only one she could remember.

"You're doing great, Joanna. We're almost done."

"Is someone helping my mommy and daddy?" she asked, when she got to the end of the song.

"The firemen are going to get them out too,

Sweetheart. I just need you to be brave right now. Okay?"

A loud noise filled the air as the car began to whine and the door pulled away from her side. Joanna could smell smoke through the blanket, but continued to sing as tears streamed down her face. She was trying so hard to be brave—like Matthew had asked her—but she was afraid. More afraid than she'd ever been in her life. She wanted to believe everything was going to be okay.

But somehow she knew something was terribly wrong.

"Okay. We got the door free," the fireman yelled over the noise and the chaos.

Matthew squeezed her hand. "Joanna, I'm going to have to let go of your hand for just a moment while the firemen move the door. But I'll be right here.

"I promise."

The blanket slipped from around her shoulders as Matthew's hand pulled away from hers. She cried out for him, scared of being left by herself. But as soon as the firemen removed the door, Matthew reached inside the car, unbuckled her seatbelt, and carefully lifted her into his arms. He pulled her to his chest, and she could feel his heart beating just as fast as hers. Slowly, he laid her on a funny mattress with wheels, but never let go of her hand. When two men in blue shirts began to touch her, she pulled away; clinging to Matthew's arm.

"It's okay, Joanna, these men are here to help you. They're doctors and they want to make sure you're okay."

As soon as she lay back down, she began to cough. But it wasn't like when she had a cold or choked on a potato chip. It hurt more than that. One of the men in the blue shirts tried to put a funny mask over her face, but she pushed it away.

"It's okay, Joanna. It's just a mask, like at Halloween. It will help you breathe and make your coughing go away."

"Is it going to hurt?"

"No, Joanna. I promise."

After the mask was back in place, one of the doctors looked at her and smiled. "Joanna, my name is Jacob, and this is Steve." He pointed to the other man standing beside her. "We're going to listen to your heart and look into your eyes, okay?"

She nodded bashfully.

Joanna tried to lie still as one doctor pressed the funny heart tube thing against her chest and the other flashed a light in her eyes. They talked about the cuts on her arms and the gash on her knee, but didn't say anything about her mommy or daddy.

"Where does it hurt, Joanna?" Matthew asked, while stroking her hair back from her face.

With her eyes closed, she pointed to her chest with a shaky finger and then to her tummy. She pulled at the mask the doctor had put on her face and asked in a quivery voice, "Where's my mommy? I want to see my mommy."

"She can't come here right now, Joanna, but I promise I will stay with you all the way to the hospital." Matthew stroked the side of her face just like her daddy did when he tucked her in at night.

Suddenly, Joanna felt very tired and no longer had the strength to keep her eyes open. The last thing she remembered was the policeman's reassuring smile as he held her hand.

CHAPTER ONE

Officer Joanna Anderson sat at a desk by herself as she listened to the morning briefing. Sgt. Blackstone paced at the front of the room as he informed the day shift officers of a few fires that appeared to be arson, another death of a prostitute in the downtown district, and the continual rise of gang activity.

"We're still hearing murmurs of tension on the west side," the sergeant said. "The Outlaws are trying to expand their boundaries but the Lost Boys and the Compadres are beginning to push back. Tensions are high, so keep your ears to the street and your presence known. Watch yourselves out there; it could get ugly."

"No uglier than it is in here," Officer Brewster said from behind Joanna as he gave her chair a shove with his foot.

Joanna ignored him, or at least she tried to. She had expected to take some heat regarding her recent actions, but she'd never expected the harassment to get this bad.

She blocked out the caustic remarks and whispered threats. She sat in her seat with her head down, eyes closed. She relived for the hundredth time her partner pushing the teenage kid through the plate glass window; and the threats he'd aimed at her if she didn't keep her mouth shut.

I did the right thing. He was out of control. I had no choice.

The noise level rose around her. She looked up to see the sergeant had finished with roll call. The briefing was over and the other officers were beginning to disperse. Sgt. Blackstone approached the desk she was sitting at and stopped.

"Anderson, Captain Armstrong wants to see you in his office."

Immediately, everyone stopped moving and looked in her direction. "Maybe the snitch is going to get a taste of her own medicine," someone mumbled.

Without acknowledging the comment, Joanna got to her feet and headed down the hall, preparing herself for what might happen. She had done the unthinkable just a month prior, and now she was going to pay for it.

She took a deep breath as she stood outside the door to the captain's office and said a quick prayer before knocking.

"Enter!" the captain barked.

Joanna swallowed hard but refused to allow his commanding voice to intimidate her. She walked into the captain's office and shut the door behind her, then stepped forward.

"Sit down, Anderson." His tone was firm.

She did her best not to look threatened by his stare or

his rank. She took a seat in one of the two worn upholstered chairs across from his desk.

"Do you know why you're here, Anderson?" he questioned.

"No, sir." *But I can guess.*

She assumed she was there once again to be interrogated about the grievance she had filed against her partner. But Cummings had given her no choice. His use of excessive force when dealing with arrests or even in the questioning of delinquents had gotten out of hand. The final straw came when he pushed a teenage boy through a plate glass window. Yes, the kid had run, and yes, they had chased him for blocks; but when Cummings had finally caught up with the teen, he wasn't satisfied with an arrest. He was angry and wanted the kid to pay.

Everyone cleared out of the laundromat where Cummings had the boy cornered. When Joanna caught up with them, Cummings was clearly assaulting the kid. She yelled for him to stop, but he was out of control. The altercation ended with Cummings pushing the kid through a large plate glass window at the front of the store. She was the only witness to the assault, and he assumed she would keep her mouth shut like she had so many times before. This time he was wrong.

That evening, Joanna had filed a grievance, stating multiple incidents where she felt Cummings had used excessive force. He was assigned a desk job until the disciplinary board could review her allegations. When they convened two weeks later, Cummings was suspended a month without pay, and Joanna had become the outcast of the department.

She was horrified when the majority of the officers—the same officers who had sworn to uphold the law and serve the community—were siding with a man who clearly abused his power. She was being ostracized and harassed for doing the right thing.

No one came to her defense. Not one person. While some expressed their hatred for her openly; others just ignored her. She couldn't believe after being in the department for three years, friends she had made since day one would so easily turn against her. She'd thought about transferring to another department, maybe even somewhere out of state. But she refused to be bullied. She had done the right thing and wasn't going to let intimidation win. Now she sat before Captain Armstrong for the second time, and wondered what kind of reprimand she was in for this time.

The captain cleared his throat before speaking.

"What I'm about to tell you, Anderson, is coming from my superiors. I don't agree with the decision and want you to know that up front. Despite what people say, affirmative action is alive and well, and breathing down our necks regarding the ratio of females in the upper divisions. You were the female that tested highest for the open detective's slot, so we have no choice. You are being promoted to detective. Effective immediately."

Joanna was shocked.

"This is *not* going to be a popular decision among the ranks," the captain continued. "I tried explaining this to my superiors, but they thought my concerns were unfounded. It will look as if you're being rewarded for your latest actions, but let me assure you, Anderson, you're not." His look fell just short of contempt. "This is a political move, a quota that has to be met." The captain eyed her, clearly looking for a reaction.

Joanna was so excited she wanted to scream and shout. But since the captain was making it very clear he didn't think she was deserving of the promotion, she kept her revelry to herself.

"I'm going to warn you," he went on. "You have a squad room of detectives to win over. They're not going to be to accepting of someone with your reputation. In fact, I doubt you'll even last the month."

He was clearly challenging her, but Joanna didn't take the bait. He might not think she was capable, but she would prove him wrong.

"Who will be my partner?" she asked, trying to invoke the sound of confidence in her voice.

"Owens."

Inwardly, Joanna cringed. Owens was one of the detectives she had already gone rounds with. Unfortunately, the captain picked up on her displeasure.

"Is there a problem, Anderson?" he asked pointedly.

"I'm not sure I'm comfortable with Owens, sir."

He laughed out loud. "Oh. I wasn't aware of the fact that I was here to make you feel comfortable. Do you want to tell me why you have a problem with Owens?"

Joanna knew the question wasn't optional.

She cleared her throat. "He's made advances towards me in the past, and I'm afraid being partnered with him might become awkward."

"Oh really?" The captain's words were laced with sarcasm as he reached for the button on his intercom. "Rose, send Detective Owens in here right away."

Joanna realized too late she was only making matters worse. She sat in silence as the captain shuffled papers around on his desk. When the door opened behind her, she sat up a little taller. Detective T.J. Owens stepped into the room and stood directly in front of the captain's desk. She chanced a glance at him while he focused on the captain.

T.J. looked like he had just stepped out of the pages of *Surf Rider* magazine. From his tousled sun-bleached hair, to his tanned complexion and baggy jeans, he looked nothing like a cop. That's why he was so good at what he did. Of course, that didn't stop him from being arrogant and obnoxious, as well.

"You wanted to see me, Capt.?"

"Sit down for a moment, T.J."

T.J. took the seat next to Joanna and gave her a sideways glance. He was clearly confused by her presence.

The captain looked squarely at T.J. and asked, "Have you made sexual advances towards Officer Anderson?"

"What?" T.J. jumped to his feet.

"Sit down, Owens." The captain's voice boomed.

Joanna spoke up quickly. "Captain, I never said he made *sexual advances*. We've just had a few awkward exchanges." She didn't dare look at T.J. even though she could feel his eyes boring straight through her.

"Okay, Anderson, let's get this straight." The captain folded his hands on his desk and leaned towards her. "What kind of *exchanges* are we talking about?"

She swallowed hard and strained to make her words sound business-like, and void of feeling. "He's asked me out repeatedly after I clearly made it known I wasn't interested."

"Yeah, well," T.J. chimed in. "I can assure you I lost all interest after you showed your true colors." He locked eyes with her to make his point.

"Officer Anderson," the captain continued, unwilling to let the situation go. "Surely an attractive woman such as yourself has been pursued before." The captain had a way of making even a compliment sound like a reprimand. "Did Detective Owens make suggestive comments about your physique?"

"No, sir." She looked directly at the captain, trying to hold her ground.

"Did he ask you to have sex with him?"

"No, sir." Joanna's answer softened as her confidence faltered. Her stare settled somewhere among the paperwork on his desk.

"Did he touch you inappropriately?"

"No, sir." Her shoulders slumped as her focus dropped to her lap; the heat of humiliation rose in her complexion.

"Good, then there's no problem, right?" He looked to Joanna for an answer.

"No problem, sir."

"Well, I have a problem." T.J. shot back. "I want to know why she's in here making accusations about me."

"T.J.," The captain looked directly at him. "Anderson is being promoted to detective. Meet your new partner."

"She's what?" T.J. once again shot to his feet. "No way! No way am I going to get saddled with some broad that screwed over her old partner and now has me in her crosshairs."

"Sit down, T.J.!" the captain barked.

"No freakin' way!" T.J. continued to rant. "I'm not

taking the chance of getting called before the review board because it's my word against hers."

"Relax, T.J." The captain stood to get his full attention. "I think Anderson can assure us that's not going to happen. Right, Anderson?" He looked at her directly.

"Yes, sir."

"Good. Then we're all clear. T.J., you can make the announcement to the rest of the men." The captain fixed his stare on Owens, daring him to balk. When it was clear T.J. was not going to show further defiance, the captain glanced between them. "That's all." He turned his attention back to the paperwork on his desk.

The matter was settled.

Joanna got to her feet while T.J. made a beeline for the door. He swung it open wide and walked out. She followed after him, expecting him to stomp off, but as soon as she stepped into the hallway and shut the door, T.J. backed her up against the wall.

"Look, I've worked long and hard to get where I am. I'm not going to let you screw it up, understand?"

"I have no intentions of screwing anything up." Her tone was as caustic as his.

"Oh sure, is that what you told Cummings right before you got him suspended?"

"Look, he deserved what he got. As long as you don't push a kid through a plate glass window, you have nothing to worry about. I'm a good cop, but I won't lie for someone who abuses their authority."

T.J.'s complexion turned red. He leaned in closer to Joanna, ready to give her more of the same, when looked to see Rose—the captain's secretary—absorbing the whole scene. His actions were harassment, plain and simple. He took a few steps back, giving Joanna some breathing room before he stormed off, expletives punctuating every step. Joanna pushed off the wall she'd been pinned against and slowly walked down the hall. *And I thought the last few weeks had been difficult. They're going to look like a walk in the park after a day in the War Room.*

There were ten other detectives besides Owens. All men. Unfortunately for her, they were all at the station for a special briefing. *Nothing like being baptized by fire,* she thought to herself as she took a deep breath and walked into the firestorm that surely awaited her.

CHAPTER TWO

Joanna felt her pulse race as she neared the briefing room—affectionately called the "War Room." She could hear the men laughing and carrying on when T.J. walked in. All revelry ceased when they caught sight of her behind him.

"Gentlemen, allow me to introduce you to my new partner." T.J.'s tone was laced with heavy sarcasm.

"You're kidding us, right?" questioned Bristol.

"Nope. I just came from the captain's office." T.J. turned to Joanna. "*Detective* Anderson," he said bitterly, "meet detectives Bristol, Barker, Rogers, Smith, Wagner, Peck, Olsen, Johnson, Martinez, and Flynn." T.J. pointed around the room as if she was staring at a group of strangers. He was only do it to patronize her since she had been worked at the same station as these guys for the last three years.

"Guys . . . this is *Detective* Joanna Anderson. Our new buddy." His teeth clenched as he took a seat on the corner of the large table at the center of the room. He folded his arms across his chest; becoming part of the gallery scrutinizing her.

She decided to take the upper hand.

"Look, you don't have to like me to work with me."

"Good!" More than one detective replied.

"But don't jump to conclusions about me either. I've been a cop for eight years, and I know what I'm doing." If looks could kill, she would be six feet under, "You can call me Jo or Joanna, doesn't matter to me."

"Oh, I don't know . . . you look more like a Benedict to me," Flynn snapped back.

"Fine! Think what you want. I may have gotten this job because I'm a woman and I'm filling a quota, but I'm just as qualified as the next guy."

Rogers approached Joanna, sizing her up like she was a piece of meat. He stood toe-to-toe with her, his sour breath warm on her face. "Don't worry, T.J., we've got you covered. We would hate for you to rely on a knife thrower as your backup."

Detective Peck finally spoke over them. He was the senior detective and had the reputation for being a pretty conservative guy. "Okay, that's enough. If the captain hears any of you talking like this, you'll get written up and you know it."

When he turned to Joanna, she smiled her appreciation. He walked over to her, she thought to shake her hand. So, she extended her hand in front of her, but he only looked at it before speaking.

"You'll have to earn our respect, Anderson, and that's not going to be easy." Peck stepped past her into the hallway, the other detectives filing out behind him. She was left standing with T.J., her pride trampled on the floor.

"Go change your clothes."

"What?"

"Your clothes." T.J. snapped. "Unless you plan on wearing your uniform your first day as a detective?"

Joanna quickly headed to the locker area–an extension of the women's restroom–to change back into her street clothes. She had worn a pair of faded jeans and a hot pink t-shirt to work that morning. She shoved her gun into the waistband at the small of her back, glad she had her denim jacket for concealment. When she looked down at the floppy sandals on her feet, she sighed. *Not the sturdiest shoes. Oh well,* She stood up straighter. *Hopefully, the day will be uneventful enough that it won't matter.*

T.J. waited for Joanna in the hallway. When she exited the restroom, he took one glance at her before turning away. She looked good. Too good. But he knew he couldn't tell her that. Try as he might to *not* like Joanna, it still didn't make her look any less enticing. Her shoulder length hair was the same sandy color as his, and her deep green eyes reminded him of the waters he'd surfed off the coast of Brazil. She definitely took care of her 5'5" frame, having definition and curves in all the right places. Joanna had a natural glow about her. He was fairly certain she liked spending time outdoors, because she didn't come across as the tanning salon type. That's why he'd pursued her when he arrived at the station a year ago. He was sure they'd have mutual interests. But Joanna had never even given him the time of day.

Joanna followed T.J. out to the parking lot behind the station and watched as he got into his car. When he revved the engine of the nondescript sedan assigned to him, she hurried her pace and slid into the passenger seat. He glared at her, obviously trying to make her uncomfortable but she refused to be intimidated. He pulled out of the lot, chirping his tires as he sped down the boulevard. After a few blocks he asked, "Where's your gun?"

She turned to him. "In my waistband, why?"

"Lucky gun," he mumbled.

"What did you say?" She turned to him, pretty sure she'd heard what he'd muttered under his breath.

"Come on, Joanna, it's probably the most action you've seen all month." His chuckle was as lewd as his comment.

She shot him a disgusted look. "What's that supposed to mean?"

"Are you kidding me?" He glared at her. "Everyone at the station knows you don't put out. Why do you think I gave up my pursuit? I wasn't going to work that hard on someone and get nothing in return."

"Good. I'm glad you know where I stand." She turned away, looking out the passenger window.

"No problem there. I'll reserve my energy for someone who appreciates it."

She didn't bother to comment. She wouldn't give him the satisfaction.

"Is it holstered?

"No." Joanna kept her answer short. She had no interest in carrying on a conversation with him.

After several minutes of silence, they pulled into the uniform shop everyone at the station used. She looked at him for an explanation.

"You need a holster," he said.

She thought about the ankle holster she had at home, the one she wore when she was off duty. But it wouldn't fit her duty weapon so she didn't bother bringing it up.

When they got out of the car, he stared at her like she was a cold beer on a very hot day.

"Had enough?" she asked as he continued to scrutinize her body.

"Do you usually wear a belt?"

She looked down at the leather belt she was wearing, puzzled by his statement.

He rolled his eyes. "I know you're wearing one now, but do you usually wear one?" he asked as he started towards the store.

"Yeah, why?"

"Because you'll need to wear one from now on to support a holster."

"Maybe I'll get a shoulder holster." *Why'd I say that?*

Shoulder holsters were pretty much a thing of the past. They were bulky and cumbersome, something only old-timers and traditionalists wore. But she knew exactly why she'd said it. She didn't want to give T.J. the satisfaction of telling her what to do.

"Are you kidding me?" He laughed. "You're too skinny to pull off the bulge under your arm and all that leather."

Joanna let the comment about her size slide as she headed to the counter at the back of the store. The clerk standing there gave her the once over, then asked, "Can I help you?"

"I'd like to see a shoulder holster." She looked at T.J. and grinned as she pulled off her jacket. The man behind the counter handed her one. After she adjusted the straps, Joanna pulled it on. The leather was stiff and the holster bulky, just like T.J. said it would be. "Do you have anything smaller?" Joanna asked the clerk.

"Nope. That's standard issue," the older man said after exchanging a glance with T.J. Something unspoken passed between the two men—Joanna was sure of it—but she let it go. T.J., on the other hand, did nothing to hide the gloating look on his face.

"You'd probably be more comfortable with this." The clerk laid a standard holster on the counter—the kind that could clip to any belt. She placed her weapon on the glass case and picked up the holster. Ignoring T.J., Joanna struggled to get the holster in place at the small of her back. When she finally had it secured, she put her gun in it and pulled her jacket on. Walking over to the full-length mirror on the wall, Joanna craned her neck so she could look over her shoulder. She tugged at the hem of her jacket and asked, "Does it stick out?"

"Does what stick out?" T.J. grinned, his eyes clearly focused lower than they should be.

"Forget it!"

She unclipped the holster from her belt and laid it on the counter. Slipping her weapon back in her waistband, she asked the clerk, "Can you hold this for me until later this evening? I don't have any money on me right now."

"Just put it on this." T.J. slapped his credit card on the counter and looked at Joanna with a grin. "You can owe me."

"No, thank you. The last thing I want is to be indebted to you." She turned to the clerk. "I'll come back for it later." She gave the man her name and number before leaving.

When T.J. exited from the parking lot, he headed west. "Do you still live in the Canal District?"

"Why do you know where I live?" she snapped.

"Research. I always make sure I know a little about my acquisitions. You just happened to be a deal that wasn't worth closing."

She was momentarily speechless. She knew he was an egotistical jerk—used to getting his way—but even she didn't know he could be so . . . so . . . blatantly arrogant. She decided the only way to deal with his narcissism was to ignore it. "What does it matter where I live?"

"Because you need to put on a decent pair of shoes."

"These are fine."

T.J. chuckled. "Don't worry, Joanna," His tone turned low and sexy. "I'll show some restraint. Believe it or not, I've been in a woman's apartment before without ever stepping foot in her bedroom."

"That's not what I was thinking." She lied. That was exactly what she was thinking. T.J. was a man with an incredibly high self-esteem, and a voracious appetite for women. She knew his type. He would use any opportunity to change her mind about him.

Joanna watched as he maneuvered through traffic.

When he got closer to her neighborhood, she gave him more specific directions.

"You'll turn right on the second street. It'll be the yellow house on the left."

T.J. pulled into the driveway and parked in front of her small garage. Her house was a quaint, cottage-style home, sandwiched between two larger houses.

"Mind if I come in and use the head? I promise to behave myself," he smirked.

Joanna just shrugged, already tired of his annoying sense of humor.

T.J. radioed dispatch that they were ten-seven in the Canal District. He then followed Joanna down the long walkway on the side of her house. Since she didn't have her keys with her, she reached for the spare she had hidden under the ledge of a nearby window. Joanna stretched her hand under the lip of the sill, felt for the key, and then moved to the front door.

"You know it's not safe to have a spare key lying around like that. It's the oldest trick in the book and the first one used by burglars."

"I know. But I jog and bike a lot. I don't want to have to take my keys with me all the time." She turned the key in the deadbolt, pushed open the door and headed for the stairs. "The bathroom is on the right." She pointed to a door off the entryway as she hurried up the stairs.

Joanna quickly grabbed her running shoes from under her bed and snagged a pair of socks from her dresser. She walked to the bottom of the steps, sat down, and tugged on her socks. She was lacing up her shoes when T.J. came out of the bathroom. She watched as he eyeballed her bike sitting in the alcove between the bathroom and the interior garage door. Then, he walked across her small living room to where French doors opened up the dining area to the patio outside. He peered out onto the deck where it sat on the edge of the canal. "Nice view."

"I like it."

When T.J. turned back to the living room, his critical eye continued around her open living space. He scrutinized the room as if it had to pass some sort of inspection.

Joanna followed his stare and looked at her living room afresh through T.J's eyes. He probably saw small and homey—maybe even run down—but Joanna saw quaint and eclectic. Though the fireplace was the central focal point of the room—with its oversized barn-wood mantel and the large maritime clock hanging above—everything else in the space fit the small cottage look she'd been going for. The over-stuffed couch of chocolate linen and hammered nail-head trim was cozy. Paired with a coffee table made from reclaimed wood, the sitting area had almost a hunting cabin's look to it. Some might consider it masculine, but Joanna didn't care. It was warm and comfortable. It soothed her at night like the chenille blanket tossed over the back of the couch.

"Please tell me you have a television in that," T.J. said, pointing to the antique armoire nestled in the corner.

"I do."

"Good. For a minute there, I thought I might've traveled back in time." He looked around some more, then asked. "Don't these old pieces depress you?"

"Are you kidding? They fascinate me. They have history and character; nothing like the cookie cutter furniture factories are spitting out today."

He shrugged. "Whatever."

Joanna was going to say more in her defense but decided against it. It wasn't worth the effort.

"Do you want something before we leave?" Joanna asked as she got to her feet.

He turned to her with a Cheshire grin and a wicked look in his eyes. "Depends on what you're offering."

"Something to drink." Her tone was clipped. "You could obviously use something to cool you down."

He grinned. "What do you have?"

"Orange juice, Grape juice; juices mostly."

"No Coke?"

"Sorry, I don't drink sodas."

"Well, any good hostess would have them on hand for visitors and unexpected guests."

His sarcastic etiquette lesson grated on her. "I haven't had much reason to entertain lately. It seems my pool of friends has dwindled."

She could tell he was about to say something, and dared him with a raised brow. He smiled instead and asked, "Got any water?"

"Sure."

Joanna walked to the refrigerator and grabbed two bottles. She handed one to T.J. before they headed out the door. She locked up the house and returned her key to its hiding place.

When they got into the car, dispatch was reporting a five-ninety-four in progress at Magnolia Park. Vandalism was on the rise and since it was usually gang related, it was a matter that was taken seriously.

"Hey, that's right around the corner from here," Joanna said as she reached for the radio.

T.J. stopped her. "What are you doing?"

"Letting dispatch know we're responding."

"I'm sure there are uniforms in the area that can respond."

"You're kidding me, right? We're right here."

T.J. slowly backed out of her driveway without answering her. Joanna shook her head in disgust. "I knew you were a screw-up but I thought you took the job a little more serious than that. I guess common day street crime is below you."

T.J. glared at her as he snatched the radio from the dash. "David Charlie Two responding Code Two." T.J. flipped the switch on the small light bar in the back window of the car and roared down the street.

Magnolia Park was huge. It had an aquatic area, multiple baseball diamonds and various play yards. As T.J. pulled into one of the parking lots, he asked dispatch for a ten-twenty on the vandals. When Joanna heard the culprits were near the retaining wall, she knew exactly where to go.

She and T.J. crept up on two guys carrying several cans of spray paint. As soon as T.J. announced their arrival, the two vandals took off in opposite directions. T.J. went right towards the water park while she sprinted after the guy headed for the baseball diamonds.

Joanna was able to gain ground on the punk—mainly because he kept tripping on his oversized jeans. She yelled several warnings, and identified herself as a police officer, but he kept running. After a few more missteps on his part, Joanna was within a few feet of catching him. He flung himself on the chain-link fence that surrounded the baseball diamond, and had almost reached the top when Joanna grabbed hold of one of his ankles. He kicked and fought to loosen her grip—but she held on. Reaching up, she latched onto the hem of his jacket, and with all her strength, broke his hold on the fence. They both fell to the ground, Joanna taking the brunt of the fall. She was momentarily dazed, but didn't let go of the vandal.

They wrestled in the dirt—each trying to get the upper hand. Joanna took a couple blows to the face before she was able to maneuver herself onto her feet. When the kid stood up, she lowered him with a well-placed knee. He collapsed to the ground—grabbing his groin—as Joanna pulled her gun from her waistband.

She panted as she drew down on him. "If you move, I *will* shoot you."

It was only a moment before she saw two uniformed officers running in her direction. Once they had control of the perp, she stepped back. After taking a couple of deep breaths, she wiped the blood trickling from her nose.

"Owens," she gasped. "He headed after the other one. Somewhere towards the water park."

"He's got back up," one of the officers said while pulling the kid to his feet.

She sighed with relief as she slumped over. With her gun still in her hand, she leaned on her knees and spit bloody saliva from her mouth.

"You okay?" Officer Dominquez asked.

She could tell he was asking out of duty. He didn't *really* care how she felt. In fact, he probably enjoyed seeing the discomfort she was in.

"I'm fine." Her words were sharp.

"Good. Then you can make your way back to the parking lot by yourself. We'll take this guy into custody and meet you back at the station." The two officers flanked the vandal as they walked towards their squad car.

Joanna waited until they were a distance away before she allowed a few painful tears to fall. Her legs felt like Jell-O after her sprint, and the weight of the kid falling on her had just about done her in. She touched the tender area at the small of her back where her gun had cut into her flesh. When she withdrew her hand, she wasn't surprised to see blood on her fingers. Pushing her hair back from her face, she took a deep breath and dusted off her clothes as best as she could. She slowly walked back to the parking lot, making sure the last of her tears were dried before she reached the car.

The look of shock on T.J.'s face told her she must look as bad as she felt. He, on the other hand, only looked winded.

"What the heck happened to you?"

"Nothing I couldn't handle," she snapped.

Joanna walked around the side of the car, slamming the door after carefully taking a seat.

T.J. got into the car and looked her over. "Are you going to be okay?"

She actually thought she detected a hint of concern in his voice. "Nothing a nice long bath won't fix."

He grinned. "Hey, I'm game if you are."

She ignored him and looked the other way.

He surprised her when he reached across the seat and tipped her head so he could see the cut she'd sustained on her forehead. "That might need stitches. I should take you to the E.R. to make sure."

She pushed his hand away and flipped down the visor. Staring into the mirror, she had a decent size cut above her right brow. "I'll be fine. I'll steri-strip it when I get back to the station." She snapped the visor shut and turned towards the passenger window.

"Suit yourself. Just don't get any blood on my car."

T.J. pulled out from the lot and headed back to the station. After a moment, Joanna opened the glove compartment and rifled through its contents.

"What are you looking for?" T.J. asked as he maneuvered through traffic.

She didn't answer; she just grabbed a few fast food napkins, then slammed the compartment shut. Reaching behind herself, she pressed the napkins to the area throbbing at the small of her back.

"What's wrong with your back?" he asked as he glanced between her and the road.

"Just a cut. But don't worry, I won't get any blood on your precious upholstery."

Her snide comment was meant to fend off any more questions. It worked. They didn't exchange another word all the way back to the station.

CHAPTER THREE

Joanna got out of the car slowly, her body already feeling stiff from wrestling with the gangbanger. When she realized T.J. was watching her, she straightened up and walked to the back door of the station like nothing was wrong.

Hopefully everyone is out in the field, she thought to herself; not wanting to face the ribbing she was sure to get if anyone saw what a mess she was.

When she turned the corner into the War Room, Bristol and Rogers were leaning over the table studying some photos. They both turned when she walked in. While Bristol looked stunned, a huge grin covered Rogers' face.

"Well, well, well, look what the cat dragged in," Rogers jeered.

Joanna ignored his comment and walked straight to the water cooler. She grabbed a disposable cup and filled it with water. She swished the water around in her mouth before spitting it back into the cup. The iron taste of blood was still in her mouth.

"So, you took a tumble with one of the Lost Boys," Rogers said as he laughed. "I heard he resisted arrest, but then again, maybe he just liked the idea of roughing up a woman."

T.J. walked into the room. Joanna was sure he'd heard Rogers' remark—but said nothing.

"Now look at T.J., here." Rogers turned and threw his arm over T.J.'s shoulders. "Not a scratch or a smudge on him. He's not going to let some lowlife get the best of him."

Joanna ignored Rogers as she crossed the room to the row of filing cabinets against the far wall. She started going through each drawer, looking for the proper report forms when T.J. came up behind her.

"If you're looking for report forms, they're in the bottom left file." He leaned against the wall, his arms crossed against his chest.

Joanna didn't acknowledge his help; she just bent down and reached for the file drawer. When she did, her jacket raised up slightly.

"Hey, you really did a number on your back. That looks pretty nasty."

Joanna quickly closed the cabinet and stood. "It's nothing."

She pushed some stray hairs behind her ear and could feel the swelling in her cheek. "Look, I'm going to take a minute to get cleaned up. I'll start on the report when I get back."

She tried to act as normal as possible when she walked past T.J. and tossed the forms on the table. Then she made a beeline for the women's restroom/locker room. Pushing the door open, she walked in, glanced around, and sighed with relief that it was empty. She crossed to her locker on the far side of the room and spun the tumbler on her combination lock. Grabbing her hairbrush and the first aid kit off the shelf, she walked to the sink, took one look in the mirror, and cringed. Along with the cut on her forehead, one side of her face was noticeably swollen, and there was blood on her lip where it had split. However, it was the pain from her back that was killing her.

Well, first things first.

She had to make herself look as presentable as possible, hoping she could keep the harassing to a minimum. Crumpling up a handful of paper towels, she held the makeshift washcloth under the faucet until the wad was completely wet. Joanna squeezed out the excess water, then pressed the towels to her face. She gently wiped at the blood and dirt smudges, before leaning in closer to examine the cut on her head. It was pretty deep. Luckily, it was close to her brow. If it did end up leaving a scar, it wouldn't be too noticeable.

She rinsed the matted blood from her hair, then quickly ran a brush through it. When she was done, she turned her back to the mirror and craned her neck over her shoulder to see how bad the abrasion on her back was. The once white napkins she had pulled from T.J.'s glove box were now red and sticking to her flesh. She gave them a quick yank, causing her to flinch. The abrasion turned bright red when a fresh rush of blood reached the surface.

Great!

She took off her jacket, unzipped her jeans, and rolled

down the waistband. She wadded up some more paper towels, and while twisting and contorting her body, she dabbed at the bloody area causing it to sting even more. After a few minutes, she had the area cleaned up as best as she could. Examining it closer, she could see that the muzzle of her gun had scraped away a patch of skin almost two square inches. It felt like the small of her back was on fire. With a square of gauze from her first aid kit and a couple of Band-Aids, she readied a makeshift patch and tried to apply it to the wound on her back.

Her first attempt was a complete disaster. Her shirt got in the way and one of the Band-Aids folded back against itself. She tried to get it unstuck, but she only made it worse. She growled in frustration and flung the twisted piece of gauze into the sink.

She took a deep breath and prepared another bandage. She rolled her shirt up to her rib cage, and pushed her jeans further down on her hips. Once again she tried to position the bandage while looking over her shoulder—using the mirror as her guide. But her sense of direction was all out of whack. As hard as she tried, her second attempt failed as miserably as her first.

"Need a little help?"

Joanna jumped at the intrusion. Looking at the reflection in the mirror, she saw T.J. standing in the doorway of the bathroom with a look of amusement on his face.

"No. But some privacy would be nice. This *is* the women's bathroom, after all." Joanna turned towards the lockers, pulled her jeans above her hips and rolled down her shirt. Leaning back against the sink, she asked, "What are you doing here anyway?"

"You were taking forever. That report is not going to write itself. And I'm not going to wait all day for you."

"I'll be right out," she snapped.

T.J. gave her one more cursory look before he shook his head. "Whatever," he huffed as he turned to leave.

Joanna picked up the first aid kit. She pulled her arm back—wanting to chuck it at his head. But she stopped herself before she let it go. *I will not let him get under my skin. He's not worth the energy.*

She turned back to the task at hand. By the time she could construct her third patch, Rose—the captain's secretary—walked through the door. "I heard you might need some help."

Rose's tone was very businesslike, but when she saw Joanna's face, and the abrasion on her back, her attitude softened. "Don't you think you should have a doctor check that out? It looks pretty bad."

"I'll be fine. I just need to get this stupid bandage in place."

"Here, let me do it."

Rose took the bandage from her hand. Joanna turned around, lifted her t-shirt slightly and bent over the sink. Rose pressed the bandage to the small of her back, causing Joanna to wince.

"Sorry," Rose apologized.

"It's all right." Joanna stood up straighter and turned around. "Thanks for the help."

"No problem." Once again, Rose was all business as she left.

Joanna fastened her jeans, pulled her shirt down, and

put her jacket on before taking one more glance at herself in the mirror. She still looked awful, but there wasn't much more she could do about it. She tossed her brush and the first aid kit back into her locker and headed back to the War Room.

Joanna took a seat at the table next to T.J., and started on the report.

"So, T.J., does the guy Anderson bagged look as bad as she does?" Rogers taunted from his corner of the large table.

"No, but from what I hear, it wasn't his face he was holding."

Bristol and Rogers winced in reflex.

"When are men going to learn, if they play hardball with a woman, she's going to go for the family jewels every time?" Bristol laughed at his own joke. "That punk is going to have a hard time living down the fact that a female cop got the better of him. Especially one her size."

Bristol and Rogers kept talking about her as if she wasn't even there. She tried ignoring their comments about her size and the way they rationalized away her ability. They made it sound as if the guy fell to the ground all by himself and she just happened to be there to detain him.

She mumbled something under her breath, and Rogers picked up on it immediately.

"What did you say, Anderson?" his tone accusatory.

"Nothing."

"Oh come on, can't you take a little ribbing? I mean, we are giving you credit for catching the guy. You're just lucky you got someone who didn't know how to climb a fence. Of course," Rogers said as he walked over and leaned on the table next to her, "Maybe he took a dive so he could roll around with you in the dirt. He knew he was caught. Maybe he just wanted a little fun for his troubles."

"That was hardly the case," Joanna shot back.

"Oh, I don't know . . . you look like you could be a good roll in—"

"Hey," T.J. interrupted Rogers. "I'd watch it if I were you. She might tell the captain you're making *sexual* advances at her, too."

"Too? What do you mean, too?" Rogers looked at Joanna with a heated glare.

"Seems Joanna couldn't wait to tell the captain I made *'advances'* towards her." T.J.'s use of air quotes punctuated his accusation. "So don't talk about how good she looks, or how much fun you could have with her. And above all, don't try to ask her out on a date or you might end up in the captain's office."

Joanna had heard enough. She leveled a look at T.J. and fired away. "Look, I didn't tell the captain you made sexual advances towards me. I just told him I knew you were interested in me socially, and I didn't think it was a good idea that we were teamed as partners."

"Don't flatter yourself!" T.J. yelled, as he shot up from his chair. "You might look good on the outside, but it's obvious your personality is flawed."

"Think what you want, T.J.! You're talking about something you know nothing about. Cummings is a bad cop and he has no respect for the badge."

"And you're a sellout. What's worse?" T.J. challenged.

"What's worse is the fact that I closed my eyes for months before I finally said something."

"No, what's worse is, not only do I have to worry about the scum I have to deal with on the streets, but now I have to worry about you sticking up for the criminals instead of for me."

"Yeah, Anderson," Rogers chimed in. "I sure hope you don't get yourself into any tight spots. It would be a shame if your backup got delayed."

Joanna didn't say a word. The threat chilled her to the bone. *Would they really hang me out to dry, just to get rid of me?*

Joanna tried to shake it off and continued with her report, praying she would never have to rely on Rogers for anything.

CHAPTER FOUR

When Joanna got home, she collapsed on her couch and reached for the cordless phone on the coffee table. She had to tell someone her good news while she still thought it was.

"Kathy, hi." Joanna could hear crying in the background. "Did I call at a bad time?"

"Just a minute, Joanna."

Joanna heard the phone thud and the crying become more pronounced before it quieted. "Sorry, Joanna, we were having a small crisis."

Kathy–Joanna's friend since the academy–was home on maternity leave. She and her husband–also a police officer–had been married a little over two years. Kathy had given birth to twin boys two months ago and was in the midst of juggling her new life.

"How are Kevin and Kyle?" Joanna asked.

"Loud," Kathy said with a chuckle.

"So I hear."

"I'm only kidding. They're doing great. Believe it or not, I'm beginning to get the hang of this. Of course, it's easier when Mike is home giving me a hand, but I really am loving it."

"That's great. Have you made a decision yet about coming back to work?"

Joanna heard a long sigh before Kathy answered.

"I'm going to resign. Mike says we can make it on one salary. So, I've decided to stay home with the boys."

Joanna wasn't surprised. Kathy was the nurturing type. As much as she insisted she'd be back in the ranks in six months, Joanna had had a keen suspicion it wasn't going to happen.

"Are you disappointed in me, Jo?" Kathy asked.

"Absolutely not! I think it's great, and I'm glad Mike's backing you on this."

"Are you kidding? It was his idea. He doesn't want the boys in daycare. And he doesn't want us having to juggle two crazy schedules. Of course, we won't be taking any trips to France or Italy anytime soon. And we're definitely going to have to rework our budget. But I think the sacrifice is worth it."

"That's great. I'm happy for you. It seems like things are working out just fine."

"And how about you, Joanna? What's new with you?"

Joanna beamed, excited to share her news. "I got it, Kathy."

"Got what?" she asked, then quickly answered her own question. "The detective's position?"

"Yep."

"Joanna, that's great! Congratulations. When did they

tell you?"

"Today."

"When do you start?"

"Today," Joanna said with a laugh as she fingered her swollen cheek. "It was effective immediately."

"That's incredible, Joanna. I can't wait to tell Mike. I thought for sure you'd blown your chances when you filed that grievance against Cummings."

"Well, I'm not the popular choice by any means. The captain sat me down and let me know he was against the decision but the brass was pushing to get females in the upper divisions. I tested highest so he really didn't have a choice."

"But you're still excited, right? I mean you're not going to decline the job based on that, are you?"

"No. I accepted. Even if the captain doesn't think I can cut it."

"What do you mean?"

"He basically said he doesn't think I'll last the month."

"Then he doesn't know you too well, does he?" Kathy encouraged. "So, who's your partner? Anyone I'd know?"

"Terry Owens. Everyone calls him T.J. I've told you about him before."

Kathy's tone turned brisk. "Yeah, he's the jerk that masterminded that prank when you wouldn't give him the time of day. How'd you get stuck with him?"

"Lucky I guess," Joanna said jokingly. "You should've seen his reaction. You would've thought he was just diagnosed with an incurable disease. It was priceless."

Kathy laughed along with Joanna. "Serves him right for the crap he pulled on you."

Joanna's tone turned serious. "It's not going to be easy, Kath. There was a lot of animosity when the decision was announced. I'll be the only female detective, and in their eyes, I've already got one strike against me. I'm not going to get any handouts or hand ups. I'm sure everyone would like nothing better than to see me fail miserably."

"But you're not going to let that happen, right?" Kathy said defensively.

Joanna smiled. It was nice having a personal cheerleader. "No. I'm going to do everything I can to prove I belong."

"Thatta girl," Kathy said just as a loud cry reverberated in the background. "Oh, that's Kyle. I need to go Joanna. I'm sorry."

"No. I totally understand."

"Hey, when are you going to come for a visit? I might live a few hours away but it's not like it's the end of the earth. I want you to see Kevin and Kyle before we send them off to college," Kathy joked as the crying increased.

"I know. I know. I want to, but I don't see any free time coming my way for a while. I promise I'll try."

Kathy congratulated Joanna again before hanging up.

Joanna could feel the smile on her face, and the pain from her swollen cheek. She was proud of her accomplishment and wasn't going to let anyone or anything diminish that.

At least for today.

CHAPTER FIVE

Joanna made it through the rest of the week. The abrasion on her back was healing nicely, though it was still tender to the touch. The cut on her head was going to leave a scar, but it followed the curve of her brow perfectly, making it look more like a shadow than a scar.

The only bright spot in her week was when she found out T.J. had not apprehended the vandal he had chased through the park. He failed to mention that until they filled out their reports. Joanna knew she shouldn't gloat, but inwardly she felt she had bested T.J., and it made her otherwise bleak week seem not so bad. T.J. had spoken to her as little as possible; choosing instead to spend his time with Bristol and Rogers. That suited her fine. The less talking, the less bickering.

In the War Room, everyone was reviewing information regarding the murder of three prostitutes. Three deaths in a month was no longer considered random. Although they were trying to keep the information under wraps, the murmurs of a serial killer had already made it to the streets and the media.

Of course, Joanna had been kept busy with every menial task known to man. She'd cleaned file cabinets—inside and out, updated records; even cleaned the water cooler. It was to be expected—being low man on the totem pole, and she was fine paying her dues. But she could do without the snide remarks and malicious stares.

She'd asked herself—a hundred times already—if it was really worth it to be somewhere she wasn't wanted. And each time she did, Matthew's face appeared in her thoughts. He wouldn't have let her talk like that. He wouldn't have let her give up or give in. Matthew had taught her how to be strong, to see things through to the end, and to rely on the Lord.

He had taught her so many things.

From the day of the car accident that had taken her parents lives, Officer Matthew Moore had become like a father to her. He had been the one to tell her that her parents had died in the accident, and had kept his promise to never leave her alone.

Matthew had told Joanna—on several occasions—the attachment he'd felt for her the moment he reached through that backseat window, and held her little fingers in his hand. After the accident he became an ever present force in her life. He fought to adopt her, but the system just couldn't see how an unmarried cop could be a stable father. Matthew didn't give up though. He visited her at the children's home every chance he could and took her to church every Sunday. He had even entertained the idea of marriage, so he would look like a more suitable candidate for adoption. But in the end, his convictions wouldn't let him enter into marriage under false pretenses.

When she was younger, Joanna loved walking to church hand-in-hand with Matthew. She couldn't wait to hear the Bible stories her teacher would read each Sunday. As she got older, she realized the faith Matthew had was something she could have for herself.

He cried the day she asked him to pray with her so she could ask Jesus into her heart.

The courts might not have allowed Matthew to adopt her, but he was the only parent she knew. She was never placed with a family. He was all she had.

He never missed a school production or an awards ceremony, and he was front and center the day she graduated from high school.

When she told Matthew she wanted to become a cop, he did everything he could to talk her out of it. Though it was the profession he had devoted his life to, he knew the dangers involved with police work and didn't want her to be a part of it. After he had exhausted every argument he could think of; he finally accepted the idea and did everything he could to make sure she was prepared for what lay ahead.

Joanna thought her future was set. She moved in with Matthew when she turned eighteen, and immediately enrolled in the Police Explorers Program. She joined the police academy three days after she turned twenty-one, and graduated six months later at the top of her class.

Her life had turned completely around.

She never would've believed she could survive after the death of her parents. But fourteen years later, not only had she survived, she had a very bright future ahead of her.

Then, one month after graduation, her world came crashing down around her. The radio call every cop dreaded to hear went out across the airwaves.

Officer down.

Matthew and his partner had been called to the scene of a reported domestic disturbance between a husband and wife; when in fact, it was a knock down, drag out fight between two crack-heads spinning out of control.

By the time backup arrived, the house was empty, except for the two police officers sprawled out on the living room floor. Matthew's partner was unconscious, shot twice in the leg and torso. Matthew had sustained a fatal gunshot wound to the head. There was nothing anyone could've done.

Joanna was given a six week leave of absence. During that time she fought with herself and God. Not once, but twice God had taken away everyone who mattered to her. In a stupor, she decided to quit the force. She wanted to let go of everything and cease to exist. She went on a self-destructive binge for three weeks–taking pills to help her sleep at night and downing alcohol to deaden the pain during the day. But no amount of drugs or booze could make the pain go away.

She thought about Matthew day and night; remembering everything he had done for her over the years. Then one day she looked at herself in the mirror and somehow felt as if she was letting him down. Matthew had invested so much time in her.

Helping her.

Caring for her.

She began to question her self-imposed destruction. Was it wrong to not want to go on? To want to just give up? Would Matthew be disappointed in her not being stronger? For turning to alcohol and pills instead of God?

Joanna had argued with herself and God for days, but in the end, she knew what Matthew would've wanted her to do. She got herself cleaned up and reported back to work; dedicated to the idea of being the best cop she could be.

Joanna stood, leaning against the rail of her deck, basking in her memories as she watched the rippling water in the canal. The sun had set hours ago, leaving the full moon to dance on the tips of the water.

I know you didn't promise me an easy life, Lord, but I could use a little help right about now.

She went back into the house, picked up her Bible from the coffee table, and headed to bed.

CHAPTER SIX

The next few weeks seemed to drag on forever. Joanna celebrated the fact she'd made it through the first month, proving the captain wrong in his assessment.

T.J. was civil and tolerated her as a partner when they were out on patrol or investigating a case. But the minute they were back in the War Room, he joined in the whispering and ribbing constantly directed at her.

Joanna did her best to ignore the comments and focus solely on her job performance, but every day was a struggle.

There were a few detectives that were decent family men and didn't buy into the harassment. However, it was obvious the intentions of the other detectives were to force her out.

They probably assumed if they made it difficult and uncomfortable enough for her, she would decide to leave on her own.

Well, they were wrong.

They had no idea how she was wired. She intended to prove to each and every one of them—the captain included—that she deserved her promotion.

No matter how much garbage they flung her way.

Cummings—her former partner— had returned to duty. He'd caught her eye on more than one occasion and smiled at her like nothing was wrong. It was obvious he wasn't going to waste his time bad-mouthing her. He was more concerned with rumor control and acting the part of the model cop. His new partner even had the nerve to pull her aside and tell her how wrong she'd been about Cummings. Joanna warned him that Cummings might have changed for the moment, but it couldn't last. His temper was too volatile; she knew from firsthand experience.

Home, after a particularly humiliating shift at work, Joanna slouched on her couch and growled out loud. "Men can be so juvenile!" she shouted as she recounted the events of the day.

She and T.J had been following a lead regarding the most recent death in the prostitute killings. The owner of a topless bar had some information for them. Since he wouldn't come out of his establishment to talk to them, they had no choice but to go in. Though Bristol and Barker could have easily taken the call, they didn't. They thought it would be more entertaining to watch her handle it.

It was exactly what she'd expected. Bare-chested young women, wearing next to nothing as they served drinks and danced suggestively from stage. T.J. slowly walked to the bar, allowing himself a nice leisurely look.

He never pretended to be a Boy Scout–that much she knew. His attitude was pretty cut and dry. If these ladies wanted to give him a free look, by all means, he was going to take it.

Joanna was sickened by the place.

Girls who couldn't have been more than eighteen walked around wearing elaborate makeup, high heels, and not much more. They were throwing their lives away and would probably never be able to dig themselves out of the filth that surrounded them.

The clientele ranged from businessmen nursing their gin and tonics–eyes glazed over in some perverse fantasy–to men old enough to be grandfathers–propositioning the young girls as they danced on stage and mirrored tabletops.

Joanna was glad she'd had a light lunch, because she was ready to puke.

She walked over to join T.J. at the bar, imagining the crud that coated it. Careful not to lean against the sticky surface, she asked the bartender, "Are you the owner?"

He looked her up and down then smiled. "Yep."

Joanna ignored his brazenness. "So, what do you have for us?"

"The girl, the one they found over by the tattoo parlor, she worked for me."

"Doing what?" Joanna asked.

He looked at her with a twisted smile. "She had her MBA and was helping me diversify my portfolio." He laughed at his own joke. "She was a waitress and dancer."

"How long?"

"She showed up a couple of weeks ago looking for work. She had a great body so I hired her."

"How do you know it was her?"

"Janice told me."

"Janice?"

He pointed to a woman in a hot pink thong and a vacant stare.

"Since Jasmine hadn't been to work or back to her room since the murder, I figured she must be right."

"How do you know where she lives?"

"I own this whole building. Sometimes I put the girls up when they need a place to stay. It's not much, but it gets them off the streets." The bartender smiled as if he was performing some humanitarian effort.

Joanna knew full well that what he was probably doing was prostituting the girls in exchange for their rooms.

T.J. finally chimed in. "Did she leave anything in her room?"

"Yeah. I haven't touched the stuff. Haven't had time."

"Mind if we have a look around?" T.J. asked politely, though it sounded more like a statement.

"Why do you think I called you guys?"

Joanna glared at the guy, realizing what he had done. Knowing the police would be showing up, he probably made sure none of his customers were upstairs. She wanted to slap the 'I'm–smarter–than–you' smile right off his face.

That's okay wise guy. Next time we'll make sure and drop by unannounced. Then we'll see how accommodating you are.

T.J. and Joanna followed the bartender up the stairs to a dingy hallway. "Jasmine's was the last room on the left," the bartender told them.

T.J. tried the handle. It was already unlocked. "Have you been in here?"

"Yeah," the bartender replied. "She was late on the rent, so I went in to get it."

"Right," T.J. said sarcastically.

The bartender stood in the doorway, watching T.J. and Joanna's every move. Joanna picked through the clothes strewn about, surprised to see designer labels and expensive accessories. She walked to the bathroom where T.J. carefully picked up wrappers with the end of his pen. He shook his head. "If she was smart enough to use protection, how did she wind up in a dive like this?"

Joanna searched the bed and found some stuff crammed between the mattress and box spring. "T.J., come look at this."

She held a student identification card. T.J. took it from her—covered everything but the picture—and showed it to the bartender.

"Is this the girl?"

"Yeah. That's her."

"Says here her name was Samantha."

"She told me her name was Jasmine, showed me a driver's license and everything. But I guess they could've been fake."

T.J. revealed the rest of the card to show it was a student I.D. for Samantha Randolph—a junior in high school.

"Hey, wait a minute." The bartender threw up his hands defensively. "I had no idea she was underage. Like I said, she had I.D. and everything."

"Was she experienced?" T.J. asked coolly.

"How would I know? I never touched her."

"Right. You have a stacked girl, prancing around in her

panties, and you never helped yourself to the merchandise?"

"She wasn't my type," he said, nonchalantly.

"Don't give me that," T.J. fired back. "Anything with a pulse is your type."

Joanna could tell from the bartender's demeanor they were beginning to outwear their welcome.

"Look, I'm the one who called you," the bartender yelled. "I tried to do the right thing. If all I'm going to get is harassed, you can get out and come back when you have a warrant." He stood at the door waiting for them to leave.

"You have any use for this stuff?" T.J. asked, waving his hand around the room.

"No. In fact, I need it cleaned out. I have another renter for the room."

"You're a real piece of work, you know that," Joanna said. "A girl is dead. But all you care about is making sure you don't lose a month's rent."

"Hey, business is business."

Joanna was ready to fire back when T.J. shot her a look of warning. "We'll give you a hand cleaning this stuff up," T.J. said, showing the utmost control.

He grabbed the duffle bag that was crumpled in the corner and tossed it at Joanna. "Go ahead and pack everything up." She looked at him questionably. When he glared at her with a look that said *don't ask*, she began loading the bag up with clothes, make-up—anything personal, while T.J. went to the bathroom and retrieved whatever he found in the wastebasket and on the floor. When they walked back through the bar on their way out to their car, Joanna noticed T.J. looked straight ahead; no longer interested in the free show playing out on stage.

Okay, maybe he isn't as heartless as I thought.

With a click of the remote, T.J. popped the trunk of the sedan so Joanna could toss the duffle bag into it. When they both got back in the car, Joanna asked, "Why didn't we just get a warrant and come back for the stuff?"

"We were beginning to wear out our welcome and we didn't have just cause for being there." T.J. pulled out into traffic as he continued explaining. "If we had waited for a warrant, you can bet half of that stuff would've disappeared. There was DNA everywhere. Maybe we'll get lucky. God knows Samantha wasn't."

"What if we just destroyed evidence?"

"Look, she's dead, and she didn't die there. We've got what we've got. The lab can run tests on all of this and see if they come up with anything. They've got the DNA that was at the scene. Chances are, her last john is most likely her killer. From the looks of her room, she made sure her customers used condoms. Since that wasn't the case at the scene, I'm going to bet the guy who rolled her is our killer."

Joanna listened as T.J explained his theory.

"Any more questions?" he snapped.

"Yeah. You didn't seem as interested in the floor show when we left. Why is that?" she asked smartly.

"Even I have my limits. It's one thing if a woman wants to flaunt her body and make a career out of it. It's another thing when some slimy bartender puts underage girls up in an apartment, so he can exploit them. Give me some credit, will ya."

Joanna could tell from T.J.'s tone he was mad, but not

necessarily at her. He'd just revealed he had a decent side, and Joanna was glad for it. She didn't want to think of T.J. being as carnal as the men in the bar. Drinking their lives away. Ruining the lives of women that saw no other way out other than selling their bodies. She knew T.J. had a little more class than that; she could see it in his eyes.

When Joanna and T. J. got back to the War Room, everyone took turns firing potshots at her.

"Hey, Anderson, we heard you had a '*bust'aling* day?" Bristol laughed.

Smith chimed in. "Did you get some coffee while you were there? They're known for their big *cup* size."

Everyone roared.

Joanna did her best to ignore their smutty humor, but it was Rogers' parting shot that hit below the belt.

"Hey, Anderson, I heard the bar was looking for some new help. Some of your credentials are a little weak," he said, glancing at her blouse. "But I'm sure they'd make an exception in your case. You definitely have the *assets* for the job."

Joanna felt degraded and exposed.

"That's enough, Rogers!" T.J. shouted.

"What?" Rogers turned to T.J. "Are you defending her, Owens?"

"No. But you're crossing a very dangerous line. You'd do good to keep your low class jokes to yourself."

"Oh, really?" Rogers stuck out his chin, rising to the challenge. "What's this all about, T.J.? You getting a little something after hours that we don't know about?"

T.J. swung at Roger's face, nailing him on the jaw. Before Roger's could retaliate, the four other detectives in the room jumped between them, preventing an all out brawl. Joanna stood by the water cooler, shocked by what was happening.

"What was that for?" Rogers yelled, while Smith and Bristol held him back. "I can't believe you're siding with Benedict."

"And I can't believe what a jerk you are. Unless you want to be written up for harassment, you'd better keep your foul mouth shut."

"She wouldn't dare." Rogers looked at Joanna, taunting her with his stare.

"She might not. But I will," T.J. said as he stared Rogers down.

Rogers shook off the guys that were holding him and straightened his shirt. He walked over to where T.J. was flanked by Olsen and Barker.

"Have it your way, T.J. I hope she's worth it."

Rogers walked away while Olsen put a hand to T.J.'s chest, holding him in place. "Let it go, T.J." Olsen gave him a warning look before he let his hand fall to his side.

Joanna quickly exited the War Room and headed for the parking lot.

T.J. rushed to catch up with her. "Joanna, wait!"

He caught her by the arm and forced her to turn around.

"Why did you do that?" she yelled.

He was clearly surprised by her tone. "What are you mad at me for? I was only trying to help."

"Well, I don't need your help, or your pity. I was handling things just fine."

"Maybe I was sticking up for myself. Did you ever

think of that? I'm not going to let my reputation be hampered just because I'm saddled with you as a partner."

"He wasn't insulting you; he was insulting me."

T.J. backed away, his hands raised. "Well excuse me for trying to help. The next time you become the target of the night, I'll just keep my mouth shut."

Joanna pierced him with an icy stare. "I've had a bull's-eye on my back since I got promoted. What makes tonight any different?"

She dared him to answer. But he just stood there.

Joanna walked to her car and pulled away, leaving T.J. standing in the middle of the parking lot.

Joanna had tried to relax when she got home, but every time she thought of Rogers' snide remarks and T.J. jumping to her defense, her anger grew.

Agitated all over again, she got up from her couch and headed for the garage. A couple rounds with the punching bag was what she needed to temper her aggravation. Kick boxing was no longer just a way to keep her physique toned and firm. It had become a sort of emotional therapy. Whenever she spent time with the bag, she had imaginary conversations with Matthew. It helped to voice her frustrations, and view them in light of the advice she thought he would give. And right now, she knew Matthew was spurring her on; telling her not to let Bristol, Rogers, or any of the guys get under her skin.

She remembered past conversations she'd had with Matthew regarding his job, Christianity, and how he blended the two. He had told her the good and the bad;

warning her she'd be tested in areas of drinking, promiscuity, and language. He cautioned her that the people she would be working with were no different than the rest of the world. They weren't superheroes. Just people with the desire to protect and to serve. Men cheated on their wives, conversations got graphic and vulgar, and excessive drinking would be commonplace for some of those she'd be working with. But he reminded her Jesus called them to "be light in the darkness" and that they were to be "*in* the world, but not *of* the world".

She could still hear Matthew saying. "We're not here to judge them, Joanna. But hopefully—in the way we live our lives—they'll see a difference."

Joanna was hot and sweaty from her workout, yet felt stronger. She was determined to do her job to the best of her ability. She wasn't being asked to concede her morals or do anything unethical. She was merely being made an example of. She refused to let intimidation take her down.

She smacked the bag one last time. *Thanks Matthew, I needed that.* A tear trailed down her face as she turned off the lights and locked the door. She missed Matthew terribly, and wished she could've had her conversation with him in person.

The phone rang just as she stepped into the shower. Her shoulders dropped. All she wanted was a few moments of peace and quiet. She decided to let the machine pick it up and would check it when she got out.

After her shower, she wrapped the towel around her and went downstairs to listen to the message. It was Kathy calling to see how things were going. It had been weeks since she'd talked to her. She always had intentions of calling Kathy when she got home from work, but her mood of late had much to be desired.

She walked back upstairs, laid across her bed and dialed.

"Hi, Kathy, it's Joanna. Sorry I missed your call. I was in the shower."

"That's okay. The boys just went down, and I wanted to see how things were going for you."

"Okay," Joanna said with a sigh.

"That good, huh? Is that jerk partner of yours giving you a hard time?"

Joanna thought about the way T.J. had come to her defense and how she had jumped down his throat because of it.

"No. He's okay. There's just a lot of stuff going on."

"Like?" Kathy persisted.

"Stuff. I don't know how to describe it. Caustic looks, off-colored jokes. It's like being in the academy again with a bunch of teenage boys loaded with testosterone, having to prove they're king of the hill."

"But are you hanging in there?" Kathy asked, clearly concerned.

"Yeah. I'm doing all right. How about you, Mike, and the boys?" Joanna needed to change the conversation. She didn't want to burden Kathy needlessly with her problems.

"Good. I've actually got the boys on a schedule and for the most part it's working out pretty nice."

Kathy and Joanna talked for about twenty minutes before they hung up. Joanna got off the phone feeling a little better. She knew she'd have Kathy and Mike's prayer support, and that meant the world to her, because she really needed it.

Boy, did she need it.

CHAPTER SEVEN

Joanna woke up the next morning anticipating two glorious days off. She had a laundry list of things she wanted to accomplish, but also wanted to just have some down time. She felt guilty she wasn't going to visit Kathy; but she really needed time to herself.

She spent Saturday cleaning her house from top to bottom, tackling all the little jobs that couldn't be put off any longer. She cleaned out the refrigerator of anything unrecognizable, and finally took the bag of clothes–that had sat in the corner of her bedroom for weeks–to the Salvation Army.

Sunday, she was able to spend in church for the first in a long time. When she'd been a patrolman, her days off never allowed her to be in Sunday morning services. But now that she had weekends off, she would be able to get back into a routine. Of course, she still allowed herself the luxury of sleeping in by going to the second service.

On her drive back from church, Joanna realized how

neglected her car looked. She drove Matthew's prized '64 Mustang Fastback on weekends and when she wanted to feel closer to him, but she hadn't had it out of the garage for a while. The Mustang had been Matthew's pride and joy, the one possession he obsessed over. Joanna was ashamed she'd let it get so dirty.

So, when she got home she grabbed a quick bite to eat—out of her now pristine refrigerator—then changed into her grubby running shorts and a tank top. With a carvac in hand, she started with the interior of the car, ridding the floorboards and mats of the built-up crud and dirt. Next, she took her time conditioning the original interior and dashboard. After washing and waxing the car, she detailed the chrome wheels and trim until they shined like new. When she was done, it looked just like Matthew had always kept it.

She stepped back to admire her work.

"Much better."

Glancing at her watch, Joanna realized there was still time to get in a quick jog before it got too late. She hurried upstairs to her bedroom and pulled on an over-sized neon pink sweatshirt. With Nike's in one hand and her Khar 9mm in the other, she sat down on the stairs to put on her shoes. When laced up and ready to go, she picked up the Khar and stroked the grip with her thumb. It too had been Matthew's. He'd worn it around his ankle as his back-up weapon. She used it as her off-duty firearm because of its compact size. It easily fit into her purse, or the pocket of her sweatshirt when she went running. Just like the Mustang, it was her way to stay connected to Matthew.

Joanna skipped her warm-up routine, already feeling

her muscles were stretched and ready to go. Starting at a slow pace, she quickly worked up to her normal rhythm. She loved the therapeutic benefits of jogging. Not only was it good for her body, but it helped channel her frustrations into positive energy. With all the stress at the station lately, she was running a lot farther these days.

Who says aggravation isn't good for your health?

The sky was just turning a dusty blue when she made it back to her patio deck. After a couple cleansing breaths, she looked over her shoulder from side-to-side, then pulled out another one of her spare keys from its hiding place. T.J.'s words of warning filtered through her head, but she quickly pushed them aside.

The automatic lights hadn't clicked on yet in her house, so Joanna walked through the living room in shadows cast from the setting sun. As she pulled off her sweatshirt and tossed it over the back of the couch, she heard the toilet flush and the creak of the downstairs bathroom door open.

Quickly, she pressed herself against the wall by the entryway, shocked that there was an intruder in her house. She strained her eyes to see where her sweatshirt had landed but didn't have time to react. When the intruder emerged from the hall, she decided to bluff.

"Don't move. I have a gun and I *will* use it."

The intruder stopped and slowly raised his hands. "Hey, I–"

"Shut up and get on your knees!" she shouted, not giving him a chance to speak.

"But–"

"I said shut up!"

The intruder continued to follow her commands, even lacing his hands behind his head. It was obvious he knew the routine.

With the trespasser on his knees, Joanna moved closer, coming within inches of her sweatshirt. Just as she reached out to grab it, the automatic lights clicked on.

The intruder used the distraction to his advantage.

Sweeping her feet out from under her, he pinned her face down against the hardwood floor. She laid there motionless hoping her attacker would think she was unconscious. If he let his guard down he would most likely loosen his grip on her arms.

That was exactly what he did.

And Joanna was ready.

She snapped her elbow back and connected with his jaw. He groaned from the impact, and grappled to regain control of her hands. He pinned her spread eagle with the weight of his body, and trapped her arms above her head.

"Knock it off before you get hurt!"

The sound of T.J.'s voice replaced Joanna's fear with anger. "What the–"

He let go of her arms and shifted his weight, allowing her to roll to her back. As soon as she turned over, she began swinging.

T.J. took a few shots to the face before he pinned her wrists against the floor above her head. He hovered over her, panting.

"What the heck do you think you're doing?" Joanna yelled, her chest heaving for air.

"I wanted to talk to you about something."

"So you broke into my house?"

"I didn't have to. I used your spare key."

He sat back on his haunches and dangled the single key in the air.

She snatched it away from him. "Get off me."

T.J. got to his feet and offered her a hand. She slapped it away and got up on her own.

"I could've killed you," she hollered.

"You didn't have your weapon."

"How did you know that?"

"Your reflection in the French doors. I saw you were only bluffing." He clicked his tongue like a teacher scolding a child.

She marched to her front door, swung it open, and yelled, "Get out!"

"I said I wanted to talk to you."

"You've done enough talking. Because of you going off on Rogers the other day, everyone thinks something's going on between us."

"You didn't deserve to be treated like that, Joanna. They were way out of line. As for their insinuations regarding us, I'll set them straight tomorrow."

"Fine. You said your peace, now leave." She pointed out the door where she was still standing.

T.J. walked to the threshold and stood. "Don't you want to hear what I have to say?"

"Not particularly."

T.J.'s hands were on his hips. He obviously wasn't budging.

"Fine," she huffed. "Go ahead and tell me, if that's the only way I'm going to get you to leave."

T.J. walked slowly back into the house and turned to

her. "Charges were filed against Cummings today. He's history."

Joanna was stunned. She closed the door slowly, and stared at T.J. in disbelief. "What happened?"

"He beat an informant half-to-death. The problem was the snitch was in his bed when he did it. In light of his other suspension, the department didn't have much choice. With your complaint on the books and now this, they decided to cut him loose."

Joanna should have felt exonerated. But inside she knew she would have to brace herself for the coming wrath. "Great! Cummings shows his true colors and somehow, someway, I'll be the one who is going to take all the heat for it. Thanks for the warning, T.J., you're a real pal," Joanna said sarcastically. She brushed past him on her way to the stairs. "You can see your way out."

When she got to her bedroom, Joanna fell back across her bed and stared at the ceiling, wondering where God was. She dug the heels of her palms into her eyes, trying to prevent tears from escaping.

"I didn't come here to warn you, I came to apologize."

Joanna thought if she ignored T.J., he'd go away. When there was a long silence, she looked at the doorway from the corner of her eye and saw him leaning against the doorjamb. He was looking around. She followed his stare, once again looking at another room in her home through the scrutiny of his eyes.

Her bedroom was a canvas of white. White wicker. White down comforter. White pillows.

It was her sanctuary.

"Nice room. A little sterile for me, but it works for

you."

She sighed, her eyes closed, the back of her hands resting on her forehead. "Why are you still here?" She didn't dare look at him. She didn't want him to see she was on the verge of crying.

"Like I said, I came to apologize."

"For what?" she snapped.

"For being so hard on you."

He actually sounded sincere. Joanna raised herself up on her elbows so she could look at him. "I can take hard. I've had to handle *hard* my entire life. I just want to be given a chance."

"Then why don't we try again." T.J. stepped forward and extended his hand. "Hi. Terry Owens. But everyone calls me T.J. And you are?"

Joanna thought it was a joke. She was sure he'd pull his hand away the minute she reached for it.

"I don't bite, Joanna," he assured her, his hand still extended in a truce. "Well, not always."

Joanna reached her hand to his. "Joanna Anderson. *Detective* Joanna Anderson."

CHAPTER EIGHT

The next day, when Joanna showed up for work, T.J. was nowhere around. She looked at the log and saw that he was needed in court on a pre-existing case, so she got herself some water and took a seat in the War Room. Minutes later, Detective Peck walked in and took a seat, a grim expression on his face.

"Anderson. We've got a positive I.D. on the "pro" found by the tattoo parlor."

"Samantha Randolph?" she asked, already knowing the answer.

"Yeah. There's no missing person on her, but we checked her school records and got an address. You and Owens will need to notify her parents."

Rogers walked in while Peck was talking to her. When Peck got up to leave, she decided to follow him out. There was no way she was going to be a sitting duck for Rogers' verbal abuse.

"Where you going, Anderson? Lost without your

bodyguard?" It was obvious he was referring to T.J. coming to her defense the other day.

"Give it a rest, Rogers. You don't intimidate me so you might as well give up trying. In case you haven't heard, Cummings screwed up again, and I had nothing to do with it this time. He just pulled more of the same old crap I put up with for months."

Joanna walked from the War Room and out the back door to the department parking lot. Irritated and angry, she decided to do something productive while waiting for T.J.

Crossing the lot to where their work vehicle was located, Joanna popped the trunk. She had noticed what a mess it was the day they had loaded Samantha's belongings into it. Fast food wrappers, empty soda bottles, and other trash littered the back. A shredded spare tire, one black high-heel boot, a spool of bailing wire, and a mangled orange safety pylon were just a few of the items weighing it down.

Joanna started by gathering the small trash together and stuffing it into a torn-up pizza box, then worked on the cans and bottles. Once the garbage was removed, Joanna turned her attention to the bigger items. She walked back and forth to the large trash bin at the corner of the lot, dumping everything but the tire and the pylon. Deciding to tackle the tire next, Joanna slowly rolled it across the parking lot, making sure it didn't brush up against her yellow t-shirt as she heaved it over the rim.

Almost done.

Before she could turn around, Joanna was thrown against the metal container. Rogers pinned her to the side of the bin, away from anyone's view.

"You think you're so smart, don't you?" He spun her around; his face twisted with anger.

Joanna tried to move, but he tightened his grip on her shoulders. She looked at him unafraid, though inside she was alarmed that he would do something so blatant where someone could see him.

"What? Going to write a grievance against me, too?" Rogers spat. "Let me see . . . that would be three complaints from you in less than two months. Do you really think that's wise?"

"What do you want, Rogers?" She shot back at him, masking her fear.

"Oh, what I want, you won't give me . . . well, at least not willingly."

She refused to acknowledge his perverse comment. "Then what?"

"Leave. Put in for a transfer and leave. You're not wanted here, and I'm the only one man enough to say it."

"And if I don't?" she challenged.

"Then things could get pretty ugly." He ran his hand down the length of her hair. "You wouldn't want things to get ugly now, would you?"

Before she could say anything, a car pulled into the lot and headed in their general direction. Rogers let go of Joanna and walked away as if nothing had happened.

She quickly walked back to the open trunk and had to hold on to the edge to keep herself from falling apart. Joanna's mind was spinning as she began mumbling to herself. "God, I don't get it? I thought this is what you wanted me to do. You wanted me to be light. You wanted me to show people that I was different. Now, I don't know what to do. If I report this–"

"Report what?"

She jumped back and nearly drew down on T.J.

"Whoa, whoa, whoa, a little jumpy this morning, aren't we?"

"Don't sneak up on me like that!" she snapped before grabbing the pylon from the trunk and flinging it to the ground. She slammed the trunk but it didn't latch so she had to try again. T.J. reached forward to help.

"I can do it myself!" She slammed the trunk a third time, forcing it to latch. She grabbed the pylon and walked it over to the trash bin, chucking it as hard as she could.

"What are you snapping at me for? You're the one mumbling to yourself and throwing things around. Oh, I get it . . . it must be that time of the month."

She looked at him with pure revulsion. "No it's not, as if that's any of your business!" She stormed toward the back door of the station.

T.J. kept pace with her. "Well, I think it is my business if you're going to be so edgy during that time."

"I said that's not the problem. I was just distracted and didn't hear you come up behind me."

She grabbed the door and swung it wide. T.J. followed her to the War Room, where Rogers and Barker were sitting.

"Problem, T.J.?" Rogers asked, deep sarcasm coloring his words.

Joanna could feel Rogers' eyes on her but refused to look at him. The smugness in his voice let her know he thought he had gotten the upper hand. She grabbed the file from on the table and headed out the door as quickly as she'd walked in.

Once in the parking lot, she walked around to the passenger side of their sedan, got in and slammed the door. T.J. followed a few paces behind her, slid in behind the steering wheel, then started the engine. "Where are we heading in such a bat-out-of-hell hurry?"

Joanna tossed the file at him. "We have to notify Samantha Randolph's parents."

"Is that what's got you so upset?" T.J. looked at her, clearly trying to figure out why she was so on edge. "Come on, what are you thinking?" he asked.

Her thoughts alternated between Rogers' threat, and the look of Samantha on her school I.D.. But she knew she couldn't talk to T.J. about Rogers.

"She wasn't even eighteen, T.J. It's just a waste, that's all."

"Hey, sometimes these kids think they have it all figured out. Then life happens and they either end up in the gutter or on a slab."

Joanna looked away. It was obvious by T.J.'s cut and dry answer he processed things differently than she did.

How can he not be affected by this? Samantha was just a girl whose biggest problem should have been picking out a dress for her high school prom. Now she's dead.

Joanna stared out the passenger window, contemplating the frailty of life.

Ten minutes later, they pulled up in front of a large Tudor-style home with a manicured lawn and two Mercedes in the circular driveway.

Joanna peered out her window. It looked like the perfect suburban house. "This is what she was running from?" Joanna said, feeling even worse than before.

"Hey, everyone has a story," T.J. said with a rather cavalier attitude.

Joanna looked at the house again. This was the part of her job she dreaded. In all her years on the police force she'd never had to make a notification. Well, her luck had just run out. She swallowed back a sickening feeling in her throat and got out of the car. She and T.J. walked up the driveway, approached the front door, and rang the ornate doorbell.

"I'll take it," T.J. said right before the door swung open.

"Yes?" A petite, Hispanic woman in a housekeeper's uniform answered the door with a pleasant smile. It disappeared when T.J. pulled out his badge.

"I'm Detective Owens and this is Detective Anderson. Are Mr. and Mrs. Randolph home?"

"Yes. Please." She motioned for them to come in. She led them to a sitting area off the main entryway. "I will get them."

The housekeeper disappeared down a large hall. T.J. and Joanna sat rather uncomfortably and waited.

A distinguished man in a business suit and a striking woman in a pink velour jogging outfit entered the room. Joanna instantly saw the resemblance between mother and daughter.

Both Joanna and T.J. stood, but T.J. did the talking.

"Mr. and Mrs. Randolph?"

"Yes," the man spoke with authority.

"I'm Detective Owens and this is Detective Anderson. We're here regarding your daughter."

"Well, if she's in any sort of trouble, we can't help you," Mr. Randolph said with disdain. "We haven't seen her in weeks."

"No, sir, she's not in any trouble." T.J. paused for just a moment. It was then Joanna saw the pain in his expression. Even though he had put on a hard exterior, she could see he was moved by Samantha's death. No matter how many notifications a person made, there was no way possible they could get used to it. You were telling someone they would never see their loved one again. How could anyone ever get used to that?

T.J. cleared his throat. "I'm sorry to have to tell you this but your daughter was found dead three days ago."

While Mrs. Randolph collapsed into the chair behind her, Mr. Randolph stood stoically, his jaw set. "Are you sure it was Samantha?"

"Yes, sir. Though she was carrying a fake I.D., we were able to identify her with a school I.D. found in her belongings. We'll still need you to come down to the county coroner to make a positive identification."

Mrs. Randolph sat with her face in her hands, her shoulders shaking under her silent cries. "How?" was the only word the woman was able to utter.

"She was strangled, Ma'am," T.J. said as compassionately as he could.

Mr. Randolph sat down and tried to comfort his wife.

"Was she . . . I mean did it look like she had been . . . sexually assaulted?" Mrs. Randolph could barely voice her fears.

T.J. glanced at Joanna. It was obvious the Randolph's weren't aware of their daughter's activities.

"Mrs. Randolph, when was the last time you talked to Samantha?"

The woman sniffed and tried to gather her composure. "She left here about a month ago. She said she was tired of living by our rules and on our terms. So, Wallace told her she was free to leave, but not to expect access to her car or bank account." The woman glanced at her husband, as if she was blaming him.

"She needed to learn respect." Wallace tried to defend his actions. "She wanted the privileges of life without any of the responsibilities."

As the shock of the moment was wearing off, Mrs. Randolph's silent tears and polite sniffles turned into raging sobs. It had sunk in. It was then that she realized her daughter was never coming home.

Mr. Randolph continued to try and console his wife, while his own eyes reddened. T.J. pulled a business card from his wallet. "Here's my card. You can call me if you have any questions that the coroner can't help you with. Mr. and Mrs. Randolph, we're truly sorry for your loss."

T.J. shook Mr. Randolph's hand before he and Joanna left.

The car was quiet for a while. Joanna glanced at T.J. seeing a look of misery. "You okay?"

He shook his head. "It never gets any easier."

"I thought you handled it very well. I saw how you intentionally avoided Mrs. Randolph's question. That was very diplomatic of you."

"Yeah, well I didn't feel very diplomatic when Mr. Randolph said he cut his daughter off to teach her a lesson. I wanted to shove my fist down his self-righteous throat. I wonder if he'll feel it was worth it when he finds out she's been whoring for the last month because he wanted her 'to learn respect.'"

Joanna could hear the agitation in T.J.'s voice, but all she could feel was pity. Pity for someone who was spoiled to the point that it killed her, because that's what had happened. Samantha's parents spoiled her until they could no longer control her. By that time, she had turned into a person that knew no boundaries. It all seemed like such a waste.

Joanna realized they weren't headed back to the station, but didn't question it. She was too busy thinking about Rogers' threat. T.J. pulled onto a dirt road and followed it to a spot that overlooked the ocean. He killed the engine and notified dispatch they were ten-seven. T.J. got out of the car, walked to the front of the hood, and leaned against it.

Joanna gave T.J. a few minutes to himself before getting out of the car and walking to the bluff's edge. She followed T.J.'s line of vision and watched as surfers cut back and forth through the pounding waves. She cringed when one of them wiped out. "I don't get it," she said, not realizing she'd spoken out loud.

"Get what?"

She turned to T.J., squinting against the sun. "Surfing. I don't get why anyone would want to fight the waves, the undertow, or the cold, all for the chance to ride a wave that could send you crashing to the ocean floor.

"That's because you've never done it before," he said with a faraway look.

"And I never plan to." She boosted herself up on the

hood of the car and rested her feet on the fender.

"Oh come on, you have no idea what you're missing. You can't write something off if you've never given it a try."

"Well, I've never gone cross-country skiing either, but I think it's safe to say I'm not missing anything."

T.J. laughed at her comparison. "That's apples to oranges. Cross-country is an endurance thing. Surfing is a complete adrenaline rush."

"Whatever." Joanna let the subject drop, but still sat mesmerized by the surfer's moves.

They watched for a few more minutes, before T.J. broke the silence. "So, what's *your* story?"

"What do you mean?" She was puzzled by his out-of-the-blue question.

"Like I said before, everyone has a story. What's yours?"

"No story." Joanna took a deep breath and inhaled the saltwater air. "I've been a cop for eight years. Transferred here three years ago."

"I know, you've said that before. How old are you? I've been with the force ten years and I'm thirty-four, but there's no way you're in your thirties."

"You know it's rude to ask a woman her age?" Joanna tried to act insulted.

"You're not a woman, you're my partner."

"Gee, thanks for clarifying." She couldn't help but laugh. "I'm twenty-nine, if it's any business of yours."

"What'd you do, join the academy on your twenty-first birthday?"

"Something like that."

"Why?"

"Why what?"

"Why police work? Is it in your family?"

Joanna thought of Matthew. Even after all this time the thought of him made her heart catch. "You could say that." Joanna knew where this was headed and didn't feel like getting into it. Her story was sad and she wasn't looking for pity; she quickly turned the questions on him.

"What about you? Are you following in someone's footsteps?"

"Yeah. My grandfather was a beat cop for thirty years and my father made sergeant before he retired."

"They must be proud."

"No, they would be proud if I cut my hair and wore a uniform. They find it hard to believe that I'm allowed to go to work looking like this."

"What—they've never heard of undercover work?"

"Oh yeah. But in my grandfather's day, that just meant a beat cop would wear a disguise and blend in."

Joanna nodded her head in understanding. She could see that T.J. had another string of questions coming her way, so she quickly changed gears again.

"We'd better check back in before Rogers tries to make something of it." Joanna got off the front of the car and walked to the passenger door.

T.J. slowly walked to the driver's door and got in. He turned the key and radioed back to dispatch that they were available. He glanced at Joanna as she stared at the ocean.

She caught him looking. "What?"

"Don't let Rogers bother you, Joanna."

"Who said I was bothered by Rogers? He's just a bully

looking for someone to pick on."

"I've seen the glares he's been giving you and heard some of the choice words he's used to describe you. Don't let him get under your skin. He can be a real jerk at times. Since he screwed up his personal life, he seems to think it's okay to meddle in everyone else's.

"I thought he was married?"

"He is, or was. His wife found out the late shifts he was putting in had nothing to do with work. He was seeing some woman that he met at a bar and got caught. So, Rogers' wife went out and got herself another man. Now she's divorcing Rogers and plans on taking him to the cleaners in the process. And to top it off, the woman Rogers was screwing around with dumped him for another guy. So you see, he doesn't have a very high opinion of women right now."

"Typical," Joanna said. "He's the one that screws around but blames it on everyone else."

"That's Rogers."

Yeah. That's Rogers, but would he make good on his threat? Joanna turned it over and over in her head. *Lord, if you want me here, you're going to have to do something to help me out.*

"So you never told me about your dad?" T.J.'s words broke into her thoughts.

"What?"

"Your dad? Was he a cop?"

"No."

"Then who?"

"Who what?" Joanna was frustrated that T.J. insisted on asking so many questions.

"You said you went into police work because of someone in your family. Who?"

Before Joanna could say anything, the radio interrupted their conversation. "David Charlie Two, what's your ten-twenty? Captain Armstrong would like to see you."

T.J. radioed to dispatch. "Ten-four. ETA in fifteen."

"What do you think that's about?" Joanna wondered, not looking forward to seeing the captain again.

"It probably has to do with the drug roundup that went down a few months back. I heard the D.A. was finally ready to take it to court."

Joanna relaxed, hoping T.J. was right, and it wasn't her being called on the carpet. She was also glad the interruption had made T.J. forget his line of inquiry. She wasn't ready to answer the questions he was asking.

CHAPTER NINE

T.J. was right. When they arrived at the station, he was the one being called in to talk to the captain. Relieved that for once it wasn't her being called on the carpet, Joanna headed for the restroom.

When she got there, Denise White was standing at the far side of the bathroom, in front of her locker. Denise and Joanna had been friends, that is, until Joanna outed Cummings. When it became unpopular to be linked with Joanna, Denise had pulled away. Joanna had been stung by Denise's rejection. She thought they had gotten to be pretty good friends. The fact that Denise decided to side with Cummings had hurt Joanna more than she had let on.

"Hey, Denise," Joanna said politely.

Denise was adjusting her gun belt when she turned to talk to Joanna. "Hey, Anderson, how's it going in the men's club?"

All the female officers called the War Room the men's club because there were no female detectives.

Until now.

"I'm doing fine," Joanna said, sounding a little more defensive then she'd intended.

Denise gave a snide smile. "I guess I would be doing fine too if I was promoted, got hooked up with a gorgeous partner, and was getting a little something extra on the side." Denise smoothed out her shirt and turned back to her locker. "I knew all that righteous crap you'd been preaching was bull. The minute you've got someone like Owens on the line, you lie down and roll over for him."

Joanna was shocked Denise would accuse her of such behavior. It took all the restraint she could muster to control her raging emotions when she spoke. "Well, Denise, once again you've chosen to listen to gossip instead of looking at the facts. I deserved this promotion, and there's nothing going on between Owens and me. That's just another rumor, that in the past, you would've known was a lie."

"Whatever," Denise said, callousness in her tone.

"What is with you, Denise? You know me better than that. I wasn't interested in T.J. before, and I'm not interested in him now."

"Then why'd he go after Rogers?" Denise snapped back.

"Because Rogers was being a jerk."

"So? There are a lot of jerks around here. You know what, Jo, I really don't care, okay? You do your thing and I'll do mine." Denise pushed past Joanna and walked out the door, leaving Joanna with a whole lot of pent up anger.

"That's it!"

Joanna marched into the War Room where she found

Rogers, Smith, and Barker. She headed straight to where Rogers was leaning back in his chair, getting so close—he almost fell over backwards—she jabbed her finger at his chest as she spit out her words.

"If you ever open your mouth about me or my private life again, I will make it my personal responsibility to see to it that you never get another woman into your bed. I will stalk you and spread rumors about you that will make it so even the "pros" won't waste their time on you. Got it?"

Rogers sprung from his chair and backed her against the wall. She heard the screeching of chairs as Barker and Smith got to their feet thinking they were going to have to break something up.

"If you think you're going to threaten me, you've got another thing coming." Rogers pressed in even closer. "If I were you, sweetheart, I'd watch my back."

"What's going on in here?" The captain's booming voice startled everyone in the room. He stepped into the War Room, T.J. at his side.

Rogers glared at Joanna, but she could read his fear. In a split second, he had let his own anger jeopardize his career. One word from her and he'd be toast, his own actions indicting him.

"Anderson?" the captain shouted at her, demanding an answer.

Rogers backed away from her as she cleared her throat. "Rogers was just showing me a situation he'd gotten himself into." Joanna stared at Rogers as she spoke.

She walked over to the water cooler, trying to act unaffected. T.J. locked eyes with her while the captain decided to let the situation go.

Rogers glared at Owens before he and Smith left the War Room. When Barker came into view, Bristol got up and joined him in the hall, leaving her and T.J. alone.

"So, are you done with the captain?" she asked as she tossed her paper cup in the trash.

"Yeah," T. J. answered. His arms crossed against his chest, clearly waiting for some kind of explanation.

"Then let's go." Joanna walked past him and headed for the car.

T.J. drove away from the station without a word, but as soon as he was in traffic he asked. "So, are you going to tell me what just happened back there?"

"Like I said, he was just–"

"Cut the crap, Joanna!" T.J. cut her off. "I didn't believe that story any more than the captain did. He only let it go so he wouldn't have to deal with it." T.J. sat staring at her waiting for the truth.

"It was nothing."

T.J. swore under his breath. "Look, I can go ask Barker or Smith, but I'd rather hear it from you."

She debated a few seconds on what she should say, and then conceded. "Rogers is telling people we're messing around."

"Messing around?" T.J. laughed. "I haven't heard that term since I was in high school."

"Oh, I'm sorry, would you like me to use a more graphic term?" Joanna could feel her skin heating up.

He chuckled. "So what. You knew that was going to happen. Let him talk. What do you care what he thinks?"

"I don't care what he thinks, but I do have a reputation that I would like to keep intact."

"Hey, I'm not bragging or anything, but being linked with me is not the worst thing that could happen to your reputation." T.J.'s look was teasing, with just the slightest bit of arrogance laced in.

"Yeah, well, you worry about what's good for your reputation, and I'll worry about what's good for mine."

"You know, your reputation could use a little softening. The guys already call you the Iron Maiden."

Joanna's jaw dropped.

"Oh come on. Don't tell me you didn't know that?"

"No, but thanks for the information." She crossed her arms and stared out the window.

Joanna was silent. She didn't know what to say. It was a compliment, whether she wanted to admit it or not. But it made her sound like she had no soul, no feelings. She wasn't that emotionally closed off or cold. She just thought sex was something more than a bartering chip in a relationship.

Listening to everyone else brag about their exploits after they came back from days off, let her know she wouldn't want to have a relationship with any of the men she worked with. So, she turned down their advances without even giving them a second thought. She had gambled when she went out with Frank Stark—a patrolman at the station. She thought he had potential, but he was just like the rest of them. That's why she never had any interest in T.J. He was too much of a playboy. She was convinced all the nice guys were already married or dead.

"So what did you tell him?" T.J. broke into her thoughts.

"Tell who?"

"Rogers"

"I told him if he said anything about my personal life again, I would make it my business to ruin his reputation, and that he'd never get another woman into bed with him."

T.J. couldn't stop laughing. "You've got guts. I have to give you that." He chuckled some more. "If you're willing to go toe-to-toe with a veteran and a guy twice your size, you have more intestinal fortitude than I gave you credit for."

Joanna didn't say anything, thinking instead about her little altercation with Rogers and how it could work in her favor. The captain had witnessed Rogers being aggressive towards her. Like T.J. said, the captain knew something was up, he just didn't want to be bothered with it. Hopefully, it would help keep Rogers at bay.

All of a sudden, T.J. slammed on the brakes and threw the car in reverse. Joanna spun her head from side to side looking for what had caught T.J.'s attention. He backed up to the alley he had just passed. Joanna looked and saw two kids huddled against the building. When the one in the red jacket saw her and T.J., he took off down the alley. The other kid slumped to the ground.

T.J. flew into action. He reversed the car all the way around the corner

"What is it?" Joanna asked, not seeing what he'd seen.

"I'm not sure, but I think he just shot that kid in the alley."

Joanna got on the radio immediately. "David Charlie Two in pursuit. Possible shooting. Alley of 2300 block of Willtern. Requesting back-up."

They saw the kid running down the alley and roared

after him. When he went up a fire escape, T.J. slammed on the brakes and got out of the car, but Joanna beat him to the hanging ladder.

T.J. watched as Joanna jumped up and grasped the bottom rung of the ladder. Within seconds, she had easily pulled herself up and began to scale the old metal frame. For a moment, he stood watching her; mesmerized by her agility and how quickly she was gaining on the kid. "Dang! What are you, a gymnast or something?" He shook his head, once again surprise by Joanna's skills.

Hurrying into action, he ran around to the front of the building. Pushing through the door of the old book store, he asked the sales clerk where the roof access was.

"What?" the clerk asked blankly.

T.J. yanked out his badge and yelled again. "The roof access?"

Startled, the woman pointed to the back of the store.

T.J. rushed up the stairs two at a time. When he got to the padlocked door, he threw his shoulder into it, splintering the wood frame. The door swung open just in time to see Joanna tackle the kid on the east end of the roof. They landed with such force, he felt the thud where he stood.

T.J. ran across the roof, watching Joanna grapple to maintain control over the kid. For a brief moment, the kid got the upper hand, slamming Joanna to the ground.

T.J. saw her head viciously snap back, and heard her cry out. He grabbed the kid by the collar and flung him face first into the gravel. With his knee in the kid's back, he pulled out his cuffs and restrained him. The punk writhed, cussing and swearing, yelling for T.J. to get off him. But T.J. didn't budge. There was no way he was going to let the kid get to his feet before back-up arrived. He could hear sirens in the distance and knew they would be there any minute.

He turned around to see Joanna slouched against one of the roof's fans. She was in obvious pain.

"You going to be okay?" he yelled.

"He threw the gun in the alley."

"You didn't answer the question."

"Just make sure someone checks the alley."

Joanna was trying her hardest to remain upright. With her eyes shut, hands braced on her knees, she tried to take deep even breaths. But every time she did, her head felt like it was going to explode.

She listened as T.J. handed off the kid to Bristol and Barker. "Here, take this piece of trash," T.J. said between heavy breaths.

"You okay, T.J.?" Barker asked; completely ignoring Joanna.

"Yeah, but do me a favor. Check the alley. Joanna said he tossed the gun."

"Sure thing."

Barker and Bristol turned to leave, with the delinquent between them, screaming police brutality.

"Hey, what about the other kid?" T.J. asked quickly.

"History," Bristol said, before the three of them disappeared into the stairwell.

As soon as Bristol and Barker left, Joanna doubled over and retched.

T.J. was quickly by her side, his hand pressed to her back. "Hey, you okay?"

She tried to say something, but hurled for a second time.

"I'm calling for a paramedic."

"No!" she managed to shout. "Just give me a minute."

Her head was swimming, and she felt like she was going to pass out. But she certainly didn't want someone poking and prodding at her.

She leaned against the fan for support, fighting for control of her body. When the worst was over, she slowly got to her feet.

"Whoa." T.J. looked at her wide-eyed. "You're one sickening shade of gray. You need to sit back down."

"Okay, but not here. The smell is going to make me puke again."

With one hand on her waist, and the other at her elbow, T.J. led her to a different vent; away from the vomit that had splashed her shoes. "Let me take a look." He reached towards her head, but she slapped his hand away. "I'm fine. I just got the wind knocked out of me when we went down, and it made me feel a little light headed."

"You're not fine." T.J. squatted down in front of her. "You just puked your guts up, and your face is the same shade as this gravel."

"I just need a minute."

Joanna took a couple of deep breaths and then tried rotating her shoulder.

Bad idea.

Pain shot through her so fast, she couldn't breathe. T.J. brushed her hair back from her shoulder, and his hand came away red.

"Hold on, Joanna. You're bleeding." When T.J. took a closer look, he cursed. "Okay, Joanna, no more macho stuff. You've got a hefty piece of glass in your shoulder. I'm going to get a paramedic up here."

"No. Just take it out."

"No way. That could make it worse. You need to be seen by someone who knows what they're doing."

"Fine. I'll let a medic look at it. But not up here."

"What is with you? Why can't you admit it when you're hurt?"

Joanna ignored T.J. and got to her feet slowly. Fighting the bile at the back of her throat, she walked to the stairwell and braced herself for the three flights of stairs. T.J. walked along side of her, holding her elbow.

The descent was slow, but she made it. When she and T.J. emerged from the storefront, Bristol, Rogers, and Smith where there going over the details of the event.

Barker came around the corner with a gun in a baggie. "Look at that," Bristol turned, causing everyone to direct their attention at her and T.J. "Once again, Owens comes out clean as a whistle, while Anderson comes out looking like crap. I don't get it Anderson, didn't your mother ever teach you that getting dirty isn't lady like?"

He laughed–along with the others. That is, until Peck showed up on the scene. Everyone was careful when he was around. Peck was the senior detective and a pretty straight shooter. He wouldn't put up with ribbing if he felt it edged on discrimination or harassment.

Joanna was glad he'd shown up because she didn't have the energy to retaliate. It was all she could do not to puke again. She needed to get out of there. But not in an ambulance. She would never be able to live it down if she did.

"Owens, what went down here?" Peck asked

"A shooter in the alley. Anderson chased him to the roof and saw him dump the gun. She apprehended him before I even got there."

Peck turned his attention to Joanna. "Good job, Anderson." He leaned closer. "Are you okay? You look a little worse for wear."

She swallowed hard refusing to admit she was in any pain. "Just a couple of scrapes. No big deal."

"Okay. But I want a paramedic to take a look at you before you leave, understood?"

"I'll make sure that she does," T.J. said in a superior tone.

Joanna glared at him, then turned and walked away.

"You can be mad at me all you want," T.J. said as he walked beside her. "But it's for your own good. Head injuries are nothing to screw around with, and your shoulder is going to need stitches."

"Fine. You got your way. I'm going. I'll be treated here. But I'm not leaving in an ambulance."

"Why are you so stubborn? It's obvious you're hurt."

"And it's obvious I'll never hear the end of it if I get carted away in the back of an ambulance."

Before she could say anymore, they were at the tailgate of the shiny white vehicle—flashing lights and all. A medic in a blue jumpsuit turned to her and smiled. "What can I do for you officers?"

⊕

Though the medic spoke to both of them, T.J. noticed he was only looking at Joanna. And it wasn't her injuries he was staring at.

"She took a pretty hard blow to the back of the head," T.J. said. "And she has a shard of glass in her shoulder. I didn't remove it because I didn't want her to bleed out."

The paramedic was listening to T.J., but never stopped looking at Joanna.

"Okay. Why don't you sit here while I take a look." He had Joanna sit on the large chrome bumper of the vehicle while he pulled on some latex gloves.

"I'm Keith, by the way." He looked at her with a smile.

Great. T.J. clenched his fists. He knew a player when he saw one. And this Keith guy was a little too smooth for his liking.

⊕

Joanna introduced herself between waves of nausea. If she hadn't felt like she was going to throw-up on his shoes, she would've tried to be a little more congenial. He was a good-looking guy, tall, with short brown hair in a preppy sort of cut; his grey-blue eyes sparkled when he smiled.

She watched as he pushed her hair back away from her shoulder and took out a pair of scissors. He pressed the scissors to the sleeve of her shirt.

"Wait a minute." Joanna put up her hand, the sudden motion making her stomach slosh. "This is one of my favorite shirts. You can't cut it."

"Well, unless you want to try taking it off, I have no choice. Besides, it's already torn and you'll never get the blood out."

"Fine," she conceded. "But don't cut my camisole. It cost me forty bucks, and I'm not about to trash it because of a little blood."

He smiled. "I think I'll be able to work around it."

Keith snipped her sleeve up to the collar, causing it to flop open and slip from her shoulder. Joanna felt exposed, even if she was wearing a camisole. She strained to see what was causing such pain, but it was just out of her range of sight. When Keith gently moved her camisole strap and allowed it to slip off her shoulder, Joanna brought her hand up to her chest, to make sure her camisole didn't shift too low.

T.J. grimaced as he watched the medic work. When Joanna turned to look at him, his face was twisted and contorted.

"Knock it off, T.J. You're making it worse."

"Sorry. I just can't believe you're sitting there with that huge piece of glass sticking out of your shoulder."

"Huge?" she repeated, feeling queasier.

"Not huge. Thick. It's a piece of coke bottle and it's pretty thick." Keith's calm tone was reassuring. Before doing anything more with her shoulder, he squatted down in front of her and looked at her eyes.

"How's the head?" he asked, flashing a penlight at her pupils.

"Still attached."

He grinned. "Humor, that's a good sign. Did you lose

consciousness at all?"

"No."

"Do you feel dizzy or disoriented?"

"A little."

"Are you nauseous?"

"Yeah."

T.J. spoke up. "She already puked on the rooftop."

Keith ignored T.J. and continued his questioning. "Are you having a hard time focusing?"

"Yeah."

"I'm glad to hear that."

"Glad?" she retorted, not sure she heard him right.

"Well, yeah. If you're having a hard time focusing, I won't take it personally that you're not looking me in the eye."

His smile was charismatic, and Joanna felt an involuntary grin crease her face as well. She saw T.J. roll his eyes but ignored him.

Keith got up from where he'd been crouching in front of her and turned his attention to the knot on the back of her head. She sucked on her teeth and pressed her lips together, trying hard to prevent herself from crying out.

He knelt back down in front of her, one of his hands brushing across the top of her knee.

She felt a spark from his touch and wished she had the energy to make a better first impression.

"You definitely have all the signs of a concussion, so I'm going to take you in. And since you're going in anyway, I think it would be better to let the E.R. doctor remove that piece of glass from your shoulder once you're there. Do you think you can last until we get to the hospital?"

Her sigh was more of a groan. "Are you sure I have to go to the hospital? I was hoping to avoid the harassment I'm going to get once I get back to the station."

"No question about it. Harassment or not, a bump on the head like that is nothing to fool around with. But if you prefer, you can sit up front with me. No gurney. How's that?"

Joanna wasn't sure which she found more appealing: not being placed on a gurney or getting the chance to sit up front with the striking paramedic.

"I guess I have no choice."

"Not exactly the answer I was looking for, but I'll take it." His smile again was charming.

"Are you sure that's wise?" T.J. asked. "Aren't there procedures that have to be followed? What about your partner?"

Joanna looked over to where the other paramedic was working on their shooter.

"Rob's used to sitting in the back. He won't mind."

Joanna saw the way T.J. was giving Keith the once over; it tickled her. T.J. made his move on women all the time, but seeing someone else take the lead was just a bit too much for his ego.

Joanna knew Keith was flirting with her, but she didn't mind. He seemed like a nice guy, was good looking, and not at all like the typical macho guys she was used to dealing with on the force. She just hoped she didn't look as awful as she felt.

CHAPTER TEN

T.J. finished up at the scene, while Joanna went to the hospital. He was angry with himself for not insisting on going with her, and irritated that the medic seemed a little too accommodating. He wasn't sure why it bothered him, but it did. Joanna was in no condition to have to fend off a Don Juan—looking to make time with her. Hopefully she had enough common sense to see through his chivalrous little act.

T.J. looked at his Nixon watch. It had taken two hours before he could break away from the station and get to the hospital. But with the way emergency rooms ran, he figured he would still have to wait for Joanna once he got there.

He walked through the sliding glass doors and up to the nurses' station. He flipped out his badge so he wouldn't get the line of questioning as to how he knew or was related to the patient. "My partner came in here about two hours ago with a head injury and a piece of glass in her shoulder.

Detective Joanna Anderson."

T.J. watched as the nurse clicked through several screens on her computer.

"She was released about thirty minutes ago," the nurse answered coyly.

T.J. was surprised. "Did you see where she went?"

"No. I just got here, myself." She batted her eyes at him and leaned on the counter in front of her. "Is there anything else I can do for you?"

"No. Thanks anyway."

Normally, T.J. would've stuck around and struck up a conversation with the nurse with the come-on eyes. She was attractive and obviously interested in him, but at the moment, he was more concerned about Joanna.

T.J. walked away a little confused. *Maybe she called a cab.* He pulled out his cell phone and dialed. When he got her voice mail, he hung up and tried her home phone. It took a couple rings before it was picked up and T.J. was greeted by a deep voice.

"Joanna's residence."

"Well, if this is Joanna's residence, where's Joanna?" T.J. said, doing nothing to hide the hostility in his voice.

"Is this Detective Owens?"

"Yeah." T.J. bristled. "Who's this?" *Like he didn't already know.*

"Detective, this is Keith Michaels, the medic that assisted Joanna at the scene."

"Yeah, I know who you are, but why are you answering Joanna's phone?"

"I drove her home after she was released. She's lying down at the moment."

"I didn't realize paramedics offered curb service."

Keith chuckled. "She didn't have her purse with her so she couldn't call for a ride, and the doctor wouldn't release her without supervision. I was at the end of my shift, so I volunteered to take her home and keep an eye on her."

"How convenient," T.J. mumbled under his breath.

"Excuse me?"

"How is she?"

"Slight concussion. Fifteen stitches in her shoulder."

"I'm leaving the hospital now. I'll be there in about twenty minutes."

"Okay. But I don't mind staying. I told Jo—"

T.J. hung up while Keith was still speaking. *I bet you don't mind.* T.J. thumped out his agitation on the steering wheel. *Who does this Keith guy think he is? And what on earth is Joanna doing? It makes no sense. The Iron Maiden letting a guy stay the night? Someone she just met? Obviously, she isn't thinking right. She has to be doped up on something.*

T.J. had to park on the street since there was a mint 69' Camaro in Joanna's driveway. He walked by the car slowly, admiring the detailing, and the perfect paint job. Now he was sure this guy was a player.

He walked the length of Joanna's house and knocked loudly on the door. Keith answered it immediately. T.J. pushed on the door, past Keith and stepped inside. He glanced around the living room. "Is she in her room?"

"Yeah. She laid down the minute she got home. I plan on waking her up in another half-hour."

"I'm sure she appreciates you driving her home, but you can go now. I'll take it from here." T.J. walked over to the couch and sat down, crossing his legs atop the coffee table, his arms spread out atop the cushions. He was dismissing Keith, letting him know who was in charge. But Keith didn't look like he was going to concede too easily.

"Well, I'll wait until six o'clock and let her know I'm leaving."

T.J. stared at the guy as he took a seat across from him. It was obvious he wasn't going to budge until he saw Joanna again.

"So tell me again what happened at the hospital?" T.J. asked.

"At the end of my shift, I went back to check on Joanna; I wanted to see how she was doing. When I got there, she was arguing with the doctor." Keith chuckled. "She definitely has a stubborn streak."

"Yeah. That's one of her better qualities," T.J. said.

Keith continued, "Anyway, the doctor wanted to admit her for observation, but she was threatening to sign herself out. I told the doctor we were friends and that I could keep an eye on her."

"So you lied?"

"I wouldn't call it a lie. Joanna and I seemed to hit it off on the ride to the E.R. I could tell she didn't want to stay in the hospital, so I volunteered to take her home."

"And Joanna went for that?" T.J. asked, completely perplexed.

"Not at first, but the doctor continued to be insistent."

"I still don't understand why she didn't call me?" T.J. asked, talking to himself but talking out loud as well.

"I asked her the same thing, since you two were partners."

"And what did she say?"

Keith hesitated. "Joanna said you hadn't been partners very long and your relationship isn't the best. She didn't want to bother you."

T.J. felt like he'd just been sucker punched. While it was true their relationship was still on shaky ground, he couldn't believe—with her puritan reputation—Joanna chose to go home with a complete stranger rather than call him. He felt like a jerk. Even worse, *Don Juan* was staring at him obviously thinking the same thing.

"Well, she was wrong. We might have our differences but I'm still her partner. I've still got her back. She was just being obstinate. As you saw for yourself, Joanna can be pig-headed when she wants to be."

The room was silent except for the ticking of the large clock hanging over the mantle. Keith seemed completely at ease, while T.J. was having a hard time sitting still. Finally, six o'clock rolled around, and Keith got up.

"Well, I'm going to go say good-bye to Joanna and let her know you're here. You sure you know what to do?"

"Yeah, I think I can handle it," T.J. snapped sarcastically.

T.J. followed Keith up the stairs to Joanna's room. Keith crossed the room to Joanna's bedside and quietly spoke to her.

"Joanna, wake-up. Joanna, its Keith."

Her eyes fluttered until she could focus. She had an afghan pulled up around her, but T. J. could see she was still wearing the same jeans and white camisole from earlier. Gone was her cut up yellow t-shirt. Her holster lay on her side table.

"Joanna, your partner's here."

She rolled herself to a sitting position, careful not to put pressure on her shoulder and looked across the room at T.J.

"What are you doing here?" She pushed her hair back from her forehead.

"I'm here to take over for *Florence Nightingale*." He shot a look of distain at Keith. It was clear Keith didn't appreciate the analogy.

Joanna looked embarrassed and gave T.J. a cold stare before giving Keith an apologetic smile.

Keith just grinned. "Let me take a look at your eyes again, and then I'm going to head home." He pulled a penlight from the pocket of his jeans.

T.J. watched as Keith went through the same routine he had when Joanna sat on the tailgate of the ambulance.

When Keith was finished, he moved in closer to Joanna.

T.J. thought for sure Keith was going to kiss her, which in that case, he would definitely know Joanna was out of her mind. But instead, Keith whispered something to her that T.J. couldn't quite hear.

Joanna nodded her head slightly. Then, they both bowed their heads and prayed.

T.J. watched in disbelief.

Oh boy. What is this guy pulling?

Keith stood and walked over to T.J. "Wake her up every hour and check her pupils. Give her two of these at nine o'clock." He pulled a white packet from his pocket. "If she starts vomiting or is incoherent when you try to wake her, take her back to the hospital."

Keith's tone was all business. T.J. took the packet and watched as Keith descended the stairs. When he heard the front door close, he turned his attention back to Joanna.

She was ticked. "Why were you being so rude? Keith was only helping."

"Oh . . . is that what you call it?" T.J. crossed the room and sat on the edge of her bed. "So, how are you doing?"

"I'm fine, I guess. I've got a headache and my shoulder is sore, but I don't feel sick anymore."

"Feel like eating something?" he offered because he was hungry himself.

Joanna thought for a moment. "Maybe some toast."

T.J. got up and headed to the stairs.

"Look, you can go home. I don't need a babysitter. The doctor was just being overly cautious." She fidgeted with the edge of the blanket.

"Oh, no, no, no. I promised *Don Juan* I'd take over. I wouldn't want him to find out I shirked my duties."

"His name is Keith. And what is your gripe with him?"

"He's an opportunist."

"He is not."

"Whatever," he mumbled as he headed downstairs. "What do you want on your toast?" he hollered up to her.

"Peanut butter," she yelled back, grabbing her head in regret.

Joanna slowly swung her feet over the side of her bed and waited, making sure she didn't feel dizzy before getting up. She crossed slowly to the bathroom and grabbed a washcloth from inside the vanity. She ran cold water over the cloth, then pressed it to her face. Running a brush through her hair took skill and precision. She could only use her one arm, and had to avoid the knot on the back of her head. She took the steps to her living room one at a time. Even though she walked in her bare feet, her steps seemed to echo in her ears.

T.J. had a carton of eggs, a loaf of bread, and a brick of cheese out on the counter.

"All I wanted was some toast," she said irritated, causing him to turn towards her.

"Yeah, but I'm hungry." He cracked the eggs while butter melted in the pan. He scrambled them and poured them into the skillet. "Should you be up?" he asked as he pushed the yellow liquid around in the pan.

"I don't see why not." She hitched herself up on one of two barstools and watched him as he worked.

When the toast popped up, he pulled the golden pieces from the toaster and put them on a plate. Joanna watched as he spread peanut butter on top of them. It was more than she would normally use, but she wasn't about to complain.

He poured her some juice, then, took the glass and plate and slid them in front of her. "Why didn't you call me? I could've brought you home." His tone was firm, and Joanna sensed he was offended.

"I didn't want to bother you. Besides, I would've had to call the station and have you paged. I didn't think that would look so good."

"Why?" he said with a scowl.

"Because Rogers already has us sleeping together. I wasn't going to give him more fuel for his fire."

"Screw Rogers!" T.J. slammed his hand on the

counter, making Joanna jump and her head pulse. "You're my partner. If you're going to continue to be my partner, you need to get something straight. We're a team. We have to work as a team and act like a team. We're going to be spending a lot of time together and work is going to naturally spill over into our personal lives. That just happens. We've got to be able to trust each other explicitly. I've got to know you've got my back and can read me enough to know how I will react in any given situation. If you think we're only supposed to be there for each other from eight to eight, this isn't going to work. A partnership is a twenty-four-seven kind of thing. Got it?"

Joanna looked at him with penetrating eyes. "So . . . do you trust me?"

T.J. returned her stare. "Yeah . . . I do. I might not understand you," he said with a chuckle, "but I trust you."

It meant the world to her to hear him say that. She felt a surge of emotion creep up inside her. She took a bite of her toast to hide the overwhelming feelings she was experiencing. She was certainly overreacting and inwardly blamed it on the medication.

T.J. served up his dinner and went around the bar to sit next to her. They ate in silence until Joanna had enough control of her emotions to asked, "So what don't you understand?"

He swallowed his mouthful of eggs. "You." He took a swig of O.J. before expounding. "You make it clear to everybody you're not interested in a relationship, and then, bam! This Keith guy shows up, you know him for all of two minutes, and you're inviting him back to your place. What's with that?"

"It was more than two minutes," she said quietly. "Besides, we just hit it off is all."

"Hit it off? You mean he hit on you, and you were too whacked to know it. Come on, Joanna, he's no different than any other man. He saw a chance to polish off his armor and play the part of the chivalrous knight and you bought it, hook, line and sinker."

"Hey." She was beginning to take offense that T.J. thought she could be so gullible. "I think I'm a better judge of character than that, concussion or no concussion."

"Oh really, and how is it that you two '*hit it off*' so well?"

"Keith and I go to the same church. He told me he had recognized me from somewhere. When we figured out it was from church, we just started talking. We hit it off."

"And you believe him? He tells you he goes to church and that gives him your stamp of approval?"

"Well, it's a start," she said defensively.

T.J. got up to take his plate to the sink. "You thought Frank went to church, too. And look what happened there."

Joanna got angry. "I was set-up, and you know it."

"You're right, you were. So how do you know this Keith guy isn't setting you up too?" T.J. started working on the dishes.

Joanna stewed over T.J.'s cynicism. She didn't want to think of Keith as an opportunist. They *had* hit it off, and he seemed like a really nice guy. "Why do you care anyway?" she asked. "You chased him away." She slid from the barstool and walked over to the couch. She curled up in a ball and closed her eyes.

T.J. turned to say something and saw that Joanna was lying down. He decided to put the rest of his lecture on hold. Glancing at his watch, he finished up in the kitchen, turned off the light, and moved to the living room. He plopped down on the opposite end of the sofa and reached for the remote. He turned on the T.V., keeping the volume low, then began flipping through the channels. He found a ball game and made himself comfortable. He turned to Joanna, and for a moment, watched her sleep. She was beautiful, and he definitely felt the same attraction for her as he did the first time he laid eyes on her.

He thought about what it would be like to be with Joanna. Some of the scenarios he conjured up got pretty steamy, that is until he remembered it was the Iron Maiden he was daydreaming about.

Get real, Owens, your ego couldn't take it.

He knew she was off limits in more ways than one. He set the alarm on his watch, crossed his arms against his chest, hunkered down in the pillows of her couch and closed his eyes.

CHAPTER ELEVEN

T.J.'s alarm startled Joanna for the second time. She was just as disorientated now as she was before. She tried to sit up but decided against it because the throbbing felt like a vice on her head.

She watched as T.J. pressed the button on his watch and yawned. He moved closer to her, perching himself on the edge of the sofa.

"How are you doing?"

"I just want this headache to stop." She closed her eyes and massaged her temples.

"Here, let me see your eyes."

Joanna stared at T.J. as he went through the penlight routine.

"What time is it?" she asked as he moved away.

"Nine o'clock."

"Good. Time for some more drugs. Maybe that will take the edge off."

"Look, why don't you go upstairs, take a nice hot bath,

and put something more comfortable on. You'd feel a lot better if you got out of those clothes and into bed."

Nothing sounded better to her than just that. "But what about my medicine?"

"I'll bring it up to you when you're done."

She slowly got to her feet; and headed to the stairs.

"Need some help?" T.J. asked.

"No," she said smugly. "I've been undressing myself for years."

"I *meant* with the stairs."

"Yeah, whatever."

T.J. heard the water running in the upstairs bathroom. He wandered around the house, looking at the art on the wall and some of the pictures Joanna had scattered about. He was trying not to think about the fact that she was upstairs, undressed, and unsteady.

He randomly flipped through the television, realizing she had none of the cable channels he was used to watching. And her video library wasn't any more exciting than her T.V.

What does she do for entertainment around here? It's one thing to abstain. But come on, you've got to have some kind of release.

He kept flipping through the T.V. channels, glancing at his watch every once in a while. When he heard the sound of vibrating pipes, he realized Joanna's tub was draining. He gave her a few minutes, for privacy sake, then with water and pills in hand, climbed the stairs. He lightly tapped on the door.

Joanna opened the door and then walked back into the bathroom. When she emerged, T.J. could see her complexion was pink and moist from the steam that had built up during her bath. Her hair was piled on top of her head and she was wearing the kind of outfit he saw all the time at the gym. Clingy pants and a tight fitting tank top. Though her face still held the strain of pain, she looked incredible.

Come on, Owens, hold it together. Nothing good can come from what you're thinking.

She pulled the clip from her head, allowing her wavy blonde hair to fall across her shoulders. She laid the clip on the nightstand before pulling back the covers of her bed.

She sat down with a sigh.

"Feel any better?"

"A little, but if this headache doesn't go away by tomorrow, I'm toast."

He sat down close to her and with a brush of his hand, moved her hair away from the bandage on the back of her shoulder.

When T.J.'s eyes met hers, Joanna became keenly aware of their closeness . . . and their surroundings. She felt him reach for her hand and knew she had to put an end to anything before it had a chance to start.

Before she could gather her thoughts to deflect what she was sure was an advance, T.J. turned her hand over and placed two white pills in it. She looked at the pills confused.

"For your headache."

She breathed a sigh of relief.

Joanna took the pills and drank the whole glass of water, hoping it would douse the feelings simmering inside her.

"Okay, it's nine-thirty now. I'll check on you at ten-thirty."

"T.J., why don't you go ahead and go home," she said as he was leaving. "One of us is going to have to get some decent sleep if we're going to be able to function at all tomorrow."

"I'll be fine. Just worry about you." He gave her a smile of assurance, then disappeared down the stairs.

Joanna was left with a head that was aching with both pain and confusion. She wasn't the Iron Maiden everyone thought she was. She did have feelings and contrary to what people thought about her, she struggled with the same issues as everyone else.

She'd found it easy to ignore T.J. in the past. His comments were always laced with innuendo; his playboy status was notorious among the ranks. But tonight, he'd been different. He'd made her dinner, and seemed genuinely concerned for her well-being. He wasn't trying to impress her, or wear her down. It was like she was seeing the real T.J. The man behind the macho, chauvinistic reputation. He wasn't out to impress the boys' club. He was only trying to help.

He was being a partner.

But better than that, he was being a friend.

CHAPTER TWELVE

T.J. pressed the alarm button on his watch. It took him a minute to get his bearings, remember where he was, and why. He got up from the couch to go wake up Joanna. But when he stood, he saw that she was already in the kitchen.

Wearing a pair of black jeans and a vintage Coca Cola t-shirt—advertising the real thing, Joanna looked as good as she had in his dreams.

"What are you doing up already?" he asked, rubbing his eyes.

"I never went back to sleep after your last wake-up call."

"Is your head still hurting?"

"You could say that." She swallowed two pain killers with a shudder.

"You know, there is such a thing as sick days." He walked over to the counter, combing his fingers through his unruly hair.

"Oh, no. I'm going to work. I'm certainly not going to

add insult to injury. . . literally."

He shook his head at her mulishness as he walked to the bathroom to relieve himself. When he returned, he watched as she massaged her neck.

"You really think you're going to be able to work feeling that way?"

"Let me worry about that, okay."

"Fine." He put his hands up in surrender. "Have it your way." He picked up his holster and badge from the coffee table. "Ready?"

"But we don't have to be at the station for another hour and a half."

"I need to go home and get showered and changed."

"Then I'll meet you there."

"You shouldn't be driving, and you know it."

"Whatever."

"Humor me, okay?" he said as he slipped on his holster and badge.

"Fine."

He waited while Joanna grabbed her purse, phone, slipped her revolver in her holster, and reached for her jacket from the back of the couch. He held the door open for her and watched as she walked away.

"Hey, aren't you going to lock it?"

"The bottom locks automatically. That's another reason I have the hidden key. I'm always locking myself out."

The climb up into his oversized truck was a challenge for Joanna. He stood by to make sure she didn't lose her balance. Of course, he got a treat as he watched her long legs stretch to make the climb. With a smirk, he scolded himself for not looking away.

T.J. drove to his apartment, which was only ten minutes away.

"You live on the marina. Nice," Joanna said as they pulled into the parking lot.

"I like it."

Once they were parked, T.J. walked Joanna to his apartment. Unlocking the door, he let Joanna enter before him. "Make yourself comfortable. I'll only be a few minutes," he said as he tossed his keys on the entry table to the left, then disappeared down the hall.

Joanna stood next to the entry table, studying the open concept apartment. She was impressed. She had expected to find leopard skins and leather but was pleasantly surprised by a masculine yet understated living space. The kitchen to the right was clean and uncluttered, the stainless steel appliances giving it a touch of class. In the living room, the brown chenille couch was inviting and the Berber carpet sophisticated. The flat screen T.V. that hung on the wall opposite the couch was large, but not overpowering for the size of the room. The only items that screamed *bachelor* was the pinball machine that sat where a dining room table should be, and the three surfboards leaning against the wall.

Joanna moved towards a set of bookshelves that flanked the T.V. Interesting artifacts and personal photographs filled the shelves. She picked up a framed picture of T.J. in his police uniform, standing with two other officers. Joanna smiled. T.J. looked young and scrawny. She figured it had to be his graduation picture from the academy because of the striking resemblance; she assumed the other two men in the picture were his father and grandfather.

There were also some pretty impressive photos of T.J. surfing. One shot was of him as he rode the crest of a wave; another showed him crouched down in the middle of a roaring curl. A picture of him, on the beach with a beautiful camera-clad blonde told Joanna where the great photography had come from.

Wooden tikis, unique bowls, and vases with tribal-looking carvings on them were scattered among the shelves. It added a touch of culture to the room. Again, not what Joanna had expected.

Moving past the bookshelves, Joanna pulled back the sliding glass door and stepped out onto the balcony. A light gust blew her hair across her eyelashes as she inhaled the smell of the ocean air. She closed her eyes and took it in. There was something about the ocean that always had a calming effect on her. That's why she lived on the canal. Although she couldn't afford a place with a view like this, being near the water was the next best thing.

"Incredible, isn't it?" T.J. walked out and joined her.

Joanna turned to see him standing behind her in a pair of baggy jeans riding low on his hips; and a towel draped around his neck. His hair was still damp from his shower and his shirtless torso was bronze and sculpted. She caught herself staring. Luckily, T.J. didn't. He was looking out over the marina, unaware she was as impressed with him as she was the scenery.

"So, you really do like to surf?" she asked.

T.J. looked confused.

"I saw the pictures of you on the bookshelf. You look like you're pretty good at it."

He looked out into the distance and shrugged. "I used to be."

She joined him in staring at the vastness of the ocean, wondering what it was about men that made them feel like they had to tame the powers of nature.

"I'll take my chances with a fleeing felon over being sucked under by a wave any day."

"There you go again." He turned his back to the rail and leaned against it, tugging on the towel around his neck. "You can't be so narrow-minded about something you haven't even tried."

"I'm not being narrow-minded. I'm using my God-given common sense to acknowledge my physical limitations."

He leaned back and laughed. "That's a pretty lofty way to say you're chicken."

"I'm not chicken," she huffed. "I just have no desire to try it."

"That's because you're chicken," he said more emphatically.

Their bantering was interrupted by the ringing of T.J.'s phone. He stepped back inside to answer it, while Joanna turned her attention to the boats moving in and out of the marina.

"Hey, Carrie . . . I know, but something came up."

Joanna couldn't help but overhear T.J.'s side of the phone conversation.

"Tonight? Sure. It's up to you." T.J.'s voice turned sultry. "We could go out for dinner, or stay in for dessert. I have a sweet tooth that needs satisfying."

"Oh, please," Joanna mumbled under her breath as she rolled her eyes.

"See you tonight, Carrie, ten o'clock." T.J. tapped on the doorframe, getting Joanna's attention.

She turned around.

"I've got to finish getting dressed or we're going to be late. I'll be right back."

Joanna felt a twinge of irritation.

Who am I kidding? Just because he showed a different side of himself at my place, doesn't change who he is. He's still a player, working his way through life, one woman at a time.

T.J. reappeared wearing a t-shirt with the picture of Kermit the frog on it.

"Nice shirt," Joanna said as she got up to leave.

"What's that supposed to mean? I love this shirt."

"That's because it suits you." *Hopping from one bed to the next.*

T.J. drove them to the station, while Joanna braced herself for the harassment she was sure to get. She did her best to walk into roll call like nothing was wrong. They slipped into the back of the room, being spotted by Peck, Smith, and Bristol. She casually glanced around, but didn't see Rogers anywhere.

Maybe today won't be so bad after all.

Roll call broke up and the detectives headed to the War Room. Joanna looked for the file on their collar from the day before and started in on her report. Everyone else was filing in when Peck walked over to Joanna and T.J.

"You guys probably haven't heard yet, but Rogers

went down last night with a minor heart attack. Well, the doctor's calling it a cardiac episode."

T.J. and Joanna were momentarily speechless.

"He's home and seems to be doing fine, but he'll be off for a week or two as a precaution, just thought you should know."

Joanna turned her attention back to her report but was having a hard time focusing. She wanted to jump for joy. She knew it was wrong, but she didn't care. Not having Rogers breathing down her neck for even a week was an incredible break.

T.J. leaned over and whispered. "You might want to wipe that smirk off your face before someone notices." His voice was teasing, but his look was serious.

She lowered her head further, intent on filling out her report, and disguising the smile that continued to pull at her lips.

She wrote down all the details of the collar, from the moment she hit the fire escape, to when Bristol and Barker took the juvenile away. The shooter was identified as one of the Lost Boys, and his victim was from the Compadres. What sickened her most was the fact that they were cousins. The shooter confessed that he was able to lure his cousin away from his posse because they were related. He told him it was a family thing. When his cousin showed up, the punk let him know which *family* he was more loyal to. One kid was sixteen and dead. The other was only seventeen being charged with murder. She knew the D.A. would push for him to be tried as an adult; she had to make sure her report was as polished as possible.

Joanna had been writing for over an hour and was

beginning to see double. Her head pounded and her shoulder throbbed. She needed something to take the edge off. She looked at her watch, then took two pain pills from her front pocket. She walked over to the water cooler and discretely got a cup of water.

When she turned to go back to her seat, Bristol shoved past her, causing her head to knock against the wall. "Hey, Anderson, watch it!" The look in his eyes told her he knew exactly what he was doing.

She thought she'd done a good job disguising her pain, but obviously Bristol hadn't been fooled. Instead of returning to her seat, she headed to the women's restroom. She went into one of the stalls and leaned against the door, taking deep breaths, willing away tears that pooled in her eyes, refusing to let them fall.

After a few minutes, when she felt she had her composure intact, she returned to the War Room and sat down to finish her report.

T.J. watched as Joanna walked back into the room. He knew she was in pain by the set of her jaw. He wanted to say something, but decided to let it go. When she finished her report and closed the file, T.J. got up. "Why don't you meet me at the car after you turn that in? There are a few things I would like to check out."

Joanna planned on leaving her report on the sergeant's desk. She didn't expect him to be there. He looked up as she tapped on the open door.

"I have the report on the Ramirez shooting," she said.

He extended his hand.

She stepped into his office, handed him the file and waited. He flipped it open and glanced over it. He was looking for mistakes. Joanna silently dared him to find any.

She had always been complimented on how thorough and precise her reports were. She'd taken extra care on this one, knowing it would come under intense scrutiny, not only from her superiors, but the D.A. as well. When the sergeant finally looked up at her, she braced herself for whatever criticisms he would have.

"What's the extent of your injuries?"

His question caught her completely by surprise, and his intense stare caused her to blank.

"You went to the hospital, correct?" His question was direct.

"Yes, sir. My injuries were minor. I was treated in the E.R. and released."

He looked over her report some more, then closed the folder. "I'm sure everything is in order." He looked at her once again. "Good job, Anderson, on apprehending the suspect. That's all."

She left his office, stunned.

Grabbing her purse from the War Room, Joanna met T.J. in the parking lot. When she climbed into the car she was unable to hide her amazement.

"What happened?" T.J. asked.

"He complimented me. He actually told me I did a good job at the scene and on my report."

"You're kidding? Sergeant Blackstone?"

"Yeah. He even asked how I was doing."

"Well, congratulations. Looks like you're making an impression on somebody."

Joanna slowly leaned back against the seat, almost forgetting about her discomfort. First, Rogers is out, then, the sergeant compliments her. A day that started out rocky was picking up by the minute.

T.J. merged into traffic.

"I saw what Bristol did. How's your head?" T. J. asked.

"I thought I was going to puke right then and there, but it's fine now."

Joanna's phone rang. She dug into her purse and slid her finger across the screen.

"Hi, Keith . . . no, I can talk . . ."

T.J. turned to her. "What's lover boy want?"

She took a swing at him, but missed.

"Actually, Keith, the last few hours have been pretty hard to believe . . . no, I'm fine . . . well, it's kind of involved . . . dinner?" She looked at T.J., seeing a flicker of suspicion in his eyes. "I don't get off until eight o'clock. Okay, let's say nine? Sure, I'll explain then . . . Bye."

She tossed her phone back into her purse. She knew T.J. was dying to say something, so she figured he may as well get it out of his system.

"What?"

"I didn't say anything," he answered sharply.

"No, but you're dying to say something, so you might as well say it and get it over with."

"Nope, I got nothing to say. You're an adult. Do what you want. I know I plan to."

"Oh that's right. You and Carrie are going to be having

some *dessert* tonight. Something about a sweet tooth?"

"Ha! I knew you were listening," he said matter-of-factly.

"I wasn't eavesdropping if that's what you mean," she said defensively. "It wasn't like you were talking quietly or anything."

"Whatever. I don't care. It's not like I'm hiding something."

"No, that's one thing you don't do, hide anything. In fact, I'm sure I'll be able to get a play-by-play in the War Room tomorrow when you're bragging to all the guys about your exploits."

"And what about Keith? Will he be bragging to his partner tomorrow?" His tone was snide.

"You're such a jerk! You know that? Must everything you do and say be motivated by sex?"

"Obviously not or I wouldn't have spent the night at your house."

His admission brought their conversation to an abrupt end.

CHAPTER THIRTEEN

T.J. and Joanna spent the rest of the day following up leads on the deaths of the other two prostitutes. They were looking for anything that would link them with Samantha Randolph.

So far, they'd found out the other two women worked the streets, while Samantha got her hookups through the bar.

Completely different routines.

Their physical characteristics didn't offer any clues either. Samantha was a blond, one woman was a strung out redhead, and the third victim was black. Their ages ranged from seventeen to twenty-seven, and none of their killings had been similar. Samantha was strangled, the redhead was bludgeoned, and the black woman died of asphyxiation. All three victims were found in a four mile radius.

Right now, the only common thread between the three women was the fact that they all died with money on them. Robbery had been ruled out in all three cases. It wasn't much to go on, but it was too big a coincidence to ignore, especially in the neighborhood they were found in.

T.J. and Joanna went back to each of the scenes, straining to find something that wasn't there. They attempted to talk with some of the regulars on the streets. Most of them just blew them off, acting like they didn't know anything. A few confided they were scared and didn't know what to do.

T.J. and Joanna were at the end of their shift, sitting at a red light, when Joanna saw a girl emerge from between two buildings. When the light turned green, Joanna asked T.J. to pull over.

He followed Joanna's sight line to see what she was looking at. "Come on, Joanna. Enough already. Let's just start fresh tomorrow."

"No, T.J., there's something about that girl, the way she's hugging the wall and not willing to come away from the building. She's scared."

"I'd be scared too if I knew there was a lunatic out preying on the likes of me."

"Come on, T.J. Last one before we call it a night." There was something about this particular girl; Joanna could sense she was afraid for reasons other than just being on the streets. The way she acted—she seemed strangely out of place.

T.J. groaned as he pulled the car over, and Joanna got out.

The girl was ready to walk away when Joanna stopped her. "Can I ask you a few questions?"

The girl stopped, looking terrified.

"You're not in trouble. I just want to ask you a couple

questions."

Joanna talked to her a few minutes about the murders, and asked her what she was doing to ensure her safety. The girl fidgeted with her tight skirt, and looked over her shoulder a lot. She really didn't give Joanna any answers; she just kept saying "the girls" were helping her.

The girl's body language was all wrong for someone working the streets. Her shoulders sunken inward, her eyes on the pavement–closed off, and the gentle way she stroked her mid-section–protective. Joanna watched her, then asked, "You're pregnant aren't you?"

The astonished look on the girl's face was answer enough.

"What are you going to do?" Joanna persisted.

The girl broke down in sobs. "I don't know; I'm so scared. I can't go home, my mother will kill me, but I can't do this either. She pointed to her scanty clothing. The other girls have been helping me, protecting me, until I adjusted to the idea. But I don't think I ever will."

Joanna was able to decipher from bits and pieces of the girl's ramblings that some hookers had befriended her and now she was trying to make a go of it herself.

Joanna didn't want her to turn into another statistic.

"Why don't you go home? It can't be as bad as this?"

"Easy for you to say." She shot Joanna a look of resentment.

"What about the baby?" Joanna asked.

"The girls think I should get an abortion, but I can't. I know I've screwed up, but I won't kill my own baby."

The girl walked over to the curb and sat down, her knees pressed together, her long legs akimbo in the gutter.

"Wait here." Joanna walked back to the car and grabbed her purse from the front seat. She sat down beside the girl and pulled a business card from her purse.

"What's this?" The girl took the card and held it up in the light of the overhead street lamp. She turned it over in her hand.

"It's the phone number of a group that can help you. You can go to them, no questions asked. They'll make sure you get the medical attention you need, give you a place to stay, and even help you if you decide to give the baby up for adoption. Their only rules are no drinking, no drugs, and no abortions. They'll help you talk to your family if you'd like, but they won't make you contact them if you're not ready."

The fragile girl turned the card over and saw the cross on the back. "Are they some kind of religious group?"

"They're Christians, if that's what you mean, but they're really cool. They won't pressure you into anything, other than taking care of yourself and your baby."

She turned the card over and over in her hand.

"What's your name?" Joanna asked.

"Michelle."

She took the card from Michelle and scribbled on the back of it. "Here." She handed the card back. "This is my phone number. If you decide not to give them a call, but you still want to talk to somebody I'd like to help."

Michelle looked at the card again, and then to Joanna. "You're sure they're not crazy people that are going to scream at me and tell me I'm going to Hell?"

Joanna smiled. "I promise."

Michelle got to her feet. Her skirt barely covered her

thighs and her halter top fell short of the pooch behind her pierced belly-button.

"Thanks. I'll think about it."

Joanna watched as Michelle walked away, praying she would call the shelter.

When she got back in the car, T.J. tore into her. "You shouldn't have done that."

"Done what?"

"You gave her your phone number, didn't you?"

"She needs help, T.J. She's just too afraid to know what to do. I wanted to let her know there are people in the world who care, regardless of what she's done."

"So where'd you refer her to?"

"It's an outreach of my church. They work with teen pregnancies and battered women. They get them the medical attention they need, counseling, legal aid, and if a girl decides to put her child up for adoption, the center helps put them in contact with suitable couples."

"How noble."

T.J.'s cynical attitude irritated Joanna. "What's that supposed to mean?"

"I just don't agree with the tactics of some of those groups."

"Tactics? What do you mean?"

"Come on, Joanna, those *centers* are usually run by zealous right-to-life groups. I just don't agree with them. I mean, in some cases abortion is the best thing for all involved."

"How can you say that?" Joanna was horrified.

"Look at that girl." He raised his voice, clearly agitated. "She's the perfect example. She knows nothing about having a baby. She's a strung out hooker stupid enough to get pregnant. Now she's carrying some trick's baby, and you want her to keep it? Give me a break. What kind of life would that kid have? Its' mother's a hooker, it will never know who its' father is, and if it isn't already infected by AIDS, it's probably addicted to the drugs its' mother uses."

"Michelle's not a hooker, she's a runaway. And stop calling her baby an 'it!' You act like you're talking about an inanimate object." Joanna took a deep breath and lowered her voice. "I didn't say she had to keep the baby, T.J. There are thousands of couples out there, wanting a child, not able to have one of their own. She can put her baby up for adoption."

"And you think one of those couples would want *her* baby? A baby who's going to have who knows what kind of difficulties. Let alone how the kid's going to react when it finds out the truth about its' parentage. The problem with you do-gooders is you only look at things through the eyes of your cause, your mission. You have tunnel vision."

"I don't have tunnel vision! I just believe in the sanctity of life. Quite honestly in scares me to think where this country is headed."

T.J. continued to drive while they debated the subject. He turned down her street, pulled into the driveway, and waited for her to get out, but Joanna wasn't finished. It took her a few seconds to work up the nerve to ask her next question, but she had to know. Her heart was racing, and her head was pounding, but she spoke with all the calmness she could muster.

"So, I guess you feel the same way about a woman

who gets pregnant by rape? She should just abort the baby and be done with it, move on with life?"

"Well, yeah. Why should she put herself through that? What kind of life would she have if she had a constant reminder of what she'd been through? And imagine the devastation that kid would feel when it found out it was a product of rape?"

Joanna chose to ignore T.J.'s use of the word 'it.' "So, again, you think that's a disposable life. A life better off not lived?"

He shrugged his shoulders. "I just don't see what good could come from that kind of life. It's a lose-lose situation."

"Well then, I guess you have a loser for a partner."

She pulled on the handle of the door and swung one foot out of the car. Before she could leave, T.J. took a hold of her arm.

"What's that supposed to mean?"

She swiveled back around and looked at him with eyes filled with pain. "*I'm* one of those babies. My mother was raped when she was in college. She had her whole life ahead of her, and could have easily used all the excuses you just rattled off, but she didn't. She valued life.

"She valued me."

Joanna stepped from the car, slammed the door, and walked briskly down the narrow walkway to her front door.

"Joanna, wait." She heard T.J.'s pounding footsteps behind her. She was still struggling with the lock on her front door when he reached her. "Joanna, I'm sorry, I had no idea."

"Of course you didn't," she said as she continued to fumble with her key. "How could you? But that's just it.

No one will ever know the potential of these kids if they continue to sacrifice them on the altar of convenience or what society deems worthy."

She pushed open the door but wouldn't allow T.J. inside.

"Come on, Joanna. At least give me a chance to apologize."

"Apologize for what? Your ignorance or your self-righteousness?"

He looked at her. "For hurting you."

"Fine. You're sorry." She started to close the door.

"But Joanna—"

"Goodnight, T.J."

T.J. stood there as she closed the door and listened as she threw the extra deadbolt. He walked away dumbfounded, not knowing how he would ever be able to make this up to her.

CHAPTER FOURTEEN

Joanna washed her face and brushed her hair. She was going through the paces, getting ready to go out with Keith, but her heart just wasn't in it. The conversation with T.J. had gotten out of hand and personal. She was mad at herself for blowing up at him, and now was in a funk. She looked at her watch. Eight o'clock. Pulling her cell phone from her purse she hit speed dial.

"Hi, Keith."

"Joanna. I was just getting ready to leave."

"About that, look . . . something came up at work tonight, and I just don't feel up to going out. I wouldn't be very good company."

"I could bring something to your place, and we could stay in."

She could hear the disappointment in his voice.

"Actually, I've had a real difficult day. I think I'm going to make it an early night."

"Are you still feeling sick or nauseous? Because if you

are, you need—"

"No, really Keith, I'm fine. Like I said, if was just a rough day."

"But you sounded so upbeat earlier."

"I know. It's just this job. Sometimes it really stinks."

"I understand."

She could tell he didn't, but she was thankful he wasn't pushing it.

"Can I call you tomorrow?"

"Sure. I'd like that."

Joanna hung up the phone, sad she'd cancelled their plans. She could tell Keith was disappointed. She was too. But she knew it was for the best. She would be terrible company tonight, and really did need to sleep.

She walked to the kitchen and threw a bag of popcorn into the microwave. Taking a bottle of water from the fridge, she waited for the microwave to ding. Exhausted, she closed her eyes and leaned against the doorway, chastising herself for telling T.J. the details of her birth. She wasn't sure if she'd done it to make her point, or just to put him in his place.

Joanna didn't like being called a zealot or self-righteous. Sure, she had strong beliefs and definite opinions, and wasn't going to just sit back and let T.J. spew his cynicism, but too many people chose sides on an issue based on ignorance. She wanted T.J. to think about what he believed and why.

When the microwave dinged, she grabbed the bag of popcorn and headed upstairs with a couple of pain killers in her hand.

A hot bath and a good night's rest, that's what she

needed. But as she crawled into bed, her thoughts traveled back and forth between T.J. and Keith.

It was going to be a long night.

When T.J. got home, Carrie was already waiting on his doorstep.

He looked at her and asked, "I thought we said ten o'clock?"

"We did." She giggled as she held a shopping bag in her arms. "But I didn't want you to disappear again like last night."

"I didn't disappear," he snapped. "Something came up. I told you that." He unlocked his apartment and walked in, Carrie following closely behind.

"Oh, sounds like my teddy bear is a grouchy bear. That's okay, I have something that will make it all better."

Usually T.J. liked Carrie's "little girl voice." He thought it was sexy. But at the moment, he just found it irritating.

"Look, Carrie, I'm not in the best of moods right now. Why don't we take a rain check? I really need to get some sleep." He walked to the refrigerator and pulled out a beer. He popped the top and took a long swig.

"But I brought something I think you'll enjoy."

Her voice was grating on him; he just wanted her to leave.

She reached into her shopping bag and brought out several small bottles, with erotic labels on them. She looked at him with a gleam in her eye. "They're edible body paints. I thought maybe we could create a masterpiece tonight."

T.J. laid in bed, wondering if Joanna's date with Keith had turned out as well as his. He laughed. He was sure by the way he gave Carrie the heave-ho she wouldn't be calling him anytime soon.

He stared at the ceiling, listening to the bell from a distant buoy. T.J. thought about Joanna, and what kind of childhood she must have had. He realized, in all their weeks together, she had never talked about her parents. He thought back to a few of the personal conversations they had. She had always turned them back on him, or somehow they were interrupted. T.J. really knew nothing about her, except of course for the gossip at the station.

His first plan of attack for tomorrow—after apologizing—would be to find out who Joanna Anderson really is.

CHAPTER FIFTEEN

"How are you feeling this morning?"

Joanna smiled at the sound of Keith's voice. "Better. Thank you."

"I thought maybe we could reschedule for tonight, if you felt up to it."

"I'd like that, but nine o'clock seems so late for dinner. Could we make it dessert?"

"Sure. You name the place."

"No, you decide."

"Okay, then. I'll pick you up between eight-thirty and nine."

"Sounds great." Joanna hung up the phone hopeful things would go better tonight with Keith. *Now to test the waters with T.J.*

She grabbed her keys and purse. Although her shoulder was still sore, her head had stopped throbbing. After a night of back and forth with her conscience, Joanna decided to apologize to T.J. It would be easier than listening to him try to defend himself. She was sorry she'd said anything at all, and just wanted to forget about it. Hopefully, T.J. would too.

When she pulled into the station, T.J. was leaning on their sedan waiting for her.

She parked her car, and walked over to him. "T.J., I'm–"

"Come on, let's go," he said with a hint of anxiousness.

Figuring they must have a lead to follow up, she got into the sedan and buckled up while T.J. drove out of the lot.

"What did you find out?" she asked, anxious to know if they had a break in the case.

"Who said I found out anything?" he asked defensively.

"I just figured you must have found out something about the case for us to leave in such a hurry."

"No. I wanted us to have a chance to talk."

Great. Exactly what she had wanted to avoid.

He was headed towards the beach, and she knew they would probably end up at the lookout they'd been to before.

"Look, T.J., let's just forget about it, okay? I'm sorry I ambushed you last night. It wasn't fair of me, and I'm sorry."

"You have nothing to apologize for, Joanna. I take the blame for my own stupidity."

"Then fine, it's settled. Let's just go about our job like nothing happened. It really shouldn't effect the way we work with each other anyway."

T.J. wasn't listening to a thing she said, he just kept driving. "I don't want to fight, T.J. I don't have the energy for it."

"We're not going to fight. We're going to listen."

He pulled onto the bluff and killed the motor. "If we're going to work together, I think we should know more about each other."

"Like what?" she asked, already exhausted at the thought of where their conversation was headed.

"Family? Friends? Hobbies? Beliefs? Why police work? Things we should know about each other, so we don't make the same mistake I did. I know I hurt you, Joanna, and I don't want to take that chance again."

"But you can't change what you believe. If that's the way you feel about abortion, you have every right to voice it. Don't apologize for your beliefs, T.J."

"But maybe they aren't my beliefs? Maybe I never took the time to think about it. I just believed what I heard, what I was told."

"Look, I don't want to talk about this right now. I don't have the energy, and we don't have the time."

"We have plenty of time. I told Blackstone we had some important information to follow up on, and we would be out of service for a while. I said we'd check back in after lunch."

"So you lied."

"No. *This* is important information."

"You don't know what you're asking, T.J. I've had a pretty screwed up life," Joanna said as she stared out across the ocean.

"That must be why you're so tough . . . and a complete

pain in the butt."

"Flattery will get you nowhere." She looked at him as he flashed his boyish smile. She hurried to look away, confused at the feelings stirring inside her.

"Come on, Joanna, we're partners. I think we should be straight with each other."

She sighed. Seeing she had no way out, she finally caved. "Fine. But I'm going to make this quick."

She said a prayer to help her get through what she was about to say, then started from the beginning.

"My parents were engaged when it happened. They were both in law school at the time. My father would take the bar that summer, they would get married that winter, and my mother would take the bar the following spring."

"She was leaving the campus library one night, when she was assaulted and raped. She never knew who did it, and was in the hospital for several weeks after. When my mother found out she was pregnant, she was devastated. But my father stuck by her side the whole time. They didn't tell anyone, not even their parents. They decided to get married right away and raise me as my father's child. When my mother got out of the hospital, they had a small wedding instead of the grand affair they had planned. Everyone was thrilled when my parents announced three months later that my mother was pregnant. Few people had known about the attack, since it happened when my mom was away at school. So no one questioned her pregnancy."

Joanna looked at T.J. and saw a hundred questions behind his eyes. She didn't stop to answer them, she just kept going.

"My mother had complications throughout the

pregnancy. She never returned to school because her health was so bad. I was delivered a month premature. Of course, everyone else thought I was two months pre-mature and touted me as a miracle baby."

"My mother never returned to law school. She chose instead to be a stay-at-home mom. I never felt anything but love from both my parents. They treated me like a princess. My mother miscarried six times after I was born. Finally, the doctors told her she would be unable to have more kids. I remember my father crying with my mother one night. I thought I had done something to make them angry. When my father found me crying in my room, he asked me why. I told him I was afraid they were angry with me. He hugged me so tight that night, as if he was afraid to let me go. He assured me he loved me and told me what a precious gift I was to him and my mother."

Joanna wiped at the single tear running down her cheek, hating herself for getting emotional.

"I cherish that conversation with my father. It was the first thing I remembered when I finally learned how I was conceived."

"How did your mom tell you?" T.J. asked softly.

"She didn't. I found out about all of this from her journals." Joanna looked at him. "T.J., my parents died in a car accident when I was seven."

"What?"

The shock in his voice was clear.

"They were killed when a drunk driver crossed the center divide. I was the only one to survive."

"Joanna . . . I don't know what to say. I had no idea."

"Few people do."

"But I don't understand. I thought you said your father was in law enforcement."

"No. *You* did. I just didn't correct you."

"I don't get it then. Why did you become a cop?"

"A police officer, Matthew Moore, helped me through the accident. He never left my side while people were shouting at him to get away. The car was on fire, and they were afraid it was going to explode. The fireman told him to get back, but he wouldn't leave my side. He stayed with me until they got me out."

Joanna stared out the windshield and saw Matthew's face staring back at her. Inwardly, she smiled.

"Matthew is the one who told me my parents had died. He accompanied me to their funeral and visited me every day."

"Didn't you have any other family?"

"I had one set of grandparents, but they were quite elderly."

"What happened to you?"

"I was put in foster care. Matthew tried to adopt me, but the county didn't think a single police officer could provide a stable home. I stayed in a children's residence until I graduated."

"But you stayed in contact with Matthew?"

Joanna nodded. "He was as close to me as a father could get. He was at every school play and every awards banquet. He took me to church and prayed with me. It was Matthew who led me to the Lord."

"So, he's why you are the way you are?"

"Don't make it sound like the plague, T.J. Being a Christian isn't a disease or a life sentence. It's a relationship."

"I guess." He shrugged, clearly perplexed. They were both quiet for a moment. Then T.J. shook his head. "I bet you were a handful."

"I had my moments."

Joanna paused for a moment and then began to chuckle. "Matthew threatened my first date within an inch of his life. I didn't get asked out by another boy for months." Joanna enjoyed the memory, but quickly turned serious. "The day I told him I wanted to be a cop, he did everything he could to talk me out of it. When he realized I'd made up my mind, he supported my decision and helped me every step of the way."

A peculiar look came over T.J.'s face.

"What?" Joanna asked.

"Nothing. I was just thinking about something. Go on."

Joanna studied T.J. for a moment before she continued, tears swelling in her eyes. "I graduated and during my first month of being a rookie Matthew was killed in the line of duty."

"That's how I know that name." T.J. shot up in his seat. "I remember hearing about it. It happened in a crack house, right?"

Joanna nodded her head.

"But I don't understand. Why did you stay with the force? I think I would've called it quits."

"I almost did. I was given time off to grieve, and I almost ended up killing myself." Joanna saw the surprise in T.J.'s eyes. "I struggled for weeks with drugs and alcohol, anything to make the pain go away. But then I realized how many people I would be letting down if I just gave up on life. My mom gave up her dream of becoming a lawyer so she could stay home with me. My father loved me more than anyone could, even though I wasn't really his child. Matthew pretty much put his life on hold for me. Helping me, nurturing me, being a father to me, even if the state said he couldn't. And then, there was my relationship with God."

T.J. shook his head, his jaw clenched. "How could you still believe in God after all you went through? I thought he was supposed to be loving and caring, a super guru that takes care of his people."

"Believe me, T.J., I struggled. When I turned sixteen, Matthew gave me my mother's journals. He had already read them and knew it was going to be difficult for me to find out about my background, but he thought I was old enough to know the truth. He sat with me as I read them. I told him I hated God, and would never believe in Him again. I cried for hours. Matthew allowed me my time of anger, but when it was all said and done, he assured me how much God loved me. He showed me how special I was. How God had given me a mother that wouldn't throw me away or dispose of me. And then, when my parents were gone, God gave me Matthew, an incredible gift. Matthew reminded me how God had brought special people into my life, not taken them away."

"But they *were* taken away," T.J. retorted.

"Yes, I know. Sin is a horrible thing. It hurts and destroys people. But Christians aren't immune to sin and its consequences."

"Then why be a Christian?" T.J. asked, clearly frustrated and confused.

"Because I don't want to travel this road alone."

Joanna looked at T.J., really looked at him, hoping she could convey to him how important her faith was to her. "I don't know where life is taking me, T.J., but I know I can't do it alone. God will always be there for me. And though I might struggle with His ways and the things He's allowed. I know He has a plan for my life. I just have to trust Him."

Joanna could see the skepticism on T.J.'s face.

"I didn't say it was easy, or that I'm a hundred percent successful. But I'm trying, and that's all He asks for."

T.J. sat in utter amazement. He had no idea, by looking at Joanna, the devastating events she had lived through. He saw her in a whole new light. Her defiance, her strong will, her commitment to her faith, they were all born out of adversity, pain, and loss.

She could've become an extremely bitter person.

Instead, she became an amazing woman.

CHAPTER SIXTEEN

"So . . . what's your story?" Joanna turned to T.J.

He looked at her, realizing his life had been a walk in the park compared to hers. "Are you kidding me? My life looks like a Dr. Seuss book next to yours."

"I didn't think this was a competition. I thought we were trying to get to know each other better?"

He reached for the ignition and turned the key. "How about we go for a walk? We've sat here long enough."

"Fine. But don't think you're going to use the beach as a distraction. I spilled my guts. I expect you to do the same."

He drove to the parking lot below the lookout. The minute he stepped from the car he took a deep cleansing breath as the ocean waves crashed in front of them. *Ah, there's nothing like that smell, that taste of salt in the air.* The love he felt for the beach, the surf, the waves, was tangible. He flipped off his shoes and tossed them on his seat before shutting the door.

"Where are we walking?" Joanna asked.

"Out there, along the water," T.J. answered as he rolled up the hem of his jeans.

He watched as Joanna took her shoes and socks off. She rolled her socks up together and leaned over to place them neatly on the floorboard.

He laughed at how particular she was, even with a pair of socks

"What?" Joanna straightened up.

"Nothing."

She eyed him, hands on her hips.

"Come on, Joanna, we don't have all day."

She stared a second longer before she leaned back against the car and bent over to roll up her pant legs. She swayed, losing her balance.

"Whoa." T.J. grabbed her forearms to steady her. "I thought your head was feeling better?"

"It was . . . I mean it is. I just kind of lost my balance."

"Here, put your foot up." T.J. patted his thigh.

Joanna hesitated before putting her sandy foot up on his leg. Carefully, he rolled up her pant leg to just below her knee.

"Other foot."

She switched feet.

The intimacy of the moment was not lost on T.J. Joanna's legs were soft, warm, tanned, and toned. He felt his pulse swell and his skin heat up. He was enjoying touching her.

Enjoying it a little too much.

"Nice legs," he teased, breaking the heat of the moment.

She tried to pull her leg away, but he stopped her. "Come on. Don't be so sensitive. You know you have great legs. Why can't I compliment you on them," he chided her, as he slowly rolled up her other pant leg.

"Because I don't want you to think you're softening me up with compliments and flattery."

"What's there to soften up?" he said as they headed across the warm sand. "You've made it perfectly clear I don't interest you in the least." He hung his head in mock rejection.

"Come on, I didn't say that. You can be a great guy when you want to be. It's just when that machismo of yours raises its ugly head you become a pain in the neck."

"Well, I have a much lower opinion of you. When you get on your high horse, you become a real pain in the–"

"That's enough." She raised her hand. "We didn't come out here to talk about me. We came out here to talk about you. So spill it."

"Really, there isn't much to tell. Like I said before, my father was a cop and my grandfather a cop before him. Naturally, I was expected to follow in their footsteps."

"Is that what you wanted to do?"

"No. I wanted to surf."

"Yeah," she chuckled slightly. "But you can't do that for a living."

"You can if you're good enough, and for a while, I was."

T.J. looked out over the horizon. Remembering how it was. Remembering the adrenaline rush of slicing through waves that could crush him.

"So, why'd you give it up?" she asked.

"I couldn't keep up. The lifestyle was killing me, or should I say the lifestyle I was choosing to live was killing me."

"What do you mean?"

"I traveled around the world from beach to beach. Brazil, South Africa, Australia, the South of France. I surfed all day and partied all night. There were girls that followed the circuit and made themselves easily accessible to us. So, we'd drink too much, have sex before we passed out, and the next day try to surf the biggest, most dangerous waves in the world. It was crazy.

"When you were doing well, a sponsor would throw a patch on your shirt and offer you their product. But have a few bad showings, and they were calling you a loser and a has-been."

When Joanna and he reached the wet sand of the shoreline, he headed south, and she fell into step alongside him.

"The guys that were smart enough to have agents and people taking care of them were the ones who succeeded. The rest of us had a lot of fun, but didn't end up with much to show for it."

"How long did you do it for?"

"About five years."

"Did you ever win?"

"Sure. I won a couple of times and placed a few dozen more."

"So what finally made you stop?"

"I almost killed myself."

Joanna gasped. "What?"

"Not intentionally."

He thought for a moment, staring at his feet and the impressions they were making in the sand. He had promised himself he wouldn't live in the past. Yet there he was, right back on that beach in Portugal, a vision of the raven-haired beauty standing before him, offering him a good time. He turned to Joanna, and saw she was waiting for some sort of explanation.

"There was this big tournament in Portugal. Through all the pre-lims, this other surfer and I were neck to neck in points. No one else could even touch us. It was all going to come down to the finals, and there was a huge endorsement deal on the line."

He shoved his hands in his pockets; the memory of the ordeal still had the ability to chill him.

Joanna walked quietly beside him, waiting for him to continue.

"The night before the finals, this incredible looking woman came up to me. She had curves in all the right places, and with what she was wearing, it left very little to the imagination.

"I'd only had a few drinks, so when she told me she had a room at the hotel and wanted some company, I was all over it. Usually, I was so wasted by the time the sex happened, I rarely enjoyed myself."

T.J. saw out of the corner of his eye, that Joanna was fidgeting with the hem of her shirt. He realized he was making her uncomfortable. "I'm sorry, I didn't mean to sound so crude."

"No problem," she said quietly.

"Anyway," T.J. continued, "we went back to her room and started really mixing it up. We were drinking and grinding and—"

Again, T.J. caught himself being a little too graphic for Joanna's liking.

"Like I said, we were hitting it off. After a while, she disappeared into the bathroom. I figured she was getting undressed, so I started taking my clothes off, when all of a sudden, my gut cramped up. I brushed it off as nothing, but then it did it again, even sharper. I felt like I'd been punched. I couldn't breathe. When it happened again, it knocked me to my knees."

T.J. stopped for a moment, recalling how he felt. The pain, the panic. "I couldn't catch my breath. I started sweating profusely, and I couldn't get my eyes to focus. That's when I knew something was really wrong. I don't remember anything else about that night."

"When I woke up the next day, the woman was gone, and the room was magically registered in my name. The finals were about to start, and I was still in incredible pain, but I wasn't about to withdraw.

"I got my gear from my room and headed for the shore. When I crossed paths with Donnie Bain—my biggest competition—he looked at me like he'd seen a ghost. That's when I knew I'd been setup. The incredible woman who had appeared out of nowhere was a plant. She had slipped me something in my drink to keep me out of the competition. Or at least that had been their plan.

But that wasn't going to happen. I was going to beat Donnie Bain, and then when we were both on solid ground I was going to beat the crap out of him and show him he was messing with the wrong guy."

"I watched as Donnie nailed his first ride. I paddled

out, and watched a few more riders call their waves. My stomach was killing me from all the cramping, and I was still seeing double. I knew I had no business being out on my board, but I wasn't going to let Donnie get the better of me without a fight. When I took a line on my first wave, I never made it to shore. I collapsed on my board and was taken under by a wave. The rescue teams had to look for me and pull me out of the water. I ended up in a hospital in Portugal, battling a parasite in my stomach."

T.J. looked at Joanna, her mouth hung open.

"That was the official end of my career. I flew back to the states after a few months, concentrated on getting well, and enrolled in the police academy. My father finally got what he wanted."

It took a moment before Joanna said anything.

"Do you ever regret not trying it again? Surfing I mean," she asked sympathetically.

"Yes and no. There were times when I'd vacation and take some really good waves. I would feel the same adrenaline rush I had felt when I was competing, and wondered if I had given up too easily. But then I'd remembered what a slow recovery I'd had. I was out of the water for six months. There was no way I would've been able to get back in competition shape. I was already twenty-four. Even if I had worked really hard and gotten back in, I wasn't going to have that many years left in me."

"But you still enjoy it?"

"Every chance I get."

They'd walked to the breakwater. He stopped and watched as a wave crashed over the rocks jetting out from the shore. "I guess we should head back."

"Yeah. Probably."

They walked in silence.

T.J. watched as Joanna followed the surfers catching some waves. She squinted her eyes, while her body moved with their motions.

"I could teach you, you know."

"What?" Joanna looked at him like he was crazy. "Oh no. Not me. I am a definite land lover."

"Come on." He laughed, unable to suppress his excitement. The thought of sharing his passion with Joanna made his heart race.

He stepped in front of her, trying to get her to stop and think about it, but she wouldn't be deterred. She marched around him, through the heavy sand towards the car.

"Just forget it, T.J. I have no desire to face plant going ninety miles an hour."

He laughed, and quickened his pace. Again, he hurried in front of her, walking backward to keep up with her determined strides.

"Let me give you a few lessons. It's really not that hard. It's mostly a balancing act. Believe me there's nothing like it. You'll love it. I promise."

Joanna couldn't believe she was actually entertaining the idea. The only reason she was even remotely considering it, was because of the smile on T.J.'s face. His features were filled with boyish charm, a nice change from the womanizing man she was used to.

But . . . if she was going to be asked to move outside her comfort zone, then she was going to expect him to take a little risk as well.

"Okay." She stopped abruptly in the sand and folded her arms against her chest. "I'll do it. But only on one condition."

"What's that?"

"You have to go to church with me." She looked at him with an arched brow and a challenging smile.

"What? Are you kidding? The wrath of God himself would rain down on me and annihilate anyone around me. I can't be responsible for that kind of carnage."

"Is that a lofty way of saying you're chicken?" Joanna challenged.

"Me? Chicken? Of a few Bible thumpers?" T.J. laughed. "Actually, I was looking out for your best interest. I believe it was you who first pointed out that I could be damaging to your reputation."

"I'm not afraid, if you're not," Joanna said as she crossed the walking path and came to rest against the hood of the car.

T.J. leaned on the car as well and started brushing the sand from his feet. As she leaned down to unroll her pants, T.J. stuck his hand in her face.

"Deal. I teach you how to surf on Saturday, then go to church with you on Sunday."

"Okay, but no backing out." Joanna took hold of his hand and shook it. "Even if I'm a terrible student, you still have to go to church with me the next day."

"Hey, I never back out on a deal."

"Then you're on."

They both got in the car and put on their shoes.

T.J. picked up the radio. "Dispatch, David Charlie

Two, we're ten-eight."

David Charlie Two, Ten-nineteen. What is your ETA?"

They were being asked to return to the station. Great, just what they needed.

T.J. looked at Joanna. "ETA in ten."

"You're the one going to have to do the talking." Joanna said. "I'm not going to get railed for being out of service."

"We weren't out of service. We were gathering important information. I think it was time well worth it, don't you?" He turned to her with a grin.

"Yeah. It was." She smiled appreciatively.

T.J. felt his heart seize. She was doing it again. Joanna was getting under his skin.

CHAPTER SEVENTEEN

When T.J. and Joanna got to the War Room, everyone was assembled, including a woman in a black suit. Joanna recognized her as Tracy Barnes, a criminal profiler. Sergeant Blackstone was passing around a new 8 x 10 glossy. That could mean only one thing. There had been another killing.

"Okay, this is what we've got," Blackstone said as he paced the length of the room. "She worked solo, twenty years old. She was found in the alley behind Emerson Street between Birch and Cedar. Cause of death was a broken neck. The I.D. found with the body says Crystal Meyers. We still need to confirm that."

"She have any money on her Sgt.?" Peck asked.

"Yep, everything's the same."

The sergeant turned his attention back to the woman in the front row. "Dr. Barnes has been working with the information from the previous killings and has put together a profile she believes fits the killer." Sergeant Blackstone turned the floor over to her and took a seat.

She stood, holding a file in front of her. "I believe we're looking for a male in his late forties to early fifties, single or divorced, probably living at home or with a family member. He feels the need to release his sexual tension, but since he can't bring women home, he uses hookers. He feels the need to kill these women because he's afraid of being identified. He's got some kind of celebrity status. He could be a politician, a businessman, someone known in the community. So in order to keep his impropriety secret, he kills them. There's no sign of a struggle, so it's obvious the women are willing participants."

"Anything else?" Blackstone asked.

"He has sex with his victims after they're dead, minimizing his need to perform."

"So he's a pervert with no get-up-and-go," Bristol popped off.

"Something like that," Barnes acknowledged blandly. "Any other questions?"

The room was quiet.

"Thank you, Tracy, for your time." Sergeant Blackstone rose, shook her hand, and waited for her to step out of the room before he snapped at Bristol.

"You've got no class, you know that?"

"Come on, we all were thinking the same thing. Well, everyone but Anderson."

Joanna looked him square in the eye. "Maybe you said it because you recognized the symptoms, Bristol."

The rest of the men erupted in laughter while T.J. looked at her with surprise.

"That's enough." Blackstone got everyone back on

track. "Okay, we now have something to go on, someone to look for. Someone who fits the profile but doesn't fit the environment. Everyone keep your eyes and ears open. Question the pros about any out of the ordinary john's or strange vehicles. That's it for now." Blackstone headed for the door. "Owens, Anderson, can I see you two in my office?"

It was a directive, not a question.

Both T.J. and Joanna got up from the desk and followed the sergeant out. They each took a seat in his office, while he closed the door. He walked around to the back of his desk and sat down.

"Anderson, we're thinking of putting you in undercover."

Joanna had seen this coming. After weeks of no leads, it was only a matter of time before a decoy was sent in. She was prepared, but somehow it took T.J. completely by surprise. She could tell by the expression on his face and the way he sat forward in his chair. He was going to say something, but she cut him off.

"When?" she asked calmly.

"We're not sure yet. We're hoping the information Tracy's provided will produce some leads. But if anything else happens or our leads run cold, we'll have to think along these lines. Are you open to the idea?"

"Yes, sir," Joanna answered.

"Good. I'll keep you posted. That's all."

Joanna and T.J. left the sergeant's office and went back to the War Room. All eyes were on them.

"You going in, Anderson?" Wagner asked.

"Possibly." Her answer was short.

"Mmm Mmm Mmm. I can't wait to see that," Flynn said. "Anderson all dolled up."

"Yeah, Anderson, do you really think you can pull off the part of a sex kitten?" Bristol sneered at her.

"I'm not worried about it," she said with a glance over her shoulder as she pulled a cup from the cooler dispenser.

T.J. wanted to jump in, wanted to slam his fist into Bristol's mouth, but he didn't. Joanna was proving to him she could hold her own with the banter. Besides, he enjoyed sitting back, watching her work the room. She was a lot smoother than he had given her credit for. Of course, there were other things about her as well that he was finding attractive. But he knew it would never work between the two of them. He had way too much garbage under his belt, and she was pretty committed to this Christianity thing of hers. That had been abundantly clear when she spoke earlier that day.

No. A partnership would have to do. He was fine with that, because he would still have the best looking partner in the precinct.

It wasn't until the end of the day that T.J. got Joanna to himself. He walked out to the parking lot with her at the end of their shift, so he could talk with her alone. He admired the great looking Mustang she was driving, looking it over as she got in. "This new?" he asked, pointing to the vintage car.

"No. I just don't drive it much."

"What a shame. So how do you feel about going undercover?" He tried to sound casual.

"I can handle it," she said through the rolled down window.

"You sure? You're not at a hundred percent physically, and I think the captain would want to know if you felt any apprehensions."

"But I don't. As long as I know I have back-up, I'll be fine." She glanced at her watch. "I've got to go, T.J."

"You have another date with Keith?"

"Actually, I cancelled last night."

"Oh." He stood with his hands in his pockets. "Then I guess I'll see you tomorrow."

Joanna almost felt guilty as she pulled away, leaving T.J. standing in the parking lot. As emotional as the day had been, it had been a privilege getting to know him better. Not the persona, but the man. The man with captivating blue eyes and mesmerizing smile. The man who looked great in jeans and a t-shirt, but even better with his shirt off.

Joanna caught herself thinking of T.J. as more than just a partner. Here she was, on her way home to meet Keith, and she was thinking about T.J. She knew nothing could happen between them. They were complete opposites when it came to their personal lives. He was everything she didn't want in a man.

And then there was Keith. She smiled at the concern he'd shown for her the day she came home from the hospital. He had looked so good in his blue jumper, but when he showed up at the hospital in jeans and a polo shirt—that fit tight across his chest and ignited his grey-blue eyes—well, he looked downright gorgeous.

By the time Joanna arrived home, she had butterflies in her stomach. She pulled her car into the garage and quickly headed for her room. She didn't have time to shower, but she hurried to change her clothes and run a brush through her hair.

She selected different shirts and slacks out of her closet, each time deciding against it and tossing them on the bed. Finally, she settled on a knit, tank-top style dress that hit right above her knees. It's light shade of blue accentuated what little tan she had. Since Keith was so tall, she decided to wear her favorite wedge sandals.

She looked at herself in the full-length mirror. She liked everything about her outfit, except the ragged gauze bandage that stuck out across the back of her shoulder. She grabbed her white button-up sweater, her little woven clutch, and headed downstairs.

She looked at the clock over the mantle, right as she heard a knock at the door. It was 8:45 p.m. Her insides were fluttering, and her palms felt a little clammy. It had been forever since her last date, which turned out to be a nightmare. She had to chuckle how that evening had ended, though. She was sure it would be one Frank wouldn't forget any time soon.

She opened the door and was greeted by a bouquet of yellow tulips and a very charming Keith. He looked amazing in khaki pants and a blue oxford shirt.

"Thank you, Keith, they're beautiful."

"I thought so, too. But next to you, they look rather

plain."

Joanna could feel herself blushing. "Come on in while I put them in water." Joanna walked to the kitchen; Keith closed the door and walked over to where Joanna was straining to reach a glass vase.

"Here, let me help you." He reached over her, brushing against her slightly, making her already heated skin tingle. He grabbed the square vase from on top of the refrigerator and set it on the counter.

"Thank you." She took the vase and put it under the tap.

"Your shoulder still stiff?"

"A little, but not too bad. Actually, the stitches are more irritating than anything. They keep poking me."

"Really? I could take a look at them. Maybe I could trim them a little."

"No, it's fine, really." She took the tulips and carefully arranged them in the vase; then carried them to her dining room table. "They really are beautiful. They're also my favorite flower."

"Really, then I guess that was luck on my part."

Joanna glanced at Keith and then looked away–afraid he was going to catch her staring.

"So, are you ready?" Keith asked.

"Sure." She picked up her purse, turned on the porch light, and closed the door behind them. She walked ahead of him on the narrow pathway, but he quickly stepped around her to open the car door.

"Thank you."

"My pleasure." He shut her door.

Joanna watched as Keith walked around the front of

the car.

When he got in the car he asked, "Did you have anything special in mind? For dessert that is?"

"No. Whatever you choose will be fine." Joanna never did get dinner, so she was starving. She would kill for a good burger, but she was the one who had suggested dessert so she didn't say anything.

"You know, Keith, I need to apologize for T.J.'s behavior the other night."

"That's not necessary, Joanna. I was glad to see he was so protective. I was a complete stranger after all."

"Yes, but at least you were polite. Thank you for helping me out. If you hadn't come along when you did, I'm sure I would've ended up spending the night in the hospital."

"You're welcome."

"I guess I was pretty out of it, wasn't I?"

"Yeah, but you sure looked cute."

Joanna was speechless, not knowing how to respond to a comment like that. *Don't just sit there, say something.* She cleared her throat, then asked the first thing that popped into her head. "How long have you been a paramedic?"

"Six years."

"Do you like it?"

"The pay isn't great, but it allows me to do what I want to do. It might change here soon, but for now, I'm good with it."

"So what is it that you like to do?" Joanna imagined him off on some wild adventure or exotic vacation. He just seemed like the athletic type, the type that would scale

Mount Everest or do the Ironman in Hawaii.

"Three times a year, I go on mission trips to offer medical aid in foreign countries."

"You mean you're part of the Life Flight Team?"

"Yeah. In fact, we have a trip coming up the end of July."

"I saw the flyer in the church bulletin. It's pretty incredible the things you are able to accomplish." Joanna looked at Keith with new admiration.

"I feel very fortunate to be a part of the team."

"So why is it that your job might change? Does it have to do with you going on these trips?"

"Yes and no. You see, I've done the paramedic thing because they valued me and let me have a flexible enough schedule to allow me to do these trips. Dr. Kline–he's the one who heads up the trips–has asked me to join his practice."

"He wants a paramedic to join his practice?" Joanna cringed. "I'm sorry. I didn't mean for that to sound so skeptical."

"It's all right. I'm actually an M.D. in family medicine," Keith clarified.

Joanna was shocked. "Then why are you working as a paramedic when you could be pulling in four times the salary in a practice somewhere?"

"It was never about the money. I always intended on going on the mission field as a doctor. I got my medical degree to help others, not to set myself up for life."

"That's admirable, but something must have deterred you?"

"My father died of a heart attack my last year of

residency. My mother was devastated. She had depended on my father for everything, and all of a sudden she was alone. When it came down to it, I just couldn't leave her."

"But I still don't understand why you didn't go into practice yourself or join up with another medical group?"

"I didn't feel it would be right to skip out on my patients or colleagues three times a year for two and three weeks at a time. It seemed irresponsible. Being a paramedic, I don't have regular patients depending on me, and the ambulance company I work for is thrilled to have me whenever I'm home."

"But now this doctor wants you to join his practice?"

"Yeah. His practice is made up of several people that take these trips with him, and alternate when they leave. If I agreed to cut out one trip a year, I could work into a rotating schedule with his existing staff."

"Sounds like a great opportunity," Joanna encouraged.

"It is, but I've gotten so attached to the people I work with in the villages we go to. I look forward to each trip with anticipation. How do I just cut out a trip and not go back?"

"I guess that would be hard."

Joanna was amazed by the depth of Keith's commitment. He was a great looking guy with a degree in medicine. He should be skating through life, but he was struggling with the idea of leaving a village of people that counted on him. He had sacrificed his dream out of concern for his mom, and now he was willing to ignore a chance at family practice so he could continue to serve others.

He really is Florence Nightingale.

Somehow, Joanna didn't feel worthy enough to be

seeing this guy. She had always felt good about her charitable contributions in the past, but all she'd given was money. Keith was giving himself.

"You're awfully quiet. Did I say something wrong?"

"No, not at all. I . . . I guess I'm just kind of in awe by what you do."

"Come on, Joanna, it's no different than what you do."

She had to laugh. She didn't feel like a humanitarian when she went to work. She felt more like a trash collector, trying to keep the streets clean so decent people could walk down them without being afraid.

Keith pulled up in front of a quaint little restaurant, advertising fondue. "I thought this would be fun since we're just having dessert."

Keith walked around, opened her door, and extended his hand. Joanna took it and allowed him to help her from the car. They walked into the darkened restaurant and approached the hostess.

"We have a reservation for nine o'clock. Michaels. We're a little late."

Joanna glanced at her watch, realizing it was already after nine. She'd been so enthralled by their conversation she hadn't noticed the passing time.

The hostess escorted them to a small booth at the back of the restaurant. The table was already set up with a little rack for the fondue pot in the middle. They scooted into opposite sides of the booth while the hostess waited for them to get settled.

"We're a little shorthanded so I'll be your waitress this evening. For dessert we have a choice of four chocolates: dark, milk, semi-sweet, or white chocolate. You can choose one or two, if you'd like."

Keith looked to Joanna. "It's your choice. I like them all."

"Are you sure? Why don't we each choose one?"

"Okay, I'll take the milk chocolate," Keith said, looking at the hostess who was smiling brightly at him.

"I'll have the white chocolate," Joanna said, noticing the hostess was still ogling Keith.

"And what would you like to drink?" the hostess asked Keith, not even acknowledging Joanna was there.

He ordered coffee and then began to fumble with his utensils. It was obvious he was uncomfortable with the woman's attention.

"I'll just have water," Joanna said quickly, as the woman walked away. She wanted to tease Keith about his admirer, but she could see he was embarrassed enough. Joanna immediately imagined how T.J. would've handled the situation. He would've totally played up to the waitress, turning on the charm.

Why am I doing this? Why am I comparing T.J. to Keith?

Keith leaned towards her to get her attention. "So why did you laugh when I compared your job to mine?"

"Because what I do has nothing to do with humanitarian reasons."

"Yes, it does. You're putting your life on the line every day for this city. It's not the best pay, and you hardly ever get a 'thank you'; but you know in your heart what you're doing is right. You're trying to make a difference, Joanna, same as me."

"That's nice of you to say, Keith, but at times I don't

feel that way."

"And at times I want to scream and holler and throw up my hands and give up. There's too much poverty and too much illness in some of these countries, Joanna. When we collapse our tents at the end of our term, there are still people waiting in line, begging for their child to be seen, or pleading with us to follow them back to their village because their people are too sick to travel.

"I feel utterly useless in times like that. We exhaust all the medication we bring and still have sick people. I want to throw in the towel. I don't want to have to witness what I can't help, but that's when I need to rely on the Lord to intervene. To heal those who He will, and to come alive in the hearts of the people that we leave behind. It's a very humbling thing to realize you can't save everyone. That's why I need to turn those people over to God."

The waitress brought their drinks, causing both Joanna and Keith to lean back in the booth. When she left, Keith reached for Joanna's hand. "Do you mind if I pray?"

"Not at all."

"Our Lord and God, thank you for allowing Joanna and I this evening where we can get to know each other better. Help us in our day-to-day jobs to remain strong and faithful. Bless this food to our bodies. Amen."

The rest of the evening was spent in never-ending conversation. Joanna hadn't been too far from the truth when she pictured Keith as the athletic type. He had in fact run a triathlon, and loved to go on long bike rides. Joanna shared her interest in biking, hiking, and her passion for kick-boxing, to which Keith assured her he had every intention of staying on her good side.

They were at the restaurant for almost two hours, enjoying their dessert and simple conversation. They had long since paid the bill and gotten the last refill on their drinks. When Joanna glanced at her watch for the third time, Keith spoke up.

"I guess it's getting late. We should probably get going."

When they turned to exit the booth, they were astonished to see the restaurant empty, chairs on top of tables, and a busboy vacuuming the far side of the restaurant. They had been so transfixed by their own conversation, they had been oblivious to what was happening around them.

They apologized profusely to the hostess as they left the restaurant. She no longer had a dreamy stare for Keith, just the tired look of someone at the end of a long shift.

Joanna felt Keith's hand rest on the small of her back as they walked towards the car. The warmth of his touch ignited a tingly sensation inside her. He held her door open and closed it once she was in. She nervously folded her hands in her lap, hoping the heat she felt in her cheeks would not show in the dim light of the car's interior.

Keith jumped on the freeway as they continued their easy conversation. He parked in her driveway and quickly walked around to Joanna's side of the car. Extending his hand to her, he helped her out of the car, and walked her to the door.

Joanna didn't want the night to end, but knew it needed to. It was closing in on midnight, and she had to work the next day.

When they got to the front door, Keith asked. "Did you

still want me to take a look at those stitches?"

She'd wanted to say yes, but she wasn't sure how far she wanted things to go this evening. And she was sure, if she invited him in, she'd have a hard time seeing him go.

"Actually, I didn't feel them at all tonight."

"Can I call you tomorrow?" he asked.

She was instantly disappointed that he didn't ask her for another date. "Sure."

"I'd love to see you tomorrow, but I already have plans."

"That's fine. I shouldn't string two late nights together anyway." She pulled her keys from her purse.

"I had a great time, Joanna." Keith stood close, his eyes trained on hers.

"Me too," she said in a whispered tone.

He took the keys from her hand and unlocked her door. Then, he stepped in closer and pressed a gentle kiss to her cheek. "Good night, Joanna."

"Good night, Keith."

She stepped inside her apartment, turned the deadbolt, and touched her cheek, feeling the warmth of Keith's kiss.

CHAPTER EIGHTEEN

After roll call, T.J., Joanna, and the other detectives gathered in the War Room. They had no new leads, but the women on the street were running scared. Those with pimps were taking their action inside. If tricks wanted a ride for the night, they'd have to go inside the bars and the clubs to find it. Martinez and Owens talked to a few independents who were still working outside. They gave the girls a warning, and by night's end, the streets were quiet.

T.J. hardly waited for Joanna to take a seat in the car before he started asking her about her date. "So, how'd it go with lover boy?" he asked.

"Stop calling him that. His name is Keith, and I had a great time."

"I guess so. You were out pretty late."

"So, you were all the hang-ups on my answering machine?" She laughed. "What, *the player* didn't have anything better to do with his time then to check up on me?

You must be slipping."

He thought about how his evening had ended the other night, or should he say never started with Carrie. Joanna was right. He was slipping, but he didn't need to be reminded of that fact.

"Hey, even a stud has to have a little time off. But don't worry about me. I've got my sights set on a young filly in my apartment building. It's only a matter of time before we–"

"Stop right there," Joanna said, with a raised hand. "You can keep your fantasies to yourself. I'm not interested in your exploits."

Joanna turned from T.J., a little disappointed. She didn't understand. He really was a nice guy. He could attract nice girls if he didn't have such a playboy attitude. If he could see women as friends and companions, instead of just playthings, he would realize there was more to life than sexual exploits or living up to the reputation he'd created. But as long as there were women out there, willing to throw themselves at men, he would never see the need to reach deeper or see past the physical.

"Come on," T.J. broke into her thought. "What did you do last night?"

"We went to a fondue restaurant and had dessert."

"And?" he pried.

"And we talked."

"Talked? That's all? You talked?"

"Believe it or not T.J., most first dates are spent talking and getting to know each other, not that you would understand that."

He rolled his eyes. "So, what did you talk about?"

"His work, my work."

They pulled up to the curb outside a laundromat. She checked the address as they got out, and climbed the stairs to the second floor apartments. T.J. knocked on the door with the number three dangling from it.

"Who is it?" A woman's voice answered, followed by a deep, moist cough.

"Police. We'd like to ask you a few questions."

Several locks turned and rattled before the door swung open. A skinny redhead with bright red lipstick and mascara-smeared eyes answered the door. She was wearing a sheer black nightie and not much else. She gave T.J. a once over with her eyes, smiled, and stepped away from the door so he and Joanna could come inside. She didn't even give Joanna a look.

"What can I do for you officer?" Again, all her attention was directed at T.J.

"Is your name Donna Delgado?"

"It's whatever you want it to be, Sweetie."

Joanna rolled her eyes, while T.J. didn't miss a beat.

"We hear you were friends with Crystal Meyers?"

Donna leaned over for a pack of cigarettes on the coffee table, giving both T.J. and Joanna an eyeful. She lit up, then took a seat on the couch. She crossed her legs as she puffed on her cigarette, her nightie riding high on her thigh. "So what. She's dead." Her tone was callous.

"Did you see anything the other night? See any of the guys she picked up?"

"No."

"You're sure?"

"Look, we weren't even working that night. This whole killing thing had us scared. We decided to lay low for a few days, except for regulars. Around eleven o'clock Crystal got the munchies and decided to grab something from the liquor store around the corner. She never came back."

"And that was the only time she left the apartment that night?"

"Yeah. We hung out here. Had a couple of friends over." She continued to puff on her cigarette, her fingers shaking slightly.

"What friends?" T.J. asked.

She flicked her ashes into an overflowing ashtray before taking another drag. "Friends. Like I said. Regulars." She stared at T.J. "Why? You interested?" She pursed her lips before wrapping them around her cigarette.

He ignored the comment.

"What time did they leave?" he asked.

"Around ten o'clock. Had to get home to the Mrs."

"What are their names?"

Donna laughed. "Like I'm going to tell you." She got up from where she was sitting and stood by the window, letting the light illuminate every line and curve of her body. It was obvious to Joanna the woman had implants. Her large breasts looked completely out of place atop her tiny waist and skinny legs.

"How do you know it wasn't one of them that killed Crystal?" T.J. continued with the questioning.

"Why would they? They have a good thing going here. Why would they mess that up?"

"So, how long have they been coming to you?"

"Since opening day."

"Opening day?" Joanna interrupted.

"Opening day. Baseball." Donna puffed on her cigarette and explained. "They tell people they're going to the ballgame. Then they come here, watch the game on T.V., have a little fun, and leave twenty minutes after the game finishes."

"Every week?" T.J. asked.

"Sometimes more."

"And it's always the two of them?" Joanna asked.

"No, sometimes Jim comes alone." Donna stiffened, as Joanna jotted his name down on her note pad. "So, his name's Jim. Go ahead and try to find him among the other millions of Jims in the city," she challenged.

"Look, sweetheart, we're only trying to help," T.J. said.

Joanna could hear the irritation in T.J.'s voice. She was surprised he wasn't acting like his charming self, especially since he had such a captive audience.

Donna smiled deeper, and gave T.J. a long seductive stare. "Maybe you should stay and protect me." She walked over to him, stopping dangerously close. "You wouldn't want to see something happen to me, would you?"

"Okay, then I guess we're done here." He stepped away from her and walked toward the door.

Joanna felt a smile crease her face. She never thought she'd see the day when T.J. Owens was embarrassed by a woman propositioning him.

"We'll be back if we have more questions," T.J. concluded.

"But what about my protection?" The woman looked at T.J. with a sultry pout.

"Keep your door shut and your legs closed. You'll be fine." He slammed the door and strode down the steps. Joanna contained her laughter but not her smile. She could almost feel the heat radiating from T.J. when they got in the car.

"She was getting to you, wasn't she?"

"Are you kidding me? She wasn't even my type." He put the car in gear and sped off.

"Busty and leggy isn't your type?" Joanna pressed the issue.

"Hookers aren't my type, thank you. Just because you think you're dating Prince Charming doesn't mean the rest of us losers are willing to settle for anyone who flashes their breast."

"Okay, whatever you say." She was sorry she'd pressed him.

Bristol and Barker met T.J. and Joanna at the coffee shop around the corner from Crystal and Donna's apartment. They kept an eye out for Donna's *regulars* hoping to pick up a lead.

"Anything yet?" Bristol asked as he swigged his coffee.

"No, but I'm not surprised," T.J. answered while chomping on a stale donut. "Donna could've warned them to stay away, or they could be afraid. I mean, after all, one of the girls they were doing is dead."

"Yeah, but that could be a turn-on for some guys,"

Barker added.

"What's wrong, Anderson, you're awfully quiet tonight? Or are you planning your line of attack for when you go undercover?" Bristol and Barker laughed. T.J. just shook his head.

"Give it a rest, Bristol," she said, acting bored by his comment.

"Oh come on, Anderson, is that the best you can do? You're going to have to sound a little more enticing than that if you're going to get johns to want to spend time with you."

"If and when I go in, let me worry about turning tricks, okay, Bristol? You just worry about grabbing the guy once we identify him."

"Oh, so superwoman's admitting she can't do it all by herself."

"Hey, I never said I could do it by myself," Joanna retorted.

"Well, you certainly didn't need Cummings. You couldn't get into his bed, so you decided to ruin his career."

Joanna jumped to her feet, knocking into the table and causing everyone's coffee to spill. "Is that what he told you? Is that what that piece of trash told you? For your information I had to shrug off his disgusting advances for months, and was willing to do it because I didn't want to cause waves.

"I stood by and watched as he bullied and coerced his way around town. But when he pushed that kid through the window, that was the last straw. I wasn't going to let him get away with it anymore. So you know what, Bristol, if you want to continue to side with Cummings after all the crap he's pulled, then I wouldn't want you as my back up. I'd rather take my chances with a killer."

Joanna stormed out with T.J. close on her tail. She got in the car and screamed under her breath. T.J. got in the driver's side and waited a moment before saying anything.

"You gonna be all right?"

"Yeah," she snapped.

"You sure?"

"I said I was fine." Her voice raised a decibel.

"Okay, okay."

T.J. started the engine and headed for the station. They'd gone about four blocks when he asked, "So, Cummings made advances at you?"

"T.J., I don't want to talk about it, all right? Just drop it."

They drove in silence until they reached the parking lot at the station. T.J. parallel parked alongside Joanna's car. When she reached for the handle of the door, he asked. "But all he did was make advances, right?"

She sighed. "I'm fine, T.J. I just wasn't going to sit there and listen to Bristol's crap. I don't care what Cummings told people, and I don't care what people think of me anymore. I'm a good cop, and until someone proves differently, I'm not going anywhere. I'll see you tomorrow, okay?"

"Sure Joanna, I'll see you tomorrow."

Joanna left the parking lot feeling beat-up and defeated. She was tired of the chauvinism and the sexism. Her energies should be spent on the cases they were working, not on watching her back from her own co-workers. She'd put on a strong front for T.J., but if things didn't improve soon, something would have to change. She wasn't going to spend the rest of her career proving her worth, while guarding her back.

T.J. was restless and didn't feel like going home. His mind wandered, wondering what kind of advances Joanna had to fight off from Cummings. If he in fact had made sexual advances, she could've easily brought a harassment case against him, but she didn't. She'd been willing to put up with his garbage, that is, until he started taking it out on others.

She had more grit than people were giving her credit for.

T.J. pulled into Scully's—the burger bar around the corner from the station—and had a great idea. He walked in, saying hi to all the regulars, then went to the counter. "Give me two combo meals with cheese, no onions, a Coors, and an ice tea to go."

T.J. went ahead and had a beer while he sat at the bar and waited. He shot the breeze with a few cops from the precinct and watched a game of pool heat up between two lieutenants.

When his order was up, he swigged the last of his beer, paid for everything, and grabbed the bags off the counter. He weaved through traffic, figuring he was only twenty minutes behind Joanna. When he got to her house, he knocked with his foot, because his hands were full. He waited a minute and then tried again. He was about to kick for a third time, when he heard a noise from inside, and saw motion through the peep hole.

"T.J. what are you doing here?" she spoke from behind the door.

He held up the bags. "I brought dinner. Scully's."

Joanna stood behind the door as she opened it. "But T.J.–"

T.J. didn't wait to be invited in, he just stepped through the doorway and walked over to the kitchen. When he turned around and saw Joanna standing with only a towel wrapped around her, it caught him completely off guard, and momentarily enjoyed the view.

She held the towel close to her chest as water dripped from her pinned up hair. "Let me go get some clothes on."

"Hey, don't change on my account," he said with a chuckle as he started unloading their food.

Joanna only got up the first few steps, when there was another knock at the door. She threw her head back and turned around. "What is this Grand Central Station?" She walked back to the door, looked through the peephole, and gasped. "Just a minute," she yelled through the door then rushed to the stairs as she spoke to T.J. "It's Keith. I need to get some clothes on," she whispered as she hurried up the steps.

T.J. waited until Joanna was upstairs, then hurried across the living room to answer the door. "Hey, Keith, come on in."

Keith looked at T.J., a little confused. "Hi. I told Joanna I would call, but I finished my other appointment and thought I'd swing by."

"That's fine. We were just going to have some dinner. Joanna's upstairs getting dressed." T.J. turned back to the kitchen, leaving Keith to digest what he'd just said.

"Look, I didn't know you two already had plans. I should probably leave." He turned back to the door, while T.J. held back a grin. Joanna came rushing down the steps, wearing shorts and a t-shirt.

"Keith!"

He glanced at Joanna. "I was just leaving." He walked out the door, leaving her befuddled.

"Keith!" She rushed after him. He was halfway down the walk before he stopped.

"Look, I should've called. I didn't mean to interrupt anything. I can see my way out." He turned to leave, but Joanna stopped him with a tug on his shirt sleeve.

"What's that supposed to mean?"

"Look, Joanna, if you two have a thing going on, I'm not gonna try and compete with that."

"A thing going on? T.J. and I don't have a thing going on."

Keith looked like he didn't believe her.

"Did T.J. say we have a thing going?"

"No, but it was obvious you were having dinner together and that you weren't . . . dressed for company."

Her eyes squinted and she clenched her jaw tight. "How do you know how I was dressed?"

"Look, it doesn't matter. I came uninvited and next time, I'll know to call." He walked away clearly upset.

Joanna stormed back into the house and slammed the door. "Okay, T.J., what did you tell him?"

T.J. started to say something, while Joanna fumed. "And don't even try to lie to me."

He just started laughing uncontrollably.

"You did say something, didn't you?"

It took him a minute to regain his composure. "Come on. It was a joke."

Joanna waited–her arms crossed against her chest– for him to explain.

"Okay, I told him you were upstairs getting dressed and we were just getting ready to have dinner." He bit into his burger but was unable to hide his smirk.

She marched over to her purse and picked up her cell phone.

"What are you doing?" he asked as she dialed frantically.

"You're going to explain to Keith your sick little joke, and then you're going to apologize."

"It was a joke. Come on, he should be able to take a joke."

"Hi, Keith." Joanna held her phone to her ear as she pierced T.J. with a death stare. "Look, T.J. has something he'd like to say to you." She quickly handed the phone to T.J., even though his mouth was full of burger.

"Hey, Keith." he said, before swallowing a mouthful. "Look, you might've gotten the wrong idea earlier. I brought dinner over to Joanna while she was in the shower. She wasn't expecting me anymore than she was expecting you. Come on, man, I was just yanking your chain."

T.J. and Keith exchanged a few more words before T.J. handed the phone back to Joanna. She and Keith had a muffled conversation before she hung up.

"Everything square?" T.J. asked, as he picked up his plate and beer and walked to the living room.

She grabbed the plate he fixed up for her, the watered down iced tea, and walked over to join him. "No thanks to you." She placed everything on the coffee table and sat down on the floor. She said a quick prayer over her cold food and began to eat.

"You know, I'm not the only one who owes you an apology." T.J. said between swallows. "I might've said what I did, but Keith believed it."

"For which he already apologized," Joanna said smugly.

T.J. grunted as he polished off his fries and crumpled up the wrapper.

After a few moments of silence, Joanna spoke. "Thanks for dinner."

"You're welcome."

They ate in companionable silence.

When T.J. was done, he leaned back against the couch and closed his eyes.

When Joanna was full, she nudge T.J.'s leg. "You want the rest of mine?" she asked, offering him half a burger and a few fries.

"Sure if you're not going to finish it."

Joanna slid her plate over in front of him. She finished the rest of her tea and began to clean up the extra wrappers. When she carried the trash to the kitchen, T.J. followed with the rest of his stuff, finishing off his beer.

"Did he ever hurt you?"

All joking was gone from T.J.'s tone.

Joanna realized T.J. was still hung-up on their earlier conversation regarding Cummings. "Come on, T.J. There's no reason to go over this." She wiped down the counter, averting her eyes.

He stopped her and with a finger to her chin tipped her face up to his. "Why didn't you ever press charges?"

"Cause I handled it," she said matter-of-factly. She tried to step around T.J., but he wouldn't let her. Her eyes were beginning to sting from bad memories. When it was obvious T.J. wasn't going to leave without some sort of explanation, she conceded.

"He got too friendly with his hands a few times. I told him I wasn't interested, and he said I was just playing hard to get."

"And?" T.J. persisted.

"We struggled one night. He–"

"You mean he assaulted you." T.J. cursed, his voice raised, not letting her finish.

"Yes, but other than getting pushed around a little, nothing happened, at least nothing sexual."

"What happened, Joanna? I want to know exactly what that lousy, no good, son-of–"

"T.J., stop!" she shouted. "I said nothing happened. I pulled my service weapon and told him I would shoot if he tried anything more. I reminded him I would have to file an accidental discharge report, explaining exactly why I had drawn my weapon. He said I was bluffing, but obviously wasn't too sure of himself. He left me alone from then on. I mean he was still lewd and made filthy comments, but he never touched me again."

"I'm sorry, Joanna," T.J. said, hanging his head.

"Hey, it's over. Cummings is out because of his own stupidity, and you have nothing to be sorry about."

"But I believed the guy. I sided with him. Everything

you said about him was true, but I was so busy nursing your rejection, I didn't see what a jerk he was."

"You were lied to." Joanna could tell that T.J. was beating up himself inside. He looked miserable about something she had already come to grips with.

"Enough with the blame okay? It's over. Let's move on." She smiled a reassuring smile and moved back to the couch. T.J. plopped down beside her.

"So, what do you do for fun?"

It was obvious T.J. was trying to change the subject, but his question came out of left field and confused Joanna. "What?"

"For fun? What do you do? I know what you *don't* do. You don't drink, you don't fool around, you don't watch cable, and the most seductive movie you have in your personal library is Pretty Woman. So, what do you do for fun?"

"Why must everything involve sex for you to consider it fun? I like biking, hiking, a good movie, a quiet dinner, a walk on the beach, those things are fun. Surely, there are things you consider entertainment that don't involve sex?"

"Surfing."

"See."

"Yeah, but even then, I can be coming in from a good wave, see some hottie in a string bikini on the beach, strike up a conversation with her, share a drink, and then bam, we're back at my apartment tearing up the sheets."

"So, everything to you is foreplay?"

"Not everything."

"You know what you need, Owens? You need to find a girl that would make you want to change your ways.

Someone that won't put up with your carousing. Someone special enough to make you see what a real relationship is all about."

"Well, I guess until she comes along, you're stuck with me just the way I am." He looked at his watch. She glanced at the clock. Eleven o'clock.

"Hey, I need to go." He abruptly headed to the door. "See you tomorrow, Anderson."

"Yeah. Thanks again for dinner."

"You buy next time."

"You got it."

He closed the door behind him and even though it locked automatically, Joanna crossed the living room to turn the deadbolt.

She went around turning off extra lights and checking the other doors and windows.

T.J. pulled out from the driveway and glanced up at Joanna's bedroom window. "If anyone could make me want to change, Joanna, it's you."

CHAPTER NINETEEN

Joanna looked at the clock on her bedside table and debated whether it was too late to call Kathy. Mike would be at work, so if the boys were down, she might actually be able to talk. But it was late and Joanna didn't want to bother Kathy if she was already in bed. She glanced at the clock one more time, then picked up the phone.

"Hi, Kathy, is it too late to be calling?"

"Not at all. In fact the boys just went down, and I was getting ready to curl up with a book and a bowl of ice cream. So, how are things?"

"Pretty good." Joanna yawned.

"You sound tired. Have you been putting in a lot of hours?"

"No more than usual."

"What have you been doing? They haven't stuck you in a file room somewhere or tried to bury you with paperwork, have they?"

"Hardly. Though if they thought they could've gotten away with it they probably would have." Joanna sighed.

"What is it, Jo, something bothering you?"

Joanna hesitated.

"Come on, Jo, spill it, or you'll have me on your doorstep by morning."

Joanna smiled, not doubting Kathy for a second. "It isn't any one thing. I've just been dealing with a lot of different issues lately."

"Personal?"

"Yes and no."

"Enough with the cryptic conversation, Jo. What's going on?"

Joanna began to explain some of the situations she was having a hard time handling. She told Kathy how hard it had been to inform Samantha's parents their daughter had been killed. Joanna explained the circumstances of the crime, and the reason Samantha was on the streets in the first place. She talked about Michelle—the pregnant girl she had stopped for questioning—and how her situation had tugged at Joanna, making her feel helpless.

Joanna went on to tell Kathy about the threats, taunts, and rumors Rogers had been spreading about her, and the fact that she was known at the station as the "Iron Maiden."

"Don't put up with it Jo, not again. You know you should've filed against Cummings, and you didn't. Don't let those chauvinist jerks get away with crap. Does anyone else know about these threats?"

"T.J. doesn't know the extent of them, but he's gotten tired of Rogers' mouth. He fired off on him the other day and let him know he would personally file discrimination charges against him if he didn't quit harassing me."

"Well, good for him. Maybe he does have some redeeming qualities after all"

"He really does, Kathy. We've had a couple of really good conversations, and I think we've got a better understanding of each other now."

"Hmm, sounds like you've had a change of heart towards him."

Joanna could hear the tease in Kathy's tone. "It's not like that, Kathy."

"So, you're not attracted to him?" she asked point blank.

"We're partners, Kathy. That would never work."

"You didn't answer the question."

"We're complete opposites."

"Yeah, well, sometimes those differences don't seem so big when you're attracted to someone. The psyche has a way of blurring the lines when we want it to, especially when you're lonely."

"Mmm . . . I'm not lonely. Not exactly," Joanna said with the slightest lilt in her voice.

Kathy gasped. "Joanna! I can't believe you've been holding out on me. You're seeing someone, aren't you?"

"I've seen him once," Joanna admitted. Before she could say anything more, Kathy assaulted her with questions. Joanna laughed because she wasn't getting a word in edgewise.

"Did you want me to answer any of those questions, or were you just going to keep rattling off more?"

"Yes. All of them," Kathy demanded with excitement.

"Okay, let's see if I remember them all in order. "Keith

. . . on the job . . . paramedic . . . Yes, he's a Christian . . . gorgeous . . . and yes, we'll being see each other again."

Kathy laughed as Joanna listed off her answers. Of course, Kathy would never be satisfied with the Reader's Digest version, so they were on the phone for another hour discussing the fine line details about how she met Keith.

"I can't believe you got hurt and didn't tell me. You're sure you're okay?"

"Yes. I'm doing fine," Joanna assured her.

"So, I guess things haven't been all heartache and sorrow?" Kathy teased.

"No. I guess there have been a few silver linings. I even had the sergeant compliment me on a report I turned in. It had to be done perfectly since the D.A. is going to push for adult charges against a juvenile. Oh, and Rogers is out on medical so I won't have him breathing down my neck for a few weeks."

As they continued their conversation, Joanna debated if she should tell Kathy about the possibility of her going undercover. It would be senseless to worry her needlessly; since it wasn't a for sure thing. Joanna decided to wait. She'd tell Kathy only if it was necessary.

When Joanna finished talking with Kathy, she felt better. She realized that with all the lows, there had been a few highs.

The only question Kathy had raised that Joanna still wasn't sure about was her growing attraction for T.J. As much as she wanted to deny it—for all the reasons she had given Kathy—there was still a part of her that felt drawn to him.

But then Joanna thought about Keith. She would be

crazy to jeopardize the budding relationship she had with him, simply because of the attraction she felt for T.J.

An attraction that could only prove dangerous.

CHAPTER TWENTY

Over the next few weeks, Joanna barely saw anything other than the precinct, the streets linked to the murders, and her unmade bed. She would collapse into it each night, then turn around and start all over again the next day.

Overtime had become mandatory as she and T.J. worked every lead that pertained to the killings. They listened to the talk on the streets, questioned registered sex offenders in the area, and ran surveillance on a few of the ones that didn't have solid alibis. They did everything short of putting the neighborhood on lockdown.

Joanna hadn't seen Keith but once or twice for lunch. And that was while they were both on duty. Since Rob—Keith's partner—and T.J. were there, they were forced to talk about superficial things before heading their different ways. To Joanna, it was nothing short of torture. To be that close to Keith, yet not able to be *near* him was harder than not seeing him at all.

Joanna would call Keith when she had a few moments to herself, but their conversations were always interrupted by one thing or another. He shared her frustration about getting some time—just the two of them—but he was always encouraging. Sooner or later, they'd get some quality time together. He promised.

No new attacks had happened since the case had become priority one status, leading them to believe their murderer might have moved on, given up, or was lying low because of all the extra eyes on the streets.

Dr. Barnes—the profiler—was sure the suspect would not completely give up. He had gotten away with four murders. He was angry and would eventually kill again. She was sure of it.

Joanna and T.J. reviewed—for the second time—file after file of registered sex offenders. They eliminated females, child predators, those serving time, those being watched by monitoring systems, and those not meeting the specifics of the profile. But there were no new leads.

Even with Dr. Barnes' appraisal of the situation, the department was having a hard time justifying all the man hours. None of the overtime at this point had produced a solid lead. It was as if their murderer had disappeared.

Joanna was sure she'd be going undercover. They had to do something to force this guy's hand. But instead, overtime was called off and everyone was to go back to their normal schedules until further notice.

Joanna was glad the O.T. was over, but hated the fact that the killer was still out there, possibly sizing up his next victim.

"What's wrong?" T.J. asked.

"Why do you think something's wrong?" she snapped as she angrily tossed one file on top of another.

"Oh, I don't know, maybe it has something to do with the way you're throwing those folders around. Or the fact that you just bit my head off for asking."

"Doesn't this frustrate you?" she asked, pointing to the folders on the table. "We separated these files into categories. Child molesters, sodomizers, rapists, and men that get off on torturing women. These men are walking the streets. They are free to commit these crimes again. Statistics show nine times out of ten, they will. But do we keep them behind bars? No! Why? Because we as a society have deemed over-crowded jails inhumane.

"Does anyone else see the irony in that?

"These men commit the most inhumane acts on innocent women, but we're worried about their comfort. I just don't get it."

"It's frustrating, I know. But it doesn't do you any good to get all worked up. We can only do what we can do." T.J. got up from the table. "Come on, let's go."

"So, do you have plans tonight?" T.J. asked with a sly grin on his face.

Joanna shrugged her shoulders.

"Don't act all innocent. I saw you texting as soon as the announcement was made."

"Yeah." she said with a smile. "Keith is coming over."

T.J. nodded. "Okay, but remember our bet. We said the first weekend after O.T. was cancelled we would settle our wager. So don't be making any plans for the weekend. Tomorrow you're mine."

"For how long?" Joanna questioned nervously.

"For as long as it takes," T.J. grinned.

"What time should I be ready?" she asked as she unlocked the car door and climbed in.

"Six o'clock."

"In the morning? Are you kidding me? On our first day off in weeks?"

"Hey, I've got to make sure you're perfectly trained before I turn you loose on those waves."

"Turn me loose?" she panicked. "I'm not going out there by myself. You said you'd teach me. You never said anything about doing it by myself." She started rambling. T.J. bent down, and with a smile he gently placed a finger to her stammering lips. She immediately stopped muttering.

"I will be with you every step of the way. I don't want you to be worried or afraid. I want you to love it as much as I do. I promise I won't let you get hurt." He allowed his finger to rest on her lips longer than necessary. "Do you trust me?" he asked in a hushed, intimate tone.

Joanna looked at him, and felt as if he was asking something more. And, there was a side of her that wanted to give him more. She caught herself and quickly broke his gaze. She started her car, while he stepped away slowly. "I'll see you at six o'clock," she assured him.

"I'm looking forward to it." he answered before she drove away.

T.J. headed for the store. He had big plans for tomorrow. He was bent on showing Joanna a different side of him.

A side that knew fun.

Fun that hinged on romance . . . not sex.

Joanna drove home, the whole time her heart racing as fast as the car engine. The attraction she felt for T.J. was hard to ignore; even though they had nothing in common. His favorite pastimes were drinking, carousing, and surfing.

How is it I have any feelings for him considering his reputation?

He thinks of sex as a recreational sport.

And the way he deals with problems is to get plastered with his buddies.

That's not going to change.

She lectured herself all the way home and finally came to a resolution. She would be T.J.'s partner and friend and do what Matthew had told her to do.

"Live so others will see a difference in you, and then when asked, let them know what that difference is."

That is what she had to do. She couldn't allow herself to be confused by her attraction for T.J.

She was so deep in her personal debate, she jumped when her phone vibrated across the dash. She looked at the display and smiled.

"Hi, Keith."

"Hi. I was just calling to see if we were still on for tonight."

"I hope so," she blurted out, then inwardly cringed. *Good move, dummy; now you sound desperate.*

"Okay, I was just making sure," Keith said. "Where are you now?"

"I'm just turning down my street. I'll be home in two

minutes."

As soon as she made her turn, she spotted Keith's Camaro. Joanna pulled into her driveway as he got out of his car and crossed the street. She watched him in her rearview mirror. He was carrying a bag of groceries as he approached her side of the car. Joanna stepped out confused.

"I don't get it? Why'd you call if you were sitting outside? Why didn't you just go up and knock on the door?"

"I thought I'd make sure we still had plans. I didn't want any surprises or awkward situations."

She blushed, remembering how awkward it had been when Keith had come over the same night T.J. brought dinner. "I'm sorry about that. T.J. really didn't mean anything by it. That's just his kind of humor."

Joanna fiddled with the lock before pushing the door open for Keith. He followed her all the way to the kitchen, then set his bags on the counter. "I think he has a thing for you. I see the way he stares at you when you're not looking."

Joanna swung around. "T.J.? No way. I'm definitely not his type."

"Why do you say that?" Keith questioned. "You're smart, beautiful, and in the same profession he is. Why wouldn't he be interested in you?"

Keith and Joanna stood in the kitchen while she tried to explain. "Because I'm not dating material."

"I wouldn't say that. I thought we had a good time when we went out."

"I had a great time with you, Keith," she stammered,

not sure how much she should say. She didn't want to give Keith a low opinion of T.J. "Let's just say fondue isn't the type of dessert T.J. is interested in."

"So what you're saying is he expects more from a dinner date than just dinner?"

"He's not as bad as that makes him sound, but yes, his expectations are different than mine."

"That's an awfully nice way of saying he's a player. Maybe I should be worried."

"Stop that." Joanna gave him a playful nudge. "So, what's in the bag?" she asked, trying to change the subject.

Keith smiled, though it was clear he knew she was ignoring his comment.

"I brought everything to make s'mores. I saw you had a fire pit on your deck and thought it would be fun."

"Sounds like a great idea."

Joanna and Keith ate s'mores until she felt sick. When he started to skewer another marshmallow, and waved it at her, she put up her hands in refusal. "No more for me. I've had way too much. And I'm not even a s'more kind of person."

"Really? I couldn't tell," he teased, putting down the skewer. He casually walked over to sit next to Joanna on the swing.

"Well, I've never had them with white chocolate before. That was a great idea."

"I thought you'd like it." He casually draped his arm on the back of the swing.

She felt his hand on her shoulder and allowed herself to lean in closer to his side. They rocked in silence, staring at the embers of the fire, watching as the light from the street lamps danced off the water in the canal.

"This was fun, Keith." Joanna's mind instantly spun back to her conversation with T.J. regarding 'fun.'

T.J. would never think marshmallows and chocolates could constitute fun.

At least not the way she and Keith had enjoyed them.

"You know," Keith said, getting her attention. "You've never shared much regarding your background. You know all about me, but I feel like I don't know much about you."

Joanna shrugged. "I've been a cop for eight years. I was promoted to detective about two months ago, much to the dismay of the other detectives. I'm still learning the ropes."

"That collar you made last month was pretty impressive for someone just learning the ropes. That had to have made some of them sit up and take notice."

"I think I'm beginning to make some headway. There will always be guys that don't think I belong, and will use every chance they get to remind me of that fact but I think I've proven myself to a few people."

"Like T.J.?"

She thought about T.J.'s reaction in the captain's office when she was first promoted, and it made her chuckle. "He was so mad when he found out I was going to be his partner. He wanted nothing more than to watch me fall flat on my face. And now he's taken some flak for backing me up." She turned to look at Keith. "He really is an okay guy. He just has to get his values in order."

"What about your parents? They must be pretty proud of you."

"My parents died when I was nine. I lived in a

children's home until I graduated. I had a very close friend who was a cop, that's why I decided to join the force."

"*Was* a cop?" Keith asked intuitively.

"He was killed in the line of duty when I was a rookie."

"Wow. Those are pretty big hurdles to have to deal with at such a young age. It's amazing you turned out as focused as you did."

"Matthew–he was my friend–had a big influence on me. He's the one who led me to the Lord."

Matthew was more than a friend, but Joanna didn't want to go into it. It would only make her sad, and she didn't want to end the evening in a sad mood.

"No other family?" Keith asked with sensitivity in his tone.

"No. My dad's parents had already passed away when the accident happened, and my mom's parents were much older and not in good health. I remember them visiting me a few times, but they were always so sad. They stopped coming after the first year. Matthew took me to their funerals when they died, and I found out they left me some money in a trust, but that is about it for my family."

"You're amazing, Joanna. You know that?" Keith looked at her with eyes of compassion and strength.

"Or stubborn," Joanna teased not wanting the heavy mood to continue.

The fire was beginning to fade. Joanna ran her hand over her arm, warding off the chill. Keith allowed his arm to enfold Joanna drawing her close. "You cold?"

She looked up at him, not wanting to move. "Not too bad." She swallowed back the butterflies that were trying to escape.

"We could go inside?" he suggested.

"No, I'm fine." She enjoyed the feel of his arms around her and didn't want to do anything to sever that contact. She looked up at him and time seemed to stand still. She couldn't break the hold he had on her, she felt captivated in his eyes.

Then, slowly, Keith bent his head down to meet hers. He brushed his lips against hers, then pulled back slightly, as if asking permission to continue.

Joanna had no intentions of stopping him.

Keith smiled, then found hers lips again, but this time it was not a glancing brush. He pressed his lips to hers and Joanna returned his affection. He held her tighter. She pressed her hand to his chest and leaned into his embrace.

Joanna could feel heat encompassing them. She knew it wasn't the fire because it was reduced to mere flickers and ash. No, they were creating their own heat. Heat she had never felt before

Keith slowly pulled away, breaking the spell of the moment. Joanna gently pushed herself away from his chest and looked into his eyes.

"I think I'd better stop right now and say good night." Keith said with a sigh.

"Me too," Joanna conceded, leaning back on her side of the swing as Keith stood.

"Here, let me walk you to the door."

Keith held out his hand to hers, she took it with a smile and walked with him through the living room to the front door. "Would it be overstating the obvious to say what a great time I had tonight?" His tone was mischievous.

"I think I got that message," she said slyly.

"Can I see you tomorrow?" Anticipation was in his eyes.

Joanna's eyes lit up momentarily, but then she remembered her surfing lesson with T.J. "I'm sorry; Keith, but I already have plans."

There was no hiding his disappointment. "What about Sunday?"

"The plans are sort of for the weekend," she answered sheepishly, knowing she should just tell him about her deal with T.J. Joanna was sure she could explain, but Keith already had a sense that she and T.J. were more than just partners. Joanna didn't want to add any more confusion to the situation.

"Will I see you in church?" she added, trying to end on a positive note.

"I'm on call until one o'clock on Sunday," he said with a slightly frustrated tone.

"You could call me on Monday?"

"Sounds good." He smiled, despite his obvious disappointment.

"Okay. Then I'll talk to you on Monday."

He leaned over and gave her an indulging kiss. The heat inside her roared back to life. When he pulled away he grinned. "That has to hold me until Monday. I hope you don't mind."

"Only that we have to wait until Monday." Her voice was sultry, surprising even herself. Keith's look was one of anticipation. He shut the door and left, but that did nothing to calm Joanna's mind.

She walked to the deck and turned on the hose. She

almost felt like using it on herself, but instead, used it on the last of the red hot embers, smoldering in the fire pit.

She felt numb by their encounter. It wasn't like she'd never kissed a guy before. Although her dates in high school were few because of Matthew's over-protectiveness; she still dated. She did her fair share of making out, but never let the physical get out of hand.

As an adult, she'd dated selectively, but seldom found herself enjoying her dates as much as they enjoyed themselves. Somehow, she always attracted the macho, lots of biceps, not a lot of brains type. Of course, since she spent her time in precincts, sub-stations, the occasional bar, and gyms, she wasn't exactly surrounding herself with single men of quality. She hadn't been able to go to church with any kind of consistency for years because of her schedule, so she'd never really been able to attract anyone there. But now, things were different. Extremely different. Keith was the complete package. He was great looking, intelligent, and had a relationship with the Lord.

And was an incredible kisser.

She laughed at herself. *An incredible kisser. I sound like I'm in junior high.*

She reprimanded herself for being so effected by Keith physically, but knew it was no use. She couldn't pretend not to feel what she was feeling. It was desire. A deep-seeded desire to see him again.

She knew her and Keith's actions were a bit accelerated because of the lapsed time since they'd last been alone together. Having to wait until Monday wasn't going to be any easier.

She locked up the house and turned off the lights. She

walked in a daze to her room and sank into the comfort of a hot bath. When she got out of the tub, her eye caught the scar on her shoulder from the stitches.

It had been a month since she'd met Keith on the bumper of his ambulance. Though they'd had so little time to see each other, she could feel her heart begin to tug in directions she'd never imagined. He was so . . . perfect. The way he carried himself, his desire to serve others, the faith they shared.

He was almost too perfect.

Joanna slipped into an oversized t-shirt and crawled between the sheets of her bed. She closed her eyes, thinking about Keith, but somehow, sometime during the night, her thoughts turned to T.J.

CHAPTER TWENTY-ONE

Joanna was up by five forty-five.

After dragging herself from bed, splashing her face with water, and brushing her teeth, she looked into the mirror and moaned.

"Why on earth did I agree to this?"

She pulled her hair back in a ponytail–taking years off her appearance–then shimmied into her modest red tankini. Her body quaked just thinking about the cold water, so she immediately pulled on a pair of sweatpants and a sweatshirt to ward off the chill. With her beach bag already packed with the essentials: lotions, beach towel, flip-flops, and sunglasses, she threw in a pair of shorts and a t-shirt, knowing the day would eventually warm up.

After making the bed, Joanna headed downstairs. She hadn't even made it to the bottom step before the doorbell chimed.

Has that always been so loud? she wondered as she

dragged herself to the door.

When she swung the door wide, there stood T.J.; bright-eyed and bushy-tailed, his expression rivalling that of a child on his way to a street carnival or the circus. "Good morning!" he said with a bit too much enthusiasm.

"Are you always this chipper at six o'clock in the morning on your day off?" she questioned, with a hint of belligerence.

"Only when I know I'll be spending the entire day surfing." He looked at her and laughed. "What are you wearing?"

Joanna glanced down at her oversized sweatpants and bulky sweatshirt; then looked at his board shorts and t-shirt. "I'm freezing. I needed to warm up."

"You look like you're dressed for the snow. Tell me you're bringing a change of clothes? It will be eighty degrees by noon."

"Yes, I brought some shorts," she said in an antagonistic tone, hoping it hid her apprehension.

"Hey, you'd better get in a better mood or I'll dump you in the middle of the ocean and let you fend for yourself."

"That's it!" She turned around abruptly and tried to storm away.

Laughing, T.J. grabbed her arm and turned her back around. "I was only kidding. Geez, lighten up."

She shuddered.

"Hey, you're really afraid, aren't you?" His tone no longer held the tease of just seconds ago. "Look at me, Joanna," he said as he stroked her arms.

She decided not to lie. She wanted him to know how

nervous she was. Joanna looked up into his eyes. "Yes, I am, and if you dare take me out in the ocean and *'dump'* me, so help me you'll be sorry."

T.J. pulled her to his side, walking her out the door. "I promise I will not do anything that you're not comfortable with. This is supposed to be fun, Joanna, not torture. Now come on, you need to lighten up. I know if you give it a try, you'll see what I'm talking about."

Joanna gathered her composure as they walked to his truck. It was loaded down with the three boards she'd seen in his apartment. She tried to calm herself so she wouldn't look like such a coward

How is it I can apprehend a criminal—with a weapon—without even thinking, but I'm afraid to go ride a wave like thousands of teenagers do every day?

Joanna continued to work on her mental state as T.J. drove to the same beach they'd been to before.

Everything looked so tranquil as she got out of the truck. She heard the waves crashing and could see there were already surfers out in the water. All of a sudden she realized if she humiliated herself, it wouldn't be a private display. Others would see her.

Her stomach rolled at the thought.

"Come here," T.J. said.

Joanna walked around to his side of the truck.

"Give me your weapon."

"She discreetly pulled her gun from her sweatshirt pocket and handed it to T.J. He flipped the backseat forward and quickly locked both of their weapons to a U-ring behind the seat.

"That's clever. Did you install that yourself?"

"No. It's the ring the seat latches on to. But it makes for a great place to stow my weapon when I'm in the water."

He handed her one of the wet suits laying on the backseat. "Here, put this on." T.J. pulled off his t-shirt. Then, without any warning, he pulled off his board shorts, revealing tight fitting, thigh hugging briefs.

Joanna didn't mean to stare. But it took her a moment before she looked away.

T.J. threw his shorts into the back of the cab and inched the wetsuit up to his hips. Then he turned to her, clearly oblivious to the awkwardness she felt.

"Come on. Put that on."

She held it up at arm's length. "It looks awfully small. I don't think it's going to fit."

"Sure it will. It was my sister's. You're about her size. You're maybe an inch taller and a little shapelier," he said with a grin, "but it will fit. Just inch it on a little at a time, like I did."

Joanna ignored T.J.'s comment and continued to scrutinize the wetsuit. With a conciliatory sigh, she laid it over the edge of the truck bed. "Okay. Here goes nothing."

T.J. watched as Joanna pulled off her sweatpants and sweatshirt. Her swimsuit was modest, as he had expected, but it still showed off every curve and asset Joanna had. Her arms and legs were toned and contoured in all the right places—obviously from her time spent in the gym. And he never would've imagined her legs could look so long. She was athletic, alluring, and had no idea how hot she looked.

A lethal combination.

T.J. watch as Joanna pulled and wiggled—inch by inch—to get the suit over her hips. Her back was to him, so she didn't realize the entertainment she was providing.

T.J. felt his endorphins raging, and had to look away. Taking a deep breath, he chastised himself. *Pull yourself together, man, before you screw something up.*

"I can't even move in this thing," Joanna said.

T.J. turned back around. "Yes you can. You just have to get used to it. Go on, finish putting it on. I'll help you with the shoulders and zipper."

Joanna shimmied further, pushing her arms into the sleeves, but before she pulled the suit over her shoulders, T.J. saw the scar from her stitches. Instinctively, he brushed his fingers across it. "It healed pretty nice."

Joanna looked at him over the top of her shoulder. "Yeah . . . not bad."

Their eyes held for a moment. T.J. felt something intense pass between them, and knew Joanna felt it as well. Without another word, T.J. helped her get the suit over her shoulders; he then reached for the long leash on the zipper and pulled.

"I feel like I am being vacuum sealed in."

"Good. That's the way it should feel. You don't want any gaps between your skin and the suit."

He stood with his hands on his waist, his heart beating in double-time. "Okay, now stretch and bend. Pull your knees up to your chest and circle your arms."

She did the calisthenics he suggested while he pulled his suit up over his shoulders and yanked on the leash. He grabbed the boards from the back of the truck and leaned them against the tailgate.

"Why three?" she asked.

"One is so we can ride tandem, until you get the feel of it. Then if you want, you can go solo." He pointed to a smaller board. "The third board's mine. Think you can carry this one?" He pointed to his board.

"Sure."

He carried it to the edge of the sand. If she buckled under the weight, he'd rather his board hit sand than asphalt. She flipped it up onto her head and steadied herself.

"Where to?" she asked bearing the weight of the board.

"Over there, between the two towers." He pointed to their left.

Slowly she headed in that direction. T.J. watched her walk away in the skintight wetsuit. His intentions for the day had been nothing but admirable. He forgot to factor in the small detail that she'd be wearing next to nothing.

He steadied the other boards under each arm and followed her to a location not too far down the beach. She carefully lowered his board onto the sand, but didn't lay it down.

"You can go ahead and lay it down, fin up," he said as he approached.

Joanna felt a cool breeze drift up from the water and wondered how cold it was. She hoped the wetsuit did its job.

"Okay. You ready?" T.J. asked, as he slapped his hands together.

"As I'll ever be." She smiled cautiously. She really wanted to try. She didn't want to disappoint T.J. by being a putts.

She followed T.J. to the wetter sand. He laid the long board down and began to explain.

"Okay. The key to surfing is where you place your feet." He stood on the board and showed her what he meant. His feet were slightly apart, actually facing sideways, knees bent, his arms out to the side. "That is really all there is to it." He stepped off the board. "Now, you try."

She felt foolish posing on the board so she stepped off quickly. "Got it."

"Okay, now this is how you're going to get up." T.J. laid down on the board. "You're going to paddle, paddle, paddle, and when the time is right, you're going to grab the rail." He showed her by placing his hands on the edge of the board. "And you're going to pop up." He did it so quickly Joanna hadn't seen what he did.

"Wait a minute. Do that again."

"Look, you can do it one of two ways. You can either get to your knee first, and then to your feet, or you can go straight to your feet in one easy motion." He demonstrated both for her, fast and then slower, until she understood what he was talking about.

"Okay, now you." He got off the board and waited for her to lie down on top of it. "Okay, I'll be saying paddle, paddle, paddle, paddle, and then when I say 'up', you pop up on your feet, making sure they're straddled slightly on the board. Okay? Let's try."

Joanna listened as T.J. gave the commands. When he

said 'up', her first instinct was to go directly to her feet. She planted herself on the board, feet apart, knees bent.

"Perfect!" T.J. yelled. "That was perfect, Joanna. Right on the money."

She felt a twinge of pride because she'd done it right, and relief she didn't look too uncoordinated or awkward.

They practiced a few more times, each time, T.J. showing more and more excitement that she was catching on so quickly. "You're a natural, Joanna."

Joanna couldn't help but smile.

"Okay, now let's try some shallow water and see how good your balance is."

T.J. walked the board out to where the water came up to Joanna's thighs. Joanna was glad for the wetsuit when she felt the cold water splash her face.

"Okay, now lay on the board," T.J. instructed, as he stood in front of her and held the long board in place.

Joanna stretched across the board, feeling unsure all over again. Even in the shallow water, she could feel how easily the board rocked against the rippling water.

"Come towards me, so that your feet aren't hanging off the end of the board. You can spread your legs apart a little bit to give yourself more balance."

Joanna carefully scooted forward, holding onto the rail, positioning her feet slightly apart. She looked at T.J. and saw the smirk on his face.

"What?" she snapped.

"Relax, Joanna, this is supposed to be fun, remember?"

His smile was contagious, but when she tried to return it, the board tipped slightly, causing her to let out a quick gasp.

T.J. just chuckled.

"Now, I'll hold the board in place, when I say 'up', go ahead and pop up. Remember how to place your feet."

Joanna nodded in agreement.

"Okay, you're paddling. Paddle, paddle, paddle, and up!"

Joanna grabbed the rail of the board, pushed herself up, got her feet under her, and froze. She couldn't bring herself to let go of the board. She held onto the sides in a squatting position and felt the board teeter from side to side.

"Stand up, Joanna," T.J. encouraged.

She sat perched on her toes, not letting go. The board was teetering harder and finally, T.J. let go of it. The long board pitched to one side, sending Joanna splashing into the water.

She came up gasping, her mouth open, and her eyes blinking. When she got her feet under her, she glared at T.J. "You did that on purpose."

"That's what's going to happen if you don't stand up."

"I wasn't ready," she argued.

"But you have to be, Joanna. You can't control the board from that position. You've got to get your feet under you and your arms out, or you'll crash every time. Once you commit, you have to commit one hundred percent."

"I can't do this." She tried wading through the water back to the beach, but T.J. quickly caught up with her.

"Hold on, hold on." He grabbed a hold of her arm and turned her around. "You really didn't think you'd be able to do everything perfectly your first time, did you?" He was being sincere.

She watched the water recede around her knees. "No,

but I didn't think I'd freeze up either." She felt like an idiot. Her perfectionistic personality taunted her.

"Come on, Joanna, let's try again." T.J. was nothing but encouraging. "And if you fall in, you fall in. It's only water."

It took her a moment to concede. She looked at the water and then to T.J. Finally, she turned around and walked out to deeper water.

CHAPTER TWENTY-TWO

"Perfect, Joanna. That was textbook."

She had the hang of it now. Joanna had gotten up on consecutive attempts and even held her balance as T.J. rocked the board.

She lowered herself back down to the board, straddling it like a pro.

"You ready to go for it?" he asked with anticipation.

Looking over his shoulder, she saw the waves breaking beyond the shore.

"Do you think I'm ready?" she asked him, completely unsure.

"You bet. There's just one more thing I need to teach you."

"What's that?"

"It's called a duck dive. Since we'll be paddling against the current, we need to get past the breaking waves. To do that we need to *duck* through them."

"How do I do that?"

"When you get to a wave, you need to press the nose of the board down causing it to cut through the wave. The more board under the water at that point the better. Lean down against the board allowing your body to cut through the wave as well. When you're through to the other side, take the pressure off the nose of the board and allow it to resurface. That's all there is to it."

She laughed. "Yeah. Rule number ninety-eight."

T.J. chuckled. "Look, we'll go out tandem. I'll be right there the whole time."

"Do we have to go way out there?" Joanna knew she sounded like a child, but she didn't care. Looking at those crashing waves made her doubt her inept abilities.

"No," T.J. assured. "We'll only go out a little way. Now scoot up so we can do this thing."

Joanna lay down and scooted towards the nose of the board, while T.J. climbed on back. She felt his chest press against the back of her legs as T.J. lay down and began paddling with her. She could only imagine the view he was getting, and was thankful to be wearing the wetsuit.

They were approaching their first wave when T.J. yelled "Duck!" She did exactly what he told her. She tipped the nose down, put her head down, and felt her body cut through the wave. When she allowed the nose to pop back up and they broke through the water, it was exhilarating!

"That was perfect, Joanna. Do it just like that again," T.J. yelled from behind her.

They continued to paddle and duck under three more waves before T.J. told her to stop paddling. He guided the board around so that they were now facing the shore. He sat up while she remained lying down.

"Now remember, we're going to paddle, paddle, paddle, and when I say 'up', you need to commit one hundred percent. Okay? I'm right behind you, and I'll help you balance, so just concentrate on getting up and let me do the rest."

She nodded her head in agreement even though she was terrified. When she felt T.J. lay back down on the board, she realized there was no turning back.

"Okay, here we go!" T.J. shouted just before she felt a sensation take hold of the board. He yelled for her to paddle, which she did with all her might. When he shouted 'up', she took a deep breath and in one fluid motion, she found herself standing on top of the board, gliding on the crest of the wave.

"Stick your arms out," T.J. yelled to her above the noise of the churning ocean. She stuck her arms out and felt his hands grasp her waist. T.J. stood pressed against her as if they were one. He held her so she wouldn't fall, but used her arms to keep them both balanced. "Bend your knees a little bit," he said over her shoulder.

"You're doing it, Joanna. You're surfing."

She could hear the excitement in his voice, and would've been excited too if it wasn't for the fact that she was concentrating so hard.

The wave began to smooth out, causing them to slow down. "Okay, lean down and straddle the board. Be careful not to let the nose dip," T.J. instructed, as his hands slipped from her waist. T.J. straddled the board right behind her.

Her heart was racing as she tried to comprehend what she had just done. T.J. let out a whoop from behind her, grabbed her arms and pulled them over her head in victory.

He scooted off the back of the board into the shallow water and came around the front of the board, a grin stretching from ear to ear.

"That was it, Joanna. You did it. You rode your first wave."

"I can't believe it. That was amazing!"

"So . . . you ready to do it again?"

"Absolutely!" At the moment, she felt invincible.

They rode tandem a few more times, each time successfully making it to shore. By the time they had paddled out for the third time, Joanna's arms were on fire. She had a new appreciation for the guys she had always referred to as 'beach bums.' She never realized what a workout surfing was.

They positioned themselves once again to mount a wave.

"Okay, this time I'm not going to hold onto you. I want you to try and balance on your own."

Joanna was a little hesitant. She'd enjoyed the feel of T.J. so close to her when they rode the waves; it made her feel safe. At least that's what she convinced herself she was feeling. Safety . . . not attraction.

They paddled feverishly and dropped into the next wave. Instinctively, Joanna popped to her feet at the same time as T.J. But without the feel of his hands on her waist, she tensed up. *You can do this. Don't screw-up.*

Joanna steadied herself on the board, tipping her arms to help maintain her balance. She was doing well–her confidence returning–when all of a sudden the board veered to the left. She felt herself falling and tried to remember what T.J. had told her earlier.

Don't dive off the board, allow yourself to fall into the water.

So, Joanna braced herself for the impact.

When she resurfaced, she saw T.J. straddling the board just a few yards away, watching for her. She swam over to him.

"You okay?" he asked as he reached out for her hand and pulled her up onto the board.

"Yeah," she said a little out of breath.

"If you're going to fall, that's the way to do it."

They paddled to shore and walked out of the surf. Joanna was glad. She really needed to catch her breath.

T.J. laid the long board down next to the other two boards lying in the sand. "So, are you ready to go solo?"

"Solo? I don't know." She looked out at the ocean, hesitantly.

"Come on. You'll do fine. It will feel just like your last ride."

"I just bit it on my last ride," she said, feeling anxious all over again.

"But you 'bit it' so well."

She glared at him.

"I'm serious. Everyone falls off. As long as you know the right way to fall, you won't get hurt."

"Give me a minute to catch my breath, okay?"

"Sure. There's no rush."

Joanna stared out into the vastness of the ocean, amazed by what she'd been doing. A small smile pushed up the corners of her lips. She now understood T.J.'s passion for surfing a little better. In the few moments between her terror and fear, she had felt the exhilaration he had spoken about.

"Hey, T.J."

Joanna turned to see two surfers approaching. They were tan, lean, and had their wet suits pulled down around their hips. They looked to be in their late teens or early twenties. It was obvious they were done for the day.

"We thought that was you." They gave him high fives and then glanced at Joanna. "A new student?" One of the guys said as he looked Joanna over with a satisfying eye.

"A friend," T.J. answered casually.

"Just a friend? Then maybe you wouldn't mind introducing us." The taller surfer looked at Joanna a little too intently.

"Not you, man. I know how you treat your women," T.J. ribbed the guy. "Besides, she's not your type."

"Then clearly you don't know my type." He continued to talk loud. Loud enough to get Joanna's attention. He walked towards her, ignoring T.J. He extended his hand and introduced himself. "Hi, my name's Andrew. Maybe when you get tired of this guy, I can take you out for a real ride?"

Joanna ignored the innuendo and gave him a polite, but uninterested smile. Though he was cute in his own arrogant way, he could easily be ten years her junior.

"As flattering as that is, Andrew, I think you should know I'm not available."

"I don't mind sharing," he persisted, while he stepped closer still.

Joanna could see T.J. was about to say something when she leaned in close to Andrew and whispered in his ear. He drew backed from her, a shocked look on his face.

"Hey. That's harsh," he said, clearly taken back.

"Yeah. But you understand where I'm coming from, right?"

"Sure . . . sure . . . totally." He seemed to stumble over his words as he signaled—with a bob of his head-to the other guy that they were leaving.

Joanna smiled as he walked away, trying to keep from laughing.

"See ya later, T.J." Andrew threw a head nod in T.J.'s direction as he walked away with his friend. His friend leaned in close to Andrew, then turned back and stole one more glance at Joanna.

When they were well out of earshot, T.J. walked over to her. "You look like the cat that swallowed the canary. What did you say to him? I've never known Andrew to give up that easy."

Joanna suppressed a laugh as she explained. "I told him my doctor had encouraged me to abstain until my tests came back. Just a precaution so I didn't spread anything contagious around."

T.J.'s shock turned into a roar of laughter.

Joanna slapped his arm. "Stop, they'll hear you."

T.J. turned to see if the two surfers were still in ear shot, but they were already to the parking lot loading their boards on top of a vintage Nova.

"I can't believe you told him that? That was cold."

"Like I was going to give him the time of day. He barely looks out of high school."

"Well, you don't look much older with that wetsuit on and your hair in a ponytail." He flicked the end of her dripping hair.

"Why didn't you just tell them I was your partner?"

"They don't know I'm a cop."

"They don't?"

He shook his head. "About three years ago there was a drug ring using the beach for contacts and drops. I worked my way into the scene and was able to finger the guys supplying the stuff. No one ever found out it was me that was the snitch."

"Were those guys involved?"

"Nah. They're boozers, but they stay away from drugs. They don't want to 'pollute their bodies'," T.J. said with air quotes.

"What? Come on, alcohol is just as bad as drugs." Joanna couldn't believe the absurdity of his statement.

"Hey, I'm just repeating you what they told me." He laughed at their stupidity. "Okay, enough about them. You've had enough time to catch your breath. So what do you say . . . are you ready to go solo?"

Joanna bit her lower lip and looked out at the waves as they swelled and crashed. She was afraid but determined. "Ready."

"Thatta girl." T.J. grinned. "Now come on, before it gets too crowded out there."

They each grabbed a board. T.J. made sure the leash was attached to Joanna's ankle before walking into the surf. They paddled out to the break point and turned around. T.J. sat up on his board. "Okay, you're going to take the first wave."

Joanna pushed herself up to a sitting position. "By myself? You're not even going to ride in with me?"

"No. It's too dangerous. You need your space. Besides,

I want to keep an eye on you, in case you need help."

"Help? You mean when you have to peel me off of the ocean floor?"

He laughed. "Don't worry, Joanna, you're going to do fine. One more thing. If you go under—"

"You mean *when* I go under."

T.J. shook his head and smiled. "*If* you go under, don't panic. Follow the pull of your leash. And, when you make it to the surface, make sure and give the thumbs up, so I know you're okay. Got it?"

She nodded, feeling slightly panicked.

What have I gotten myself in to?

They both watched the waves as they swelled and then died down behind them. When they saw a wave that was gaining momentum, T.J. yelled at her. "Get ready! This is all you."

Joanna lay down on her board and said a quick prayer. She heard T.J. yelling at her to paddle, so she began lapping at the water as quick as she could. When she heard him yell 'up,' she sprung to her feet, bending her knees, holding out her arms. She rode the wave for what felt like only a few seconds before she felt herself falling. Trying not to panic, she allowed her body to lean back into the water. The jerk of the leash pulled at her ankle as she was swallowed by the wave

Joanna swam in the direction her ankle was being tugged. When she broke through the surface of the water, she threw her arm across her board and gave the thumbs up.

After taking a minute to catch her breath, Joanna heaved herself up on the board and sat up. When she turned around, she saw T.J. was coming in on a wave of his own.

She watched as he cut through the water, making sharp, slicing turns. He was all over the wave; it was hypnotizing to watch. When his wave finally smoothed out, he pushed the tail of the board down and lay down. He paddled over to where she was drifting.

"That was incredible!" she said.

"So you enjoyed it even though you crashed?"

"Not me stupid, you. The way you rode that wave; it was amazing!"

"That was nothing. You should see the waves in Baja or Victoria Bay. *Those* are incredible."

"Well, I think I like these just fine."

"And I think you did great."

"I didn't do great. I barely made it at all."

"Patience, Joanna, patience. Now, are you ready to do it again?"

CHAPTER TWENTY-THREE

Joanna and T.J. rode the waves for another hour. Even though she had just as many wipeouts as rides, Joanna was loving every minute of it. Her arms burned from paddling and her legs felt like rubber, but she didn't want to quit. Not yet. T.J. was having such a good time; she wasn't going to let a little fatigue get the better of her.

She watched as T.J. flawlessly rode another wave. He paddled over to her when he was done.

"Well, I think we'd better call it quits for now. You look tired."

"Me! I'm not tired." She tried to put a perky smile on her face. "Are you tired?"

"No, but I'm use to this kind of exertion."

"So, you're saying I'm out of shape?" Joanna slapped water at him.

"No, but come on, you've got to admit it, this takes a lot more energy than jogging or riding a bike."

"You *do* think I'm out of shape," she said feeling

irritated. "Well, I feel fine. I could ride all day." To prove it, Joanna lay down on her board and began to paddle out against the tide.

"Come on, Joanna. You don't have anything to prove."

Joanna heard T.J., but didn't stop. She continued to paddle.

When she got to the break point her arms felt like flaming noodles.

What was I thinking? This is stupid. My energy is shot.

She looked at T.J. straddling his board in the surf, his arms crossed against his chest.

One more time. I can do this.

She waited for the perfect wave.

When she saw one approaching, she began to paddle, but quickly realized she wasn't going to get enough speed to ride the wave. When she felt the opportunity pass, she sat up on her board knowing she had to concede.

"I give up," she yelled to T.J. "So, how do I get in now?"

"What?" T.J. hollered.

Joanna framed her mouth and yelled, "I admit it. I'm too tired. How do I get in?"

She couldn't hear T.J., but he was pointing behind her. She shook her head and threw up her arms. "I concede. I can't do it."

When T.J.'s shouting turned frantic, Joanna turned, but it was too late. She saw the wave just as it crashed down on top of her.

Joanna hit the water hard gulping a mouthful of saltwater and churning sand. She tried not to panic as she felt herself being pulled under, the leash yanked from her ankle. The water was murky and black as it rolled her around, turning her world upside down. She lost her bearings and no longer knew which way was up. Her lungs began to burn as she fought through the water to find the surface.

Her mind was racing.

Terror seized her.

She was panicking.

She couldn't breathe and she couldn't see a way out. Her arms flailed, but she felt as if she was getting nowhere. Finally, her lungs exploded, releasing what precious air she had left. Pinpricks of light danced before her eyes, and her limbs went limp. She was sinking and there was nothing she could do about it.

She felt a yank on her foot and then an arm wrapped around her middle. She was being propelled upward.

When she burst through the surface of the water, Joanna gasped for air, her chest heaving for oxygen. But she couldn't catch her breath. She was choking on the water that had filled her lungs. As hard as she tried, she couldn't control the coughing that racked her lungs and chest.

"I've got you, Joanna. You're gonna be okay."

T.J. pushed her onto his board and climbed on behind her. He paddled feverishly while she laid there gagging and coughing. She could hear T.J. trying to soothe her and wanted to tell him she was okay, but she couldn't. She didn't have the air she needed to breathe.

"We're almost there, Joanna. Hang on."

Hearing his deep concern, she forced herself to speak. "T.J.," she sputtered. "I'm fine."

She continued to cough, her chest burning, her throat raw.

When they got to the sand, T.J. lifted her off the board. Joanna caught sight of another surfer beside them as T.J. ran up the beach. When he got to where his long board was laying in the sand, he collapsed beside it. Still holding her close to his chest, Joanna continued to cough and sputter. Gently, T.J. laid her down, cradling her head on his lap. She tried to talk but couldn't.

The surfer dropped beside her with a bottle of water in his hand. "Here." He thrust the bottle at T.J.

T.J. supported Joanna's neck so she could try and drink some water. She was able to take a few sips in-between coughs. Finally, she began to feel air fill her lungs. She lay still for a few moments with her head resting on T.J.'s lap. She closed her eyes and took a couple of deep breaths. Her lips tasted like saltwater, and her chest stung from the strain on her lungs. When she was finally able to focus, she saw T.J. and the other surfer hovering over her.

Her embarrassment told her to get up and shake it off. She tried to sit up but felt T.J. restrain her.

"Not so fast, Sparky. You need to rest a minute."

"I'm fine." She tried to sit up again, but T.J. pressed his hands to her shoulders, keeping her in his lap.

"Just rest a minute, will ya?"

Joanna laid her head back down in T.J.'s lap and closed her eyes.

T.J. turned to the teen kneeling beside him. "Thanks for your help. I owe you."

"No problem, man. When I saw that wave drill her, I knew she was gonna be hurtin'."

T.J. had seen this kid and his friends on the beach before. He was a decent surfer. Decent enough to have gotten T.J.'s attention a time or two. T.J. was impressed with his willingness to help out a stranger. Most kids his age were usually self-absorbed, not willing to do much for anyone but themselves. This kid was different.

"Why don't you hang around a minute; let me go to my truck and get you a couple bills. My way of saying thanks."

"No way, man. You don't need to pay me. I'm just glad I could help." The kid shook T.J.'s hand. "The name's Justin."

"T.J."

"I know. You're T.J. Owens."

Shocked, T. J. asked, "How'd you know my name?"

"I've come here surfing with my older brother before. He recognized you. Said you were an awesome surfer until an injury took you out in some big competition. I watch you when you come. You've still got some sick moves."

T.J. was embarrassed by the admiration and tried to shake it off. "Come on, let me give you something. Someone willing to help out like that should get some kind of reward."

"I don't want your money. But, if you're serious, there's something else you can do to thank me," Justin said, squinting against the intensifying sun.

"Sure. Name it."

"How about teaching me a few of your moves, a couple of your tricks?"

T.J. stared at the teen, feeling flattered and awkward at the same time.

"You got it."

"Really," Justin said with a laidback smile. "That'd be sick."

"Well, I think Joanna and I are going to call it a day, but give me your number. I'll call you sometime when we can cut it up."

Justin stared at the waves and shook his head, clearly disappointed.

"Look, I'm not blowing you off. Joanna took a pretty good hit, and I want to make sure she's okay."

"Would you stop talking about me like I'm not even here," Joanna grumbled.

The young surfer looked at Joanna and then to T.J. again. "It's cool." He smiled. "We can hook up another time." He got to his feet and brushed the sand from his knees. "Yell if you need some more help."

"Sure thing, Justin, and thanks again."

Joanna was staring at T.J. when he turned his attention back to her.

"How are you doing?" he asked, brushing her bangs back from her forehead.

"I feel like a fool. I can't believe I ate it out there in front of everyone. What an idiot. All because I refused to admit I was tired."

"Well, good! I'm glad you learned something." T.J.'s voice was stern, his eyes filled with concern.

She grimaced as she tried to sit up.

"Take it easy, Joanna, you really did take quite a beating out there."

T.J. helped her to a sitting position. Joanna could feel his hand on the small of her back as she rotated her neck around and allowed her head to drop forward to her chest.

"You gonna be okay?" he asked again, as he put his hands to her shoulders and began massaging them.

"Ah . . ." Joanna stuttered and swallowed hard. Even through her pain, she could feel the warmth of T.J.'s hands–strong yet gentle–kneading her shoulders. "Actually, it's my neck that hurts."

He began to rub her neck gently. "You probably snapped it back when you went under."

"Probably," she said, trying to ignore the awkwardness she felt. She knew T.J. was just trying to make her feel better, but she immediately pictured Keith and wondered what he would think if he saw them.

T.J. massaged her neck a little longer before he crawled around to sit in front of her. "I've got everything in the truck for a picnic lunch. But I think we should call it a day."

Joanna could see the disappointment in his eyes. He had planned a whole day for them, and she didn't want to spoil it. "No, I'm fine, really. I mean my mouth tastes like a saltshaker and I'm a little stiff, but other than that, I'll be fine. In fact, if you wanted to go do some surfing with that guy, I'll just lay her and soak up some sun."

"I don't think so. You need to go home, take a nice hot shower, and relax."

"T.J., really, I just got the wind knocked out of me and swallowed too much water. I'm fine. I've been in worse pain after a day at the gym."

"I don't know . . ." T.J. glanced over to where Justin was just mounting a wave. Joanna could see T.J. didn't want to end his day in the water. "Look, if you'll just go get my bag out of your truck, I'll be fine here on the beach."

"You're sure?"

"For the third time, yes. I'm sure." He gave her a hard look—the one he used when he questioned someone he didn't believe. "Would you knock it off." She gave him a playful shove and then wished she hadn't. She hid her wince behind a shallow chuckle. "Now, go get my stuff."

"Man, you are so stubborn!"

"And that's one of my finer qualities." She grinned at him, one eye closed against the sun.

He shook his head and sighed. "Fine. I'll be right back."

Joanna watched as T.J. jogged across the sand to the parking lot. When he returned he was loaded down with Joanna's bag, a huge cooler full of stuff, his shorts in his teeth, and a picnic blanket tossed over his shoulder. T.J. plopped the cooler down in the sand and handed Joanna her bag. He stretched out the blanket and weighed down the corners with a handfuls of sand. T.J. tossed his shorts on the blanket—his keys slipping from the pocket—and asked again. "Now, you're sure you're going to be okay?"

Slowly shifting her weight to the blanket, Joanna reached for his keys and looked up at him. "If you ask me one more time," she dangled his keys in front of her, "I'm going to drive myself home and leave you stranded. Go on. It will be nice to relax here for a little while."

T.J. smiled and reached for his board.

"Just do me a favor before you go?" Joanna asked.

"What?"

"Unzip this thing for me."

Joanna pulled her ponytail over her shoulder and waited for T.J. to free her from the crush of the wetsuit. T.J. dropped to his knees behind her and tugged on the leash. Joanna inhaled, well, as much as she dared, then sighed when she felt the suit give way. "Much better." She inched the sleeves down, then pushed the suit to hips.

Wincing slightly at the pain in her neck, she glanced over her shoulder to where T.J. was still sitting. Joanna looked at T.J. looking at her. The same intensity she had felt earlier passed between them like an electric shock. "What's wrong? she asked."

"Ah . . . nothing . . . I . . . ah, was just making sure you were okay."

T.J. got to his feet, pushing his hair away from his face. "If you start feeling worse, just give me a wave." He tucked his board under his arm and jogged to the water.

Joanna finished peeling the wetsuit off and tossed it on the corner of the blanket. Adjusting her swimsuit, she sighed when the warmth of the sand radiated up through the blanket. She rotated her neck slowly, trying to loosen her knotted muscles. *Boy, am I going to be sore tomorrow.*

Not wanting to dwell on the negative, Joanna tipped her head back and allowed the sun to shine on her face. It felt glorious; it was a beautiful day. Hot, but not too hot. A slight breeze kept the heat off her skin and filled her senses with all the smells unique to the beach. She put on her sunglasses, closed her eyes, and lay down on the blanket, allowing her body to sink into the comfort of the molding sand.

As much as Joanna tried to concentrate on the heat of the sun, the feel of the sand, and the brush of the breeze, her thoughts kept drifting to how it had felt to be in T.J.'s arms, her head in his lap, his hands massaging her shoulders and neck.

Get a grip, Joanna. Nothing good can come from what you're thinking.

Joanna disciplined her thoughts and focused on the cawing of the gulls overhead. Their simple tones served as the distraction she needed. Before long, she felt herself being lulled to sleep.

Slowly, T.J. walked over to where Joanna was lying in the sun. Her eyes were hidden under her sunglasses, but from the rise and fall of her chest, he could tell she was asleep. Quietly, he set his board down and walked over to the side of the blanket Joanna was lying on. Then, he shook his head violently, allowing the water from his hair to sprinkle onto Joanna's exposed skin.

Joanna shrilled and jerked from the cold and the surprise. She yanked off her glasses to see T.J. hovering over her. "That was cruel, T.J! I was sleeping."

"I know. That's what made it so funny." He laughed.

Stretching slowly, Joanna winced at the muscles in her neck. They were so tight, they felt like rubber bands ready to snap. She brushed the water from her legs and arms, as T.J. pulled at the leash on the zipper of his wetsuit.

"How are you feeling?" he asked.

"Okay. My muscles are stiff and my chest still feels tight, but no more than when I've been swimming all day."

T.J. plopped down on the blanket next to her and began to strip away his wetsuit. His cavalier attitude towards his dress—or should she say state of undress—irritated her. She tried not to stare when he reached over for his board shorts, but she was only human. His tanned physique and corded muscles were very impressive, and hard not to notice.

He rolled onto his shoulder blades and pulled his shorts up over his hips. He was tying them when he said, "It's nice to know you're not completely dead."

"What's that supposed to mean?"

"I saw you staring."

"Well, if you didn't want me to stare you shouldn't have stripped in front of me."

"Who said I didn't want you to stare?" He laughed, making her blush.

She slapped at his arm. "Why do you do that? Why do you say things like that?"

He leaned over on one elbow and stared at her intently. "Because whether you're willing to admit it or not, you're attracted to me."

She laughed at his arrogance in an effort to hide the truth. "You are so full of it, you know that?"

Heat ignited inside her and it had nothing to do with the sun. She knew what she had with Keith was something with potential, but her attraction to T.J. continued to perplex her.

"Ah, but you didn't deny it?" T.J. teased.

His smile was making it hard for Joanna to think, let alone breathe.

"My ego couldn't take it even if I was attracted to you. I know you're not a one-woman man. And I don't believe in sharing."

T.J. turned serious. "Maybe I haven't found that *one* woman yet."

His eyes revealed a vulnerability she hadn't seen before. Joanna could sense they were crossing over into dangerous territory. Knowing their conversation was about to go in a direction she wasn't ready for, she steeled herself and went into defense mode.

"I thought you brought me out here to learn how to surf and have some lunch." Her tone was sharp, "If this is some kind of high pressure sales pitch to wear me down, I'm not buying." She crossed her legs and tried to get up, but T.J. yanked her back down.

"Why do you always get so defensive? Lighten up." He laughed, as if nothing had happened, but she knew what she had seen in his eyes, what she had felt. That's what worried her.

"I'm hungry, how about you?" T.J. switched subjects seemingly unaffected by their banter. He got on his knees, opened the cooler and started unloading the feast he had brought.

Joanna tried to shake the unsteadiness she felt, glad for the distraction. She watched in amazement as T.J. set out sandwiches, potato chips, and little cartons of potato salad, macaroni salad, and fresh cut fruit, as well as a bakery box filled with different kinds of cookies. The food just seemed to keep coming.

"Okay, you've got your high cal, low cal, low carb, no carb, and," he reached back into the cooler. "your non-carbonated, non-alcoholic fruit drink." He looked at her and smiled. "Bon appetit."

She looked at the array set out in front of her and grinned at his commentary. She knew if it had been up to him, he would have been satisfied with a beer and a hoagie, but he had brought things he thought she might like.

"This looks great, T.J., but there's no way we're going to be able to finish it all."

"Then we'll take it back to your place for dinner," he said as he started opening cartons and unwrapping sandwiches.

"So, tell me about your sister," Joanna asked. She'd been curious ever since T.J. mentioned having one. "If she's anything like you, she must be a handful."

"She was a photographer." His tone was even. "She died two years ago."

"T.J., I'm . . . I'm sorry." Joanna cringed, not knowing what else to say, especially after making such a smart-aleck comment.

T.J. was quiet while he ate. He looked out over the ocean and the waves as if he was in search of something. Poking at her food, Joanna waited for him to say something more. When he didn't, she asked, "She was the girl in the picture with you, the one with the camera, wasn't she?"

It took him a moment to answer. "Yeah. Chrissy would sometimes go on tour with me. Until she got sick."

"How'd she die?" Joanna whispered.

"Ovarian cancer, same as my mom."

Joanna could tell T.J. didn't want to talk about it. She

knew how difficult it was for her to talk about Matthew so she let it go and quietly ate her lunch. T.J. changed the subject to surfing, letting Joanna know how impressed he was with her efforts.

At first their conversation felt stilted and awkward, both of them aware of what it was they *weren't* talking about. But soon, they were talking about work, the prostitute killings, and the everyday stuff that occupied their minds twenty-four-seven.

It was after three o'clock when they packed up for the day. Joanna knew she'd gotten a little too much sun because her shoulders were already turning pink. She had intended to use sunblock after lunch, but had forgotten when she and T.J. got lost in conversation. Slipping her shorts on, Joanna felt a slight sting on her legs, but ignored it as she helped T.J. load everything back into the truck.

Not wanting the day to end, T.J. took his time loading everything back into his truck. He carefully secured his boards, shook out the blanket, and stealthily retrieved their weapons from his hiding place.

He knew Joanna was fighting the attraction she felt for him, he could feel it. And he knew—given enough time—even with all their differences, she would have to admit there was something between them. He hoped to use the rest of the day to prove just that.

Although T.J. was sure he could wear Joanna down, his conscience was waging its own internal struggle. Joanna was out of his league. She was so much more than the usual women he wined and dined. What if he pushed too far and screwed-up things for good? What then?

He knew he was taking a gamble, but he felt it was worth the risk.

He had to see if they had a chance.

"Want to take a walk on the pier?" he asked as they pulled out of the parking lot.

"Sure. I haven't been to the pier in forever."

T.J. beamed. *His plan was working.*

Once they were parked at the pier, T.J. grabbed his sweatshirt from the back seat and put it on. He quickly slid his weapon into the waist of his board shorts and pulled his sweatshirt down around it. Joanna slipped her weapon into her sweatshirt pocket before getting out of the vehicle.

The pier was crowded with an eclectic group of people. Two street musicians—one with an old saxophone, another with a guitar—played their instruments as families walked by. A group of teenagers hung out by a tattoo parlor, obviously trying to hook up before the day was over, while street vendors displayed their talents of jewelry, pottery, and other trinkets.

T.J. and Joanna strolled through the crowd, stopping to wander through each store and mingling among the art booths. They stopped to buy a churro before continuing down the weathered planks. When a mime began to approach them, Joanna ducked behind T.J., clutching at his sweatshirt. "Keep walking," she said, her voice strained.

T.J. laughed. "What's the matter? You're not afraid of a mime are you?"

"Don't let him near me, T.J." She was adamant, pressing herself even closer to his back, his sweatshirt balled in her fists.

They walked quickly away, the Charlie Chaplin-looking performer twisting his black lips into a frown.

"I hate those guys. They always make a person look stupid."

"Oh, and clinging to the back of my sweatshirt and walking sideways around him looked much better?" T.J. joked.

Joanna realized she was still holding onto him and quickly let her hands drop to her side.

"Hey, I wasn't complaining." His boyish smile instantly turned into a seductive grin.

"Never mind," she said lengthening her stride.

They reached the end of the pier and looked out over the old wooden rails. There were a few surfers riding close to the pillars and Joanna watched them, shaking her head.

T.J. bent down close to her ear. "The wet suits are in the truck. We could join them if you'd like?"

"Humm . . . maybe next time," Joanna said with a mocking tone and a smile.

"So, there might be a next time?" he asked.

"Maybe." She inhaled the breeze and closed her eyes.

T.J. just smiled. She had enjoyed herself. Even with her wipeout and the aches and pains, she was sure to have tomorrow; he saw the look in her eye that let him know he'd introduced her to a whole new high. One even she could enjoy.

As they walked back the length of the pier, T.J. had to fight the urge to reach for Joanna's hand.

I know she feels it, too. I saw it in her eyes. How is she able to ignore her feelings when I am ready to bust out of my skin?

The drive back to her place was done in a comfortable silence. When they pulled up outside her house, T.J. got out of his truck and walked around to open her door. "Are you still up for leftovers?" he asked, referring to the extra food from their picnic.

"Why not? No sense letting good food go to waste."

Joanna helped T.J. carry in the cooler, then excused herself to the bathroom. When she looked at herself in the mirror, she slipped the strap of her swimsuit to one side. Her glowing skin confirmed what she already knew.

When she returned to the kitchen, she saw T.J. had gone out on the deck. Her thoughts went places she didn't want them to go.

What am I doing? How can I have these feelings for T.J. when it's clear we are complete opposites? His morals are that of an alley cat, and he has absolutely no interest in God. But people can change. She argued with herself. *Don't be stupid, Joanna.*

He's not going to change for you.

She walked outside and joined him on the deck. "Did you want to eat out here?" she asked.

"Sure. I'll get the cooler. I can let the excess water drain while we're eating."

T.J. carried the cooler outside. He drained the water before they started rummaging through the leftovers. Joanna took the fruit, and some of the macaroni salad, while T.J. finished off the last sandwich. He offered her the potato salad before polishing it off himself.

The sun was setting quickly, so T.J. offered to build a

fire. Joanna agreed because they still needed to discuss the details of his end of the bet. While he stoked the logs to life, Joanna moved to the swing.

"So, about tomorrow. Why don't you plan on picking me up around ten o'clock. My church is pretty casual, so you won't need a suit or tie. Jeans and a polo shirt will be fine."

"I don't know," T.J. said as he stretched and moaned. "I'm pretty tired from all that–"

"Oh no you don't!" Joanna stopped him. "You're not backing out on me. So help me I will drag you out of bed myself if I have to."

T.J. slid onto the seat next to her. "That sounds like fun, too." He teasingly raised his brow. She was ready to rain all over him when he stopped her. "I was only kidding. I already told you I don't welch on bets."

"Good," she said firmly.

They sat in silence as the sun drifted beyond the horizon. Joanna shuddered, her sunburn causing chills to race across her arms.

"You cold?"

"Not really, but I did get a little more sun than I expected."

T.J. turned towards her and moved the strap on her suit, slightly. "Wow, I guess you did."

When their eyes caught, Joanna felt more than chills travel through her body. Before she knew what was happening, T.J. leaned in close to her and pressed his lips to hers. For a moment, she responded to his kiss, wanting to know what it would feel like, but then she caught herself and pulled away.

"T.J., don't," she whispered under her breath.

"Why?" His face was still dangerously close to hers. "I know you feel it to."

"We just can't. It wouldn't work."

"You think too much, Joanna. Why don't you just go with your feelings for once." His fingers brushed her cheek and his thumb caressed her lips. He leaned in closer.

"I can't do this T.J." Joanna got up from where she sat and walked into the house. Her heart pulsed violently as she paced the living room. She jumped when the automatic lights clicked on, washing the living room in a soft glow. Taking a deep breath, she sunk to the stairs just as T.J. walked in.

"Tell me you don't have feelings for me, Joanna, and I'll leave you alone." The tension in his voice was palpable.

Joanna held her head in her hands, not sure what she should say. "We're partners, T.J. Of course I have feelings for you."

"That's not what I'm talking about, and you know it."

"But that's what I'm talking about," she said, looking up at him. "I don't know how to explain how I feel, T.J."

"Try." His frustration was apparent.

Joanna said a quick prayer that she would be able to explain her feelings and her reservations without hurting T.J. She wrung her hands in her lap as she tried.

"Okay, T.J., I admit I'm physically attracted to you, and I've seen a different side of you since we've become partners. But our interests are too different, and how we view life is polar opposite of each other. There are too many other things that are involved in a relationship besides physical attraction that we don't have in common.

And to me, the obstacles are too big to ignore."

"It's the church thing, isn't it?" he said bluntly. "I said I would go with you."

"But that's not what church is, T.J. It's not a bartering chip or a wager in a bet. It's a part of my life; a very important part."

"But I could go tomorrow and like it. Then this whole conversation would've been unnecessary."

She rose from the steps, frustrated she wasn't making her point clear. She paced to the living room, twisting the hem of her tankini in her hand. "But it's more than that, T.J. There's the drinking, the carousing, the swearing, the women. Don't you see how different we are?"

T.J.'s jaw was set and she could see contempt in his eyes. "Yeah, I see the difference. While I've chosen to live life and have fun, you've chosen to judge everyone and everything."

She hung her head, the pain from his indictment sharper than the pain in her neck. She let out a low breath, before speaking again in whispered tones. "I'm not judging you, T.J., I'm only doing what's right for me. And those are not things I want in my life."

"And since that's what I represent to you—drinking, carousing, having fun—you don't want me either, is that it?"

She rubbed at her face knowing she was in a no-win situation. "T.J., I care for you. I really do, but as a partner and as a friend."

He stalked over to where she was standing—and with his hands to her forearms—pulled her close. She ignored the pain of her sunburn, but wasn't so sure she could ignore the pain in T.J.'s eyes.

"But I can change, Joanna. I was only filling time until the right woman came along. But now you're here. You said it yourself. Someday I would find the right girl, and I would want to change."

Joanna was frustrated T.J. was being so stubborn. He knew they were as different as night and day, but he was refusing to admit it.

"What do you see in me, T.J., that makes you want to give up all your favorite pastimes?"

"What do you mean?"

Her question had obviously caught him off guard.

"What makes me so different, so intriguing? It can't be my looks, because I've seen the women you attract. Most of them have me beat hands down. It can't be our similar interests, since we don't have any. It can't be the way I get along with your friends, since most of them hate me. So what is it? Tell me that."

T.J. looked at her dumbfounded, but it was Joanna that answered for him.

"You're not interested in me, T.J., you're intrigued by me. It's the mystique, the unknown. You found a woman that wouldn't roll over for you and you found it entertaining. That is, until Keith showed up."

"This has nothing to do with Keith." He pointed a finger at her, his temper flared.

"Yes, it does. You were perfectly content to tease me and rib me, treat me like the "Iron Maiden." Then when I showed I could be interested in a man, you got ugly. You nearly threw Keith out of here like he had tampered with your property. Then you scolded me like some naïve adolescent, insisting I was being played."

"Because he's a man, Joanna," T.J. shouted. "And you were acting like he was some sort of superhero that could do no wrong. I don't care what you say. He is still a hot-blooded, male who probably dreams at night about getting into your pants. Just because he hasn't come right out and said it, or done anything about it, doesn't mean he's not thinking it."

Joanna was pacing, doing what she could to control her rage. She knew T.J.'s character assassination of Keith was just his way to get her angry. He was trying to throw her off the track of what they were really talking about. And what they were talking about was them, not Keith. She decided to lay it out for him as clearly and as calmly as she could.

"You wanted me when you first got to the station, T.J. That was obviously lust since you didn't know a thing about me. After I reported Cummings, you wrote me off as a snitch and had no problem saying lewd things about me or to me. Then we became partners. Even though you hated the idea, you knew you had to get on board. A civil relationship begins to develop between us and the back-stabbing stops. We get to know each other and feelings start to develop, but that's because we work with each other T.J. It's a normal reaction to the environment. We were forced to make this relationship work, and we have. We never would've traveled in the same circles, or chosen each other for friends if it wasn't for the job."

"But I don't see why that's wrong," T.J. argued. "You're right. Everything you said is spot on. We never would have chosen each other as friends. But we are friends." He moved closer to her. "Good friends. Why can't we just see where that takes us?"

"Because I know where it will take us. I'll cave-in. Abandon my principals; and end up in bed with you."

He looked shocked.

"What? Does that surprise you?

"I'm human, T.J. I have the same feelings and desires you do. I also have insecurities and fears. If we were to have a relationship, we would be in a no-win situation. Either I would end up in a sexual relationship with you, totally disregarding my beliefs. Or, we would try to have a platonic relationship, and I would always be wondering if you were getting it from somewhere else. I would either be trying to live up to the women you've been with, or I would turn into a jealous, untrusting woman. Our relationship would end in shambles, and we would end up hating each other. I don't want to jeopardize our friendship like that. It means too much to me.

"You mean too much to me."

Tears slipped down Joanna's face, causing T.J. to look away. He wanted to be mad at her, but he couldn't. He knew on some level, she was right. The sexual attraction between them was too great to think they would be able to have a romantic relationship and still remain platonic. And as much as T.J. knew he cared for her, he couldn't say for sure that it would last forever. He would like to think it would, but he had to be honest with himself knowing that even the best of things don't last forever.

Joanna was waiting for T.J. to blow-up. She'd seen the

flicker of anger in his eyes, and knew it was right below the surface. So, she was not expecting what happened next.

T.J. stepped forward and drew her into a hug. He kissed the top of her head and then lowered his lips to her ear. "You're right. As much as I want to be with you, Joanna, I don't want to hurt you."

Joanna held on to T.J., aching inside. Not just because of the hurt she'd seen in his eyes, but because of the feelings she had for him. She knew her attraction for T.J. stemmed from rebellion that stirred in her. A part of her wanted to dive into a relationship, a sexual relationship. But, it was her faith and commitment to God that kept her from doing something she could never undo.

T.J. pulled back from her and looked into her eyes. "Don't think I'm not going to still try and hit on you in the future. I'm admitting it probably wouldn't work out. But my mind isn't always in sync with my hormones."

She chuckled at his attempt at humor.

"And," he continued, "don't think I won't be watching Keith like a hawk. I care for you, Joanna. And you can bet if I'm willing to sacrifice a relationship with you to make sure you don't get hurt, I'm certainly not going to stand by and let someone else hurt you."

T.J. gently placed a kiss to her lips. It was slow and tender and something he would always savor.

He was letting go of what could have been.

He was doing the right thing for once, and it was tearing him up inside.

He stepped away from Joanna and rubbed his hands

together.

"I need to go. Just let me get the cooler, and I'll be out of here."

"Just leave it, T.J. I'll clean it out and you can get it tomorrow when you pick me up for church. We're still on for church, right?"

"Yep. Lucky me. I lose the girl, and I still have to sit through a church service."

She frowned and hung her head.

"I was only kidding. Geez, cut me a little slack. I don't take rejection well." He walked to the door and turned as he opened it. "Good night, Joanna."

"Good night, T.J."

T.J. closed the door, and stood on the porch until he heard Joanna turn the deadbolt. He walked away with a heavy heart. T.J. knew he had done the right thing for Joanna's sake, but he'd lost in the deal. He felt like going out and getting hammered, anything to kill the pain. But that wasn't the answer, and he knew it. Besides, if he showed up for church the next morning with a hangover Joanna would never forgive him.

Joanna cleaned up the deck, the cooler, and her bedroom she'd left in disarray earlier that morning. The whole time she cried at the pain she felt in her heart. She really did love T.J. She knew that now, because of the pain she was feeling. But her love for him was deeper than a physical love; she cried for his soul. She knew he needed the Lord. But with his reputation and his cavalier exterior, she knew it would be nothing short of a miracle, and the

Lord had yet to perform a miracle in her life.

Or the lives of those she loved.

Joanna finally fell asleep with a heavy burden pressing at her heart.

CHAPTER TWENTY-FOUR

Joanna hurried to get ready for church. She'd relived her conversation with T.J. a hundred times since last night, and wasn't sure how she would handle seeing him.

She slowly pulled on a pair of khaki slacks and a new light green, sleeveless, v-neck sweater she'd bought on clearance at J. Crew. Stepping into a pair of slip-ons, she pushed her hair off her sunburned shoulders. She looked into the full length mirror, not sure she liked what she saw. Joanna was about to change for the third time, when she heard a knock at the door. She glanced at the clock on the bedside table and smiled. T.J. was right on time.

"Hi," she said as she opened the door.

"Ready?"

Joanna couldn't help but stare at T.J. She thought he looked great yesterday in a pair of swim trunks. But nothing compared to how he looked leaning against the frame of her door, in tailored jeans—nothing like the baggy ones he wore to work—and a fitted white polo that showed off his physique, as well as, their day in the sun. He looked downright gorgeous.

"What?" T.J. said nervously, looking down at his jeans and preppy loafers. "You said it was casual. Is this not good enough?"

"No! You look fine."

Real good, Joanna. Add a little drool to that stare and you'll look like a high school freshman gawking over the senior football star.

"Ah . . . let me grab my purse."

Joanna gave T.J. instructions to Covenant Christian Church. She was quiet while he maneuvered through traffic, wondering if he felt the same awkwardness she did.

"So how do you feel about yesterday?" T.J. asked.

"Yesterday?" Joanna didn't know what to say. She had hoped they had said all they were going to on the matter.

"Yeah. You've got to admit it was quite the workout. And there's the matter of your little wipeout. Are you sore at all?"

Surfing. He's talking about surfing.

"No. I feel pretty good," she lied. "You forget, I jog, bike, and kick box every week. I'm not some couch potato that just sits around all the time."

Of course, she didn't tell him she had to stand under a hot shower this morning just to get the kinks out of her neck, and the reason she'd chosen slip-ons was because she couldn't bear the thought of bending over to buckle her favorite sandals.

T.J felt nervous pulling into the parking lot of Joanna's

church. He'd never been to church before and didn't think his normal icebreakers would be appropriate. He got out of his truck and walked around to help Joanna down. As they walked up the front steps, T.J. leaned over and asked. "I'm not going to have to do anything, or wear a stupid badge because I'm a visitor, am I?"

"Oh, didn't I tell you? You have to go up front and introduce yourself."

"I what?" He stopped cold in his steps, his voice drawing the attention of those around them.

"I was only kidding," she whispered, and politely smiled at the people staring at them.

They both received bulletins and warm handshakes as they walked into the foyer. Joanna led T.J. to a pew on the right-hand side, towards the back. T.J. thumbed through what he thought was a program, and was amazed by all the other groups that met throughout the week.

He leaned over to her and said, "There's a group here for everything; divorce, single-parents, teen mothers, substance abuse recovery groups. I thought the church looked down on all this stuff?"

"Not the people, T.J., just the sin. There are many hurting people out there, and the church doesn't want to condemn them. They want to help them if they're sincere about getting help."

T.J. was surprised. It wasn't what he was expecting.

The choir made their way on stage while the congregation quieted. T.J. followed Joanna's lead and stood when the choir director instructed them to do so. He listened as Joanna sang the worship chorus being projected onto large screens on either side of the stage.

Man, she's even a good singer.

He felt himself being enticed by Joanna all over again. Seeing how she looked today, her skin glowing from being in the sun and remembering how she looked in her tiny red swimsuit.

Give it a break, T.J. You're in church for heaven's sake. Show a little self-control.

They sat through the announcements and a special number by a guest soloist, before the preacher took the pulpit. The preacher wasn't at all what T.J. was expecting. He thought he would be older, but this guy looked to be only in his late forties. He didn't have the perfect hair and fake smile he was expecting either. He wasn't even wearing a jacket and tie, just a dress shirt and slacks. The preacher somehow looked familiar, but T.J. couldn't see how that was possible.

I must be confusing him with someone else.

The preacher set a small box on top of the pulpit before he prayed.

Joanna prayed intently that T.J. would listen to the pastor's preaching. When she had looked at the title of the message in the bulletin, she thought for sure God had orchestrated what the pastor would speak on. It was exactly what T.J. needed to hear.

Joanna kept glancing at T.J. during the service, trying to read his expression and his body language. He wasn't fidgeting in his seat or looking at his watch. He actually seemed to be listening.

"So you see," the pastor continued, "we all have a

God-shaped hole in our lives. I brought this box to represent our lives."

The pastor opened the small gift box and removed the contents. It had a coffee mug and several pieces of packing popcorn in it. "This cup represents God, while this packing material represents the things we think will make us happy.

"I know some of you have probably told yourself you'll have more time for God later–once you get your life in order–but first, you need to take care of business. So, you work twelve-hour days at a high paying, high profile job."

The pastor picked up a piece of popcorn and put it into the box. "Then, you get the high-end car so you can show off your success. You worked hard for it and you deserve it, right?" He put more packing material into the box. "Then it's the house, the club memberships, and the recreational vehicles." The pastor continued to fill the box. "The happiness you experience doesn't last, so you continue to find new things to fill the box.

"But none of those things are making you happy. So you have to look for new ways to fill the box.

"As you search for that unattainable thing that will make you happy, you start filling your life with things that have no business being there. Alcohol. Drugs. Gambling. Pornography. Pretty soon the box is filled and you've left no room for God."

The pastor picked up the cup–the representation of God–and tried to put it into the box filled with packing material. "You see your box–*your life*–is filled. And, with all the garbage you've put in your life, you can't see what's missing. But you know something is."

The pastor looked out over the congregation making sure they were all taking it in. Then, he dumped the popcorn out of the box and started over.

"But you see, the thing that was missing all along was God." He picked up the cup and put it in the box, upside down. Then, he lifted the box up so everyone could see inside. There was little room left for the packing material. "Instantly, your life is full. By the presence of God alone, you have filled the emptiness in your life." He paused before making his next point.

"Now, I'm not saying that God doesn't want you to have things like a nice car and a nice house. I'm just saying they are no longer necessary in order for you to experience fullness in life.

God has replaced those 'things' with what is important." The pastor held up a piece of packing material. "Like *love*–the love for your family." He placed the piece of packing material in the box and picked up another. "*Joy*–the joy of friends." He picked up yet another piece of packing material. "*Peace*–peace that God will provide for your needs. *Patience*–through the hard times. *Goodness, kindness, gentleness, and self-control.* These are the things that are important and are to be valued. God fills you up completely, from the moment you accept Jesus into your life." One by one, the pastor filled the box.

"So you see, you cannot experience fullness of life unless you start with God. Now I know there are probably some of you out there thinking I don't have a clue. You think I just don't understand the pressures of the world or the stress you're under. But those of you who know me, know that isn't true." He smiled at the congregation. "And those of you who don't know me, will have to come back and hear my testimony at another time.

"The decision to be made today is between you and God."

The pastor paused, and Joanna prayed.

After a short moment of silence, the pastor stepped out from behind the pulpit. "There are others here today that would like to talk to you, if you still have questions regarding your relationship with God. We encourage you to make a decision today.

"You never know if you'll have this opportunity again."

Joanna stole a glance at T.J. He was still listening intently as the pastor spoke. She just hoped he *heard* what he was saying.

Finally, the congregation began to file out of the sanctuary. Joanna instinctively reached for T.J.'s hand so she could thread him through the stream of people heading for the exits.

Keith watched as Joanna led T.J. from the sanctuary. She hadn't seen him standing in the corner. He had stopped in on his lunch break, hoping to see her. And what he saw only confirmed what he'd already suspected.

He slipped out the side entrance, feeling like a fool.

Joanna and T.J. walked to his truck in silence. As they waited to exit the parking lot, an ambulance passed in front of them. Joanna immediately thought of Keith. She missed him and looked forward to hearing from him tomorrow.

Joanna waited until she and T.J. were out of the bustling parking lot before asking what was on her mind.

"So, what did you think?" she said, anxious to hear what T.J. would say.

"It was different than I expected."

"How so?"

"The pastor for one. I figured he'd be in his seventies, and tell me I was going to Hell."

She laughed at his explanation. "I guess Pastor Grant isn't your typical pastor."

"So, what did he mean by 'his testimony?'"

"It's his story of when he realized he needed Christ in his life."

"He made it sound like it would surprise people. Do you know his story?"

"Yeah."

"So?" T.J. was waiting expectantly.

"He was imprisoned for embezzlement when he was in his thirties."

T.J. looked at her with surprise.

"I guess he was some kind of whiz kid in the financial world, and got caught up in a huge scandal."

"That's why he looks familiar," T.J. said. "He was plastered all over the news back when the story broke. Didn't he go to jail?"

"He did. He accepted the Lord through a prison ministry and studied to become a pastor while still in jail."

"So I guess he knew what he was talking about when he said people are trying to make themselves happy with 'things.'"

Joanna beamed inwardly and smiled. "So you *were* listening."

"I caught the gist of it," T.J. said casually.

"So, what do you think?"

"I think I'm hungry. Where should we eat?"

"How about Antonio's?"

It was a little Italian place Joanna thought would be quiet enough so they could continue to talk if T.J. felt like it.

"Sounds good to me." T.J. turned at the next intersection.

"Now back to what Pastor Grant said, what did you think?" Joanna didn't want to be pushy, but she did want to know what T.J. thought of the message. A message perfectly suited for where he was in life.

"I think he made some valid points."

"Such as?"

"People looking for something but never being satisfied."

T.J. continued to keep his eye on the road.

"So he didn't offend you?"

"No. Everyone's entitled to their opinion."

Joanna decided not to push further. It was enough that T.J. had gone and that he'd actually listened. She would pray that he would think about what he'd heard. And if he had questions, he'd be willing to talk to her.

They sat down for lunch. T.J. crossed his arms and looked at Joanna. "So, about last night," T.J. started.

Joanna held her breath. She didn't want to have this conversation. Things had gone so well today. She didn't want to take a step backwards.

"I thought we cleared everything up last night?" she said quietly.

"Everything except how you feel about Keith."

She dipped her head. "I don't think we need to talk about Keith."

"Why? Aren't you going to see him again?" he persisted, just before the waitress came to take their order.

"I'll have the chicken Alfredo with penne pasta, and lemon water," Joanna said, the waitress not even looking at her.

"I'll have the lasagna with a side of tortellini's," T.J. said.

"And to drink?" the waitress asked, with a flirtatious smile.

I'll have . . .," T.J. looked at Joanna before he ordered his drink, "a Coke."

The waitress gave him a long, lingering look before she walked away with their menus.

Joanna smiled at T.J. "You didn't have to order a coke on my account." She knew he would've preferred something stronger.

He shrugged. "It sounded good."

"So, when do you think the O.T.'s going to kick in?" Joanna said, trying to change the subject to something other than Keith.

"Why? Are you worried about going undercover?"

"No. I just didn't know—since we don't have any fresh leads—if the brass would consider it a cold case and let it go."

"I don't think that's going to happen. There's been too much media attention given to this case. Some womens' groups are getting up in arms claiming we're not doing everything we can, because the victims were prostitutes."

The waitress brought their drinks and a basket of fresh sourdough bread. T.J. pulled it apart, releasing steam from the warm loaf.

Joanna decided to test the waters. "Would you mind if I prayed for our food?"

In the past, Joanna would've quietly prayed to herself, but she decided she needed to be bolder about her faith. She needed to let T.J. see that it was a part of her everyday life, not just a once-a-week thing.

"Sure," he answered with a clipped tone, but Joanna knew it was because he was caught off guard.

She bowed her head slightly. "Thank you, Lord, for this day and this food. Bless it to our bodies and keep us safe as we do our best to serve this city. Amen."

She opened her eyes only to see that T.J. was staring at her. He poured some olive oil on the plate of bread, dipped a piece, and then before bringing it to his lips asked, "So, you're not going to talk about Keith with me?"

"I didn't say that."

"You're right. You didn't say anything."

"Fine, what do you want to know?" She decided she might as well answer his questions, knowing he would just continue to badger her.

"Why is he driving an ambulance?"

"What do you mean?"

Joanna saw a flicker in T.J.'s eye.

"Oh my gosh! You ran a check on him, didn't you?" She sipped at her water, trying to control her temper. "When did you do that?"

"Last night. I had a little extra time on my hands."

She knew he was referring to the end of their 'date.'

"Why did you do that?"

"I needed to find out what this guy is all about, and you weren't telling me."

"So, you know he's a doctor."

"Among other things."

Joanna knew T.J. was getting at something, but she wasn't going to bite. She didn't want to give him the satisfaction.

"He works for the ambulance company because it gives him the freedom to go on missions trips throughout the year. He goes to foreign countries and provides medical aid."

T.J. acted unimpressed while he chomped on his bread.

Joanna was about to concede and ask T.J. what else he'd found out, when the waitress brought their meal. T.J. dug right in, seeming to let the conversation about Keith drop. So, Joanna decided she wouldn't bring it up if he didn't.

They enjoyed their meal without further talk of Keith. T.J. dropped her off at home and didn't even needle her for an invite in.

She could tell he was trying.

Their weekend had definitely had both highs and lows. Surfing was amazing, and seeing T.J. in church was a miracle in itself. Even their argument over their relationship had ended well. So, after a few stuttered stops and starts, Joanna was ready to deem the weekend a success.

Joanna pulled her cell phone from her purse and

realized she had forgotten to turn it back on after church. She pressed the button and watched it come to life.

No messages.

Keith had told her he was on call until one o'clock. She glanced at the clock on the wall. *One twenty-three.* She decided to chuck decorum and give him a call. Joanna scrolled through her contacts, pressed the number she had stored in her phone, and waited for him to answer. When it went to voice mail she shrugged in disappointment and left a message.

"Hi Keith, its Joanna. My weekend plans are over, and I thought if you weren't busy, you might want to come by for dinner. Call me when you get this message. I hope you're having a good day."

Joanna was frustrated she wasn't able to talk to Keith. She decided to fill the time–until he returned her call–with a call to Kathy.

A weekly update Kathy was sure to enjoy.

T.J. walked into his apartment feeling a strange sense of emptiness. He shuffled over to the refrigerator and instinctively reached for a beer; but decided instead to have one of the fruit coolers from the six-pack he'd bought for Joanna.

Taking a swig of the tart drink, he walked out onto his balcony and leaned against the rail. He watched the boats as they glided in and out of the marina and listened as the buoy clanged in the distance.

He replayed the pastor's message in his mind. It hit home. He'd been looking for happiness in the exact things the preacher pointed out. Women, alcohol, a self-centered life. All he had to show for it was . . . nothing.

He was empty inside.

He told himself he was having fun, but was he?

Why did he drink?

Why didn't he stick with any one woman?

Why was he even in his job?

T.J. began to question everything about his existence. If he could only walk away quietly from it all, he would.

But he couldn't.

He had a reputation. Certain things were expected of him. What would the guys think if he gave up drinking and didn't hit the bars with them at the end of the shift? What would they do if he declined their set-ups? Or he didn't give a play-by-play on his latest conquest? The guys were always making wagers on how long it would take T.J. to make time with a woman. What would they do if he no longer played the game?

He leaned against the wall, his eyes closed, feeling overwhelmed. This was not the life he wanted. He was almost thirty-five years old and had nothing to show for it. At the rate he was going, he'd end up forty and alone.

He thought about Wagner and Olsen. They were good family men. He watched the way they beamed when they pulled out pictures of their kids or talked about their wives. Their job was their job, and they were good at it. But their families were their life; they knew what was important.

T.J. had joined the force because it was expected of him, and he was good at it. He was good at anything he put his mind to. But the police force was an easy solution to get his father off his back.

He hadn't had the perfect family life. Maybe that's why he hadn't thought family would be important to him. But now . . . now he wasn't sure what was important at all.

He leaned against the rail, straining . . . peering into the distance; as if the answers to life were written in front of him if he just look hard enough.

There's got to be something more.

Kathy laughed while Joanna explained her adventure in surfing. "You should've seen me, Kath, it was incredible. And T.J. was so patient. Come to find out, he was actually a champion surfer in his younger days. You should've seen the way he sliced through those waves. It was amazing."

"Sounds like you've changed your tune about T.J."

"What's that supposed to mean?" Joanna asked.

"I'm just saying you sound different."

"Come on, Kath, we are *partners*. Besides, he's not as bad as he would like people to think. That macho persona of his is just a cover. He's actually a pretty decent guy. And, he held up his end of the bet."

"So, he went to church with you? How'd that go?"

"Better than I expected. He actually listened. When I asked him what he thought about Pastor Grant's sermon, he said he thought the preacher had made some valid points. The message was tailored just for him. It was like God orchestrated the whole thing. I just hope some of it sinks in and T.J. realizes what's missing in his life."

"Is that all it is, Joanna? You're just concerned about T.J.'s spiritual condition?"

"What do you mean by that?" Joanna answered, annoyed with Kathy's tone.

"The way you're talking about him is so different than just a few weeks ago. I think you're falling for the guy."

"Kathy, I—"

"I'm just saying watch yourself, Joanna. You know he's a player. Just make sure you don't get played while on your way to saving him."

Joanna thought about the kiss she and T.J. had shared. She'd allowed it, wanting to satisfy her own curiosity. But the minute she realized what she was doing, she knew it was wrong and put a stop to it.

"Kathy, I admit I've been struggling with my feelings for T.J. But I realized this weekend it would be a mistake to get involved with him on an intimate level.

"He needs someone who will be a real friend to him, not a buddy who gets drunk with him, or a lover who preoccupies him. He needs someone who will be there for him. Someone who will ask him the hard questions, and set him straight when he starts veering in the wrong direction."

"From what you've told me, he's more than veered," Kathy said, judgment in her tone.

"But I think he's beginning to do some soul searching. Today was the first step. I just want to be there for him when he's ready to take the next one."

"Just as long as you don't become collateral damage in the process."

"Don't worry, Kathy, I'll be fine."

CHAPTER TWENTY-FIVE

Joanna got ready for work the next morning, frustrated she'd never heard back from Keith. She had left two more messages for him the night before, but he never returned her call. She knew his work was just as unpredictable as her own, but somehow that didn't make her feel any better.

He probably just got busy with overtime. Or covered someone else's shift as a favor.

Joanna convinced herself to let it go. She was sure she would hear from Keith as soon as he had the chance.

"What a lousy day! And it's not over yet."

Joanna tossed her purse onto the passenger seat before getting into her car and slamming the door. She rubbed her forehead, trying to massage away her headache, then looked down at the stain on her favorite jacket.

She was so mad, she cursed under her breath. Bristol had intentionally bumped into her, causing her cup of coffee to splash down the front of her jacket. "Stupid jerk!" she yelled, then gunned it from the parking lot.

Joanna told T.J. she would go home to grab a bite to eat and change her jacket. He asked to come along, but she told him no. She needed some space. Changing her jacket wasn't the only reason for going home. She needed time to get her attitude in check. She'd been short-tempered all day and knew exactly why.

Keith still hadn't called.

In spite of making excuses for him, and wanting to give him the benefit of the doubt, Joanna was mad. If Keith wanted to call it quits between them, then fine. But he could at least be man enough to do it in person, or return her call and give it to her straight. The silent treatment was so juvenile. She thought Keith was a little more mature than that.

Just then, her phone rang.

Joanna quickly dug it out of her purse, a part of her hoping it was Keith. He would tell her how sorry he was for not calling, and explain that his phone had died or he'd lost it. But when she looked at her phone, there was no caller I.D.

"Anderson."

"Joanna?"

A female voice was crying hysterically into the phone. Joanna strained to hear. "Who is this?"

"It's Michelle. You . . . you talked to me a while ago. You said to call if I . . . if I needed help."

Instantly, Joanna remembered the pregnant girl she and T.J. had questioned on the street. "Yes, Michelle, I remember. What's wrong?"

"I think it's the baby. It hurts really bad. I'm scared." Michelle's words sounded more like convulsions.

"Where are you, Michelle?" Joanna had to concentrate to make out what the sobbing girl was saying

"I'll be right there, Michelle. Hang on. I'll be right there."

Joanna repeated the address in her head as she speed-dialed Keith's number. He still wasn't answering.

"Keith this is an emergency, so if you're at work pick up." She waited a second, hoping to hear his voice, but got nothing.

"Keith, I need your help. If you get this message, I'm at 334 Holloway St. Apt. E. If you're not at work, call it in for me, or bring your medical bag."

Joanna hung up the phone and dialed T.J. When he picked up, she didn't give him the chance to say hello.

"T.J., you need to meet me at 334 Holloway St. Apt. E."

"Joanna, what is it, what's wrong?"

"It's Michelle. Remember the pregnant girl I questioned the other day? Well, she just called me, hysterical. She's hurt. And from the sound of it, she's hurt pretty bad. I'm on my way there now. I called Keith to meet us."

"I'm on my way. And Joanna, be careful. If this is our guy, and he's left a witness, he might still be around waiting to finish the job. So keep your eyes and ears open."

Joanna frantically wove in and out of traffic. When she got to Holloway Street, she slowed enough to follow the street numbers, then double-parked alongside a broken-down Impala. Throwing her emergency placket against her windshield, Joanna ran up the stairs of the shabby building. When she got to the apartment, the door hung slightly ajar. With her weapon in hand, Joanna cautiously pushed it open.

A single bare bulb hung from the ceiling casting uneven shadows around the room. Michelle was lying on the floor in a fetal position, a tattered blanket covering her. Joanna wanted to go to her, but had to clear the apartment first. She didn't want to get blindsided by whoever had assaulted Michelle. Once she knew the apartment was clear, Joanna hurried to Michelle's side. When she brushed back the girls stringy black hair from her face, Joanna cringed.

Michelle was a bloody mess. She had a nasty gash across the bridge of her nose, and her lip was split wide open. Her face was swollen; smeared with tears, mucus, and blood. Her eyes were squeezed shut in obvious pain.

"Michelle, it's Joanna. I need you to talk to me. I need you to tell me what happened."

"My baby," she cried out. "He killed my baby." With her arms wrapped around her mid-section, Michelle continued to sob.

Joanna leaned closer to the girl, so she could look into her eyes. "Michelle, I'm right here." Joanna spoke it a soothing tone. "I'm going to help you, but I need you to look at me."

Michelle's eyes fluttered open, but she was having difficulty focusing.

"I know you're in a lot of pain, but I want you to try and take a couple deep breaths, okay?"

Michelle just cried.

Joanna reached for the girl's hand and gave it a squeeze. "Come on, Michelle. I know you can do it."

Michelle's breathing was shuddery at first, then, became a little more even. Soon, she was following Joanna's lead and taking deep, cleansing breaths.

"That's it. You're doing great. Slow, even breaths."

With Michelle distracted, Joanna lifted the blanket from the girl's body.

Tears stung Joanna's eyes.

Michelle laid there naked. Even though she only had the light from the overhead bulb, Joanna could see the bruises and welts that covered Michelle's body. But it was the small puddle of blood, pooling under her thighs that caused Joanna to almost loose it.

God, no.

Joanna heard sirens in the distance, thankful help was on its way. She looked around the dingy apartment for a towel, a rag, anything. But everything she saw was filthy. Quickly, she took off her jacket and rolled it into a ball, then pressed it between Michelle's legs.

Michelle was quiet.

Too quiet.

"Michelle, are you still with me?"

"Come on, Michelle, I need you to open your eyes."

Nothing.

"Michelle!" Joanna grabbed her hand again and gave it a squeeze.

It was lifeless and clammy.

Joanna heard a rumble on the stairs and looked up to see Keith burst through the door. He had on his blue jumpsuit, a medical bag in his hand, his face pale. When their eyes locked, Keith released a breath, then hurried to Joanna's side.

"She's been beaten, and I think she's miscarrying," Joanna quickly explained.

Keith hunched down next to Michelle. "Joanna, you scared me to death. From your phone call, I thought it was you that needed help." Keith was talking to her, but looking at Michelle.

Keith's partner rushed into the room and took his place on the other side of Michelle. "Joanna, this is Rob; Rob, Joanna." Keith made introductions, while assessing Michelle's condition.

"Michelle, I'm Dr. Keith Michaels. I need to see what's going on here, okay?"

Michelle was unresponsive.

"She was hysterical when I got here and I thought she was going to hyperventilate," Joanna explained. "So I did what I could to calm her down. She stopped responding just before you–"

Joanna's voice cracked.

Keith put his hand over Joanna's, the one holding Michelle's. "It's okay, Joanna. You did great."

Joanna scooted out of the way, but didn't let go of Michelle's hand.

Keith pulled back the blanket, exposing Michelle's nakedness and her wounds. He moved Joanna's bloodied jacket out of the way as he continued to assess Michelle's condition. "How do you know her?" he asked.

"T.J. and I talked to her a few weeks ago about the murders. When I found out she was pregnant, I gave her a card for Horizon House and my phone number."

"Do you think she's using?" Keith questioned.

"I don't know. She didn't seem like the type."

Rob quickly checked her arms for drug use and pulled back the lids of her eyes. "Doesn't look like it," he said, as he hurried to set up an I.V.

Joanna grabbed a packet from Keith's medical bag and ripped it open with her teeth. Using the sterile piece of gauze, she mopped Michelle's forehead and cheeks.

Keith examined Michelle's pelvic area while Joanna kept her eyes riveted on Michelle's face. She continued to stroke Michelle's skin, trying to bring her comfort. When Joanna stole a glance at Keith, she whispered. "The baby?"

He shook his head somberly.

Joanna pushed back her tears and continued to wipe the damp cloth across Michelle's forehead.

T.J. ran into the room, out of breath, sweat glistening on his forehead. Joanna looked at him, tears running down her face. T.J. glanced quickly at Michelle, then back to Joanna. They spoke without saying a word. Joanna watched as his shoulders slumped and emotion twisted his face.

"What can I do?" T.J. asked.

"Help me with the gurney," Rob said.

"Yeah, sure thing."

Rob and T.J. disappeared into the hallway, leaving Joanna and Keith with Michelle.

"Is she going to be okay?" Joanna whispered to Keith.

"She's lost a lot of blood," was all he said.

There was a flurry of commotion when T.J. and Rob returned with the gurney. The four of them lifted Michelle onto the gurney; Joanna never let go of her hand. Keith and Rob readied Michelle for transport while T.J. stood out of the way.

By the time they were ready to leave, Michelle was conscious and sobbing. Joanna knew it wasn't from the pain, but because of her loss. She squeezed Michelle's hand, letting her know she was there.

"It's my fault. I should've gone. I should've done what you told me. It's my fault."

Joanna tried to calm her. "Michelle, this is not your fault. I'm sorry this happened, but it's not your fault."

"I killed my baby. I killed my baby." Michelle's weeping was more pronounced, causing her to become hysterical.

"Listen to me, Michelle. If you had wanted to kill your baby, you would've done it months ago. But you didn't."

"Then why? Why did I have to lose my baby?"

Joanna allowed silent tears to fall down her face as she looked intently into Michelle's eyes. "Michelle, I know you loved your baby, but so did God. You were headed for such a difficult road, maybe God in His incredible compassion decided He would care for your baby for you. He loves you, Michelle, and He wants to help you. He's not punishing you. He's reaching out to you. Let Him help you Michelle. Let God help you."

T.J. turned away, rocked by the situation.

Just a few weeks ago, he thought the girl would've been better off with an abortion. Now he found himself choked up because the baby was dead. The same baby he'd felt was a disposable inconvenience.

He felt repulsed with himself.

T.J. and Joanna followed behind Keith and Rob as they carried the gurney down the stairs. Outside the apartment a crowd gathered, everyone wondering if Michelle was another victim of the Prostitute Murderer. Two squad cars were there, the officers doing what they could to keep the crowd a healthy distance away. T.J. also spied Bristol and Barker out of his peripheral, leaning against their sedan, looking as if the whole scene was a waste of their time.

"Can I ride with her?" T.J. heard Joanna asked Keith.

"Yeah. Just give us a minute to get her hooked up."

T.J. held out his hand to Joanna. "Give me your keys. I'll take your car back to the station."

"Thanks, T.J." She handed him her keys but her attention was still on Michelle. When T.J. gave her hand a squeeze, she turned back to him.

"You going to be all right?" he asked.

Joanna stared at him, making him feel uncomfortable, like she could read his mind. "Yeah, but are you?" she asked, turning the tables on him.

"I'm fine. Just worried about you."

Her look told him she wasn't buying it. Before she could say anything more, Keith signaled for her to get in the ambulance.

"Call me if you need a ride," T.J. yelled, right before the ambulance doors were shut.

He watched as they pulled away, lights flashing, siren blaring, then walked over to where Bristol and Barker were standing.

"So was it our guy?" Bristol asked.

"No. It's not the right M.O. He's not going to strike in broad daylight."

"She's lucky," Barker said.

"Yeah," T.J. said sarcastically. "I'm sure that's exactly what she's thinking right now. That she's real lucky."

"Here, do me a favor." He tossed his keys to Barker. "Drive my truck back to the station."

T.J. walked over and got into Joanna's car. Sitting with his head against the headrest, his eyes focused on the ceiling; he stared at nothing, wishing he could feel the same.

After he felt like he had his emotions in check, he reached to buckled his seatbelt.

That's when he saw it.

A small black book wedged in the middle of the front seat. When he dug it out, he read the cover. <u>New Testament, Psalms and Proverbs</u>.

T.J. brushed his thumb across the lettering on the cover. Then, put it on the seat beside him before pulling away from the curb.

CHAPTER TWENTY-SIX

Joanna sat to the left of the gurney and did what she could to comfort Michelle. She stroked her pallid forehead and continued to use soothing words. But when Michelle's eyes fluttered shut and she stopped responding, Joanna looked at Keith.

Keith continued to work on Michelle. And though his words were calm and encouraging, Joanna could tell by the crease of his brow something wasn't right.

"What is it?" she asked.

Keith glanced at Joanna, then to the monitors.

"What is it? What's wrong?"

Before Keith could answer, the monitors hooked to Michelle went berserk. Keith became a blur of activity, while Joanna yelled at Michelle not to give up.

By the time they reached the hospital, Michelle was once again stable, but still unconscious. When Keith and Rob rolled Michelle through the emergency room entrance, a team of nurses and a doctor were waiting for them. Keith relayed Michelle's stats to the E.R. doctor before the gurney disappeared behind the two large white doors.

"I'm going to refill our supplies," Rob said as he left Joanna and Keith standing in the hallway.

Keith glanced at Joanna, but didn't make eye contact. After his initial conversation with her at the scene, he hadn't really spoken to her at all.

"You going to be okay?" Keith asked, sounding detached and cold.

"Yeah. I think I'll just wait here for a while and see if I can talk to her some more."

"Well, I have to go back out. I'm on shift today."

"I thought you were going to be off?" she asked quizzically.

"I picked up an extra shift since I had nothing else to do."

"Oh," Joanna said, feeling completely shut out. "Maybe we can talk later?"

"Maybe. But I don't have a lot of spare time right now. I leave in two weeks on our next trip, and I have a lot I still need to get done."

Joanna watched in silence as Keith walked away. She had never felt a brush off so cold and unfeeling before. Walking to a seat in the waiting room, she slowly sat down, feeling numb and dejected. She had no idea what had gone wrong between her and Keith, but it was obvious he was no longer interested.

When T.J. arrived at the hospital about an hour later, he was surprised to see Keith was still there. T.J. pulled into a parking slot reserved for police and emergency vehicles and got out. Keith looked at him from the back of the ambulance, but ignored him as he walked around the side of the vehicle.

T.J. followed. "Can I talk to you for a minute."

It wasn't really a question.

"I'm pretty busy," Keith answered back.

"I think you can make time for me," T.J. challenged.

Keith glanced at Rob. "I'll be right back. Go ahead and pull it over there." Rob got in the driver's side and pulled the ambulance to a designated parking zone.

Keith followed T.J. to a bench at the right of the emergency entrance but didn't sit down.

"What's this all about? I have a job to do." Keith's attitude was coarse, no longer the accommodating EMT technician of before. The hostility in his words only proved T.J.'s point. Keith was not the saint Joanna believed him to be.

"I wanted to talk to you about something before I spoke to Joanna."

"Hey, you know what," Keith threw up his hands in surrender and backed up a few steps, "she's all yours. I don't have time for this. End of discussion." Keith turned to walk away.

"What's that supposed to mean, lover boy?" T.J. snapped.

Keith stopped in his tracks.

T.J. could read the agitation in Keith's taunt shoulders and clenched fists. He didn't think—with Keith's beliefs and all—that he would throw a punch, but from the look on his face when he turned around, T.J. wasn't so sure. Besides, men were all the same, Christian or not. Find their weakness and they would pounce. With the anger mixed with frustration in Keith's eyes, it was obvious Joanna was his weakness.

"Look, I'm not going to play games, okay, "Keith said, his tone controlled but belligerent. "I asked Joanna point blank if you two had something going on. She told me no. But after what I walked in on the other night in her living room and what I saw yesterday, it's obvious she doesn't know what she wants. So, if you're asking me for some space, you've got it.

"She's all yours."

Keith walked away, almost reaching the passenger door of the ambulance when T.J. yelled. "Or maybe you know she'll eventually find out about your little run-in with the cops and she'll dump you anyway."

Keith stopped where he was, rage coloring his face. "Those charges were dropped, and you know it."

"So they were dropped. Charges are dropped all the time, but that doesn't mean the person is innocent. So, I thought I'd give you a chance to tell your side of the story. But since you're not interested in Joanna anymore, I guess it doesn't matter."

Keith stormed back to T.J., meeting him toe-to-toe. "I know she spent Saturday and Sunday with you. I saw you."

T.J. crossed his arms against his chest and spoke matter-of-factly. "True. She did. We're partners. We're going to spend a lot of time together."

"That's not what I mean, and you know it."

"So you don't trust her, is that what you're telling me?"

"I saw you two in church together. You were holding hands. Partners don't hold hands."

"You didn't answer the question." T.J.'s voice raised in agitation. "Do you or don't you trust her?"

"I trusted her when she said there was nothing going on between you, but seeing you two together yesterday let me know things have changed. Look, T.J.," Keith said with a conciliatory sigh. "I care for Joanna. I really do. But I'm no good at playing games. I take my relationships too serious for that."

T.J. could see Keith had feelings for Joanna. Genuine feelings. The old T.J. would've taken delight in breaking them up, showing Joanna she could be duped. But he couldn't do it. He wanted to protect Joanna, not hurt her.

So he decided to let Keith off the hook.

"Look, Joanna and I had a deal. She had to learn how to surf, and I had to go to church with her. I won't lie. Our feelings for each other was a topic of discussion over the weekend, but we decided it wouldn't work. I have too much garbage I have to work through in my life. Joanna and I are friends. *Good* friends. That's why I wanted to talk to you before I said anything to her."

Keith looked at him intensely. It was clear he didn't trust T.J. It was also clear by the resolve in his eyes, he had no choice but to tell T.J. what he wanted to hear. "Fine," Keith said. "What do you want to know?"

"You were charged with having sex with a minor. Is that true?"

"The charges were dropped. You know that."

"So, the charges were dropped. You could've had a good lawyer that got you off on some sort of technicality.

I'm asking you if it happened." T.J. clenched his jaw, preparing himself for the answer.

"No."

"Then why were charges filed in the first place? You had to have done something."

Keith walked back over to the bench and sat down. T.J. chose to remain standing. Keith steadied his elbows on his knees, his head hung low between his shoulders.

"Natalie was a girl in the youth group where I volunteered. Come to find out, she was struggling with some major issues at home. Anyway, I was taking a bunch of kids home in the church van that night–"

"Let me guess,' T.J. interrupted. "She was your last stop." He shook his head. "I would've thought you were smarter than that."

"But that's just it," Keith fired back. "I was always careful not to let a girl be my last stop. Natalie was supposed to be sleeping over at Heather's–another girl in the youth group. But when I pulled into Heather's drive, Natalie didn't get out. She told Heather she had decided to go home.

"After a few minutes of driving, Natalie moved from the bench seat in the back of the van to the passenger seat. She asked if we could pull over and talk for a minute, that what she had to say was private, and she didn't want anyone else to know. I asked if it could wait until the following day because I really needed to get her home, but she began to cry, saying she was afraid to go home.

"That's where I blew it."

Keith looked up at T.J. "I immediately assumed she was being abused at home and that was why she was afraid.

Even though I knew better, I pulled over. But I made sure we were in a clearly lit area, around the corner from her house.

"When she stopped crying, she told me she was pregnant and didn't know what to do. Her parents didn't even know she had a boyfriend. I told her she needed to go to them and be honest, but she started crying again and told me I didn't understand. I tried to calm her down, but she became angry. I told Natalie she needed to get counseling from someone more equipped to deal with her issues."

Keith paused, staring at his hands as he twisted them together. T.J. could tell he was reliving the event.

Keith looked up at T.J., and then to the ground. "She went ballistic. She started yelling and screaming, accusing me of being like her boyfriend. Saying we used girls and then threw them away. Natalie said some pretty horrific things before she got out of the van and ran home.

"It took me a minute to react, and when I did, I followed her in the van to make sure she made it home. When I saw her climb the steps to her house, I left.

"I drove back to the church parking lot to get my car; by the time I got to my apartment, there were two cop cars waiting for me." Keith leaned forward, his hands clenched together.

"Natalie told her parents I raped her.

"Apparently, before she went inside her house, she tore her clothes to look like she'd been attacked. Since she was clearly hysterical, her parents believed her. By the time the police talked to her, she had changed her story and said we'd had consensual sex, and it wasn't the first time. She obviously realized they were going to find out she was pregnant, and if she didn't change her story fast, there were going to be a lot more questions."

"So, I was jailed for having sex with a minor. But thankfully, her story didn't hold up long. She was interrogated three times, and each time her story changed. Then, one of her friends came forward and told Natalie's parents that Natalie was seeing another guy, and that she had already admitted to being pregnant. The police told Natalie she was going to have to take a lie detector test. That was it. She caved.

"She admitted I never touched her, that she was seeing another guy, and that she was three months pregnant. Her parents were horrified, the charges were dropped, and the church showed compassion toward everyone involved."

Keith looked at T.J. "So . . . now you know the truth. I never touched her. That's why the charges were dropped. I'm sure that's not the story you were looking for, but it's the truth." Keith massaged the back of his neck, his eyes locked on the pavement of the parking lot.

"Believe it or not," T.J. said. "I was hoping it was something like that. I wasn't looking forward to telling Joanna something I knew would hurt her."

"So, what *are* you going to tell her?" Keith asked, sounding wounded and dejected.

"What does it matter if you're not going to see her anymore?" T.J baited Keith, knowing he was still clearly interested in Joanna.

Keith didn't look up, but asked, "So there's no chance of you two getting together?"

"I wouldn't say 'no chance,' but I would say the chances are slim." T.J. was being honest. In the back of his mind, he didn't want to relinquish the idea of him and Joanna possibly having a relationship in the future.

Keith stood and walked towards the E.R. entrance instead of the ambulance that was waiting for him.

"Where you going?" T.J. yelled after him.

"I have some groveling to do," he said as the electric glass doors slid open.

"Hey, Keith, we have a call," Rob yelled from the ambulance. "A multi-car collision with fatalities."

With the lights flashing, Rob whipped the ambulance around towards the ER entrance and came to a screeching halt alongside Keith.

Keith turned to T.J. before getting into the ambulance. "I want to be the one to tell her.

"That is, if she'll even speak to me again."

CHAPTER TWENTY-SEVEN

T.J. glanced around the hospital waiting room. Joanna sat in the far corner with her head down. He was pretty sure she was praying. He walked across the waiting room and quietly took a seat next to her. She turned to look at him.

"Sorry," he said. "I didn't mean to interrupt."

"You're not." She leaned back in her chair, resting her head against the wall. "What are you doing here?"

"I figured you would eventually need a ride."

Joanna didn't say anything, she just stared straight ahead.

"Any news?" he asked.

Joanna pushed her hair back from her face with a sigh. "She's going to be okay."

They sat in a moment of silence, T.J. watching as Joanna fought to hold her emotions in check.

"Has anyone contacted her parents yet?" he asked.

Joanna shook her head. "She insists she doesn't want to see them. And since she didn't have any I.D. on her, there's no way to track them down. For all I know, she could've lied to me and Michelle isn't even her real name."

T.J. reached for Joanna's hand and squeezed it. "I'll go back to the scene. See what I can find out. I'll also run a check on any missing persons named Michelle or someone fitting her description."

"Thanks, T.J."

"No problem." He let go of Joanna's hand and got to his feet. "I'll call you if I find anything."

She just sat there, staring at her hands.

T.J. squatted down in front of her, tipping her chin up so he could look into her eyes. "Are you sure you're going to be okay? I could get someone else to do the digging while I stay here with you."

She attempted to smile. "I'll be fine."

"You'll call when you need a ride?"

"Sure."

Joanna had to wait a while longer before she was allowed to see Michelle. When she walked into the girl's room, she could hear her quietly crying. Joanna walked around the side of the bed.

"Hi, Michelle."

"Hi." Her voice was so childlike. With no make-up on, Joanna could see how really young she was—even with all the bruising on her face.

"How old are you, Michelle?"

"Fifteen."

"Michelle, I know your parents have to be worried about you. Won't you let me call them?"

"No!" Her words were abrupt and filled with fear. "I can't go back there. My mother hates me. Don't make me go back there."

Joanna realized it wasn't just fear in Michelle's tone—like any teenage runaway would feel when they knew they'd have to go home—but terror. Michelle had run away from home for a reason and Joanna had a sick feeling she knew what it was.

She sat on the edge of the bed while Michelle wiped away the tears in her eyes.

"Michelle, I want to help you. Do you believe me?" Joanna waited for the girl to look at her.

"Yes."

"So you trust me?"

"Yes."

"Then tell me why you ran away from home."

Michelle burst out crying again. "It wa . . . wasn't my fault. I tried . . . tried to stop him. But he was drunk and forced . . ." Michelle's sobbing cut off her words.

Joanna pulled Michelle into her arms and held her close. "Trust me, Michelle. I promise I won't let whoever hurt you do it again. But you have to tell me who it is."

Joanna held Michelle until she was able to calm down. Then she asked again. "Who are you afraid of, Michelle?"

"My step-dad."

Joanna waited until Michelle fell asleep before she left her room. She took a few deep breaths before talking to the nurse at the front desk. She could hear the anger in her voice, but she was doing her best to keep her composure.

After leaving explicit instructions with the nurse, she called T.J.

"Can you come pick me up?" she snapped.

"Sure, but what's wrong?"

"I'll explain when you get here."

It took T.J. fifteen minutes to get to the hospital. Joanna was pacing the breezeway when he got there. She got in the car and slammed the door.

"What's up?"

"We need to get an arrest warrant for Raymond Henderson."

"Who's he?"

"Michelle's step-dad.

"The child she was carrying was his. He raped her five months ago. When Michelle found out she was pregnant, she told her mother and her mother kicked her out of the house, calling Michelle a liar and a tramp. When Michelle went to Henderson, saying she was going to tell his boss, he threatened her. So, she asked for money for an abortion instead. That's what she's been living on. When the money ran out she was forced to turn to the streets."

"That would explain why we have no missing persons report," T.J. said.

"You got it. And why Michelle was too afraid to go home."

"What about today? What happened?"

"She picked up a guy that liked things rough. She told him she wasn't into that kind of stuff, so he got even rougher. When she started to hemorrhage, he split. That's when she called me."

"Can she identify him?"

"Not really. She said he was older. Dressed nice. Tall. But she never got a good look at his face. He approached her, asked if she was available, and followed her up the stairs. Once inside, the apartment was too dark for her to see anything else."

"Back to Henderson," T.J. asked. "How do you know she'll press charges? If he threatened her once, he'll do it again."

"Because she has a brother and an eleven-year-old sister at home, and she's afraid the same thing will happen to her."

They worked the rest of the day and into the night trying to secure a warrant, but it was harder than usual. Henderson was a lawyer and belonged to a prestigious law firm. His stellar reputation in the law community made it difficult to find a judge willing to overlook who Henderson was. But T.J. pulled in some favors and finally got the ball rolling.

Joanna went home and changed out of her bloodied clothes before she went back to the hospital to take Michelle's formal statement.

Joanna arranged for Irene Kemper–a psychologist from Horizon House–to be present during Michelle's interview. Even though she felt Michelle trusted her, she was still a cop; that could be scary to a fifteen-year-old girl who had adults in her life shatter her trust. Joanna wanted to make sure Michelle knew she had an advocate on her side.

Irene introduced herself to Michelle and explained she did not work for the police but was there to support her. She further explained to Michelle that the questions Joanna would be asking would be very personal in nature, even embarrassing, and that it was very important she be specific and not withhold any information. Irene also assured Michelle that if she felt uncomfortable, pressured, or confused, she could stop the interview at any time.

Joanna was glad Irene was there. Her reputation as an advocate for victims was stellar. Irene knew how important it was for Michelle to feel a sense of control during the interviewing process. Rape was not only a sexual crime, but a psychological one as well. Michelle's step-father had stripped her of any control. To return control back to Michelle was very important in order for her to cooperate.

For the most part, the interview went well. At times, Michelle would freeze up. But Irene did a great job of calming her down and getting her to reconnect with Joanna. At one point, Michelle became defensive because Joanna had repeated some of the same questions. Irene assured Michelle it wasn't because Joanna didn't believe her; she just needed to make sure she had the facts straight before an arrest could be made.

Just after midnight, with an arrest warrant in hand, T.J. came to the hospital and picked up Joanna. When she was getting into the car, she noticed Bristol and Barker pull up behind them.

"Are we expecting trouble?" she asked.

"Not necessarily. I just wasn't sure where your head would be."

"What's that supposed to mean?" she snapped. "Are you saying you don't think I can handle my job?"

T.J. kept his attention on the flow of traffic. "Let's just say you're a little more involved in this case than you probably should be."

"So you *don't* think I can handle it! Thanks a whole heck of a lot! So nice to know you have such a low opinion of me."

"That's not what I meant and you know it, so stop trying to pick a fight with me."

Joanna stared out the passenger window, knowing she needed to get herself under control before they reached the Henderson's.

"So are you going to tell me how it went?"

Joanna shook her head. "Michelle told her mother about the rape, but she refused to believe her."

"Why?"

"Because Henderson's rich. She was tired of being a single parent struggling from paycheck to paycheck. She wasn't about to give up her new lifestyle. So she told Michelle if she didn't like the living arrangements she could leave."

T.J. clenched his jaw. "So her mother did nothing about it?"

"Nope. I guess Michelle blamed her mother when her father walked out on them two years ago. So her mother accused her of trying to sabotage her new marriage.

"Michelle said she did everything she could to stay out of Henderson's way. But when her mother went out of town on a retreat, Henderson came home drunk that night and raped her. When Michelle told her mother, even showed her the bruises on her body, Henderson said she was lying. Said she'd made the whole thing up to cover her own wild behavior."

T.J. chanced a look at Joanna. "Don't hate me for

asking, but do you think Michelle could be lying to you?"

"No way." Joanna shook her head. "If you could've seen the fear in her eyes, T.J., you wouldn't be asking."

T.J. maneuvered through a high-end neighborhood, then pulled into a beautifully lit circular driveway. Bristol and Barker pulled in behind them. When T.J. got out of the car, he walked over to Joanna and stood directly in front of her. "Are you going to be able to handle this?"

"Absolutely. I wouldn't think of doing anything to jeopardize this arrest."

"Good girl."

T.J. knocked on the door firmly. There were lights on throughout the house—even at this late hour—but no one answered. He looked at Joanna then knocked again with the side of his fist. A moment later the lock clicked and the door opened cautiously. A tall, distinguished looking man answered the door. He wore dress slacks and a designer shirt, his tie loose around his neck.

"Yes?"

"Are you Raymond Henderson?" T.J. asked bluntly.

"Yes. What's this about?"

"I'm Detective Owens and this is Detective Anderson. I have a warrant for your arrest. If you'll come with me, you can call your lawyer from the Twenty-seventh Precinct. Unless you decide to represent yourself."

"This is preposterous. I'm not going anywhere with you without an explanation."

"I just told you, I have a warrant. You *will* be coming with us." T.J. took a step forward.

"What's going on?" A woman's voice drifted from the house. She stood beside Henderson—tying the sash on her silk robe—and demanded an explanation.

"Are you Mrs. Henderson?" T.J. asked while Joanna struggled to even look at her.

"Yes."

"You have a daughter named Michelle Brown?" T.J. asked.

"Well, yes, but Michelle doesn't live here anymore."

"Well, of course she doesn't," Joanna said, doing nothing to hide her sarcasm. "You kicked her out of the house two months ago."

The woman brought her hand up to her chest; acting horrified by Joanna's accusation. When she realized nobody was fooled, her eyes turned vicious.

"Michelle is no longer welcome in this house because of her illicit behavior."

"Then you should have kicked him out, too." T.J. turned Henderson around and slapped handcuffs on him. "Your husband is being arrested for the rape of Michelle Brown. We're taking him to the Twenty-seventh Precinct. You might want to call his lawyer."

"But I *am* a lawyer!" Henderson shouted.

"Then I'll be sure to read your Miranda rights nice and slow so there's no room for error."

T.J. led Henderson down the stairs and to the back of their sedan. Joanna turned to Mrs. Henderson and said, "In case you are wondering where Michelle is, she's at Mercy Hospital. She was beaten up earlier tonight, because the guy who paid to have sex with her liked it rough."

Joanna walked away, leaving Mrs. Henderson standing with her mouth hanging open.

CHAPTER TWENTY-EIGHT

T.J. decided it would be best if he was the one to question Mr. Henderson. Though Joanna argued, she finally agreed. He had more experience—and at the moment—a cooler head on his shoulders. So Joanna conceded to watch from the observation room.

T.J. was introduced to Donald Carter—Henderson's attorney—before taking his seat. Carter looked pretty sharp for two in the morning, putting T.J. on alert. He would have to be on his best behavior and do everything by the book.

He proceeded to ask Henderson a litany of questions. Mr. Carter interjected legalese or conferred with his client before allowing him to answer a single one. Finally, T.J. had enough. He stood so quick, his chair shot out from under him and crashed into the wall. Slamming his hand down on the desk, T.J. hollered. "Let's cut the crap here. You came home drunk. You raped Michelle when nobody was in the house. Then, you threatened her, telling her you would do the same thing to her sister if she told anyone."

"Michelle has quite the imagination, doesn't she?" Henderson said coolly.

"Well, her *imagination* got five hundred dollars out of you for an abortion," T.J. said matter-of-factly.

"That? She told me she needed the money for some camp thing she was going to. She was having an argument with her mother at the time so she came to me. I thought I was being the nice guy. I had no idea she would try to use it against me."

T.J. wanted to punch the guy. He acted so calm and collected, like they were discussing something of little importance.

"You have nothing on my client. You're just phishing. I demand he be released."

"We want a DNA sample before we release him," T.J. informed them both.

"What for?" Mr. Carter demanded.

"Michelle Brown was raped earlier today. She said it was her step-dad who did it. That he was punishing her for running away. We need a DNA sample to confirm or deny her allegations."

"No! Absolutely not!" Henderson answered tersely. "I have an image to uphold. I can't let my reputation be questioned by submitting to such scrutiny."

"Fine. But you know as well as I do that I can hold you for forty-eight hours on probable cause. What do you think *that* would do to your reputation?"

Mr. Carter leaned towards Mr. Henderson and whispered. He then looked at T.J. "I need a few moments alone with my client."

T.J. left the room, knowing by what he saw in

Henderson's eyes, he was guilty as sin.

Joanna stepped from the observation room due to attorney-client privileges.

"You lied. Henderson had nothing to do with Michelle's attack today and you know it."

"Hey . . . all's fair in the interrogation room."

"But I don't understand. Why accuse him of something you know he had nothing to do with?"

"He thinks Michelle had an abortion months ago and he knows he didn't rape Michelle today. Henderson thinks he's in the clear; we won't be able to match his DNA to Michelle's assault. But what he doesn't know is we can match it to the DNA of Michelle's fetus."

Joanna squeezed her eyes shut. "You mean baby. Michelle was carrying a baby."

"I'm sorry, Joanna. Her baby."

"So what do you think he's talking to his lawyer about?"

"I think he's telling him the truth. He's admitting to raping Michelle. But since he thinks she had an abortion months ago, he's asking his attorney if there is any way his DNA will be found on Michelle."

The door to the interrogation room opened. "You can come back in Detective Owens," Mr. Carter said smugly.

Joanna went back to the viewing room.

Mr. Carter paced the interrogation room as if he was in court. "Mr. Henderson has decided to submit to a DNA test, as long as it is held in the strictest of confidence. He sees no reason why his reputation should be dragged through the mud on account of his step-daughter and her rebellious behavior."

T.J. pressed the intercom button next to the door. "Detective Anderson, would you please have the crime lab technician come to interrogation room three."

Joanna went and got Sonya Ortiz. They had asked her to be on standby in case Henderson consented.

T.J. introduced Sonya when she walked into the interrogation room.

In a matter of seconds, she had swabbed the inside of Mr. Henderson's cheek, then left.

"Now you realize, Mr. Henderson's submission is to be held in the strictest of confidence." Carter wagged his finger at T.J. "If I even here a hint of a rumor regarding this, I will sue this department so fast you—"

T.J. quickly cut him off. "Don't tell us how to do our job, Mr. Carter. We are well aware of Mr. Henderson's rights. Believe me, we're not going to do anything to jeopardize Michelle Brown's case."

A look passed between the attorney and his client, the cocky smile slipping from Henderson's face.

"I see no reason for my client to remain in custody. He's cooperated with you completely. I want him released into—"

"Save your breath, Carter. Henderson isn't going anywhere."

T.J. watched as Joanna paced like a cougar in a cage. Neither of them had gone home last night, Joanna refusing to leave the station until the DNA tests were confirmed.

"Go ahead and check in on Michelle. I'll call you the minute the results are in."

"Are you sure?"

"Yeah, I'm sure."

Joanna prayed all the way to the hospital.

She prayed for Michelle's fragile heart and that God would make Himself known to her. When she got there, she was surprised to see Michelle's mother waiting in the corridor. Joanna had no intention of giving the woman the time of day, so she walked right by her without saying a word.

"They won't let me see my own daughter because of you."

Joanna stopped in her tracks and turned around. "That's right. I didn't want anything to interfere with Michelle's recovery."

"You can't do that! I'm her mother."

"I can! And I did!" Joanna turned to walk away.

Mrs. Henderson grabbed Joanna's arm and yanked her around. "Who do you think you are?"

Joanna jerked her arm free from the woman and got in her face. "I'm the cop your daughter turned to because her mother called her a tramp and kicked her out of the house. I'm the woman who held Michelle's battered and bleeding body because she had to turn to the streets to survive. So, if you have something to say to me lady, bring it on. The way I see it, you're an accomplice to your husband's despicable crime. And if I have any say in it, you'll be going to jail, too."

The woman glared at her. "I wouldn't hold my breath."

Joanna took a step towards the woman, but before she

could do anything, Keith appeared of nowhere and stepped between her and Michelle's mother. With his hands on her waist, he gently pushed Joanna back, putting some distance between the two women.

"Come on, Joanna, leave it alone," Keith whispered, trying to calm her.

"You saw her, right? You saw her threaten me," Mrs. Henderson barked at Keith. "That's police harassment."

"Lady," he turned to face the woman. "I saw you yank Detective Anderson's arm. In my book that's assault. So I don't think you want to make an issue out of this, because I'll tell the cops exactly what I saw."

With his hand pressed to the small of her back, Keith walked Joanna over to an alcove on the far side of the hall. "You need to calm down, Joanna. Picking a fight with the girl's mother isn't going to do any good."

"Her name's Michelle," she snapped.

Joanna walked back and forth with her hands on her head and her eyes closed, trying to calm herself. "What are you doing here, anyway?" she asked Keith.

"I wanted to talk to you about something. I called the station. T.J. told me you were here."

"So, what did you want to talk about?"

"It can wait. Right now, you need to calm down before you make another scene."

Keith leaned against the wall and waited Joanna out. "So, what was that all about, anyway?" Keith asked.

"Michelle's step-dad raped her, and her mother sided with him. She sacrificed her own daughter because she didn't want to lose her rich husband. Can you believe that?"

Keith didn't have a chance to answer before Joanna turned to the sound of clacking heels behind her.

"I want to see my daughter," Michelle's mother insisted.

"Fine," Joanna spat back. "But you're not going in there alone. If you upset Michelle in the least or she asks you to leave, you're out of there." Joanna took a step, when Keith stopped her. Bending his head down close to hers, he spoke softly but his words were stern. "Keep a cool head, Joanna. Don't do anything that's going to get you in trouble."

Joanna looked at the concern in Keith's eyes. "I'll behave. I promise." She did her best to give him a reassuring smile.

The woman followed Joanna to Michelle's room. "Wait here," Joanna snapped.

Joanna pushed the door open and quietly crept into the room. Michelle turned to look at her.

"How are you feeling this morning?" Joanna asked.

"Horrible," Michelle said, pressing her fingers to her swollen lip.

Joanna walked closer. "How do you feel about seeing your mother?"

Michelle's eyes froze in place. "She's here? How did she know I was here?"

"I told her."

"You told her! What about him?"

"He's in jail, and you don't have to see your mother if you don't want to."

"What does she want?"

"She says she wants to see you."

"Well, I don't want to see her. I just want to know where Marci and Mark are. I want to know my brother and sister are okay."

Joanna knew Michelle was terrified on behalf of her sister and brother. Unfortunately, she didn't have any answers for her. "I don't know where they are. But you could ask your mother. I won't leave, Michelle. I'll be here the whole time if that's what you're worried about."

"I just want to make sure Marci's okay. That he hasn't done something to her."

"Okay, I'll let her in, but you say the word and she's out of here."

Joanna walked to the door and pushed it open. "She said she'll see you."

"I knew she would," the woman huffed, and pushed past Joanna.

Joanna looked at Keith still standing in the hall. "Are you going to be here for a while?" she asked, wanting to talk to him.

"As long as I don't get a call," he answered with half a smile.

Joanna closed the door and saw that Michelle's mother hadn't approached the bed. She wore a look of shock as she stared at her bruised and beaten daughter. When she finally got up the nerve to step closer to her daughter's bedside, Michelle just glared at her.

"I want to see Marci. I want to make sure she's okay."

"She's in school. And she's fine," Mrs. Henderson answered curtly.

"How do you know that? You wouldn't have believed her even if she had told you something. Just like you didn't believe me."

"Now, Michelle, don't start that. I know you don't like Raymond. But these lies you've told about him are going to get you in serious trouble."

"You still don't believe me, do you, Mom?"

The woman looked at her hands.

"He gave me money for an abortion," Michelle said, her tone pleading for her mother to believe her.

"He told me about that. He said you'd gotten yourself pregnant by some boy, and he was only trying to help. He was hoping you'd see him as an ally instead of the enemy."

"And you believed him. You believed him over me. Why?"

The woman's look was cool and controlled. "Michelle, I don't think we want to get into this right now."

"Why? Why won't you believe me?"

"Because you were looking for trouble!" The woman raised her voice and then quickly gathered her composure. "The way you were dressing, and the friends you were hanging out with. It was only a matter of time before someone took you up on what it was you were offering in your short shorts and skimpy tops."

"Yeah, your husband!" Michelle shouted back, then broke down.

"You're just saying that to get back at me. You still blame me for your father leaving. You've ruined your life, and now you're trying to ruin what I've worked so hard to get."

Michelle got a cold, mean, look on her face and wiped the tears from her cheeks. "I don't care if you believe me or not, all I care about is Marci and Mark. I won't let him do to them what he did to me. You think you're doing the right thing by standing by your man. Well, how are you going to look when he's proven guilty and people find out you had the power to stop him, and you didn't? That you sacrificed your own children for a rich lifestyle. I'm not ruining your life Mom. You are."

The woman had nothing left to say. She stormed from the room allowing silence to rest on Michelle and Joanna. Joanna walked to Michelle's bed and reached for her hand. "You're going to make it Michelle. And I promise not to let anything happen to your brother and sister."

"What happens now?" Michelle asked, looking helpless.

"Mr. Henderson has agreed to a DNA screening."

"Why would he do that?"

"He doesn't know about the baby, Michelle. He thinks you had the abortion. He thinks we're trying to charge him for the attack on you yesterday. He's going down, Michelle. He won't be able to hurt anyone anymore."

Michelle's eyes welled up, and she clutched her abdomen. "What happens to my baby now?"

"We can have a service for her," Joanna said through her own tears. "If you'd like."

Michelle nodded, bursting into tears. Joanna allowed Michelle to cry. She needed to get it out. She needed to grieve.

Joanna sat with Michelle for some time, going over the details for the baby's service, her case, and her future. When Michelle drifted off to sleep, Joanna slipped out of the room, feeling wiped out.

She glanced up and down the corridor looking for

Keith.

Her shoulders were heavy as she walked to her car alone.

CHAPTER TWENTY-NINE

T.J. saw Joanna as she entered the War Room. She looked beat. He brought her a cup of water and waited for her to sit down, but she didn't. She was too agitated.

"Where are we?" she asked, needing to get caught up.

"Henderson's out on bail."

Joanna was ready to pounce, but T.J. raised his hand, stopping her long enough for him to explain what she already knew. "Until we get back the DNA results, we have nothing to hold him on. It's his word against hers."

"Then we need to get Child Protective Services over to his house and get Michelle's sister and brother out of there right away."

"We're already on it, Joanna."

"Good. What now?"

"We wait."

Joanna closed her eyes in frustration.

"Have you eaten anything today?" T.J. asked.

"I'm not hungry."

"That's not what I asked. Come on, let's get out of here and go get something to eat."

T.J. gave Joanna a nudge towards the door, while asking Peck to call them the minute things were ready. He could tell Joanna really didn't want to go, but she didn't have the energy to argue. They both climbed into T.J.'s truck and headed around the corner to the coffee shop.

T.J. ordered a burger and fries. Joanna opted for just the fries. Their drinks came, and Joanna played with the straw in her ice tea.

"What are you thinking?" T.J. asked as he fiddled with the saltshaker.

"Michelle wants a service for her baby."

T.J. nodded.

Joanna continued to stare into her drink, talking out loud, but not really talking to him. "She's going to have a tough time of it. She doesn't want to go back to school. She's too embarrassed by what she's done. She's thinking about getting her GED. She doesn't want to go home. Even if Henderson isn't there."

The waitress brought their food and asked if there was anything else she could get them. When she left, Joanna continued.

"I thought maybe she could stay with me for a while. Until she has a plan and gets back on her feet."

T.J. swallowed hard and reached for her hand. He leaned in close across the table and quietly spoke to her, hoping to be the voice of reason. "Joanna, that's not a good idea, and you know it."

She tried to refute him but he persisted.

"I know you feel a connection with Michelle. But it

wouldn't work. Even if she's the victim in all this, you know nothing about her. Her friends. Her habits. Her behavior."

"She's hurting, T.J. She needs to know someone cares." Joanna's tone was determined.

"I know. So why not that Horizon House place?"

Joanna looked up at him and glared. "I thought you didn't like places like that. You know . . . do-gooders with tunnel vision, blinded by their cause."

He sighed, knowing Joanna was using his own words against him. "Okay, I deserve that. But like you said, she's hurting and she's going to have a lot of issues to work through. Michelle will need professional help for that, Joanna. People who are trained. By all means, I think you should stay in contact with her, help her, and be her friend. Just leave the rest of it to the professionals."

Joanna knew T.J. was right. As much as she wanted to believe she could help Michelle, the girl was going to need a lot more help than she could provide. She would talk to Michelle tomorrow and see what she thought about a place like Horizon House. In the meantime, she'd call the director and see if they had the space and the resources for Michelle's situation.

Joanna smiled at T.J., thankful for his input. She fiddled with her fries, eating them one at a time.

"So, have you been able to talk to Keith at all today?" T.J. asked.

"Not really. But I get the impression maybe things weren't going as well between us as I thought."

"Why do you say that?"

"When we transported Michelle to the hospital, he was very aloof. He acted like he didn't want to talk to me."

"He probably was just in work mode."

"Maybe." She pushed her fries over to T.J. so he could finish them, then sat back against the booth. "He showed up at the hospital just in time to keep me from decking Mrs. Henderson."

"What?" T.J. looked at Joanna in shock. "Tell me you didn't do anything stupid."

"Gee, thanks for the vote of confidence."

"Joanna, you didn't–"

"Don't worry. Nothing happened. She didn't like me ignoring her so she got in my face. Well, I got right back in hers. That's when Keith stepped in and made sure I calmed down."

"Good thing someone was thinking clearly," T.J. added as he pushed the extra fries around in a pile of ketchup. "So, was he there to see you?"

"I don't know. When I was done with Michelle, he was gone." Joanna saw the perplexed look on T.J.'s face and knew something was up. "Why all the questions about Keith?" She stared at him intently. "You know something, don't you?"

T.J. leaned back against the booth and rubbed the back of his neck, clearly uncomfortable. "Keith saw us in church on Sunday."

"What?"

"He saw us holding hands. He figured you changed your mind about me . . . and about him."

"He told you that? He just walked up to you and said

he was no longer interested?"

"Actually, I approached him about something else. But the bottom line was, he wasn't going to play games and that if we had a thing going on, he was bowing out."

Joanna slumped in the booth and thought back to how Keith had acted at the hospital. It explained a lot. "So, you set him straight, right?"

"Actually, I told the guy off for not trusting you. Then I set him straight."

"Saying?" Joanna wanted to know exactly what T.J. had said.

"I told him we were partners and good friends, nothing more."

"And he believed you?" Joanna prodded.

"Yeah."

Joanna stared at her silverware, running her finger up and down the handle of the fork.

"What are you thinking, Joanna?"

"This is why I don't have a personal life," she blurted out, clearly frustrated. "It's too complicated. There are too many unanswered questions and misunderstandings. Missed signals. Misinterpreted signals and unspoken expectations. It's just too much."

She crunched on an ice cube and then continued. "You know, I've bagged on you for your womanizing, going from one woman to the next. No ties. No commitments. Maybe I was wrong. Maybe you've got the right idea. If you don't get serious with any one person, you can't get hurt."

T.J stopped her before she could continue. "Don't talk like that, Joanna. I've made a mess of my life, and now I realize because of my reputation, I'll never find a woman like you."

T.J.'s confession surprised her. He sounded like he'd been doing some soul-searching and was beginning to see he needed to change things.

"So, give Keith a chance. I know he cares for you, and I know you care for him. You just have to know he's still a man. He's protective, jealous and insecure. Just like the rest of us."

CHAPTER THIRTY

Joanna finally dragged herself home after thirty-six hours without sleep. She had made sure she was present when Child Protective Services showed up at the Henderson house to take Marci and Mark into protective custody. The lack of emotion on their faces at having to leave their mother chilled Joanna. Something wasn't right. What child willingly left their mother?

A child that was abused.

Joanna could only pray they didn't have stories of their own to tell.

Later that day, Joanna was with Marci and Mark when they went to visit Michelle. For the first twenty minutes they did nothing but cry and hug. Mark and Marci cried because their sister was beat up and in the hospital, but Michelle cried tears of joy knowing her brother and sister were safe. No one talked about the abuse. That would be up to the psychologist assigned to the case. For the moment they were just thankful to be together and away from their step-father . . . and mother.

Joanna and T.J. worked long and hard to make sure the Henderson case was getting through all the proper channels as quickly as possible. Joanna wasn't going to rest until she knew Henderson was behind bars.

When she finally got home, Joanna closed the garage door, stepped into her house, and collapsed on the couch. Never had she felt so drained—physically, psychologically, and emotionally.

She must have fallen asleep, because the sound of the answering machine picking up her phone, stirred her. "Hi, it's Keith. I thought you'd—"

Joanna scrambled for the phone. "Hi, Keith."

"Screening your calls?" he joked.

"No, I must've fallen asleep. I didn't even hear the phone ring."

"So, I guess you're pretty tired."

"Not too tired for company," she volunteered.

"So, you wouldn't mind if I came over for a little while?"

"No, not at all. In fact, I really wouldn't mind if you came over and happened to have a half-gallon of cookie dough ice cream with you."

He chuckled. "Okay then, I'll see you in about twenty minutes."

Joanna got up from the couch and jogged upstairs. She pulled off her jeans and t-shirt then jumped into the shower. She knew she would have to be quick, but she needed it to help wash away the emotions of the last two days.

After running a brush through her hair and pulling on a pair of her nicer workout pants, Joanna grabbed a t-shirt from her dresser and hurried downstairs.

She looked around her house, making sure it was presentable. She straightened pillows and dusted tabletops with the palm of her hand. A knock brought her frenzy to a stop. Joanna opened the door and smiled.

Keith wore a pair of relaxed jeans and a tight-fitting t-shirt with his department logo on it. His eyes looked bluer and held more feeling than she'd ever seen before.

He stepped into the house, but before Joanna could even close the door, he pulled her close and pressed a take-your-breath-away kiss to her lips. When he finally pulled back, he looked at her and smiled. "I didn't think I'd get a chance to do that again."

She looked at him wanting him to know she felt the same way. "I'm glad you did."

"I'm sorry for the way I spoke to you at the hospital. I was having some real issues that I've been told were unnecessary."

Joanna's smiled. "T.J. told me you two talked." She took the grocery bag Keith was holding and walked to the kitchen. Keith followed.

"What all did he tell you?" he asked.

"That you saw us in church and got the wrong impression." Joanna pulled the carton of ice cream from the bag and removed the lid.

"Is that all?" he pursued further.

"He said I should be angry at you for not trusting me."

"He's right," Keith conceded.

"I was mad at the start. Angry you were so willing to dump me."

"Is that what T.J. said? Because I never said that. I just

told him I wasn't going to play games. And if he was going to make a play for you, I knew I couldn't compete."

She handed him a bowl of ice cream. "Living room or deck?"

"Living room's fine."

They walked over to the couch together and sat down side by side.

"So you're not mad at me?"

"It takes too much energy to be mad." Joanna slid a spoonful of ice cream in her mouth and moaned, clearly enjoying it.

They each ate their ice cream in a companionable silence. When Keith was finished with his, he set his bowl on the coffee table. "Sorry I wasn't at the hospital when you were ready to leave."

"I understand. You have a job to do."

"So, where do things stand with Michelle?"

Joanna explained all the steps that had been taken to ensure Michelle's recovery, and the safety of her brother and sister. When Joanna was done with her ice cream, she set her bowl next to his. Folding her feet up under her, she sat back against the cushions of the couch.

"Tell me about your day." She smiled.

"Actually, I'd like to talk about something else."

She sat up straighter at his serious tone. "Sure . . . what?"

"It's kind of a long story, but I want you to know about it. It doesn't affect us, at least I hope not. T.J. found it in my record, and I didn't want you to stumble across it someday or be taken by surprise."

She'd stopped listening as soon as he'd said the word

'record.' "You have a record?"

"No, I didn't mean record. I guess I meant 'file.' Well, wherever you would look to find out information about people that had charges against them dropped."

"You were charged with something?"

"Joanna, let me explain, okay? Then, if you have any questions, we can talk about them."

Keith spent the next hour explaining to Joanna about Natalie and the charges that had been filed against him. And how they had been eventually dropped.

Joanna sat dumbstruck through most of it, letting Keith talk uninterrupted. When he was done, he waited for her to say something. Joanna couldn't imagine how hard it must have been for Keith and his mother to sit by while someone accused him of such a heinous crime.

"That must have been devastating for you and your mother," she finally said, sympathetically.

"It was horrible.

"I was fingerprinted, had mug shots taken, and spent the night in jail. My mother was beside herself not knowing what to do to get me out. Finally, one of the elders stepped forward at the prodding of the pastor. Pastor Thomas tried to remain neutral in the situation, but he knew me well enough to know I would've never done such a thing. The elder helped my mother with the bail, and I was released the next day. Two days later, the charges were dropped. I was just thankful Natalie had told someone else about being pregnant. If Donna hadn't come forward, things could have gotten really ugly. As it was, the whole church knew about it, but because of the quick dismissal, people understood I was wrongly accused.

"Well, most people."

"Were there still people at your church that thought you were guilty?"

"Yeah. A handful of people left. Some even blamed the pastor for not having more control over his congregation. They felt if he'd been doing his job as a spiritual leader, none of it would have happened."

"They were living in the clouds," Joanna chided.

"I know. But eventually things returned to normal. That was seven years ago, but every once in a while I still think of what could've happened." Keith looked at Joanna. "So, are you horrified?"

She sat up straighter. "Absolutely not. You didn't do anything wrong."

"I know. But it's still not a very pretty story to have to tell someone you care about."

"Well, I'm glad you told me. Not that I would've done a background check on you like T.J. did. But, I have to admit, it would've been shocking if it came up without me knowing about it."

Keith leaned back on the couch, clearly relieved. "So, how was surfing?"

Joanna's eyes popped. "I guess you two talked about a lot?"

"T.J. told me about the deal you struck. You had to learn to surf; he had to go to church."

Joanna smiled at the memory. "It was fun. A lot of work, but fun. Even the fact that I almost drowned wouldn't stop me from doing it again."

Keith raised an eyebrow. "He also said the topic of you two getting together came up."

"What was T.J. doing, spilling my guts for me?" she said, trying to hide her surprise with humor. When she saw that Keith wasn't laughing she got serious.

"Keith, I have feelings for T.J., I admit it. But it's not what you think. I care for him a lot. That's why I made a deal with him. I wanted to get him to come to church. I wanted him to hear what Pastor Grant had to say about life and where Christ fit into the equation, and it worked. T.J. listened. Really listened. I just want him to know there's more to life than women, drinking, partying and going home lonely. Do you understand?"

"Yeah, I understand. It's just you spend so much time with him already. What's to say if he starts changing, your feelings for him won't deepen. Then what?"

Joanna stared at her hands, thinking about what Keith was asking. She wondered if she could even be certain of the answer. He brushed back the hair from her face, pushing it behind her ear. He tipped her chin up so he could look at her eye-to-eye.

"I leave at the end of the month, and I'll be gone for two weeks. I just need to know if we should wait until I get back before we start a relationship. Maybe we need to give this a little more time."

Joanna knew at that exact moment what she wanted. She leaned forward and kissed Keith passionately.

Their kiss lingered, but when Joanna finally spoke, her voice was whisper soft. "I'd like to know where we stand before you go, so I have something to look forward to when you come home."

Keith pulled Joanna into his arms to show her he felt exactly the same way.

CHAPTER THIRTY-ONE

The week had been full of highs and lows, leaving Joanna short on sleep.

The DNA results had come back positive, proving Henderson had fathered Michelle's baby. Knowing there was no way he could refute such evidence, Henderson changed his story. He now claimed he and Michelle had engaged in consensual sex.

He explained that on the night in question, he'd come home from an office party, admittedly inebriated. He insisted Michelle took advantage of his impaired condition and seduced him. He went on to explain that Michelle blackmailed him in exchange for her silence. He insisted the five hundred dollars he'd given Michelle was only the first of many times she'd demanded money from him. When he refused to give her anymore, she changed her tactics and accused him of rape.

Henderson was very convincing, leaving Joanna to defend Michelle to others who decided to weigh in on the case. Though others were being swayed, Joanna knew Michelle wasn't lying. She'd seen firsthand the fear and terror in Michelle's eyes when talking about her stepfather and what he had done to her. The panic Michelle had displayed regarding her sister and brother's safety was palatable. It wasn't until she'd seen Marci and Mark with her own eyes that Michelle had finally been able to calm down.

Joanna knew Michelle was not the master manipulator Henderson was making her out to be. But that didn't make it any easier on Michelle when Henderson's arrest made front page news.

When the story hit *The Daily Reporter*, Henderson turned the tables on Michelle and portrayed himself as the victim. He claimed—in a moment of poor judgment—he'd succumbed to Michelle's seductions. Admitting his actions were inexcusable, Henderson argued it was his impaired condition that had allowed him to make the mistake of a lifetime. He'd even proceeded to tell the reporter that when he refused Michelle's continued overtures, she'd left home, and now prostituted herself on the streets.

Joanna saw right through Henderson's act. He was showing how easily he could discredit Michelle in the eyes of the public. The same public the jury pool would be drawn from. He was using intimidation to bully her, victimizing her all over again.

And it worked.

When Michelle learned what Henderson was saying about her, she told Joanna to drop the charges. She was terrified to face Henderson in court, convinced she couldn't win. It would be a case of he said—she said. And what juror would believe her—a prostitute—over a prominent attorney?

But Joanna explained to Michelle, that even if she dropped the charges, the state would have no choice but to prosecute Henderson. The DNA results proved he had engaged in sexual relations with a minor. Consensual or not, it was still statutory rape. Henderson would be convicted, but his sentence could be diminished to probation with minimal or no jail time. If he was convicted of forcible or aggravated rape, his jail time would be greatly increased, and Michelle would be exonerated of his vicious lies. At least in the eyes of the law.

After a very long, emotional conversation, Joanna had convinced Michelle not to withdraw her charges.

Michelle was going to stand up against Henderson.

Someone had to.

Before Michelle was released from the hospital, Joanna arranged a private service for her baby in the hospital's chapel. She knew it was important for Michelle to have some closure before she could move on. Joanna was touched when Michelle told her she'd named her baby after her. Anna Marcella.

Joanna, along with Marci and Mark, stood next to Michelle as she said a tearful good-bye to her daughter. Both T.J. and Keith had offered to be there for emotional support, but Joanna convinced them she'd be okay. Besides, it wasn't about her, it was about Michelle. She didn't want her to feel uncomfortable.

After leaving the hospital, Michelle moved into Horizon House. She was disappointed when she found out Mark and Marci could not stay with her. She begged and pleaded, but Irene, the director of Horizon House, explained that it just wasn't possible.

Knowing Michelle's emotional state was key to her recovery, Irene worked tirelessly on Michelle's behalf to keep Mark and Marci together. In the end, they were placed in a home with a middle-aged couple who had an excellent reputation. It wasn't the solution Michelle had hoped for, but at least she knew her brother and sister were safe.

Dealing with Michelle's ordeal was not the only thing vying for Joanna's attention all week. Things at the station had heated up as well.

Another murder had put everyone in a tailspin. When Joanna got to the station, she was immediately called into the captain's office and told she would be going undercover. She would get the next two days off, but come Monday, she would work as long as necessary in order to catch the killer that was terrorizing the city.

T.J. had been in a pensive mood all week. Joanna had tried to find out what was bothering him, but he just kept brushing it off as stress and fatigue. She didn't buy it. In the past, he would've relieved his stress with the guys down at the corner bar, or with one of the many women he had on speed dial. But he'd chosen to keep to himself and go home each night alone.

The only bright part of Joanna's week had been spending time with Keith. They'd both been working long shifts, but always managed to see each other, even if for just a few hours each night. He would be leaving soon, and the thought of him traveling to a foreign country triggered a new set of fears for Joanna.

Keith's team would be going into an area known for political unrest. There had already been reports of humanitarian groups being caught in the crossfire. Keith assured her his team prepared for such things, but it didn't help in the least. All she knew was he'd be a sitting duck for two weeks.

They'd had more than one tense discussion about it, but in the end, Joanna knew she had to support Keith in what he wanted to do, and leave the rest up to God.

Joanna was looking forward to the next two days. It had been what got her through the week. Keith had switched shifts with a few guys so he could have the entire weekend off. It meant working double shifts up until the time he left on Wednesday, but they had felt it would be worth it to have two uninterrupted days together before he left.

Now Joanna was going to have the unwelcome task of telling him about her assignment. She could only imagine how he was going to take it. Probably not much better than T.J. had.

T.J. walked Joanna to her car at the end of their shift. "You and Keith have plans for this weekend?"

"Sort of. We plan on spending it together if that's what you mean."

"Are you going to tell him?" T.J. looked at her intently.

"I don't know how, but yes, I'm going to tell him."

"How do you think he'll take it?" T.J. leaned against the hood of her car.

Joanna fiddled with her keys. "Horribly."

"Yeah, I can only imagine."

"What about you, do you have plans for the weekend?" Joanna needed to change the subject. She couldn't let T.J.

see the anxiety she felt.

"Surfing, mostly. You remember that kid, Justin? We're going out on Saturday."

"Sounds like fun."

"You're welcome to come—you and Keith. I'll show him the ropes. And I promise to be nice." T.J. smiled deviously.

"No, thank you," she laughed. "I don't know when I'll have days off again. I'm certainly not going to spend these being beat-up and washed out to sea."

"Okay," he chuckled. "But you know where to find me if you change your mind."

She got into her car and rolled down the window. He leaned on the frame and looked at her, all kidding gone from his expression. "It's okay to be afraid. You know that, right?"

She looked at her lap and then to him. "Yeah. It will keep me on my toes."

"I'll be right there, Joanna. I won't let anything happen to you." The concern in his voice was almost more than she could bear.

"You bet you will be, partner. I'm going to make sure you're working just as hard as I am." She laughed, trying to hide her fears. "Now, I've got to go. I'll see you on Monday."

"The team won't meet until seven o'clock. How about if I come over around six o'clock and make sure you're doing okay?"

"Sounds good."

Joanna pulled from the station, rehearsing how she was going to tell Keith about her assignment. She didn't want to ruin their evening, so she decided she would tell him tomorrow.

Her phone rang, making her purse vibrate on the front seat. She smiled even before answering the phone. The ringtone was exclusively Keith's.

"Hello."

"Where are you?"

"We got out a little late. I'm a few blocks away."

"Okay, I was just checking before I put the steaks on."

"I'll be home in five."

Joanna hung up her phone and tossed it on the passenger seat. In doing so, she glanced at the seat again and noticed her New Testament wasn't where she usually had it. Shoving her hand in between the leather upholstery, she felt around for it. *When did I see it last?* She wasn't sure with all that had gone on lately. Joanna looked at the floorboards but still didn't see it anywhere. When she pulled into her garage, she killed the engine and immediately began looking for her Bible.

"What are you doing?" Keith asked.

Joanna could hear him laughing. She imagined how she must look, sprawled out on the front seat of her car, head on the floorboard.

"I can't find my New Testament. I usually have it tucked in my seat, but I can't find it anywhere." Her words were sharp as she hung her head over the seat, looking on the floor again, feeling every nook and cranny. "This is ridiculous! I always leave it in the car."

After a few more minutes of searching, she scooted out of the car and slammed the door. Her hair was askew and her jaw was set. "I can't believe this. I always leave it on the front seat."

Keith looked at her and smiled while he straightened her hair. "I'll buy you a new one."

"No!" she snapped. "Matthew gave it to me. I don't want a new one, I want to find mine. I just can't remember the last time I saw it."

Keith pulled Joanna against his chest and wrapped his arms around her, holding her close. "It's okay, we'll find it," he said in a calm voice. "But why do I get the impression you're agitated about more than just your Bible?"

Joanna held on to him a second longer and a little tighter than usual. It wasn't just the Bible; it was knowing she would have to tell him about her assignment.

"The steaks!" Keith took off through the house.

Joanna shook off her anxiety, frustrated she'd almost ruined the evening. She welcomed the moment alone to take a deep breath and adjust her attitude before walking out to the deck. It was dark but she could see Keith's silhouette as he pulled the steaks from the grill and set them with the rest of the food assembled on the table. A table beautifully set with linens, candles, and a bouquet of yellow tulips.

Keith turned to see her reaction and grinned. "From the smile on your face can I assume everything meets with your approval?"

"Everything looks wonderful."

Keith pulled out her chair, placing a kiss on her cheek. He took the seat opposite her and reached out for her hand to pray.

When she opened her eyes, she took in the beauty of

Keith's special touches.

"What are you looking for?" Keith asked as he looked at her through candlelight.

"Nothing. I just can't believe you went to all this work."

"This is our last weekend together before I leave. I wanted to make it special."

Joanna's heart sank. She wanted it to be special too, but knowing she had to tell Keith about her assignment was weighing heavily on her.

She dished up her plate quietly even though her appetite was nonexistent. Keith had gone to a lot of trouble and she didn't want his efforts to go to waste. She was nibbling on her corn when Keith asked about work. Not wanting to ruin dinner, she tried to side step the question.

"I got a call from the D.A. today. He's going to press charges against Michelle's mother. He thinks he can get her on child endangerment."

"That's good."

"Yeah, now Michelle doesn't have to worry about her brother and sister being placed back in the home."

"What about Michelle, how's she doing?"

"She called this afternoon. Even though she has a long road ahead of her, I think she's going to be okay. Michelle's tough."

Keith nodded, acknowledging Joanna while continuing to eat. Joanna picked at her baked potato and pushed her steak around on her plate. She cut off a piece of it and placed the larger portion on Keith's plate. He looked puzzled at the gesture.

"I had a big lunch today, and I don't want to let this

amazing meal go to waste." She forced a smile as she watched the candles flicker inside their glass holders and fingered the petals of the tulips.

"You know, you could go with me?" Keith said.

"What?" Not sure she'd heard him right.

"On the trip. You could go with us. One of the people on our team had to back out, so we have an open spot."

She shook her head. "I can't get the time off, especially not now."

"Something happen?" He lifted his eyes to meet hers.

She'd spoken what she had hoped to put off until tomorrow. Now she had no choice; she needed to be honest with him. Keith deserved that much. Joanna calmly took a sip of water before answering.

"There's been another murder."

CHAPTER THIRTY-TWO

Joanna told Keith she didn't want to ruin dinner with talk about work. But now that dinner was over and they had moved to the comfort of the living room, she knew she wouldn't be able to put it off much longer.

Keith had insisted on doing the dishes and was just finishing up in the kitchen. Joanna prayed for the right words, and that Keith would have a receptive attitude. He walked into the living room juggling two bowls of cookie dough ice cream, water for her, and coffee for him. He sat everything down on the coffee table and snuggled close to her.

"Now, where am I supposed to put that?" she teased. "You already stuffed me like a Thanksgiving turkey."

"No, I tried to stuff you. You ate next to nothing." His look told her he'd seen right through the facade she'd been wearing.

"Joanna, what's wrong? Something's been eating at you since you got home. Is it the trip? If it is, we've been over this a hundred times. We're there to provide aid. If at any time we feel as if we could be in danger or a danger to those we're helping, we'll pull out."

"No, it's not the trip. Though I still will be on edge until I know you're home safe."

"Then what is it?" He reached for her hand and brought it up to his lips, pressing a kiss to the back of her wrist. "I was hoping tonight could be spent doing things other than talking." He grinned making her blush, smile, and want to cry all at the same time. She had wanted a romantic weekend as well, not one that would add more strain to the tension they were already feeling. She pulled her hand away slowly, trying to concentrate on what it was she had to say.

"We're stepping up our efforts in the prostitute killings."

"That's good. It's about time something more was done. You said it yourself, you guys have hung back for too long."

"That's what the brass is saying, too. So, starting Monday, we're going to be implementing an undercover sting operation." She looked at her lap, not able to look at Keith. "I'm going to be the bait."

"What?" Keith tipped her chin up forcing her to look at him.

"Starting Monday night, I'll be going undercover on the streets."

He shook his head in objection. "No. You can't do that. It's too dangerous! This guy is a killer!"

"It's my job, Keith," she said quietly, trying to get him to lower his voice.

He jumped from the couch, still shaking his head, his tone near shouting. "Then they can get someone else! You need to tell them no!"

"I already said yes, Keith. The operation is already in motion."

"What were you thinking, Joanna? You can't do this. This is ridiculous. This is way out of your league."

Joanna was beginning to take offense at the fact Keith was questioning her abilities.

"Keith, I'm a trained police officer. I am more than capable."

"Police officer, yes. Hooker, no. Didn't you even think about what you would have to do while on this kind of assignment? Joanna, you're going to be setting yourself up for men sizing you up, groping you. How far will you have to let your charade go before you collar the guy?"

"Keith, I'm not compromising my standards for this. It won't even get that far. As soon as a guy propositions me, he'll be arrested. We're going to be doing a sweep operation, hoping to find our killer. Everyone that is arrested will have to submit a DNA sample. Those will be compared with the DNA we have from the victims. I will have back-up the whole time. T.J.'s not going to let anything happen to me."

Keith stopped pacing and turned around in a huff. "T.J. sees no problem with you flaunting yourself all over the streets, being manhandled by perverts just so you can catch this guy?"

"It wasn't T.J.'s decision, it was mine," she said firmly.

Keith was staring out the window when Joanna got up

from the couch and wrapped her arms around him. "I'm sorry you don't approve, Keith, but this is part of my job. I need to do this."

"No." He turned around to face her, anger in his eyes. "You don't *need* to do this. You *want* to do this. You're trying to prove something, Joanna." He started pacing again. "You want to save the world, and now you're risking you're life to do it."

"Isn't that what you're doing?" she shot back. "Aren't you flying off to some war-torn country, putting yourself in harm's way because of your altruistic attitude? What is it you were telling me? *'You're doing what you can with your training, trying to make a difference in the world'?"*

"That's different! I'm not walking into that country, looking for trouble. You're going out on those streets, alone, with a target on your back, looking for a killer."

Joanna slumped onto the couch and buried her face in her hands.

Keith softened his tone and knelt in front of her, resting his hands on her knees. "Five people have already been killed by this guy. This isn't a game, Joanna."

She looked at him through watery eyes and held his hands. "I know. It's my job. I have to do this. With or without your support."

He pushed himself back onto the coffee table and sat across from her, staring at the carpet.

"Maybe it's better this way, Keith. Maybe it's better this happened now. This is a part of my job; assignments like this will always be a possibility. I know this isn't what you bargained for. But if you're not going to be able to adjust in a situation like this, we need to decide now if we have a future together."

"Don't say that, Joanna."

"But it's true." She got up from the couch and walked away.

Joanna was leaning on the rail of the deck when Keith walked out to join her. He had sat in the living room sulking for close to an hour. When she heard his footsteps behind her, she closed her eyes and took a deep breath, preparing herself for what she assumed would be a final good-bye.

"What are they going to do to ensure your safety?" Keith asked, his words heavy with emotion.

His question surprised Joanna. She turned to him, wiping her runny nose and watery eyes. "I'll have a wire that T.J. will be monitoring. The minute anything happens, he'll signal the surveillance team and they'll move in."

"Will anyone be watching you?"

"T.J. will. I'll be wearing a camera so he will be able to see what I see."

Joanna could see the redness and struggle in Keith's eyes. She hadn't meant to put him in this situation, but it was something they would have to face if they continued seeing each other. Law enforcement would always be central in her life. It's who she is. But she had never thought a relationship would make her question that.

Keith walked over to her and wrapped his arms around her waist. "I hate this, Joanna, I really do. I wish you'd reconsider." She began to pull away but he held her tighter. "But, I'm not going to stand in your way if this is something you feel you have to do."

Joanna stared at him, trying to absorb what he was saying. *He wasn't going to stand in her way. Did that mean he was going to walk away?*

"So . . . where do we stand?" Joanna asked, trying to be stoic.

"Well, I don't know about you, but I'm shaking like a leaf." He gave her a weak smile. "I guess that won't go away until I know this guy is caught and you're off the streets."

"But us, where do we stand?" She needed a more definitive answer.

Keith pushed her hair back over her shoulders and framed her face in his hands. "I have no choice, Joanna. I've fallen in love with you. I can't walk away now. God knew about this when He brought us together. If He thinks I can handle this, then I need to step up to the plate and put my faith where my mouth is."

Joanna could not believe it. Keith loved her. Her eyes were bloodshot and overflowing, her nose running; she knew she was a mess. Not the picture-perfect moment a girl dreams of when a man tells her he loves her, but she'd take it anyway.

She wrapped her arms around his neck. "I love you, too, Keith. I'm sorry I've put us in this situation."

He hushed her. "No, don't be sorry. Just get the job done and get out of there, okay?"

"I will," she whispered.

The kiss they shared was almost painful. They both felt the uncertainty of the future, and the urgency to know everything was going to work out.

CHAPTER THIRTY-THREE

Joanna and Keith's weekend hadn't gone exactly as she had expected. Highs and lows had peppered their time together.

Friday night, Keith left around two in the morning. They had spent much of the night holding each other, comforted by the joy that came with knowing their relationship had moved to the next level. But there was also the uneasiness of knowing it would be tested far beyond what most relationships had to endure.

Today, they had agreed to not think or talk about anything but each other and their day spent together. Try as they might, they couldn't push their fears far from their thoughts.

They biked along the canal and strolled through the Farmer's Market. But the tension of what *wasn't* being said continued to fill the silence.

When they stopped for caramel apples at a cute little candy store, they sat on a bench outside and basked in the afternoon sun. Joanna closed her eyes, wishing she could do something to eliminate the pall that hung between them.

At the strum of a guitar, Joanna glanced up. A street performer—a kid in his late teens or early twenties—smiled. "A beautiful song for a beautiful lady?" He was asking permission to play.

Keith nodded his approval.

The kid played a beautiful romantic song. He didn't sing, but his guitar did. The song was rich and intense, like the score of an epic movie. When he was done, Keith thanked him and handed him a twenty.

Keith tugged on Joanna's hand, "Come on, let's go home."

They rode their bikes back to her house, then decided to go to his place for an afternoon swim and a movie. The temperature of late July was escalating, and the pool at Keith's apartment sounded inviting.

When they got to his place, Joanna went into the bathroom to change. She slipped off her shorts and t-shirt, and pulled on a black halter-style one-piece suit. She tied a sheer black sarong at her waist and stepped into the living room.

Keith watched Joanna from across the living room and smiled. He was a lucky guy.

Joanna was the most amazing woman he'd ever met. She was the whole package: she loved the Lord, was feisty as all get out, and an incredible cook. She laughed at his corny jokes and liked watching cartoons, but was extremely intelligent. She had an admirable career, one he should be proud of, not intimidated by, and she was flat out gorgeous. He didn't think she realized how beautiful she was. In fact, her unassuming ways made her even more attractive.

"What?" she asked

"Oh nothing. Just thinking." He went into the other room and pulled on his trunks. He grabbed two beach towels out of the hall closet and tossed one at her.

"Ready?" he asked.

"Are you kidding? I feel like I'm melting."

They walked to the pool just around the corner. There were already several people lounging on the deck. Some sunbathed on chaises, while others sat on the rim of the pool, dipping their feet in the water.

Keith waved to a few people he knew as they walked over to two empty chairs and laid out their towels.

Jerry–a guy Keith played hoops with–walked towards him and asked, "Where've you been?"

When Jerry's eyes veered before he could answer, Keith turned to see what had caught his friend's attention. Joanna had removed the sarong from her waist and set it on the chaise. Jerry was leering at Joanna and did nothing to hide it. Keith clenched his fist, fighting the sudden pang of jealousy.

"So, this is why you're no longer playing hoops with me," Jerry said in a friendly tone as he continued to eye Joanna.

"Hi, Jerry." Keith turned to Joanna, wishing she was wearing more than a swimsuit. "Joanna, this is Jerry. Jerry, this is Joanna."

Jerry stuck out his hand. "Nice to meet you, Joanna. I had no idea the choirboy had such good taste." Joanna took the complement with a smile, while Keith gritted his teeth.

"See you around, Keith. But then again, maybe not." Jerry winked at Keith, then took one more look at Joanna before walking to the far side of the pool.

"Jerk," Keith muttered under his breath.

"Ready to go in?" Joanna asked, as she eyed the pool.

"Sure."

They walked over to the stairs and began their slow descent. Keith glanced around at the men sitting poolside and felt as if they were all staring at Joanna. She stood on the third step—splashing her arms and face—as she got used to the water. Keith watched . . . no, more like scrutinized the way she bent to scoop the water and allow it to trickle down her body. Her moves seemed seductive. Sensual.

Don't be an idiot, he chastised himself. Jealousy was an ugly thing and right now it was really messing with him.

Already in the water, Keith was irritated she was taking so long. "Come on, Joanna, just get in." His words sounded sharper than he intended.

She took the next few steps a little quicker and then glided over to where he was. She rested her elbow on the edge of the pool and pushed her hair back from her face.

"The water feels great." She smiled.

"Then what took you so long to get in?"

She looked at him oddly. "I always take my time getting in."

"And why is that?" he bit back.

"What?"

"Nevermind." He smiled, trying to control his

irritation.

They swam back and forth the length of the pool without any interruption, just like they'd done numerous times before. After they completed several laps, they stopped in the deep end of the pool and rested against the edge.

"I'm going to go ahead and get out now," Joanna said with a kiss.

"Okay. I'll join you after a few more laps," he said, stealing another kiss.

Instead of swimming back to the shallow end and using the stairs, Joanna thrust herself up onto the cement nearest their chairs and climbed out.

Keith heard one of the men on the side of the pool whistle under his breath. He turned and saw them watching Joanna as she walked to her chaise.

She dried off her face, and slicked back her hair from her forehead. She patted her suit and legs with the towel, before straightening it out and lying down in the sun. Keith watched the interaction between the two men on the side of the pool. He imagined what filthy things they might be saying, and couldn't take it anymore.

He swam to the side of the pool, hoisted himself up, and stalked over to where she was laying. "Come on, let's go."

She shielded her eyes from the sun and looked at him dumbfounded. "But we just got here."

"I don't care. We need to go," he hissed through clenched teeth.

"Keith what is it? What's wrong?"

"Let's go." He grabbed his towel, pushed his feet into

his sandals, and waited for her to gather her things.

Joanna quickly got up, pulled her sarong around her waist, and picked up her sandals and towel.

Keith stormed to his apartment, unlocked the door, and left it hanging open for Joanna. He tossed his towel on the dining room table, then spun around when he heard the door close.

"What were you doing out there? Practicing?"

She stood there stunned. "Practicing? What does that mean?"

"Come on, Joanna. Every eye out there was on you, and you know it."

"Keith, what are you talking about?"

He looked at Joanna's clueless expression, dropped his head in disgust, and sighed. *What am I doing?* He massaged his brow, trying to rein in his anger. "I'm sorry, Joanna, just forget it. I was overreacting."

"You were overreacting to what? What did you think I was doing?"

"Joanna, I said I was sorry."

"Sorry for what?" She crossed her arms.

"It's me, okay? It was me having a problem out there. You did nothing wrong; it was me."

He sat on the couch dragging his fingers through his wet hair. "I saw how some of those guys were ogling you, and it made my skin crawl. I thought about you on the streets, men leering at you, and I guess I kind of lost it. You're a beautiful woman, Joanna. Of course guys are going to stare at you, but I just kept imagining . . . well . . . imagining more."

She sat next to him, resting her hand on his knee.

"Joanna, you didn't even notice. You don't even notice the way men look at you. I just can't imagine how it's going to be for you on the streets, wearing something like you're wearing now. Or maybe I *can* imagine and that's what's got me all twisted up inside."

"Keith . . . I'm going to be all right. T.J.'s not going to let anything happen to me. Nothing. You know that. What can I say to make you understand that?"

He grasped her hand. "You can't, Joanna. There's nothing you can say that will take away this knot in my stomach. I just need to work through it. I just want it to be over."

"Then we'll pray it's over before you leave. You leave on Wednesday; a lot can happen between now and then."

"That's what I'm worried about."

CHAPTER THIRTY-FOUR

Joanna stayed at Keith's to watch a movie. He would catch her looking at him, knowing his empty gaze gave away his thoughts. He tried to shake his ominous feelings, only to look at Joanna and see her gaze set on some faraway object.

Keith hated himself for his earlier outburst. It had been unfair to lash out at Joanna because of his own insecurities. He'd apologized a hundred times over, and each time, she was more than willing to let the situation drop, telling him she understood.

But he didn't want to let the subject drop.

He wanted to be angry and argumentative.

There was a part of him that thought he could talk her out of the assignment if he could just make her understand how dangerous the whole thing was.

But deep down he knew that wasn't going to happen. She was too stubborn and too committed to her job.

After they watched their second movie, they languished on the couch. The credits had ceased and the screen was blank, but neither of them moved.

Finally, it was Joanna who broke the silence. She sat up on the couch and faced Keith. "You need to talk to me. I need to know what you're thinking."

"You know what I'm thinking. I don't want you to do this."

"Okay, then tell me why. Tell me your fears, and I'll tell you how we're going to guard against them."

"I don't want men touching you," he said with a stone face.

"They won't. Professionals don't let men touch the 'merchandise' before getting paid or seeing they have the means to get paid. The minute I'm offered money, I'll take them to a designated room and I'll ask them what they expect for their money. Once they've told me, my back-up will be waiting in an adjoining room where they've heard and recorded everything. The men won't even have a chance to put their hands on me, Keith. The john will be quietly escorted out a back entrance. After an appropriate amount of time, I reappear back on the street. Business as usual."

"And it doesn't bother you that men are going to say the filthiest, vilest things you could imagine?"

"Keith, do you think I've lived in a bubble my whole life? I've been verbally accosted before. I've been propositioned, glared at, and even had to get myself out of a few tight situations. I've even been set-up by the guys I work with. But each time I was able to keep a level head and defend myself."

Keith considered Joanna's argument. It didn't make him feel any better, but he knew she was prepared for what it was she was being asked to do.

"What else . . . what else are you thinking?" Joanna grabbed his hand and stroked it.

"I guess I'm jealous," he huffed. "There, I said it."

"Jealous?" she said indignantly. "Jealous of what?"

"Not really jealous, but resentful." He got up from where he was sitting, knowing he wasn't going to be able to make his point clear. He crossed the room, walking with clenched fists. He looked at Joanna, sitting on the couch, waiting for an explanation.

"I'm angry, Joanna, all right! I'm angry that every man who propositions you, every man that sees you—your police buddies included—will be having sexual fantasies about the woman I love and want to protect. And I can't do a frickin' thing about it."

Joanna hung her head. "I know what you're saying, Keith. And believe me I took all that into consideration when I chose my team."

"What do you mean, *you* chose your team?"

"The captain let me choose the men that would be working on this assignment. He realized it would be important for me to have faith and trust in the men who would be my back-up. Besides T.J., I chose Wagner, Peck, Olsen, and Johnson because they are all family men, with wives of their own. Peck is a veteran. A real standup guy. He doesn't allow foul language in his presence, and he's treated me with nothing but respect since I made detective."

Joanna walked over to Keith, laying her hand on his forearm. "I'm sorry, Keith. I know this is difficult for you, but you have to trust me. You have to let me do my job."

He pulled Joanna close, wrapping her in the protection he wanted so desperately to give her. "I'm considering staying home. I don't think I should go on this trip. Not now."

Joanna took a step back and looked him in the eye. "No. You need to go, Keith. What would you do if you stayed home?"

"I don't know, but at least I'd be close by if you needed me, if something happened."

"Nothing is going to happen. You've got to believe that." She paused for a moment. "Would you feel better if you met the guys that will be working with me? Would that help?"

"No." He pulled her close. "Just let me hold you."

Joanna melted in Keith's embrace, hating the emotion she heard in his voice.

She was having second thoughts.

She'd been selfish.

She'd been so bent on proving her worth, and so excited when the captain let her pick her own team, she hadn't taken into account the personal consequences.

She hadn't stop to consider how serious she and Keith had become, or how difficult this would be on him.

Now, she could think of nothing else.

Her tears wet the front of Keith's t-shirt. He pulled away to look at her, sadness in his eyes. "Don't cry, Joanna."

She moved from him, sitting on the edge of the couch,

her head in her hands. "It's just that I don't know what to do. I was so sure of this, and now I'm not."

Keith sat next to her, framed her face with his hands, and brushed her tears away with his thumbs. "You're going to get this guy, that's what you're going to do. You're going to nail him to the wall."

Keith bent to press a kiss to Joanna's lips. A kiss that turned into much more. He felt Joanna's body next to his and pulled her closer. They slowly sank into the cushions of the couch. He wanted to drink her in; never let her go. He felt an urgency to experience love with Joanna. That if he claimed her as his own, maybe he wouldn't feel so vulnerable at the prospect of losing her.

Joanna knew what Keith was doing, but did nothing to stop him. She wanted him to know she was completely his. She had vowed she would never give up her virginity outside of marriage, but words didn't seem enough to express what she was feeling. It was an excuse and she knew it, but she didn't care. It was her decision to make. At the moment she wanted Keith to know how very much she loved him.

Joanna's body was intoxicating. Keith's lips traveled to the nape of her neck and his hands roamed freely over her exposed skin. He was fighting the warning bells going off in his head. His conscience was causing his heart to constrict. What he was doing was wrong, and he knew it.

But the rebellious, belligerent side of him no longer wanted to do what was right, true, and honorable. He wanted Joanna for himself.

He was turning a deaf ear to the standards he'd held himself to since adolescence, when he felt a shudder travel the length of Joanna's body. In an instant, he realized what he was doing. He was taking advantage of her; he was doing to Joanna what he feared would happen to her out on the streets. The accusations he'd lowered against her co-workers, and the men who would proposition her, he'd just committed himself.

He stopped, tucked her head to his chest, and held her tight. "I'm sorry, Joanna, I don't know what got into me. I was angry and hurt. But the person I wanted to protect the most, I just took advantage of. I'm so sorry."

"I understand, Keith. I wanted it as much as you did. Even though I knew it was wrong."

They laid, holding each other for a while longer. Keith didn't want to let Joanna go; if he did, he was afraid he might never hold her again. Playing with the wisps of hair that hung around her forehead, Keith looked outside through the open drapes and saw a darkened sky. He looked at the clock on the wall and wondered where the time had gone. They hadn't even eaten dinner, not that he'd had an appetite.

"I should probably take you home."

Wearily, they both sat up. Keith stood, pulling Joanna to her feet. He looked at her, his eyes pooled with emotion. "I know I said it before, but I want you to hear it again. I love you, Joanna. I can't bear to think of what might happen. What could happen."

She pressed her fingers to his lips. "Then don't. Think instead of the time we'll be able to spend together when you get back. I'll get some extra time off once this is all over. Maybe we can take a vacation somewhere."

He raised his brows with a mischievous smile.

"With separate rooms, of course," she added.

"Of course." He agreed, as if gentlemanly thoughts were the only thing to cross his mind. "Unless we were celebrating something special. Like an elopement, maybe."

Her eyes brightened, totally shocked by Keith's declaration. "An elopement could be fun."

"Well, then, you'll have to come up with a list of locations while I'm gone."

"Are you serious?"

"I guess you'll just have to wait and see."

The drive to Joanna's was quiet. Keith walked her to the house, but when she opened the door, he remained on the porch. "I don't think I'd better come in. We avoided disaster once tonight. I don't know that I'll be strong enough to do it again."

She stepped close to him, laying her head against his chest, slipping her hands in the back pockets of his shorts. He stroked the back of her head, enjoying the silky feel of her hair against his fingers. He placed a kiss on the top of her head.

"I'll be by tomorrow at ten o'clock to pick you up for church."

"You could come by earlier, and I could fix you breakfast," she offered.

"Okay. I'll be here at eight."

CHAPTER THIRTY-FIVE

Joanna watched the amber lights on her nightstand clock tick off every minute until the wee hours of the morning. Dawn was just breaking when she kicked off her covers and swung her feet to the floor. She wasn't getting any sleep, so she figured she might as well do something productive. Still missing her New Testament, she decided to give her car a thorough shakedown.

Joanna covered every inch of her car's interior. When she came up empty, she finally decided her New Testament must be lost.

She watched as her tears hit the floor of the garage. She knew she was overreacting. She had other mementos that had belonged to Matthew, but her emotions were raw; her sensitivity level heightened by all that had transpired yesterday. Wiping the tears from her eyes, she spoke to herself. *Just let it go. It will show up eventually.*

Joanna got cleaned up and pulled on an old pair of

sweatpants and a t-shirt. She headed to a twenty-four hour market so she could make a big breakfast for Keith. Roaming the aisles of the store, she finally decided on waffles, eggs, and apple-wood bacon.

Joanna was busy in the kitchen when she heard a light knock at the door. Licking batter from the side of her hand, she hurried to answer it.

Keith stood there, dressed for church, looking incredibly handsome. How could he make a simple white dress shirt look so good? It amazed her. After a quick kiss and a "good morning" greeting, Joanna hustled back to the kitchen before the waffles burnt.

Keith followed her to the kitchen and watched as she juggled a pan of eggs, a griddle of bacon, and the waffle press. After rescuing the waffles from the iron, Keith pulled her to his chest.

"What are you doing?" She held her batter-caked hands away from his shirt. "You're going to get something on you."

"I'm willing to take my chances." He bent down and kissed her then smacked his lips and smiled. "Strawberries."

They had a wonderful breakfast together; enjoying the outdoors, a beautiful morning, and conversation that had nothing to do with her assignment. When they were done, Joanna got ready for church, while Keith cleaned up the kitchen. She told him to leave the mess for later, but he did it anyway.

Joanna walked down the steps and was greeted with an appreciative smile on Keith's face. Her navy wrap-around dress fell just above her knees, showing off what little tan she had. When she walked to the entry table to grab her purse, Keith stepped up behind her and wrapped his arms around her waist. Placing a kiss on her neck, he said, "You look beautiful."

"I'm glad you approve."

Joanna couldn't help but notice that Keith pulled her a little closer, held her a little tighter than usual as they walked to his car. He was scared. She could feel it. And it made her think—just for a moment—what her life would be like if she decided to leave the force. She had never considered doing anything else, but maybe—with the right person in her life—she would be willing to leave it behind.

Keith quickly found a parking spot in the church lot. With clasped hands they walked in together and slipped into the back pew just as the music was starting. They remained standing for worship, Joanna drinking in the peace the songs conveyed.

As they bowed their heads to pray, Keith nudged her slightly to make room for a few latecomers. When she opened her eyes, she looked past Keith to see T.J., Justin, and another man sitting next to him. She was stunned. When their eyes met, T.J. reached across Keith's lap and handed Joanna her New Testament.

"I've been meaning to get this back to you," he whispered, smiling.

She looked at the little black book and then to T.J. "How long have you had it?"

"Long enough to finish it," he said with a wink. When she went to ask him something further he put his finger to his lips, turning to the pastor who was addressing the congregation.

Joanna sat back in the pew in disbelief. She felt Keith squeeze her hand, and she looked at him with a stunned expression. He just smiled, then turned his attention back to the pastor.

Joanna couldn't seem to focus on what Pastor Grant was saying. Her mind was too busy trying to figure out what was going on with T.J. *Surely, he hadn't come to church just so he could return her Bible?* She glanced over at him and saw his eyes focused on the pastor; he was listening intently. There was no question he was hearing what was being said.

Joanna had a hard time sitting still while the pastor concluded his sermon. She needed to talk to T.J. She needed to know exactly what had brought him to church.

After the congregation sang the closing song, they began to filter out. Joanna knew there was no use trying to talk to T.J. while in the building, so she followed Keith, T.J., Justin, and the other man out to the parking lot.

T.J.'s truck was in the visitor parking, up front, near the sanctuary. When they reached it, Joanna caught T.J.'s eye, and started to say something. But he quickly turned his attention to the other man and made an introduction.

"Joanna, you already know Justin." She smiled at the teenager who had helped her on the beach. "But, I'd like to introduce you and Keith to Jeremy Bush, Justin's brother."

Everyone shook hands.

T.J. continued. "Come to find out, Justin goes to youth group here." T.J. looked from Justin to Joanna. "He and I've been surfing in the mornings and got to talking. He asked me to come to church with him, so I figured, why not."

Joanna could see Jeremy looked a little uncomfortable. His shaggy brown hair and flip-flops clued Joanna to the fact that this was probably the surfer brother Justin had spoken about.

After a few minutes of light conversation, Justin and Jeremy left, with plans to meet T.J. at the beach the following week. As the two walked away, Joanna turned her attention to T.J. She didn't want to put him on the spot in front of Keith, but she had to know what was going on with him. What had made him want to read her New Testament and come to church?

"Hey, Joanna, I see Dr. Kline over there," Keith said as he pointed to a small cluster of people near the sanctuary. "I have a few questions for him about the trip. I'll be right back."

She watched as Keith walked up the steps to the tall man in the suit and tie, then turned her attention back to T.J.

"Surprised?" he asked with a grin on his face.

"To say the least." She moved closer to him and with a low serious voice asked, "What's this all about, T.J.?"

He shrugged his shoulders. "I guess I liked what the preacher had to say last time, so I thought I'd give him another listen."

"And my Bible?" she asked, holding up the small black book in her hand.

"When I took your car back to the station the day you rode with Michelle to the hospital, I saw it lying on the front seat. I started thumbing through it to see if I could find what the preacher had talked about that Sunday. I didn't find that, but I found myself reading it anyway. I can't say I understood it all, but a lot of it seemed to make sense."

"And?" Joanna wanted to know where T.J. was going with this.

"I'm not completely sold on it yet, if that's what you're asking. But I'm interested enough to want to know more."

Impulsively she hugged T.J., feeling tears pool in her eyes. He held her tight for a moment, then let his hands slip away. Joanna turned to see what T.J. was staring at and saw Keith, standing on the steps with Dr. Kline. T.J. was being sensitive to Keith, and it made her want to hug him all the more. When Joanna stepped back from him, he asked, "Have you told Keith yet?"

"Yeah." She glanced back to where Keith and the doctor were talking.

"How'd he take it?"

"Not too well." She rubbed her thumb across the worn leather cover of her Bible. "We've had a pretty stressful weekend."

"When exactly does he leave on his trip?"

"Wednesday."

Keith walked over to them, putting a proprietary arm around Joanna's waist. "T.J., why don't you join us for lunch?"

"Thanks, Keith, I appreciate the offer, but I know you'll be leaving this week. I don't want to take up any of the time you have left to spend with Joanna."

"But I'd like to talk to you, if I could. I'm not thrilled with Joanna's assignment."

"Keith, I promise you everything is going to go by the book. I'm not going to let Joanna out of my sight."

Keith looked at T.J. intensely. Joanna couldn't tell if T.J.'s words comforted Keith, or put him more on edge.

"Keith, Joanna means a lot to me." T.J.'s look was hard as stone. "Believe me, I'm not going to let anything happen to her."

CHAPTER THIRTY-SIX

Joanna and Keith spent Sunday afternoon together much like they did on Saturday. There were times when they would just hold each other, and others when neither of them could sit still; their anxieties too much to handle.

Joanna shared what she and T.J. had talked about in the church parking lot. She was excited about the flicker of change in T.J., and hoped it would continue.

Keith saw a different side of T.J., too. He was being protective of Joanna, not possessive. T.J. was respecting Keith and his relationship with Joanna; he was stepping aside.

Dinner was pizza delivery. They ate it in front of the T.V. watching a sappy movie from the forties on one of the classic cable stations.

Keith had his feet up on the coffee table while Joanna was tucked up against his chest.

"So what time does all this start going down?" It was the first time Keith had mentioned the operation since talking with T.J.

"We get together at seven o'clock to go over all the details one more time. We should be in place by eight."

"And what time will you call it quits?"

"It's hard to say. It depends on how things are going."

He dropped his arm from the back of the couch to pull her closer to him. "And you're going to call me the minute you're out of there, right?"

"Absolutely."

Nothing more was said. About an hour later, Keith got up from the couch and pulled Joanna up next to him. He wrapped her in his arms, his chin pressed against the top of her head. "I think we should pray," Keith said softly.

Joanna nodded against his chest. "Can you?" Her voice quivered. "I don't think I can talk right now."

Keith squeezed her tight and began. "Lord, Joanna and I come before you with heaviness in our hearts. We need Your help. We know we are Your children and You've already planned out our days in advance. Help us, Lord, to remember You're in control of all things. Protect Joanna. She's putting herself in harm's way and she'll need Your protection. Help T.J. as he watches out for her. Help him to be alert and cautious. And Lord, we see T.J. is allowing your Word to work its way into his life. Let it penetrate. Let it take root. We ask Lord, that he comes to know You as the Savior he needs. And Lord, protect the team and I as we travel. Let our efforts reflect your love. May we bring more than medicine to these people who know so little of your love, and struggle to feel love at all in a world of sickness and depravity. We're yours, Lord. Use us as You desire. In Christ's name. Amen."

Joanna lay awake Monday morning, refusing to get out of bed—but unable to sleep. After having a hypothetical conversation with Matthew, she cried. She missed him in times like these. His pep talks, guidance, and love had been pivotal in her life. He had gotten her through the death of her parents, her awkward teenage years, and had challenged her to never settle. 'Be your best, Joanna, and let God do the rest.' It had been his motto in life, and the creed Joanna had chosen to live by. *I'm trying, Matthew, really I am.*

Joanna decided to call Kathy and let her know about the assignment. She didn't want to worry her but she could sure use the prayer support. Kathy had numerous questions about the assignment and Joanna's safety. Joanna explained as much as she could while Kathy listened quietly.

"Don't worry, Kath. Everything's going to be okay. I've got men I trust looking out for me, and T.J. is going to be right there. I'll be completely safe."

Kathy acknowledged everything Joanna was saying, but Joanna could still hear the worry in her friend's tone. So she decided to change the subject and gave Kathy a quick update on her relationship with Keith.

She explained she and Keith were still very much an item, but didn't tell Kathy how serious they were. Kathy was a wonderful friend, but had a knack of over analyzing everything.

"Be praying for us, Kathy, this assignment is definitely going to test our relationship. As much as I will miss him, I'm relieved Keith will be out of the country. I have to keep my mind in the game, and I don't know if I could do that with Keith scrutinizing my every move."

"But he realizes how important your career is to you, right? Because if he is asking you to choose between him and your job, maybe he's not the right man for you. Being a cop is part of who you are, Joanna. Don't go losing your identity because of some guy."

Joanna smiled. "Let me ask you this, Kathy, why did you quit the force after having the boys?"

"I told you, Mike didn't like the idea of the boys being in daycare."

"So you *sacrificed* your career because of Mike?"

"No. I did it because I love Mi—oh my gosh!"

Joanna laughed. She could almost picture the wheels spinning in Kathy's head.

"You're in love with Keith!" Kathy said, clearly astonished. "Why didn't you tell me you two were that serious?"

"Because it's kind of freaking me out. We haven't known each other that long, so I don't know if I'm being impulsive or if this is the real thing."

"Does he feel the same way? Not the impulsive part, the love part?"

"Yes." Just saying it made Joanna's heart race.

"Have you talked marriage?"

"Let's just say the word elopement has been thrown around."

Kathy squealed with excitement. "Oh, Joanna, I'm so happy for you. Of course, if you marry this guy before I'm able to give him the second degree, I'll shoot you where you stand."

Laughing, Joanna said, "I wouldn't think of it. Look,

after this assignment is over and Keith gets back, we'll get together. I would love for you to meet him."

Joanna heard a cry in the background. "Sounds like you need to go."

"Yeah, I better."

"One more thing, Kathy, being praying for T.J." Joanna quickly told Kathy about T.J., her New Testament, and his appearance in church. "He's searching, Kathy, and he has a lot of questions. Just pray I can make it clear to him what's missing in his life."

The cry in the background turned to a wail.

"I gotta go, Joanna, but you can bet Mike and I will be praying . . . about everything."

After her phone call with Kathy, Joanna cleaned her house from top to bottom, ending with her bedroom closet. She pulled out blouses and skirts she hadn't worn in months—even years—and started putting together outfits she could use during the weeks ahead.

Nothing she had was sexy or trampy enough on its own. But a few adjustments to hem lines and how they were worn would do the trick.

With a stack of outfits in the corner of her room, Joanna glanced at the bedside clock. She wasn't expecting T.J. for a couple more hours, so she headed to the mall to take care of a few last minute preparations.

When Joanna returned home from the mall, she felt wiped out. She looked at her watch, then to her latest purchases when her phone began to ring; digging it out of her purse, she answered.

"Hello."

She sighed at the sound of Keith's voice and sat carefully on the edge of the bed. "Hi. Are you home already?" she asked.

"No. I just had a break and needed to hear your voice."

"You sound tired." Joanna could hear the heaviness in his voice.

"I'm all right, how about you?" he asked.

"I'm okay. But the waiting is driving me crazy. It's like I know what I have to do, and I just want to be given the chance to do it and get it done." Joanna heard a radio chirp in the background.

"I've got to go, Joanna, but I get off at midnight. I want you to call me as soon as you're home, okay?"

"I will. I promise."

When T.J. arrived at Joanna's house, his face was stoic and he looked at her with a piercing stare.

"How are you doing?" he asked.

"Okay, but I really wanted to talk to you before we head to the station." She waived him into the house and shut the door. "How are *you* doing?"

"Me," he said with a questionable laugh. "I'm fine. I'm not the one who's going to be slinking around downtown, playing dress-up . . . or should I say dress-down?" He joked, but there was an edge to his voice.

"You know what I'm talking about, T.J. I want to know what made you want to come to church yesterday."

"Curious, I guess." He tried to shrug it off as nothing too important.

"Curious about what?"

He walked to the kitchen, opened her refrigerator and then closed it. "I don't know, Joanna; I guess I got to thinking about my life and what I'm doing with it. It all just seems like a waste of time." He leaned back against the counter, folding his arms against his chest, his attitude reflective.

"What do you mean?"

"Come on, Joanna, look at me. My personal life sucks. I'm not doing what I want with my life. But I do the job because I'm good at it, and it's what's expected of me."

"That's not true, T.J. You wouldn't be as good as you are if you didn't care." She spoke to him from across the kitchen bar.

"I don't know . . ." T.J. pushed away from the counter, not finishing his thought as he walked to the living room and plopped onto the couch.

"So how is it that, you, Justin, and his brother ended up in church together?"

"Justin and I have been spending a lot of time hanging out in the mornings. It started with surfing, but there have been days when we've ended up doing more talking than surfing. He's a great kid, Joanna, nothing like most kids his age. He's not into the party scene. And when I asked him about drinking and drugs, he told me he was a Christian and he didn't buy into those things."

"Really?" Joanna said, slightly shocked.

"Yeah. We've had some pretty deep conversations about life, the future, and where he thought God fit into all of it. He told me his life is steady, but his brother's life is pretty screwed-up. Jeremy drinks and parties a lot. He's already gotten two girls pregnant, and is seeing someone Justin describes as a real skank. He's worried his brother is ruining his life and is going to self-destruct."

T.J. chuckled and shook his head. "It was a real eye-opener, Joanna. Here I thought I was being a role model to Justin. You know, surfing icon, hot-shot cop. Then, I realized, for a high school kid, Justin had a better head on his shoulders than I did."

"So how'd you all end up at church?"

"Justin asked if I went to church. So I said sure, I'd been to church." T.J. looked at Joanna and grinned. "I know, I know. I knew that's not what he meant, but I didn't want to disappoint him. I was no better than his brother. Someone he described as a screw-up that needed to be saved.

"Justin asked if maybe I would be willing to go to church with him. He thought he would be able to convince his brother to go if he had the chance to meet me. You know . . . the big surfing superstar." T.J. mocked himself.

"So, the three of us surfed all morning then headed to church. Imagine my surprise when Justin gave me directions to your church."

"Do you think it helped? With Justin's brother, I mean," Joanna asked, but she was more interested in what effect it had on T.J.

"I don't know. I hope so."

"And you?"

T.J. looked at her and shrugged. "I know I've got to make a change. My life as it is now is getting me nowhere."

Joanna felt a thrill in her heart because of the change she was seeing in T.J., but she didn't want to push him.

"You know, T.J., I'm always here if you have any questions."

"I know. I'm counting on it. But right now, we need to concentrate on you and what's going down tonight. I don't want you to be distracted in the least, understand?"

"Yeah." Her stomach tightened.

T.J. glanced at his watch. "You ready?"

"Sure." She went upstairs and got the duffle bag she had packed. She planned on getting dressed at the station. There was no way she was going to take the chance of being seen leaving her house in what she would be wearing tonight.

When she shut the door behind them, she felt T.J.'s arm come around her shoulder. She knew he was trying to offer her comfort and support, nothing more. Their relationship was on a different level now.

They were partners.

Better yet, they were friends.

CHAPTER THIRTY-SEVEN

When Joanna and T.J. got to the War Room, everyone was assembled. Joanna glanced around and cringed when she saw Rogers. Ever since he'd come back from medical leave, he'd been more caustic and aggressive than ever. But something had changed. The other detectives no longer backed him up. In fact, most of the men had gotten fed-up with his behavior.

Rogers' looked at her with sheer hatred, but she didn't care. She refused to allow him to intimidate her. Instead, she glanced around the room at the other men. Some of them met her gaze and nodded, even offered her a smile of reassurance. The mood in the room was different. It took her a few minutes, but she realized what the difference was.

Respect.

The men finally looked at her with respect.

The captain immediately started going over every plan and detail of the evening. Everyone involved knew their assignment and understood she'd be depending on them.

Rogers, Barker, and Bristol hung back on the fringe of the room, listening to the details, knowing they weren't involved.

It was easy to read their body language. They were ticked-off they weren't part of the operation, but had no one to blame but themselves.

Their intimidation and harassment had back fired. Joanna had surrounded herself with men she could trust.

They were now the ones on the outside looking in.

When everyone had their assignments, the noise level went up a notch. Joanna rose from where she was sitting and was heading for the locker room when Rogers cut her off.

"You haven't welcomed me back, Joanna. Why is that?" he said snidely.

"I'm not the lying type . . . or the cheating type for that matter."

She knew she'd gotten her point across when his complexion flared red, but she didn't wait for his rebuttal, just continued towards the bathroom. She had other things to think about, more important things than his juvenile bullying.

Once in the bathroom, Joanna pulled a few items from her bag and hung them in her locker. Then, she stood in front of the sink and wedged her make-up bag between the mirror and faucet.

She artfully applied smoky shadow, mascara, and liner to deepen her eyes; a vibrant red stained her lips. Feeling she had achieved the sensual look she was going for, she moved on to her hair.

Bending forward at the waist, Joanna let her hair hang

free. Using hairspray and a product that guaranteed maximum volume; she sprayed, teased, and scrunched her hair. When she stood upright, she caught a reflection of herself in the mirror, amazed at the transformation.

Next, Joanna got undressed in one of the stalls and put on one of her newly altered outfits. Tonight, she would wear a jean skirt with snaps up the front. Of course, it was now eleven inches shorter than its original look and pushed down low around her hips.

The red silk blouse she'd chosen to go with the skirt used to be one of her favorites but had been ruined by a stain. Ignoring the buttons, she simply tied the hem in a knot against her ribcage, allowing the black lacy bra she was wearing to peek out. She had her limits on how she would dress—braless being one of them. Instead, she decided to wear sexy lingerie and make it work as part of her look.

She attached strappy high-heeled sandals to her feet before gathering up her clothes from the back of the toilet. She put her street clothes in her locker, purposely avoiding her reflection in the mirrors above the sinks. When she was ready, she turned to the full-length mirror on the back of the bathroom door.

She was repulsed by what she saw.

It took her a moment to adjust to how she looked. Her hand traveled across her abdomen and fingered the glittery charm dangling from her belly-button. It was still tender to the touch.

The piercing wasn't anything she found attractive, and she would remove it as soon as the assignment was over. But she thought it would be an important accessory to her overall look. The same with the exotic henna tattoo that was now inked across her right shoulder.

Joanna walked back to her locker and grabbed the warm-up jacket she'd worn earlier. She put in on, closed her locker, then took a slow, even breath. "Help me, God," she whispered as she opened the bathroom door.

T.J. was leaning against the wall in the hallway, across from the bathroom. When he saw her, he stood straight, clearly shocked by her transformation.

Joanna did a slow turn. "Well, am I every man's dream?" Joanna said sarcastically, fighting her compulsion to throw-up.

"No." T.J. shook his head, reaching for her hand. "That's who you are naturally."

Joanna cringed. "Okay, T.J., that's enough of that. If you're going to go all soft on me, I'm not going to be able to get through this."

"Okay, would you rather I proposition you right here in the hallway?" he said, with a wink and a smile.

"Actually, yes. I could use the aggravation for motivation."

"You mean like talking to Rogers?"

Joanna could tell by the look in his eyes, T.J. wanted to know what had been said.

"You know what—try as he might—I'm no longer going to allow him to get under my skin. He's not worth it. Besides, I've got more important things to do."

"Come on," T.J. said, giving her hand a squeeze. "let's do this thing."

When Joanna walked into the War Room, she decided to take the bull by the horns. "Okay, gentlemen, do all your ogling now and say whatever tacky comments are on your mind. Because the minute we hit the streets, I want to know you've got my back . . . not fantasizing about it."

She got a few cat-calls and a 'come over here honey,' but nothing vulgar or crude. She actually laughed, knowing the men were truly teasing. They were doing their best to distract her, not insult her. When they filed out of the room, they were all encouraging and showing her their support.

Her thoughts fast-tracked back to just a few months ago, when she first walked into the War Room and was met by angry, indifferent stares. She no longer felt like the odd man out.

She had done what she set out to do.

She had proven she belonged, and had earned their respect along the way.

The ride to the stakeout area was done in silence. T.J. wanted to say something to ease the tension, but when he looked over at Joanna, her eyes were closed. He didn't know if she was praying or not and didn't want to interrupt.

When they got to the dingy apartment where the command room was set up, a technician was waiting for them.

"Hi, I'm Detective Owens, and this is Detective Anderson," T.J. introduced them as he reached for the young kid's hand. The techie introduced himself as Paul. He shook hands with T.J. and Joanna, but his eyes never veered from Joanna's short skirt.

"Had enough?" T.J. asked the technician, irritated the kid had the audacity to leer.

"Sure . . . yeah." He spun around towards his table covered with electronics, and clapped his hands together. "Let me show you everything."

Paul turned towards Joanna, holding a little black wire attached to a cylinder the size of a AAA battery. "Okay, this is what you're going to be wearing. This is a one-way radio. You'll slip it into your bra, making sure this end is positioned so it can transmit."

"So, I can hear Joanna, but I can't talk to her?" T.J. clarified.

"Right. In situations like these we find it safer not to have a two-way radio on the target. It cuts down on the chance of the bug being detected and outside interference accidentally being transmitted."

Both Joanna and T.J. nodded, this was information they'd already been told.

"Detective Anderson, all you have to do is whisper and Detective Owens will be able to hear you. This is a very powerful receiver.

"Now, this," Paul pulled out a black barrette with rhinestones attached to it, "believe it or not, is a camera." He held it up facing T.J. and pointed to the video console behind them. T.J.'s face filled the screen. "You'll just slip this in your hair and Detective Owens will be able to see everything you see."

Joanna took the small device and pulled back a few strands of hair over her right ear, then looked at the monitor. "Amazing." She swiveled her head, making the video screen look like it was swaying back and forth.

At the console, Paul explained to T.J. where each of the four monitors were positioned.

"So, you already know this one is connected to the barrette." Paul pointed to the first monitor, then moved on to the second. "This one shows the room Detective Anderson will take the johns to. See that door?" Paul pointed out on the monitor. "It connects to the room Peck and Olsen will be in. All you have to do is give them the go, and they'll move in to make the arrests."

"The second camera is in the stairwell, and the third camera—"

"Wait a minute," T.J. interrupted. "There are two stairwells leading to this floor."

"Yeah, but the second connects to the alley out back. Detective Anderson has no reason to use that one. Like I was saying," Paul continued, "the third camera gives you a visual of the sidewalk out front. You'll have eyes on Detective Anderson at all times. And see that old beater van parked down the street? That's where Wagner and Johnson will be. If anything goes down on the street, they'll be able to get to Anderson in seconds."

Paul went on to explain the radio systems, and Joanna's wire. T.J. asked for clarification here and there, but everything was pretty straight forward.

"I'll be here tonight," Paul said, "to make sure there aren't any glitches and to sharpen camera angles if necessary. But after tonight, you'll be on your own."

Budget constraints wouldn't allow Paul to be there throughout the entirety of the operation. But T.J. felt confident the equipment wasn't anything he couldn't handle.

After everything was explained, and everyone was in position, T.J. turned to Joanna.

He placed his hands on her biceps and gave them a squeeze, trying to read the blank expression on her face. The light was gone from her eyes, and she looked like an empty shell of a person. If she had a game face, T.J. was convinced she was wearing it.

"Are you ready?"

"Yeah."

"Remember, if at any time you feel uncomfortable or something doesn't seem right, if the john isn't cooperating or you can't get the info we're looking for, just say "you're wasting my time." That's the signal, and no matter what, we'll be there in seconds. Okay?"

"Yep." She took a deep breath and removed the jacket that had been covering her mid-section. When T.J. saw the glitz hanging from her naval, he couldn't hide his surprise.

"Is that real?"

"Real annoying," she said belligerently.

He raised a brow and grinned. "I think it looks pretty sexy."

"That's what I was going for."

Joanna walked to the door and slipped out into the hall of the seedy apartment. She leaned against the wall momentarily, taking a deep breath.

Okay, Lord, here I go. Please God, let this guy hit on me tonight. I want this over with.

Whatever the cost.

She stood up straight, threw back her shoulders, and pretended to be every vixen she'd ever seen portrayed in the B-rated movies she'd watched on TV.

CHAPTER THIRTY-EIGHT

T.J. and Paul focused on the monitors as a beat-up caddy pulled to the curb. "That didn't take long," T.J. said, as he watched Joanna amble over to the side of the car and lean down to get a look at the guy. His stomach constricted as he saw the slimy looking guy practically drooling over Joanna.

"Whatcha looking for, Mr.?" Joanna's tone was pure silk.

"Whatever you're offering, sweetheart."

"Oh, baby, what you're lookin' at ain't free. If you ain't got the money, then I ain't got the time."

"I've got the money, sweetheart, hop in." The man was nearly panting and T.J. was ready to jump out of his skin.

"No, baby, you've got me all wrong. If you want some backseat action, then you can go on down to the high school." She turned from the vehicle but he quickly whistled her back.

She leaned on the window frame again.

"Then where?" he asked anxiously.

"Upstairs. Room B. I'll be waiting."

T.J. watched the monitors and keyed the radio. "She's got one. Peck, get ready."

"Say again. You've got static," Peck answered back.

"Get ready," T.J. repeated.

"Wagner, you got the car?"

"Got it."

T.J. was sure this wasn't their guy. The victims had never been found inside. And the fact that this guy was willing to follow Joanna to her room didn't fit the profile.

Instinctively, T.J. knew the most they would get this guy for was solicitation. But that did nothing to calm his racing pulse. He watched the monitor and saw Joanna burst into the room. She was wringing her hands and taking deep breaths.

"Oh man, she's going to blow it," Paul said, as he sat with his eyes glued to the surveillance screen.

T.J. grabbed the kid's collar and gave it a yank. "Shut up!" He gritted between his teeth. "You put your butt on the line with a killer and see how calm you are."

T.J. quickly turned his attention back to Joanna.

"T.J., I don't think this is our guy. He was too willing to come inside." Before she could say anymore, there was a knock at the door.

"Come in." Joanna's sultry voice was back.

The man walked into the room and lunged at Joanna, but she stopped him before he could lay a hand on her.

"You get nothing until I see some cash."

The man pulled crumpled up bills from his pocket. He counted it and then asked, "What will fifty dollars get me?"

"You tell me?" she enticed him.

T.J. clenched his fist in approval. She was handling herself perfectly. Joanna knew the customer had to offer her money and tell her what he wanted. If she volunteered any information it would be considered entrapment.

The man slinked over to Joanna and tossed his money on the bed. He pulled at her ear with his lips and told her what he wanted. The minute T.J. heard the man's depraved suggestion, he jumped.

"Peck, move in. We got it."

Before T.J. could finish the transmission, he saw Peck and Olsen bust into the room. The john didn't even have the chance to exhale. His face was up against the wall and his hands were cuffed against his back. T.J. rushed into the room and grabbed Joanna.

"You okay?"

She was rubbing at her ear like she was trying to scratch away the filth of the man's lips. "Yeah, I'm all right." She took a few deep breaths and paced the room. Olsen took the guy in cuffs down the back steps to a waiting, unmarked car. Peck turned to Joanna.

"You okay, Anderson?"

"Yeah. I'm fine."

Then he turned to T.J. "You've got static in your radio. It keeps cutting in and out. You might want to see if the techie can get it fixed."

"Yeah, sure. I'll talk to him."

It took forty-five minutes before Joanna was calm enough to hit the streets again. Their suspect would be held until the end of the shift, when T.J. could bring in the tapes that would incriminate him. The perp's car was hooked-up for impound, and Olsen was back from the station. Everything had gone like clockwork, except for the static in T.J.'s radio. But Joanna's equipment worked perfectly, and that's what mattered.

Everyone was back in place, and Joanna was back out on the streets. She prayed the whole time she walked up and down the pavement, T.J. hearing every word she said.

It was nearly four in the morning, and Joanna hadn't gotten any more hits. She got a few drive-bys from high school delinquents shooting off their foul mouths, but no more paying customers. T.J. drove her straight home. He would handle the paperwork at the station, but nothing she needed to stick around for.

As he walked Joanna to her door, T.J. held her close to his side. He took her keys from her hand and unlocked the door. The minute they stepped inside, Joanna broke down and cried. T.J. pulled her to his chest and held her tight, his emotions raw.

Joanna finally stepped away from him, wiping at the mascara running down her face. "I'm sorry. I just couldn't hold it any longer."

"Joanna, don't be sorry. You did great tonight. You were able to keep it together when you needed to. You were incredible."

"Thanks."

T.J. didn't know how to fill the silence. Finally, he pressed a kiss to Joanna's forehead. "Try to get some rest. I'll see you tomorrow around seven." He walked to the door, then turned around before leaving. "Are you going to be okay?"

"Yeah. I'm going to call Keith, and then I'm going to

take a scalding hot bath." She smiled. It was a weak smile, but he gave her points for trying.

He said goodnight then slipped out the door.

Joanna walked upstairs, grabbed her cordless and dialed Keith's cell phone. She dropped to the side of the bed and listened as his voicemail picked up. Squeezing her eyes shut in frustration, she left a message, trying to hide the disappointment in her tone.

"Hi, Keith, I thought you'd be home by now. I'm home. Everything went fine tonight. I'm going to take a nice hot bath, then go to bed. Call me when you have the chance.

"I love you."

She hung up the phone, feeling cheated. Keith was supposed to be off by midnight. She had wanted to talk to him and hear him say I love you before she went to sleep. Feeling tears sting her eyes, she got up and dragged herself to the bathroom.

Running the water, she filled the tub with the sweet smelling bubble bath she'd purchased at the mall. Not only had she bought things to make her look the part of a prostitute, she also picked up a few items to pamper herself with when she got home each night.

She was just getting ready to pull the plug on her bath water when her phone rang. She sighed in relief at the ringtone. She picked it up from where she'd laid it on top of her towel.

"Hello?"

"Hey, it's me."

At the sound of Keith's voice, Joanna relaxed back into the warm, soothing water.

"I'm sorry I missed your call. I ended up doing a swing shift. We were working an accident over on Clover Street."

"That's all right. It's just good to hear your voice." Joanna knew she'd be able to go to sleep now; hearing Keith's voice made all the difference in the world.

"So, how'd it go? Are you okay?" His words were urgent.

"Everything went fine. Like clockwork."

"Were any arrests made?"

Joanna knew Keith didn't care about the arrests. It was just his way of asking if she'd had to deal with any perverts.

"One."

Keith sighed. "And you're okay?"

"Fine."

"Can I come over?"

"Are you off now?"

"Not until eight o'clock."

Joanna was torn between what she wanted and what was practical. "Keith, as much as I want to see you, I can barely keep my eyes open now. There's no way I'll make it until eight o'clock."

"That's okay. Go ahead and go to bed. I'll use your spare key and let myself in. I'll sack out on your couch and wait for you to wake up."

Joanna closed her eyes, thinking how wonderful it would be to wake up and have Keith beside her. Wonderful but dangerous. "I don't think that's a good idea, Keith. I think we'd be playing with fire." The phone was silent, and

Joanna knew she'd insulted him. "Keith, it's not you, it's me. I'm feeling too vulnerable right now. I don't think I'd have a lot of self-control."

"Then let me be strong enough for both of us."

"No. That wouldn't work, and you know it."

"So you're saying I can't see you before I leave?" Keith's voice raised slightly.

"I'll see you at the airport. Like we planned." Again the phone was silent. "Please don't be angry, Keith. We've already been over this."

"I'm not angry." His tone softened. "It's just that I haven't even left yet, and I'm already anxious to get home."

"I know, Keith. I feel the same way." Joanna clutched the phone to her ear while a silent tear fell to her chest. "I'll meet you Wednesday night at the airport."

"My plane leaves at eight."

"And I'll meet you at six."

"You're sure you know where?"

"Keith . . ."

"I know, I know." Keith was silent for a moment. When he spoke again, Joanna could hear the emotion in his words. "Joanna . . . I love you."

"I love you too, Keith."

Joanna pulled the plug on her tepid bath and moved with heavy steps to bed. She fell asleep praying about her present circumstances . . . and her future with Keith.

CHAPTER THIRTY-NINE

When Joanna's alarm went off at four in the afternoon, she groaned and tossed one of her pillows across the room. She was exhausted. Nightmares and bizarre dreams had attacked her unconsciousness, and whenever she woke, it was hard to get back to sleep because of the afternoon sun lighting her bedroom. The stupid belly ring hadn't helped much either. It was still tender, making it hard for her to find a comfortable position.

Getting out of bed, Joanna decided to go a few rounds with her punching bag. She needed somewhere to channel her pent-up aggression. And since her house was already spotless, there was nothing left for her to do except work up a good sweat. But, even with all her efforts, the day ticked by with incredible slowness.

T.J. was right on time; the drive to the station quiet. Joanna went directly to her locker and put on another tasteless outfit. This time, she remembered to bring her street clothes with her to the apartment. Otherwise, she was going to end up with a locker full of clothes.

When she and T.J. got to the apartment, Joanna took off her jacket so she could get wired. Her halter top revealed the tattoo of a fairy-like nymph on her shoulder.

"Is that new, too?" T.J. asked, as he handed her the small transmitter.

"Yeah, but it's not permanent. It will wear off eventually." Joanna slipped the transmitter into her halter and adjusted the mic.

⊕

T.J. glanced over Joanna's outfit. It was more revealing than the night before. She was trying too hard, but he thought it best to keep his observations to himself.

They were in position a little after eight and stayed in place until three in the morning without as much as a single hit. T.J. drove Joanna home, sensing her disappointment. He pulled into the driveway and turned off the car. "Joanna, you're doing fine. We can't expect this guy to materialize overnight."

"I know. I guess I just want this to be over with."

"We all do Joanna, but . . ." T.J. wasn't sure how to say what was on his mind.

"But what?" She turned to him.

"Joanna, I just don't want you to think it's you."

"What do you mean?"

"Well, it's just that I don't want you to think it's the way you look . . . or act, or the way you dress. You're doing a great job. Don't think you have to dress more provocatively to get this guy's attention."

She grinned. "Is that what this is all about? You didn't like the way I looked tonight." She chuckled. "Since when are you the fashion police?"

"I just don't want you to think you have to try so hard. You're a knockout Joanna, and you know it. I don't want you to do anything you're not comfortable with. We just need to be patient."

"I know." She looked down at the small purse in her hand and fiddled with the strap.

"Same time tonight?" T.J. asked, as he started the car.

"No. I'm seeing Keith off at the airport tonight. I'll meet you at the station."

"Okay, I'll see you then."

Joanna ran her bath water and dialed Keith at the same time. "Keith?"

His voice was groggy. "Hey, Joanna . . . what time is it?"

"Three-thirty. We cut out a little earlier tonight."

All of a sudden Keith sounded completely awake. "Why, did something happen?"

"Nothing happened. That was the problem. We didn't get a single hit."

Keith sighed. "Look, why don't I come over let's say about three o'clock tomorrow. You could drive me to the airport and then take my car home for me."

Joanna stepped into the tub as she and Keith made plans for late afternoon. After hanging up phone, she slowly sunk into the warm, bubble-laden water.

T.J. headed for the beach after he dropped Joanna off and checked in at the station. It was his way of winding down.

He met up with Justin and surfed until the tide went out, then planned on crashing until his alarm clock woke him. But he didn't need his alarm. His jumbled thoughts kept him awake.

He pulled the Bible he'd bought at Wal-Mart off the nightstand and flipped through some of the marked pages. Some of it was difficult to understand. But there were other sections that made him realize even some of the people in the Bible had screwed-up pretty bad and God still forgave them.

Maybe it wasn't too late for him after all.

Joanna looked through the peephole at two in the afternoon, surprised to see Keith standing on the porch, a single yellow tulip in his hand. She pulled her robe tightly around her and tied the sash before answering the door.

"You're early."

She reached out for the flower and gave him a quick kiss. His eyes said he wished she would have lingered. "Let me get dressed, and I'll be right down."

Joanna rushed up the steps and quickly pulled a floral sundress from her closet. It was one of her favorites because of its slender cut, shear material, and little flounced sleeves.

She tossed her robe on the bed and slipped the dress over her head, the pull at her naval reminding her of the new piece of jewelry.

She looked at herself in the full-length mirror and turned. She made sure the short scallop of her sleeve covered her tattoo. She didn't want Keith to see either one of her new additions. She wasn't sure how he would react, and didn't want to ruin the afternoon.

Keith was waiting for her at the bottom of the stairs when she was done dressing. He reached out for her and pulled her close. When she winced, he quickly backed away. "What's wrong?"

"Nothing." She returned his hug, prepared for the pain this time, and added a firm kiss.

"You sure look pretty. You're going to make it even harder for me to leave."

"I just want you to remember what you're leaving behind. Just in case you decide to extend your trip." She hung on his neck, eyes transfixed on his.

"That's not going to be a problem." He kissed her again . . . and again.

The phone rang, interrupting them.

"Let it ring," he said placing yet another kiss on her lips.

She giggled. "I've got to—"

He wouldn't let her speak. He just kept dotting her lips with kisses. She finally broke his hold and went to check her voicemail. It had been Michelle. Worry extinguished her happy mood. "I've got to answer this," she said as she pressed a few buttons.

"Hi, Michelle, it's Joanna. Sorry I couldn't get to the phone in time. Is everything okay?" Feeling a sense of relief, Joanna smiled at Keith; everything was okay.

Joanna watch as Keith moved to the couch and made

himself comfortable. She continued her conversation with Michelle, pacing the living room as she spoke. After a few moments, Keith got up from where he was sitting and whispered in her free ear.

"I'm going out on the deck to cool off. The floor show is driving me crazy." Keith pointed to her dress, and she realized what he was talking about. The afternoon sun filtering through the windows accentuated the transparency of her dress. Joanna felt her cheeks flush, but Keith just laughed as he moved out onto the deck.

When Joanna finished her conversation with Michelle, she joined Keith outside.

"So, how's Michelle doing?"

"Pretty good. It's going to take a while for her to recover from everything she's been through."

Joanna leaned on the rail next to Keith. "So, you're going to call me when you can, right?" she asked as she looked at the water drifting in the canal.

"Every day."

Keith caressed the small of her back. Joanna closed her eyes at his touch, wondering what she was going to do the next two weeks without him. The case would occupy her mind, but Keith would occupy her heart.

He snaked his arms around her waist, pulling her back against his chest. Her gasp didn't go unnoticed, and he quickly let her go. Keith turned and looked Joanna in the eye. "That was the second time you did that. You're hurt, aren't you? What aren't you telling me."

"No. I'm not hurt." She looked at him; deciding how best to explain. She figured the easiest thing to do would be to just show him.

Taking Keith's hand in hers, she gently laid it on the soft material of her dress and slid it over to where the jewel poked out slightly. "I pierced my bellybutton, and it's still a little tender."

He pulled his hand back, "Why'd you do that?" He said, disappointment in his tone.

"Because it's expected, if you're working the streets." Joanna cringed at how tacky her own words sounded. She could tell Keith was trying not to let it bother him.

But it did.

"Come on, Keith, don't let this ruin our time together."

She looked at the simmer in his eyes as he put his finger to her chin and lifted her lips to touch his. "Is there anything else I should know?"

She smiled weakly. "A Henna tattoo, but that's it."

"Where?"

Joanna lifted her sleeve and turned so he could see it. Instead of getting angry or voicing more disappointment like she expected, Keith surprised her by placing a gentle kiss where the nymph was delicately tinted.

"You're driving me crazy, you know that don't you?" Keith spoke between kisses. Kisses that traveled up the nape of Joanna's neck. "I thank God every day for bringing such a beautiful woman into my life. I love your strong will, enthusiasm for life, dedication to your job, and the passion you have for God. And I know God doesn't tempt us beyond what we can handle. But I'm telling you Joanna, He's giving me a lot more credit than I deserve."

Keith's words thrilled her, because he loved her as she was, and didn't have plans to change her. Sure, they would have disagreements regarding her work. But he knew that was a part of who she was, and he accepted it. He might not always like it. But he accepted it.

The day went by too quickly and before Joanna knew it, they were standing in the airport terminal holding hands, not wanting to say good-bye.

"Remember, call my cell phone no matter what time it is. I won't have it on me at work, but I'll check it for messages whenever I can." Joanna acted like a mother hen, giving him last minute instructions, straightening his collar, and wiping her lip gloss from his cheek.

"I will, Joanna." Keith grasped both her hands, stilling her nerves. He looked at her with his piercing blue eyes. "Be careful, Joanna. Please don't do anything foolish or risky. Don't try to be a hero . . . and listen to T.J. I know he's a good man and will be looking out for you while I'm gone."

She swallowed hard. "I will. Everything by the book. I promise."

Their kiss was as intimate as a busy airport would allow. Joanna stood back and watched as Keith passed through security, then headed up the ramp to his gate where the rest of his team waited. He didn't look back, but she understood why.

When Keith was out of sight, she turned to walk away, tears blurring her vision. She'd been strong in front of him, not wanting him to remember her with tears in her eyes. But now that she was by herself, the torrent she had held at bay, flooded her lids and spilled down her cheeks.

She never would've thought that love . . . love for a man, could be so painful. She knew the pain she felt at the death of her parents, and the loss of Matthew, but this was different. She kept reminding herself it was only for two weeks.

Two weeks.

"I can do this!"

Joanna arrived at the station a little early. The captain cornered her and asked her how things were going. Since she knew he was briefed daily, she assumed his real question was *how was she doing?* Once she convinced him she was fine and committed to seeing the assignment through, he walked with her to the War Room.

The other men slowly drifted in, bantering to keep the mood light. She glanced at the clock on the wall, knowing it was time to transform herself.

As she headed to the locker room, she saw T.J. come in the back door and stopped. He glanced over her and grinned. His appreciation made her blush.

"I'd like to think you got all dressed up for me, but who am I kidding." He smiled the smile that had charmed dozens of women. "Did Keith get to the airport okay?"

"Yeah."

"And you're going to be able to keep your head in the game tonight?"

"Absolutely!" she answered with certainty.

Joanna stepped into the locker room and psyched herself up to become her alter ego. After teasing her hair and applying make-up, she scooped up her costume for the night and dropped it on the back of the toilet in the bathroom stall.

Joanna pulled on the rhinestone studded crop top she'd bought on clearance at a lingerie store, and a pair of black spandex pants she had to slither into to get them over her hips.

Between her short top and her hip-hugging pants, a good portion of her mid-drift was exposed. That's when Joanna realized she'd forgotten to bring a jacket. Getting Keith to the airport had distracted her enough that she hadn't thought past their good-bye.

Without a jacket on, Joanna felt extremely self-conscious as she stepped from the locker room. It was one thing to look like this under the cast of a street light, where shadows help to masked some of her embarrassment. But in the fluorescent lit hallways of the station, she felt over exposed.

Rogers was standing outside the War Room, talking to Frank. Joanna gave Frank one of her penetrating stares and watched as he quickly walked away. Rogers on the other hand, looked at her with an unsettling gleam.

Joanna knew he was trying to intimidate her, but it wasn't going to work. She stared right back at him. She wouldn't give him the satisfaction of looking away. But when he stepped into her path, Joanna had no choice but to stop.

"Got a problem?" she said defiantly.

"Yeah. I'm looking at it."

"Don't give me too much credit. I hear I'm not your only problem."

He took a step closer. "What do you mean by that?"

Joanna refused to back down. She wanted Rogers to know she wasn't going to take his harassment any longer. "You screwed-up your personal life, and now you're looking for someone to take it out on. Well, I'm not going to be your whipping boy. You're a sorry excuse for a man and a cop, and I'm not going to put up with your garbage anymore.

"If you want to tangle with me, go right ahead. I'll file against you just like I did Cummings. I think I have enough clout on my side now. I won't have any problem getting the captain's attention."

"Don't push me, Anderson, because I'll push back."

"Go right ahead. You'll be pushing yourself into an early retirement."

She stepped around him and into the War Room, leaving Rogers with his veiled threats.

T.J. looked at Joanna and had to fight the sickening feeling that assaulted his stomach. It was as if God was using her to show him the depths of his own depravity. In the past, he thought nothing of staring at women who dressed to entice. If they wanted to showcase their bodies, he was more than willing to be their audience. But now, seeing Joanna dressed that way disgusted him.

Why?

Because Joanna was a person. A person with feelings. And he realized the women that walked the streets were real people, too. No hooker or stripper grew up saying:

When I grow up I want to be a hooker and let strange men have sex with me because I have no other source of income.

Or. *I want to be a stripper so men can get their thrills staring at me, not caring that I'm a person who had higher goals but this is where I ended up."*

T.J. realized women made themselves objects out of

desperation—when they felt they had no other choice, or because they'd been told that's all they were good for.

He realized he had perpetuated that feeling in women by the way he took advantage of them, never really giving a relationship a thought. All he wanted was to feel good for the night.

God was doing a number on him.

He was slowly chipping away the things T.J. thought had made him happy. He hadn't had a beer in days, the taste of alcohol no longer giving him the buzz that usually relaxed him. And now, God was using Joanna to show him how wrong it was to use women to satisfy his emptiness.

The preacher had talked about the many things people use to fill the void in their lives. God was showing T.J. he was guilty of the very same thing. He was trying to fill his emptiness when God was the only one who could.

T.J. continued to wrestle with his feelings as he drove through back streets to get to the apartment building. He glanced at Joanna, wanting to talk to her, but the distant look on her face let him know her thoughts were faraway—probably on Keith—and he didn't want to interrupt.

They climbed up the back steps and entered the room with all the electronic equipment. Joanna slipped her transmitter in place while T.J. looked the other way.

"I saw you in the hall with Rogers and Frank. Everything okay?"

"Yeah. I told him I wasn't going to put up with his crap anymore. And to stay away from me."

"Do you think you got your point across?" T.J. asked as he checked their devices, making sure everything was working.

"As much as I could with a jerk like Rogers."

"I saw the way Frank bolted when you walked up. You never did tell me what went on between the two of you."

"Nothing. Why? Did he say something else?"

"No, that's just it. He refuses to talk about it. He won't say a word. Not even to—"

T.J. stopped before he incriminated himself.

Joanna leaned on the console and grinned at T.J. "Not even to the guy that set me up? Is that what you were going to say?"

"You knew?" T.J. was shocked Joanna knew he'd been the mastermind behind the prank, but had never confronted him.

"Of course I knew."

T.J. hung his head out of embarrassment. "Just tell me nothing happened, and I'll leave it at that. I feel horrible I set you up, and I just want to know that Frank didn't try anything."

Joanna's stare was cold, her expression tight. "He didn't try anything. Satisfied?" She turned around and, adjusted the clip camera in her hair.

"That's it? You're not going to tell me what happened?"

Joanna paused for a moment then glared at him. "Your bet was that he couldn't get into my bed, right?"

"Right." T.J. could actually feel himself blushing.

"Well, he was smooth. I'll give him that. Frank was the perfect gentleman, until we got back to my place."

Now T.J. wasn't so sure he wanted to hear anymore. To think he'd been responsible for setting the whole thing up made him feel like a jerk. "But nothing happened, right?"

"Oh, I wouldn't say that," Joanna snickered.

"Come on Joanna, this isn't funny. Tell me what happened."

She broke out in laughter. "You should have seen him running around my neighborhood buck naked."

"What?" T.J. was thoroughly confused.

"He did end up in my bed, T.J. So technically he won your little bet. When we got back to my place, I went upstairs to use my bathroom. When I came out, he was lying in my bed, his clothes piled on the floor."

"You're kidding?" T.J. didn't understand why Frank wouldn't have bragged about that. "And he didn't tell any of us?"

"Oh, he could have. But when I threw his clothes out the window, I told him if he dare lie to anyone about what went on, I would tell the entire station how he slinked away from my house buck naked, his shortcomings tucked between his legs."

T.J. was laughing. He couldn't help it. The mental picture of Frank running down the street naked was just too much.

"I'm glad you think it's funny. I was never more embarrassed in my life."

"You're a pretty tough, chick, you know that." T.J. draped his arm around her shoulder. "Not many people could've put up with the abuse you have over the last year. And you know what? I know of at least seven guys that have really come to respect you for it. No one deserved the detective's position more than you."

Joanna sighed, pride lighting her face. She pulled the clip through her hair one more time, making sure it was in position. When she turned to T.J., he gave her a smile, hoping it let her know just how much she meant to him. "You ready?"

She nodded. "Let's get this done."

It had been a busy night. Joanna had been propositioned several times, though not every one of them led to an arrest, however three men were in custody.

Joanna was getting more resilient, being able to get back out on the street without much down time. Her demeanor was getting more calloused and her comments more caustic. Seeing the transformation in Joanna made T.J. realize how women could turn off the emotional side of being used by men.

Of course, Joanna had back up and knew there was no way anyone was going to use her. But seeing the Joanna he knew fade behind the clothes and the makeup each night bothered him.

It was getting late, and T.J. was ready to call it quits when a late model Buick pulled up where Joanna was standing. She leaned on the window frame and began her routine. T.J. was glad he was the only one who could hear Joanna and the filth she had to put up with.

The trick quickly parked his car and followed Joanna inside. When they walked into the room, the man was immediately on Joanna, pressing her against the wall with his body. T.J. jumped from his seat waiting for Joanna to use the signal. *Say it Joanna. Say it.*

She pushed at the man's shoulders putting some distance between them. "Your tab's running, baby, and you don't even know what it's costing you."

"I don't care. Name your price." He pressed his face against her neck.

T.J. watched the screen, as the man began to grope her. "Come on, Joanna, get out of there," he gritted under his breath.

T.J. raked his hands through his hair, knowing what Joanna was thinking. She knew they couldn't let this guy go and take the chance of him ruining their entire set-up. But she had also been warned if she used entrapment he'd be on the streets in an hour, exposing their sting.

She was trying to get him to say something, but was allowing too many liberties in the meantime.

Finally, she pushed him away roughly. "No freebies, mister! Just tell me what you want and how bad you want it."

He spun Joanna around, pushing her down onto the bed. He pounced on top of her and said, "I've got a hundred bucks and two hours–"

Before the man could say another word, T.J. gave the signal. Peck and Olsen broke into the room, throwing the guy onto the floor. T.J. busted through the door, picked up the guy, and slammed his face against the wall.

"You're under arrest, you filthy piece of trash."

Peck pulled T.J. off the guy while Olsen applied the cuffs. "Go check on Joanna, T.J. We've got this covered." But T.J. lunged at the man again. "Get out, now, T.J.!" Peck stood between T.J. and the man. "Check on Joanna. She's in the surveillance room."

T.J. stalked into the surveillance room and slammed the door. "What the hell did you think you were doing?" he yelled at Joanna, his concern replaced with anger.

Joanna paced back and forth, her breathing labored. "I had to get him to name a price. I couldn't take the chance of screwing-up and letting him get away."

"You let it go too far, Joanna. You can't do that." His voice was still raised.

"I can handle it," she said defiantly, and pushed past him.

T.J. reached out and grabbed her arm, jerking her around to face him. "I don't want you to handle it. I'll use my own judgment next time. If things get too hot, I'm putting a stop to it, signal or no signal."

She pulled her arm free. "T.J., I have a job to do. We need to catch this guy before he murders someone else. I can handle a little pawing. Trust me. I know what I'm doing."

"Fine. You can handle it, but that's it for tonight. I'm calling it quits."

T.J. got on the radio, and through all the static and squawking on his handheld, he let everyone know they were packing it up for the night.

He and Joanna didn't exchange another word.

When they returned to the station and Joanna saw Keith's car in the parking lot, her heart constricted. For an instant she thought he was there, but quickly remembered she'd driven his car to work, and he was thousands of miles away. She rummaged around in her purse for her cellphone, turned it on, and checked it for messages.

Nothing.

When Joanna got home, she hurried to check her landline for messages–on the outside chance Keith had confused the two numbers.

Nothing.

He said not to expect a call the first few days.

Keith had warned her they had thirty flight hours, not including layovers and travel time from one connection to another. He had told her the earliest to expect a call was Friday, but she stared at her phone anyway.

Joanna took an extra long bath before climbing into bed. Tonight had taken a lot out of her. She was exhausted physically and emotionally.

When she closed her eyes, she prayed for Keith and his team–for a safe trip and a rewarding mission. She prayed for T.J. realizing he was struggling with the operation more than she had expected. She also prayed for his soul, knowing he was searching for answers regarding life. She closed her prayers with Michelle; she was young and had her whole life ahead of her. "Make yourself real to her, God. Be her rock."

CHAPTER FORTY

The rest of the week had its ups and downs. Thursday night had been so quiet, Joanna was convinced their operation had been compromised. But Friday night was a revolving door of perverts, drunks, and tweakers looking for some cheap action. It had been their busiest night yet, with five hook-ups before two in the morning.

Friction between she and T.J. was building. He was mad at her for taking what he considered were unnecessary risks and she argued she was doing what needed to be done.

He'd snapped at her more than once tonight and she'd pretty much told him off. She reminded him his job was to mind the monitors, hers was to get the perps to name their price and fetishes. If he didn't like his assignment, she'd get someone else to replace him.

They hadn't spoken the rest of the night.

But Joanna knew T.J.'s attitude wasn't the only thing contributing to her bad mood. She hadn't heard from Keith until early Saturday morning. And by then, she was climbing the walls with worry.

When she'd finally spoken with Keith, he apologized profusely and explained his team had encountered some unexpected delays.

Political tensions had risen in the area where they usually set up camp, causing his team to travel to an underdeveloped region in the south. Keith assured Joanna he and his team were perfectly safe, but because of the unforeseen change, his phone use would be extremely limited. When he told her he would not be able to call every day like he had promised, Joanna's heart sunk. She understood his need to conserve his phone batteries for emergency situations, but it did little to minimize her disappointment.

Choking back tears, Joanna had kept her voice strong and steady. Voicing her frustration would've only make Keith feel worse. A guilt trip when he was thousands of miles away was something Keith didn't deserve—especially since the circumstances were beyond his control.

Joanna assured Keith she understood, and his safety was all that mattered to her. They'd hardly gotten the chance to talk about anything else before their connection was lost.

Joanna felt cheated.

She hadn't gotten the chance to say 'I love you.'

Burying her emotions, Joanna hit the streets on Saturday night with a vengeance. The weekend had been much like Friday. Everyone was out looking for a party and she was the entertainment.

If Joanna had been a part of a typical sting operation, the weekend would've been seen as a great success. But that wasn't Joanna's reason for being on the street night after night. Her purpose was one dimensional.

She was looking for a killer.

Every night that she failed, she gave the killer a chance to leave another victim behind.

By Monday, Joanna had hit a wall. Emotionally she was wrecked, physically she was dragging. The operation was taking its toll on her. Losing sleep and weight, she felt completely wiped. When T.J. insisted on driving her home Monday night, she conceded without a fight. He walked her to the door, but instead of wishing her a goodnight, T.J. followed her in and sat her down.

He explained that he was genuinely concerned about her health and was questioning her ability to continue the operation. He wanted to call it quits, and was ready to go to the captain and tell him that.

Joanna was shocked and felt betrayed.

She knew T.J. was right. She was exhausted both physically and mentally, but that didn't give him the right to go to the captain behind her back. Fired up, she let him have it with both barrels.

She told T.J. in no uncertain terms that if he wanted to call it quits, he had every right to walk away. She also reminded him it was *her* operation, not his. She would decide if and when to scrap it.

T.J. argued that her stubbornness was blinding her to the physical signs of exhaustion. If she continued to push herself, she was going to suffer a physical breakdown.

She insisted he was being overly dramatic and that it was insulting for him to question her abilities.

They continued arguing for over an hour before T.J.

stormed out, leaving Joanna to wonder if he was really going to go to the captain.

An hour later, T.J. called. He apologized, not for his feelings, because he was convinced she was headed for a breakdown. But, he agreed not to go to the captain. At least not yet.

Joanna's compromise was that she would make a concerted effort to get more sleep and not skip meals.

T.J. seized the opportunity and insisted on fixing her dinner. "I'll be back at five o'clock. Be prepared to be amazed."

"That isn't necessary, T.J. I can fix my own dinner. I don't need a babysitter," she snapped, feeling as if he didn't trust her.

"It's not up for discussion. I'll see you at five."

Joanna was on the phone with Keith when T.J. arrived to fix dinner. She gave him an irritated glance as she let him in, then walked out onto the deck. She talked to Keith in a soft tone, not wanting to be overheard. When she walked into the kitchen and handed the phone to T.J., he looked at her, a confused expression on his face.

"Keith wants to talk to you to make sure I'm not hiding anything." She crossed her arms and raised her brow, her way of warning T.J. not to say anything that would bother Keith unnecessarily.

"Hey, Keith, how you doin'?"

Joanna listened to the one-sided conversation. T.J. did a good job of assuring Keith everything was okay. "Don't worry, man, everything here is fine." He glanced at Joanna with a deadpan look. "Sure. See you soon."

He handed the phone back to Joanna. She stepped away to finish her conversation, then walked back to the kitchen.

"Thanks for being supportive," she said to T.J.

The tension between them had not eased completely, and she knew T.J. had masked that while talking to Keith.

"I didn't want him to worry. I know how I feel sitting in the next room. I wasn't going to tell that to a guy thousands of miles away."

"But you're right, everything here is fine," Joanna said.

"Right," he said sarcastically.

"What's wrong, T.J.? Everything is going as planned."

"You're taking too many chances." He crossed from the kitchen to the open French doors. Walking outside, he started to prepare the coals in the barbeque.

She walked after him, leaning on the doorframe. "How can I take too many chances with you in the very next room?"

"I just don't like what you're letting scum get away with." He poured on the lighter fluid and struck a match. Flames leapt three feet in the air."

"Hey, would you mind not taking your aggression out on my grill. We're cooking a few steaks, not a side of beef."

He ignored her.

"Your overreacting, T.J."

"Am I?" He turned and got right in her face. "Or maybe you're enjoying it." He pushed past her.

"What is that supposed to mean?" she asked, as she followed him back to the kitchen.

"Come on, Joanna, admit it. This is exciting for you."

"What are you talking about?"

T.J. whirled around, pointing a dogmatic finger in her face. "You. I'm talking about you pushing the boundaries of your virginal lifestyle. Your ridiculously high standards would never allow you to compromise your morals. But now . . . now you can be daring. Push the envelope. All in the line of duty."

Joanna opened her mouth to say something but T.J. continued, waving his arms as he spoke, the veins in his neck bulging. "You can do the things you've never allowed yourself to do before. You can play the part of a tease, of a seductress. You can throw yourself at a man knowing nothing's going to happen to you. You're completely safe. You've got back-up."

Joanna stood with her mouth hanging open, utterly shocked by T.J.'s accusations. "I can't believe you're saying these things to me. I thought you knew me better than that. What was last night all about? Your concern for my health, my well-being? Was that just a lie? Or maybe you were embarrassed by the way I was *throwing* myself at those men?" Tears fell over her heated cheeks. "You're nothing but a—"

"Joanna, I'm sorry, I didn't mean—"

T.J. reached out for her arm, but she jerked it away and marched to the front door. Swinging it open hard, it slammed into the wall, causing the door knob to embed itself into the plaster. "I think you should leave. I would hate for you to think I was trying to seduce you."

T.J. walked over to the door, pulled it from the wall, closing it softly. He leaned his head against the door and sighed. "Joanna, I'm so sorry. I don't know why I said those things."

"Well you certainly thought them!" she shouted, her voice quivering.

"I'm sorry," he said softly, then walked to the foot of the stairs and sat down. He rested his elbows on his knees, and clenched his hands together. "It's me, Joanna. I'm trying to find excuses for what I've done."

"What to do mean by that?" she asked, belligerently.

"I've used women my whole life, Joanna. I've always told myself they were having just as much fun as I was. That it was mutual. But seeing you with those men, knowing you're just playing a part, makes me wonder. Were the women I've been with playing a part, too? Being who they thought I wanted them to be? Did they feel like you do at the end of the night, used, dirty . . . emotionally exhausted? I realized I was doing the same thing to the women I dated, as the men in that apartment are doing to you. The only difference is I didn't offer them money."

Joanna's anger was immediately replaced with compassion.

With an aching heart, she sat down next to T.J. and laid her head on his shoulder. "T.J. you're being too hard on yourself. I know you didn't take advantage of anyone, you're not that type. The women you've been with were willing partners." She laid a reassuring hand on his forearm. "But you can see now why God set sex aside to be experienced by two people. Husband and wife. In marriage, you don't question the actions or motivations of the other person. You know that person is with you because of love and commitment, not just gratification."

"Then explain to me divorce and affairs?"

"I'm not saying every marriage is perfect, T.J. But you can see how if you hadn't had these previous relationships you wouldn't be questioning your motives. Selfishness is usually what breaks up a marriage more than anything else. If God is at the center of that relationship, selfishness has a harder chance of creeping in."

He laid his hand on top of hers. "I'm so sorry for saying those things to you Joanna. That was inexcusable of me. I guess I just wanted to blame you for the turmoil I'm feeling."

"You blame me?" Joanna's heart plummeted.

"No." He gave her hand a squeeze. "I said I *wanted* to blame you. But I can't. I made my choices, and I have to man up and take responsibility for them. It's just being with you, talking with you, going to church with you . . . it has me rethinking everything in my life. I've screwed-up so much, and it's killing me to think about the people I've hurt along the way."

"You need to talk to someone about it, T.J. God is trying to break down the barriers you've put up, but they've been there for so long they're difficult to get through. I bet if you made an appointment to talk to Pastor Grant, he'd be able to give you some real perspective on what you're going through. Remember, he's been there before."

T.J. squeezed Joanna's hand. "I don't know if I could talk to a perfect stranger about the crap I'm dealing with."

"But promise me, you'll at least consider it."

He sighed.

"Come on, T.J., you can be frank with him. And I know he'll be honest with you. Pastor Grant doesn't pull any punches. He's not going to sugarcoat what he has to say just to make you feel comfortable. If anything, I think you'll appreciate his straightforwardness."

T.J. sat, stroking the back of Joanna's hand.

After a minute, she gave him a little nudge.

"Okay, I'll think about it."

CHAPTER FORTY-ONE

Joanna had a static-filled phone call from Keith on Thursday. Other than the change in location, his trip was going as planned and he would be home in less than a week.

She assured Keith she was fine, but heard a marked difference in his tone when she told him there were no plans of pulling back. She quickly changed the subject to T.J., giving Keith the Reader's Digest version of their conversation, and that T.J. was considering meeting with Pastor Grant when their assignment was over.

Keith was telling her about a young boy he had treated, when the static became so loud, she could no longer make out what he was saying. Frustrated, she strained to hear him, but it was no use. She kept talking to him with the hopes he could hear her, but after five minutes with no response, she finally disconnected his call.

Joanna was in a melancholy mood the rest of the day, contemplating what her future looked like. She was in love with Keith. That much she knew. But she also recognized he struggled with her line of work. He was supportive, and she didn't think he'd ever ask her to choose between her job and him, but could she expect him to put his anxieties aside if their relationship became permanent?

She was already stressing about how Keith would handle her assignment once he got home. He would be shocked to see the way she had been dressing, and the emotions she dealt with each night when she came home—Joanna wasn't sure she'd be able to hide them.

She knew she was only playing a part, but her self-esteem was taking a major hit. She couldn't even look at herself in the mirror anymore, and her energy level was at an all-time low.

Joanna now understood why so many prostitutes were drug addicts. The last few nights she'd had to resort to taking sleeping pills. It was the only way she could erase the leering eyes and silence the vile comments she put up with before a trick indicted himself.

She could only imagine how hookers must feel after sacrificing their bodies for a few dollars, pulling their clothes back on, only to turn around and do it all over again.

It wasn't a lifestyle. It was a death sentence.

It was Friday night and proving to be busier than the last. Everyone on the team was worn and irritable; morale at a dangerous low.

Joanna couldn't help but feel responsible. She had purposely chosen family men to be on her team to protect her dignity. She hadn't stopped to think of the time it would require them to be away from their own families. She'd apologized each night, feeling like she had failed. But each time that she did, they assured her this was part of the job, and she had nothing to be sorry about.

Of course, it didn't improve their dispositions any.

Keith had called her Sunday morning, apologizing for interrupting her sleep. He explained why he hadn't been able to talk on Saturday, and confirmed he would be coming home on Tuesday. He asked if she would still be on assignment. She reluctantly told him that they were in place for another week.

Hearing the disappointment in Keith's tone was the straw that pushed her over the edge. Joanna tried to muffle her tears, but it was no use. When Keith realized she was crying, he immediately asked her what was wrong. What was she hiding? It took her several minutes to assure him the only thing wrong was that she missed him terribly.

He promised to call her as soon as he was stateside, which, if all their connections were made, should be sometime early Tuesday. He told her how much he missed her and reminded her how much he loved her. She was telling him the same when static took over the line and it eventually went dead.

Early Monday morning, Joanna was leaning against a street sign, her mind on Keith. She'd played their conversation over and over in her head, hearing the disappointment in his voice each time. Her eyes started to well up.

Just then, Johnson drove by flashing his lights once—their signal they were done for the night. Surprised they were shutting down so early, Joanna looked at her watch. It was only two o'clock. When she walked around to the back steps, she saw Peck and Olsen on their way down.

"Hey, why is T.J. calling it quits so early?" she asked.

"Frustrated like the rest of us, I guess," Olsen said, then quickly apologized. "I'm sorry, Joanna, I didn't mean to snap."

"Hey, you have every right to be frustrated. You both have a wife and kids to go home to. And every night you're out here with me, is more time away from them. I get that, and I'm sorry."

Peck put a hand to her shoulder and gave it a squeeze. "We're a team, Joanna. *You* have nothing to apologize for. Hang in there. We're going to get this guy."

After their little pep talk, Peck and Olsen each gave her a hug and wished her goodnight.

Joanna watched as they got into their beat-up sedan and drove away.

She really did have a great team. In time, all their efforts were going to pay off.

Joanna walked up the steps tired and weary. She walked into 'her' apartment and headed to the adjacent room where T.J. would be waiting for her. She opened the door and froze in horror. T.J. was lying on the floor, his shirt covered in blood. She dropped to his side, hearing him moan in pain.

"Well, hello, *Detective* Anderson."

Joanna spun around to see Rogers standing behind her. Gun in hand.

She quickly reached for T.J.'s weapon, but Rogers grabbed her by the hair and pulled Joanna to her feet. She threw her elbow back connecting with his nose, trying to break free.

He moaned in pain and shoved Joanna forward against the console of equipment, knocking the air from her lungs.

But he didn't let go.

He took his cuffs and smacked them against her wrists, clamping them so tight Joanna could feel them cutting into her skin. He spun her around as she screamed for help. His fist plowed into her jaw, knocking Joanna to the floor. Without her hands to break her fall, her head crashed against the wall before she crumpled alongside T.J.

Her vision blurred and dimmed, but Joanna fought to keep from blacking out.

Rogers tied something around her mouth, and began to drag her into the other room. Joanna looked at T.J. one last time.

No God. Not like this.

Throwing her onto the bed, Rogers' straddled Joanna, his heavy body pinning her against the mattress, blood from his nose dripping on her face. He pressed his hand against her neck and squeezed.

"Surprised?"

He laughed, and Joanna realized it was him.

Rogers was the Prostitute Killer.

The recognition in her eyes made Rogers smile. "Yep. You guessed it. I've been under your noses the whole time."

Joanna struggled under his weight, but his hand squeezed her neck even tighter. "Uh, uh, uh, I wouldn't do that if I was you."

Joanna lay still for a moment trying to comprehend

everything that was happening. She glanced at the door to the adjoining room. T.J had been shot and laid in the other room dying and there was nothing she could do about it. Rogers' eyes glanced in the same direction, reading her mind.

"No, he's not dead. But he will be. He'll bleed out before anyone finds you."

Rogers ripped at Joanna's blouse, tearing it to shreds. Then he pulled the wire from her bra and the clip from her hair. "I'll take these. I've already destroyed the rest of the equipment, but I'm not sure what the storing capabilities are in these things." He shoved them into his pocket, then stared at Joanna. He began stroking her hair and ran his fingers over her lips.

"The other women I killed first. They disgusted me. I didn't want to hear them fake their enjoyment. But you, I'll get a keen satisfaction knowing the last thing I took from you before you died was the last thing you would ever want to give away."

Rogers yanked at Joanna's skirt then smothered her with his body. Knowing she was going to die, Joanna pled for T.J.'s life.

God, please don't let T.J. die. He doesn't know You yet. You have to give him more time.

Joanna's head was spinning. Rogers still had a grip on her neck, squeezing the life out of her. Joanna closed her eyes. *And God, let Keith know how very much I loved him.*

Just then, Joanna heard a single gunshot and felt Rogers' dead weight collapse on top of her. She struggled under his bulk until his lifeless body fell off the side of the bed.

Joanna looked across the room and saw T.J. propped up against the doorjamb, his shirt drenched with blood and his skin the color of stone. He dropped the gun he was holding as his head fell back against the door.

Joanna screamed against the gag in her mouth. She knew she was watching T.J. bleed to death, unable to do anything about it.

With her hands still cuffed behind her back, Joanna tried to sit up. Unable to do so, she finally rolled herself off the side of the bed falling face first onto the floor. She shook off the pain and quickly got to her feet.

Joanna sunk to her knees beside T.J., powerless to do anything.

Please God.

Please.

Stumbling to the other room, Joanna looked everywhere, finally spotting T.J.'s handheld radio on the floor amid the debris of smashed equipment.

She crawled over and picked up the radio with her bound hands. She dropped it more than once, trying to get her finger on the button. She pressed the button and held it for as long as she could, then waited.

"T.J., is that you?" Joanna squealed when she heard Peck's voice. Peck had complained about the static from T.J.'s radio every day. Joanna had never been more thankful for a crappy piece of equipment.

She held the button again.

"Come on, T.J., just use the phone!"

Joanna pressed the button again, this time trying to use Morse Code. *Come on Peck, figure it out.* She messed up the code and had to start over. Then dropped the radio and watched it slide away from her. She could feel blood on her hands from the cuffs, making the radio hard to hold onto.

She picked up the radio again, her hands shaking so badly, she could barely hang onto it. Before she pressed the button, she heard Peck's transmission.

He was on his way.

Joanna's relief lasted only a second. She quickly crawled over to where T.J. lay, slipping on the trail of blood left by his wound. Joanna had to fight the nausea turning in her stomach at the sight of T.J.'s blood smeared all over her legs. Bending over, she pressed her ear against his chest and prayed for a heartbeat.

It was thready. But there.

Hang on, T.J. You've got to hang on.

Joanna was pleading, crying, and praying at the same time. She knelt next to T.J., rocking back and forth. She struggled against the cuffs on her wrists, crying at the pain.

When she heard approaching sirens, she silently pleaded for them to hurry. But it was an eternity before they grew louder.

Don't you dare give up, T.J. I need you here with me.

When she heard pounding on the stairs, Joanna looked up just as Peck busted into the room. He and Olsen surveyed the room, weapons drawn, shock registering in their eyes.

Peck got to Joanna first and removed the gag. "Joanna, what happened? What's Rogers—"

"T.J.'s bleeding to death," she gasped and choked. "help me stop the bleeding!"

Peck pulled his sweater off and immediately went to work on T.J.

"It was Rogers all along," Joanna cried hysterically. "He's the killer. He shot T.J. and was going to kill me."

With his weapon trained on Rogers, Olsen knelt down and pressed his fingers to his neck. "He's dead."

With the threat neutralized, Olsen hurried to where Joanna knelt next to T.J. He pulled out his cuff key and freed Joanna's hands. She pulled her arms around, crying at the excruciating pain in her shoulders.

"Joanna, look at me," Olsen said.

But she didn't take her eyes off T.J.

"Joanna, you're covered in blood. Where are you hurt?" Olsen asked.

Joanna glanced down, seeing not only the blood covering her body, but her exposure. She tried to pull her blouse shut, then realized her skirt was in shreds.

She looked up at Olsen. Without a word being said, he took off his jacket and wrapped it around her.

"Thank you," she whispered.

"Joanna, let me help you." Olsen tried to help her up, but she shook him off. "I'm fine. I want to stay here. I want to make sure he's okay." She watched as Peck pressed his sweater against T.J.'s side, trying to stop the bleeding.

Joanna took T.J.'s hand and gave it a squeeze. "Hang on T.J. I'll never forgive you if you die on me," she cried.

When the paramedics entered the room, both she and Peck were asked to move back. But she didn't budge.

"Ma'am, we need you to move back."

Peck gently pulled her to her feet and held her firmly to his side. "Come on, Joanna, they're going to do everything they can for T.J., but we've got to give them space to do it."

Peck led Joanna over to the bed and sat her down. He looked at her face and then held out her hands.

"Can we get a paramedic over here?" he asked quietly.

"No. I'm fine." Joanna pulled her hands away. "It's T.J.'s that's hurt. They need to help him." She tried to stand, but with his hands resting firmly above her knees, Peck held her in place.

"Joanna, you're hurt," he said calmly. "We're going to get a paramedic over here to take a look at you."

A female attendant knelt in front of Joanna.

"I'm fine," Joanna said, tears in her eyes. "You've got to help him."

"Miss, they're doing all they can. Let me help you."

When Joanna looked at the attendant in her blue jumpsuit, she thought back to the first time she'd met Keith.

And then she heard Keith's voice.

I love you, Joanna.

Joanna spun around looking for Keith, but couldn't find him.

"Joanna, what is it, what's wrong?" Peck asked.

"Where's Keith?"

Peck looked at her confused. "He's overseas, right?"

"No." She looked from side-to-side. "He's here. I just heard him."

Joanna was disoriented and confused. She was sure she'd heard Keith's voice, but how was that possible when he was thousands of miles away?

"He's going to be all right," Joanna heard someone say.

"Thank God," Peck said, emotion thickening his

words. "Joanna, did you hear that? T.J.'s going to be okay."

"I want to go with T.J. I need to be with him." Joanna tried to stand, but her legs gave out.

"It's okay, Joanna. Everything's going to be okay."

CHAPTER FORTY-TWO

Joanna didn't remember passing out or being taken to the hospital. She knew she was in the E.R. when she saw the same doctor that had treated her concussion standing over her.

"Come here often?" he said humorously.

She shot straight up. "T.J.?"

The doctor placed his hands on her shoulders and lowered her back to the examination table. "He's going to be fine, Detective Anderson. He's lost a lot of blood, but he was lucky. No vital organs were hit."

She relaxed against the table. "And you, my dear, have only a few nasty cuts and bruises. From what I hear, you were pretty lucky as well."

Joanna knew it wasn't luck. God had seen them both through a horrible ordeal. He wasn't finished with T.J. yet, and apparently He wasn't done with her either.

Although the doctor had preferred Joanna stay overnight for precautionary reasons, she had refused. She needed to see T.J. and wouldn't be able to if they stuck her in a hospital room.

Joanna was loaned a pair of surgical scrubs since the clothes she had been wearing were destroyed. She was embarrassed when she thought of the condition Peck and Olsen had seen her, but thankful beyond words they had shown up when they did.

When she was finally allowed in to see T.J., she walked quietly over to the side of his bed, not wanting to disturb him. He opened his eyes slightly and reached out for her hand. He looked at the bandages that covered her wrists.

"Are you okay?" he asked, his voice shaky.

"Better than you," she said with a smile, pushing a lock of hair from his forehead.

"It was Rogers all along," T.J. said.

She nodded, not trusting her voice.

"He told me what he was going to do to you, and that no one would even suspect him. I could hear him in the other room. I was afraid I was going to be too late. He didn't . . . he didn't hurt you, did he?"

"No." Joanna wiped the tear running down his face. "I'm fine, T.J. A little banged up, that's all. You were right on time."

"I prayed, Joanna. I prayed God would save you."

She smiled. "And I prayed He would save you."

"He has Joanna." T.J. squeezed her hand. "But not just physically. I told Him . . . if it wasn't too late for me . . . I'd like to get to know Him better."

Joanna collapsed against T.J.'s chest in tears. He moaned, causing her to sit up quickly. "I'm sorry."

Joanna's eyes scanned the bandage across his chest. "I didn't mean to hurt you."

"You could never hurt me, Joanna. In fact, you saved my life . . . in more ways than one."

Joanna watched as T.J. slept. When she was convinced he was going to be all right, she decided to go home and change. Keith would be home soon and she didn't want him to see her like this. She would explain to him what happened, but certainly didn't want him to see it firsthand.

When Joanna stepped out into the hallway, she saw Pastor Grant approaching, his expression grim. She was surprised he had already heard about T.J.'s accident—and by the look on his face, she knew no one had told him T.J. was out of danger.

"Pastor Grant, I can't believe you've heard already." She reached out her hand to shake his, emotion in her eyes.

"Then you know what happened?" he asked.

"Know . . . I was there."

The blank expression on Pastor Grant's face caused a coldness to run through her veins. "You're here to see T.J., right?"

"No, Joanna. I called your station looking for you and was told I could find you here." He stared at her, his eyes swollen and red. "Joanna, there's been an accident. The plane that was chartered for Keith's team went down. There were no survivors."

EPILOGUE
FOUR YEARS LATER

Joanna watched T.J. from the parking lot before walking across the sand. Smiling, she watched him do what he loved most.

She remembered the disappointment she felt when he told her he was quitting the force. She was afraid it was a knee-jerk reaction to being shot. But when he told her what he wanted to do, she was stunned.

The following year, T.J. started a surfing ministry. He wanted to take kids that were latch-key or in difficult situations and try to improve their quality of life. Along with the support of the church and some of his surfing buddies, he was able to finance what he considered his dream job.

T.J. had no idea God would use his willing heart to create a whole new ministry. Now he traveled to different churches and youth facilities, telling others how God got a hold of his life and turned him around.

He was having an incredible impact on the youth culture in their area. No one was more proud of his accomplishments than Joanna.

She watched T.J. as he rode a wave, a boy no more than four-years-old balancing on the board in front of him. There were a dozen kids running around and at least three other instructors helping on this Saturday morning.

T.J spotted Joanna the minute he hit the sand. He waved at her quickly before huddling the kids and instructors together for a closing prayer.

Joanna still felt a tingle whenever she was around T.J. She couldn't explain it and no longer tried to figure it out. She just smiled as she walked towards T.J., her sandals dangling from her fingers, her face turned toward the sun.

The kids dispersed—some with parents, others with instructors. Justin waved at Joanna as he collected the boards and other equipment; she smiled and waved back. Justin had turned out to be an amazing young man. He'd been ready to hit the pro circuit when T.J. explained to him his vision. Once Justin heard about it, he wanted in. He attributed T.J with saving his brother's life and wanted to give back. T.J. didn't take credit for the change in Justin's brother, knowing it was God that had saved him, but he had been thrilled to have Justin as a partner.

T.J. walked over to Joanna and gave her a big hug. He was still wet but she didn't care. She took in the scent that was uniquely his—something between sunscreen, seaweed, and board wax. When she saw the scar on his chest, she remembered that horrific day, four years ago. The day she thought her world had come to an end.

T.J. held her tight, walked over to the guard station, and sat on the stairs with her.

"What brings you out here?" He smiled at her, warily.

"What? I can't stop by just to say hi," she teased, knowing he knew her too well.

"Not usually."

It had taken a long time for Joanna to recover from the news of Keith's death. She swore it was him that whispered to her in that shabby apartment as T.J. lay close to death. She didn't feel abandoned by God, just confused. She couldn't understand why the people most important to her kept being taken away. It was T.J.–with the help of Pastor Grant–who had helped her through it.

She continued with the force after a short absence. They were both recognized with a commendation for their efforts in the Prostitute Killings. Everyone was shocked when all evidence–including DNA–proved it was indeed Rogers that had been responsible for the prostitute murders. Dr. Barnes figured it was the break-up of his marriage and his over-the-top macho image that led to his demise. Something inside him snapped and a vicious cycle was set in motion.

Even getting awards from the city council and governor's office did nothing to change T.J.'s mind about the future. God had finally broken through to him, and he had to make a change in his life if he wanted to do the things that God had laid on his heart.

"Earth to Joanna." T.J. waved his hand in front of her face, bringing her back from her daydream.

Sorry. I guess I kind of zoned out for a minute." She smiled at him and brushed some of the sand from his shoulder.

"Joanna, what is it?" T.J. looked at her, and Joanna could see concern in his eyes.

"I've been seeing someone and I'd like you to meet him."

"Oh . . . looking for some brotherly approval, are we?" He nudged her slightly, making her blush.

"Maybe." Her tone was serious.

"How long have you been seeing him?" he questioned.

"Five months on and off."

"Go on."

T.J. was surprised.

Joanna hadn't really seen anyone since Keith's death. She had taken it hard and had refused to let anyone else get close to her.

Though Joanna naturally sought refuge in T.J.'s arms, they quickly came to the conclusion that what they had was so much more than a romantic relationship. T.J. was there for her through the dark time, but they decided not to jeopardize what they had with an intimate entanglement that might not work out.

They were family.

They bickered like brother and sister at times, but loved each other fiercely.

T.J. had been seeing someone steady for almost a year. Joanna had given him her complete approval except for the way he was dragging his feet when it came to popping the question. Anna was a great woman with a nine-year-old son. She'd never been married, just gone through a few difficult situations; an unplanned pregnancy being one of them. T.J. got along with Scott like he was his own son, and Scott worshipped the ground he walked on.

"Five months on and off, because you weren't sure or because of your schedule?" T.J. questioned, getting his mind back on what Joanna had come to talk to him about.

"Because of our schedules. Sam's with the DEA."

T.J. raised a judgmental brow.

"I know, I know, I said I would never get involved with anyone in law enforcement, but it just kind of happened."

"How?"

"Working that trailer park sting. Remember, I told you we were tipped off about a meth lab out there. Sam was one of the agents sent in to assist us on the operation."

"And he's been assisting you ever since." T.J. gave Joanna a playful jab to the ribs.

"Come on, T.J., I'm serious." She got up from where they sat and started wringing her hands, a habit of hers that gave away how nervous she was.

"Why is this the first I'm hearing about him?" T.J. asked.

"Because it just kind of happened. I wasn't looking for a relationship; it was just all of a sudden there. I guess I wanted to make sure I knew how I felt before I told you."

T.J. got up and dropped an arm around her shoulder. They started walking down the beach.

"I assume he's a Christian?"

"Of course."

"Hey, just checking. If I remember correctly, you weren't completely immune to the charms of one overly handsome, rough around the edges, smooth-talking cop."

She smiled.

"Okay. So, when do I get to meet this guy?"

"I thought maybe you and Anna could come over on Tuesday for dinner."

"And does Sam know he's going under the microscope? Because I'm going to grill him, you know that, right? As far as I'm concerned there isn't a guy in the world good enough for you. Nothing short of a knight-in-shining-armor will garner my approval."

"Don't you dare be rude to him!" She punched him hard in the arm. "And stop being so obstinate. If you plan on scaring him off we can just forget about it."

T.J. laughed. "Come on, I'm just teasing. Well, sort of."

"T.J., this is serious. I've told Sam a lot about you, and he'd like to meet you. But not if you're going to give him the third degree."

"Okay, okay, I'll give the guy a shot." T.J. smiled at her and gave her a squeeze. He was glad to see the spark in Joanna's eyes. It had been absent for a long time; obviously this guy was special.

"Dinner sounds like fun," he continued. "I'll double check with Anna and make sure it's okay with her."

"Now you know, I'd normally invite Scott, too, but I thought it would be better if it was just us adults. You understand, don't you?" Joanna looked around. "Where is Scott anyway?"

"He and Anna went shopping for my birthday," T.J. said sheepishly.

Joanna gave him a fallen look. "Oh, T.J. I'm sorry,

with everything I have going on right now I kind of . . . forgot."

If Joanna wasn't mistaken, she saw just a hint of disappointment in T.J.'s expression. He tried to mask it but she knew him too well. It took everything in her to hold back the smile pushing at the corners of her mouth.

"Come on, Joanna, birthdays are for kids."

"But I feel so bad. It's just—"

"Like I said, Joanna, it's no big deal."

They walked and talked for a while until they ended up back at the guard shack. Justin was already out in the water, catching waves of his own, and Joanna could see T.J. was restless to do the same.

She glanced at her watch. "Well, I have a meeting in thirty minutes."

"On a Saturday?"

She just shrugged.

T.J.'s expression turned serious.

"Don't worry. It's nothing dangerous."

"And you'd tell me if it was?"

"Yes. I would need the prayer support."

"Good." He pulled her into a hug.

"You know, T.J., I would've never made it through everything if it hadn't been for you."

He chuckled. "I can't imagine where I would be if it hadn't been for you. Actually, I can, and that scares me even more." He pulled back and look into her eyes. "Funny how life turns out, isn't it?"

"Yeah," she sighed, looking out at the water. "Who

could've imagined you would be the one in ministry with a promising relationship, and I would be the one still trying to clean up the streets, going home alone every night."

"You're not alone, Joanna, and you know it." She looked down, but T.J. pushed her chin up, looking her in the eyes. "That's what makes you so strong."

"Well, I'm getting tired of being strong, T.J. I'd be willing to let someone else shoulder the weight of the world for a change."

He grinned and tipped his head towards the waves. "I've got an extra board. You know when you're surfing you forget about everything else."

She laughed. "That's because I have to hang on for dear life."

T.J. had a gleam in his eye that Joanna knew meant trouble. Slowly, she started backing away from him, knowing he was up to no good. Sure enough, before she get to far, he had his hands around her waist and was dragging her near the water's edge.

"T.J., I have a meeting in twenty-five minutes. I don't have time for this." She pleaded between peals of laughter.

He conceded, but only when she promised to go surfing with him sometime next week. Joanna had actually gotten pretty good but didn't do it nearly as much as she would like. But she had to admit, when T.J. did get her out on the waves, the rest of the world disappeared.

"Okay, then," she said, with a smile. "I'll give Anna a call to confirm Tuesday. Just in case you forget." She hugged him before she turned to walk away.

"Joanna . . ."

She turned back to look at T.J.

"I'm praying for you. I know God has a plan for your life. Look what he did with mine."

She waved good-bye and headed for her car. She had to fight back the tears because it was true. God had already done incredible things in her life. Even through loss and struggles, the thing that kept Joanna strong was knowing God had used her to bring T.J. to Him.

The chain of events in her life—the death of her parents and Matthew, following in Matthew's footsteps becoming a cop, being partnered with T.J. It had all been a part of God's plan. If she had rebelled at any one point, things might've turned out completely different. She knew God could have used anyone to come into T.J.'s life and shown him the truth. But she felt honored He had chosen her, and she had gotten an invaluable friend in the process.

She still struggled with the loss of Keith. She didn't know why God had taken him from her, and so far she hadn't seen the good, if any, that had come from the loss of people doing the Lord's work. But she tried not to dwell on the unknown.

She looked back at T.J. as he waited astride his board for the perfect wave. She laughed at her deception. She wasn't sure she could pull it off. The look on his face when he thought she'd forgotten his birthday was priceless.

She and Anna had been planning his surprise party for weeks. Kathy and Mike would be there with the boys, so would Pastor Grant, Sergeant Peck, some of their mutual friends from church, and of course all of T.J.'s students. It was going to be the first time she ever pulled something over on T.J., and she wasn't going to let him forget it.

Joanna was in a reflective mood the rest of the day.

The events of four years ago were never far from her mind, but time had lessened the pain.

God was healing her.

Joanna would've never believed it was possible for her to love again. But when she thought of Sam, she smiled and felt her heart race.

Sam was a great guy. A man of God. A man of principle. And as handsome on the outside as he was on the inside.

She had told him on numerous occasions she wasn't interested, but he never gave up. He was very persistent.

Lucky for Joanna, one of Sam's other attributes was patience.

They'd been taking it slow, partly because of their schedules, but also because of Joanna's fear of being hurt again. Each time she'd felt herself getting closer to Sam, she'd back off and become distant. She'd even encouraged him to see other women. But he'd endured her moments of panic, and assured her he wasn't going anywhere.

Now they were to the point of talking commitment.

Although Sam could be quite romantic, he promised not to blindside her with a proposal. He didn't want her to feel cornered or pressured, but he'd made it very clear he loved her, and was convinced she was the person God had chosen for him.

Having T.J. meet Sam was huge. By doing so, Joanna was admitting to herself she was ready to take the next step. T.J. was the most important person in her life and it was important he meet Sam. She knew he would give Sam the third-degree and be possessive but only because he cared.

Joanna was confident T.J. would see what she saw.

A man of integrity and faith.

Smiling to herself Joanna took a deep breath and whispered. "Mrs. Samuel Connors.

"I like it."

ABOUT THE AUTHOR

Tamara Tilley writes from her home at Hume Lake Christian Camps, located in the beautiful Sequoia National Forest. She and her husband, Walter, have been on full-time staff at Hume for over twenty years. Tamara is a retail manager and an active book reviewer. You can read her reviews on her blog at http://tamara-tilley.blogspot.com Along with reading, spending time with her grandkids, and crafting cards, she loves connecting with readers at www.tamaratilley.com.